Trouble in the China Sea

An unexpectedly large oil discovery in the Philippines
triggers geopolitical tensions.

BOOK SEVEN OF THE GEOPOLITICAL TECHNO-THRILLER SERIES

ANDREW B. LOUIS

Copyright © 2023 by Andrew B. Louis

For information regarding permission, please write to:
info@barringerpublishing.com
Barringer Publishing, Naples, Florida
www.barringerpublishing.com

Cover, graphics, and layout by Linda S. Duider
Cape Coral, Florida

ISBN: 978-1-954396-57-9
Library of Congress Cataloging-in-Publication Data
Trouble in the China Sea / Andrew B. Louis

Printed in U.S.A.

DEDICATION

To my old friend, Pat, who was once my boss and taught me about oil exploration and production.

OTHER BOOKS BY THE AUTHOR

Other novels by Andrew B. Louis include:

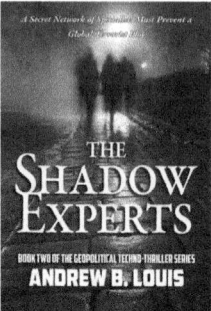

Operation Kovesh, The Shadow Experts, Below the Surface, The Crypto Trap, Escaping the Bear, Glitter and Smoke, The Improbable Collector, Seven Miracles to Save the World, A Crooked Few and *Tough Choices* available at Amazon.com.

www.AndrewBLouis.com

ACKNOWLEDGMENTS

Though all the writing and errors are solely my own doing, a number of people contributed to the creation of the text. I would like to thank the numerous friends and family members who were kind enough to comment on various drafts and led me to make material changes for the better, especially Jeff, Patrick, and, as usual, my dear wife.

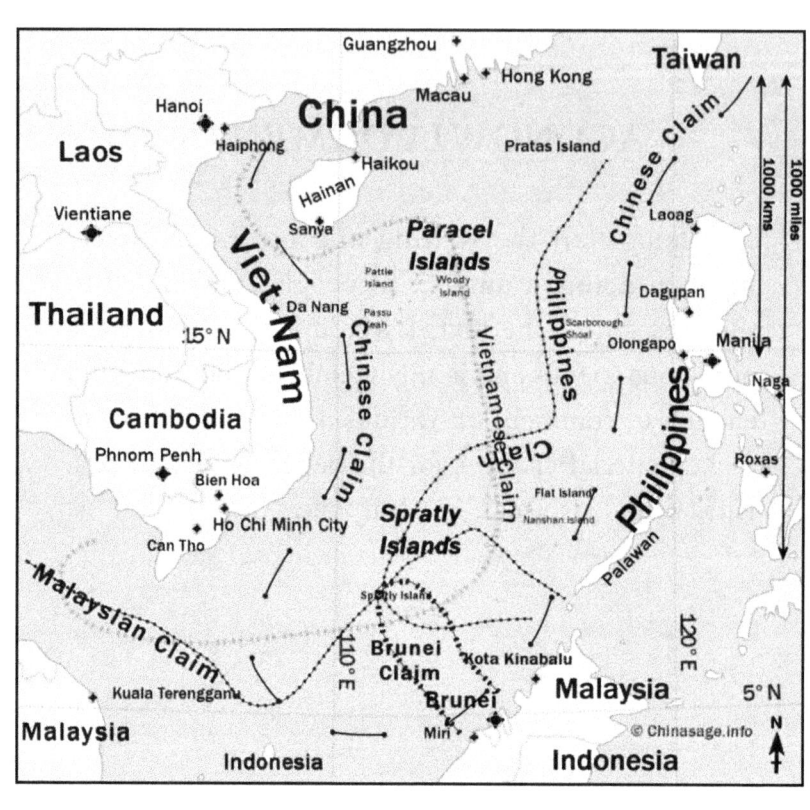

SYNOPSIS

Indications of a new, potentially quite significant, hydrocarbon discovery in the Philippines brings a wealthy Filipino businessman to seek the help of a Manilla-based *Mossad* agent with whom he has struck a friendship, without knowing of his role. Though *Mossad* initially expresses only a limited interest in providing the help the businessman seeks, it eventually agrees to assist with the creation of self-defense mechanisms for the oil production platform. Subsequent developments broaden the assistance provided, as a few incidents create a potentially more critical dimension to the current problem. Terrorist acts involving the use of biological agents cultivated to be particularly harmful force the hand of *Mossad*, who feel they must help uncover the source of a mysterious disease initially affecting fishermen in the Spratly islands. This requires Mossad to invite *The Shadow Experts* to join the undercover operations. As improbable as it might seem, in part because of the physical distance between the Philippines and Israel and in part in view of the lack of a direct geopolitical interest in the South China Sea on the part of the Hebrew state, an alliance forms which demonstrates how discreet, and laser-focused help can achieve what might otherwise appear impossible.

Disclaimer: All the parties to this story are totally fictitious and if there was some resemblance with individuals or institutions, it would be purely coincidental.

PROLOGUE

MANILA, THE PHILIPPINES
FALL 2022

The sun was setting on Manila Bay, a famous attraction in the capital city of the Republic of the Philippines, which comprises myriads of islands strewn about in the middle of the South China Sea. Numerous, tall coconut palm trees etched their fronds in black against the changing fiery sky. The initially bright white disk had gradually and inexorably gone through all the nuances of yellow and orange to take a deep red color as it sank into the sea. Though he did not see the green flash that some people claim to have seen as the sun finally disappears into the sea, the poetic beauty of the scene was not lost on Ehud Shamir. Officially, Ehud was a military attaché at the Israeli Embassy. That evening, he was finishing his first cocktail with Luis Ramos De Ayala, a powerful local businessman.

They were sitting in Luis's majestic two-story penthouse apartment. The home occupied the 51st and 52nd floors of the South Tower of Pacific Plaza, one of the most desirable, and probably most expensive, condominium complexes in Manila. Luis's penthouse being nearly 180 yards up offered a distant, but still almost full view of Manila Bay and its famed sunset when the air quality was good; and today, the air quality was exceptionally good.

Pacific Plaza comprised two towers, slightly angled to the northwest, and each with its own heliport on the roof. The twin towers sat due east of the Manila Golf and Country Club, reputedly the most exclusive and quite possibly the most expensive golf course in the country. Westerly facing apartments in these towers afforded a wonderful view to their owners, who were quite often more than willing to show them off to visitors. Distant perspectives of Manila Bay and the luxuriant palette of all kinds of greens with a variety of seasonal flowers on the golf course in the foreground were a very hard spectacle to beat. Additionally, as Luis had said more than once, he saw the golf course as his insurance that nobody would ever build anything on these grounds. His glorious perspectives were safe, for him and future generations.

Before moving to the covered terrace, which was an extension of the large living room, the men spent a few minutes in the adjoining bar selecting and pouring their drinks. Every time he visited Luis in his penthouse, Ehud was impressed by the fact that the living room had very high ceilings, as it was two-stories high. The second floor of the apartment had a balcony which looked down into the living room. The feeling of space was quite impressive and complemented the outside views from the large bay windows: Manila Bay in the distance, The Manila Golf Club down below, the whole city extending to the Bay. Once the drinks were poured, they moved to the terrace, where they sat down in the dark bamboo sofas with plush orange cushions, Ehud had immediately jumped on the reason for their meeting:

"Your phone call seemed quite urgent, Luis! What's going on? How can I help?"

"You said it, my friend. It's quite urgent. In fact, urgent may not even be strong enough a word. Fabulously exciting might be better."

Luis paused and looked straight at Ehud, he then added:

"You know I'm involved in oil exploration, right?"

"Sure do. Why, you even told me a month ago that you had finally started drilling a well in your largest drilling permit; I think you called it your service contract."

"Good memory. Good memory. We call that area a service contract because we signed a contract with the government that grants us the drilling rights there in exchange for some set share of the production if we hit oil in commercial quantities. Currently, they don't ask for too much, only 7.5% of the value of the oil and gas we would produce."

"I see. Why didn't you call me earlier?"

"Well, I did not call you when we first hit oil, because I wanted to be sure."

"Sure of what?"

"That we had hit a large enough oil reservoir. That we could produce commercial quantities of hydrocarbons. There's been no question that we did strike oil. But the question quickly morphed to a different one—how big? And, believe me, I think we may have hit a real gusher."

"You sure?"

"Well, as sure as you can be in this business. But that's not all. Recent technology allows us to drill directionally and as such to get a much better sense of what we actually hit. Well, it not only confirmed our hit, but more than that. It's suggesting that the field could be quite large."

Luis explained that, as is typical, they had started drilling the well vertically. As is also standard operating procedure, they had run wireline tests at various depths as they kept drilling. The results of these tests were their first indication that there was oil and some gas there. As they should typically have done, they kept drilling down until they found themselves below the reservoir. That classic strategy gave them a sense of the thickness of the oil-bearing rock layer. They could, in Luis's words, have kept going to see whether there was oil further below, but, following their geologist's advice, they elected to stop there. Casually, he added with a wink of his right eye:

"For the time being."

Ehud noticed Luis's side note but elected to stay quiet at the time. There was no point in his view sidetracking the conversation. Luis then turned to the newer technology which allowed them to do much more. Having elicited from Ehud that he was not familiar with what horizontal drilling meant or involved, Luis explained that the process really comprises three stages:

"First, you drill a small diameter pilot hole along a designed directional path. Then, you enlarge the pilot hole to a diameter suitable for the installation of the pipeline. Finally, you pull the pipeline, the equivalent of casing in vertical drilling, back into the enlarged hole."

Thus, as Luis was telling it, after they hit the oil, they backed up the drill bit until it was near the top of the oil-bearing layer. There they started to drill "horizontally" though the section does not really start truly horizontally but is angled down so that the drill bit gradually slides down into the oil deposit. This made it possible to determine the horizontal extent of the reservoir in the direction they had chosen, driven by their geological analyses. He concluded:

"With the rig we had, we could not drill more than 3,000 feet horizontally. Yet, believe it or not, we found we were still getting oil all along the horizontal section as well. It's entirely possible that the reservoir extends further than what we tested."

He paused for a second and added:

"You know what? The odds are it does."

"What does that tell you?"

"I don't want to be too optimistic but given what we know of the geology of the area and the result of this first wildcat well, we may have found a major reservoir. This may even be bigger than anything that has been found anywhere in Northwest Palawan and thus in the Philippines—ever . . ."

■ ■ ■ ■ ■

Though the connection with the Apiado De Ayala family, one of the most prominent family groups in the Philippines, had surely become more and more distant, Luis had elected to keep the "De Ayala" in his name. Cynics would argue that his rationale for doing so was a mix of arrogance and desire for recognition: Ramos was quite a common family name in the Philippines, while De Ayala was one of the most admired and wealthiest family groups. Luis, they opined, simply wanted to stand out in the crowd, to be taken more seriously than his initially modest station warranted. There was most probably some truth to this narrative, at least at the outset. Luis, when asked, would simply reply that he kept the "De Ayala" to honor Celeste De Ayala y Roxas, his great-grandmother on his mother's side.

Luis's family branch went back to the first daughter of Miguel and Celeste and was thus still quite wealthy by local standards though it had not been as successful as the Apiado De Ayala branch until Luis took the business over. Cynics would even now concede that he no longer needed the reference to the "De Ayala" connection to be recognized as a successful entrepreneur. Luis's business enterprises were varied, and his fortune had arisen from logistical activities including all forms of shipping, as well as selected local manufacturing and insurance businesses.

Further and more critical to the recent developments, he had been fascinated by the hopes born in the late 1970s and early 1980s that the Philippines could one day become first self-sufficient in energy and eventually even a net exporter of oil. Though his first investments in the hydrocarbon area had not yielded terribly visible fruit, it certainly had planted a seed which would mature over time. Luis's financial group had initially invested in all four of the main local listed companies that participated in the Nido project. He then added a new line to his own business, investing alongside those whose shares he had initially only purchased: he would typically buy a minor participation in the service contracts which any one of these companies would purchase from the government. But, by now clearly infected with the "oil bug," he kept wanting to become more involved searching for oil and gas in his native country; that led him to grab the lead investor and operator roles in service contracts offered for sale whenever he could.

While these activities were not immediately rewarding, things had changed for the better in the more recent past. If confirmed by one or two other wells, Luis stood at the very start of a new and massive fortune. Further, it would compound into making him a national hero who was helping The Philippines become self-sufficient in oil and possibly even an oil exporter. His desire for fame in his own right, distinct from the senior branch of the family, would finally be met.

■ ■ ■ ■ ■

Though officially a mere commercial attaché in the Manila Israeli Embassy, Ehud had a more important but also quite secret role. He was the local head of *Mossad*, the Israeli Secret Service. In that role, he was to develop and manage local contacts, and forward any useful intelligence to Tel Aviv. Ehud had cultivated a relationship with Luis after he had casually been introduced to him at some official diplomatic function. He quickly realized that Luis was able and willing to provide him with quite a lot of information which could be and had several times proved to be quite important.

Israel had been aware of the numerous geopolitical issues which were playing out in the Pacific Basin, starting with the substantially increasing regional economic integration that was taking place as China's economy had boomed in the prior twenty years. It knew full well that China could and in reality, had interfered in regional issues within the Middle East.[1] These interferences, usually amounting to a tacit or even visible support of certain of Israel's enemies, were of major concern to Israel. They fit quite nicely with Ehud's official and not-so-official roles. Everyone understood that a stronger economy gave China the wherewithal to seek a greater role in the Pacific region, which memories of its history naturally kindled. China indeed was the world's leading superpower well over 1,000 years ago. Though there were periods of time where civil wars weakened it, China was the largest, strongest, and most populated country in the region that encompassed Europe and Asia; and the United States at that time were but a glimmer in the eyes of old-world explorers, such as John Cabot, Christopher Columbus, Vasco de Gama, or Amerigo Vespucci.

While certain of China's activities made a lot of economic sense, even if they seemed oddly aggressive, it was equally clear that others had geopolitical dimensions, causing potential conflicts with existing powers such as the U.S. For instance, the decision by Beijing to violate the agreements it signed with the U.K. (when Her Majesty's government decided not to renew the lease on the New Territories and thus agreed in 1984 to return the whole Hong Kong Colony to China in 1997) served directly or indirectly as an important reminder to all related parties that the country offered both substantial economic growth opportunities and material geopolitical risks.

Beyond China, though the situation had seemed to calm down somewhat in the more recent past, Ehud and Israel could not ignore the Islamic terrorist activities which had plagued the Island of Mindanao for nearly a half century. Israel needed to monitor all contacts between the Moro Islamists and Palestinians. The recriminations of the two groups might be different, and they were at least as much as the differences in purposes between Palestinians and Islamists in Africa.

---

[1] From the same author, see "Below the Surface," Barringer Publishing 2022.

However, the fact was that they proceeded from a common initial viewpoint: ethnic recriminations leading to territorial claims and a search for self-government. These at times totally natural and even fully understandable tensions had traditionally been a routine entry point for superpowers such as China, the Soviet Union for as long as it existed, Russia since the Soviet Union disintegrated in 1991 and even the U.S. Proxy confrontations were infinitely preferable to direct warfare: a fight at the margin, where convenient denials could always be offered if things turned out poorly or even just embarrassing.

Interestingly, the relationship between Israel and the Philippines went a long way back. The Philippines were the only Asian country to agree with the creation of the State of Israel. It supported U.N. Resolution 181 on the partition of Palestine and the Creation of the State of Israel in 1947. Diplomatic relations between Israel and the Philippines followed in 1957 and a friendship treaty in 1958. More recently, the aggressivity of China and in particular its claims on the Spratly Island (partially claimed by the Philippines as well), motivated the Philippines to seek even closer relations with Israel, which was known as an ally who was anything but fickle. While the Philippines could not reasonably expect that Israel would come to its aid should China attack it militarily, the local government knew very well that *Mossad* would provide at least as good intelligence as the CIA and would do it with no material risks of leaks, which could not be said about the CIA, or even the local U.S. military command structure in the Philippines.

In short, the relationship which Ehud had been building looked like it had the potential to work to the benefit of both parties.

■ ■ ■ ■ ■

Luis's announcement on that day was ostensibly providing excitement but could also potentially cause a major crisis. Could it be enough to incite China to meddle visibly into the Philippines oil industry? Could this meddling go further and extend to issues of ethnic strife? Were Luis's expectations reasonable from the point of view of Israel? Even if they were, was Israel in a position that it could deliver? Could any cooperation be official, or did it have to be secret? Could secrets be kept in the Philippines?

CHAPTER.01

TEL AVIV, ISRAEL, MANILA, THE PHILIPPINES, AND SOMEWHERE IN THE AUSTRIAN ALPS

A couple of months after the drilling of the second well into Luis's hydrocarbon reservoir had started, he placed a frantic phone call to Ehud Shamir:

"Something very strange is happening. I need your help . . ."

"Can you tell me more?"

"Not on the phone. Can you have lunch here? I can send the helicopter if that helps . . ."

"Lunch it is. Your helicopter will be welcome, though I can always use ours. From my office window, traffic looks crazy. Not a surprise, by the way; just a casual observation . . ."

He paused with a short laugh and continued:

"Have your pilot let me know when your bird is a couple of minutes away. I'll go straight up to the helipad, and we can turn around and fly off immediately."

■ ■ ■ ■ ■

Luis was awaiting Ehud at the helipad, rather than down below in his living room. As Ehud landed on the helipad of Pacific Plaza South,

Luis's face told the whole story. Whatever he needed to tell Ehud had to be both quite serious and probably bad. They only exchanged a solid handshake and did not start a conversation as the noise caused by the engine of the helicopter was just too loud. Nobody could hear anything, and Enrique, Luis's pilot, could not turn it off as he would need to vacate the helipad and fly the copter to its normal hangar.

Once they had reached Luis's penthouse, his message was quite serious:

"Several fishermen have been reported sick and a few of them died suddenly. They all lived on the north end of Galoc Island."

"The same Galoc as in the oil fields? As the area where you're drilling?"

"One and the same! In fact, the same Galoc as quite close to our own reservoir!"

"Any idea what happened?"

"It's been kept out of the news by government order, but you can imagine that I have good contacts. They would talk to me; I have too much at stake for them to keep me in the dark. They told me two things. First, the common element in all those who got sick is that they often went fishing near the two Twin Islands, aptly named North Twin Island and South Twin Island, the southern tip of Popototan Island. They are both less than a mile from a small fishing village on the north coast of Galoc Island."

"Symptoms?"

"The only thing I know is that the victims complained of flu-like symptoms, with a high fever. I'm told the few that died did so within less than a week of the first symptoms."

"What is there on either of these two islands? Any national secret?"

"Secret? No! Next to nothing! Nice place to fish or to scuba dive, very small beaches, but no permanent establishment. Not even a cabin on the beach. In the greater scheme of things, they're tiny and uninhabited, save for a few turtles, birds or even maybe rats."

"Any lead?"

"Frankly, none that I know of."

"What's the government doing?"

"As much as they can, which is unfortunately not much. They've flown the sick to the ACE medical center in Puerto Princesa, you know, the largest city in Palawan."

■ ■ ■ ■ ■

Having been in the Philippines for a while, Ehud did not need Luis to explain to him what and where Palawan was. The Province of Palawan is a province of the Philippines that is in the region of Mimaropa. It really is an archipelago, comprising a myriad of islands. Moreover, from a total area standpoint, it is largest province in the country comprising 10,000 square miles. The capital city is Puerto Princesa.

■ ■ ■ ■ ■

Luis continued:

"You may not believe it, but Puerto Princesa even has an international airport. The hospital is part of a nationwide chain of private hospitals founded by medical doctors. Officially, they're considered at least as good as the three government-owned establishments there, but many people think they're the best."

"How far is it from the fishing village?"

"Less than 150 miles as the crow flies."

"Did they isolate anyone who has been in contact with the sick?"

"I don't know, but I sure hope they did."

"What do you want us for?"

"I don't know for sure. I have little if any confidence in our government's efforts frankly. For instance, I have not heard of any contact with foreign medical authorities to investigate.

"That's serious."

Ehud paused and just said that he would contact Tel Aviv, though he could not promise anything. He added:

"You know I must go through my own hierarchy. I'm a military attaché, not someone involved in health matters. So, I must go through the Defense Department, though I'm sure you're aware that we have excellent medical care within the various branches of the military.

■ ■ ■ ■ ■

Back at the office, Ehud immediately called Mark Levi. He had no idea whether *Mossad* had any experience which might be applicable there, but he was pretty sure that Mark would know a lot more than he. They had met casually a few years earlier and had developed some affinity for each other.

■ ■ ■ ■ ■

Mark Levi had rapidly risen in the ranks after he captained a very difficult but, in the end, extremely successful operation that had involved him impersonating a terrorist. During the mission, he had been able to locate and deactivate a series of explosive devices that were paired to small glass containers filled with biological agents. He had subsequently captained at least three very important missions and always managed to exceed both Simon's and David's expectations. Simon Rabinowitz was initially the head of the *Disruption* division of *Mossad*, while Dabid Heller was his number two. Thus, though Mark's young age, not even 40, would seem not to preclude further promotions, he found himself quickly becoming the right-hand man of David Heller when he succeeded Simon Rabinowitz, just as Simon had been the right-hand man of Ariel Landau, *Mossad*'s overall Head, before succeeding to him.

■ ■ ■ ■ ■

Ehud could not have been luckier, as Mark had played a crucial role in a mission which might have some relevancy here.[2] Mark's immediate reaction was to laugh heartily, then he simply said:

"Well, I don't know what this is, but if there is some poison or virus involved, I do have experience. Listen, I can probably help, but I can't do it alone: I'll need someone to help me. I can't say anything now, but I already have a couple of thoughts as to who might be the right partner. Can you send me a summary of what you know, and I'll discuss it with a couple of people. If we're lucky, we may have a straightforward way of helping. At the same time, I've got to tell you that, if my suspicions are anywhere near the mark, we are talking about something quite serious. Not an act of war per se, but well within the sphere of terrorism."

"Terrorism?"

"Can't say anything more now because I'd only be speculating. Yet, let's only note that this may be a first step in a campaign waged by people working for China."

"China?"

"Yep. You know the worries which Luis had at the outset?"

"Sure do."

"Well, this could be a first salvo. A not-so-veiled threat. I doubt anything further will happen before I'm back with you. But tell Luis to call you the moment someone contacts him with an expression of interest in purchasing some or all his investment in the consortium."

---

2 See "The Shadow Experts" by the same author, published by Barringer Publishing 2021.

"Wow. Now that you've said this, I can begin to build a storyline in my own mind. I think I see where you're going. Not fishing for more than I should get, but still—could the trigger have been the fact that the second well did hit oil?"

"Bingo! Don't go any further."

■ ■ ■ ■ ■

Within minutes, Mark was on the phone with David Heller, the Head of the *Disruption* Group of *Mossad*. He asked if he was available for a few minutes:

"I've got information, which is not ready for prime time, but could be quite serious."

"Come right in. I'm waiting for you."

As was his habit, Mark went straight for the cream-colored leather sofa in the corner of David's office, expecting, correctly as it turned out, David to sit in one of the two matching chairs. He immediately asked:

"So. Tell me. What's up?"

"Well, first let me preface the whole thing with a big caveat. I need way more info to begin to support my intuition."

"Understood. So, what's up given what you know?"

"I fear that China, directly or through some surrogate, fired the first salvo against the Philippines."

"You'll explain that. Right?"

"Sure. I wanted a headline to tell you why I'm disturbing you."

"You never disturb me, my friend."

Mark smiled and continued:

"Well, you remember that the field which our "friend," or rather Ehud Shamir's friend in the Philippines discovered, looks increasingly as if it is really a major find. Anthony Stacey, Countess Renate's petroleum engineer, feels that the results of the second well are very, very promising."

"I do. I do. But tell me, why can't Anthony be sure?"

"He needs the two horizontal extensions of this second well, and probably a third well altogether; at least that's what he says."

"I see. Sorry I cut you off."

"No worries. Well, we have reasons to believe that someone on the drilling team is a mole, or at least someone who is not good at keeping secrets. I'm told it's not unusual as speculators love to have their own sources; few people pay much attention to insider trading issues . . . That's the only source we can think of unless Luis himself or his top petroleum executive Angelo is doing the leaking."

"Why would they do that?"

"Money, my friend, money. There are so many nominee companies around here that you could assume that the leaker could be paid with additional shares placed for him in a nominee name."

David replied with a smile:

"I see. Interesting. Interesting. But back to the key issue. What else?"

"Ehud has just heard from Luis that a few fishermen have become sick, with a few of them dying within days."

"What? Dying? That's serious. What do you think? Biological warfare or coincidence?"

"At this point, again, I'm only speculating. But I feel that one could easily assume that some form of virus or other pathogenic agent has been released near where the fishermen operate. Ehud tells me of a couple of tiny islands, the largest of the two is about 25,000 square yards, less than 1% of a square mile. Only fishermen who operate in that area have fallen sick. All the others are just fine."

"And you assume it is some sort of intimidation?"

"Precisely, but the key word here is 'assume.' I've told Ehud to watch for any unsolicited offer for someone to buy Luis out of his investment."

"Can't have that. By the way, Eli Abelman is in the midst of that too. Right?"

"Absolutely. That's why I am reacting without having all the information."

"What do you think you need?"

"I'd like to discuss this with Countess Renate. She has at least two associates, or more precisely *suspected* associates who could help. The Frenchman . . ."

"Dr. Armand Duchemin?"

"Yes. That's him. The other is his Japanese colleague. He also helped us in the virus mission. Koichi Oshima is his name if I'm not mistaken."

"What could they do?"

Mark explained that this was precisely what he needed to discuss with Countess Renate. His intuition was telling him that there was some urgency reaching those sick people who had not died yet, as well as anyone they might have been in contact with. Further, they might be able to administer some generic drug that would improve the prognostic for the sick. David nodded his agreement and simply said:

"I know I am preaching to the choir, but make sure to draw a big distinction between what is fact and what we might call various forms of informed or rank speculation . . ."

■ ■ ■ ■ ■

Countess Renate immediately understood the urgency of the situation. With her relationship with *Mossad* sufficiently developed over the last several years that she did not need to negotiate anything upfront, she decided to contact the people in her network. Mark surprised her when he added:

"One thing I would suggest, Countess. I think Dr. Duchemin would be the best alternative in the short-term."

Countess Renate sounded surprised, particularly given the fact that Tokyo, where Professor Oshima was located, would be closer than Paris, the home and workplace of Dr. Duchemin. Mark explained that the relationship between Japan and the Philippines, or more precisely between the Japanese and the Filipino peoples was not simple. Countess Renate interrupted:

"The Pacific war?"

"Absolutely. But there is more. Though things have improved vastly in the last twenty-five years, The Philippines were just like Thailand: a preferred destination for Japanese 'sex-tourism.' So, you can bet that there's a bit of a love hate relationship."

"Are you being philosophical or was that a joke?"

"Neither really. The Philippines knew of the so-called touristic activities, and officially disapproved of it. Yet, that was a lot of money accruing to the country's overall tourist trade accounts. So, they hated it on principle but tolerated it because of the money."

With a wry smile, Countess replied:

"So, you really mean a tolerance hate relationship, if that phrase exists."

"Right."

Countess quickly regained her always serious and businesslike demeanor. She asked whether Mark would be able to get an invitation for Dr. Duchemin, suggesting:

"Could your friend Luis Ramos De Ayala set that up?"

"Sure. Yet, it might be better if he was a guest of our Embassy. Officially, our embassy is involved through Ehud Shamir, the military attaché. Luis has a good relationship with him, and that's how we found out about the problem. It might be more prudent not to raise any flags until we know a lot more."

Mark paused for a second and smiling added:

"And I suspect that we cannot wait until we know everything we need to know. Fortunately, Palawan Island is only sparsely populated, but with the sick having been flown to Puerto Princesa, the local metropolis, I am concerned that the more we wait, the greater the potential damage."

"Can't fault your logic Mark, as usual I should add. Let me get on it right away."

She paused and felt she still needed to ask:

"You're not going to do this without Luis knowing anything, are you?"

"No. He will be in the loop, if only to get us access to the sick. We'll also need interpreters. But I do not think he should be our official 'sponsor' in this mission."

"I see that. But how are you going to play this with the Filipino Government?"

"That's the key. We will offer to contact someone who has helped us in the past, without mentioning your name or your group. We will mention the experience we have had with something that might be a lot more similar than at first blush."

"What if they turn you down?"

"I asked Ehud that question, hypothetically. At first blush, there're no reason. However, he made the point that the whole thing had to be managed carefully. He says that Filipinos do not appreciate being talked down to. But they would likely appreciate the help, as I'm sure they are wondering what this really is. That's why someone like Dr. Duchemin would likely be welcomed with open arms."

He paused and almost dejectedly added:

"And if all else fails, we'll get Luis to invite us to look at the issue from the point of view that it may well have a direct impact on his business."

CHAPTER.02

MANILA, THE PHILIPPINES

The history of oil exploration in The Philippines has been mixed at best. It got under way in 1899 with the first hole drilled onshore in Cebu Island—Toledo 1—by Smith Bell under a Spanish royal grant. Though some 300 wells were drilled onshore after that, they produced little oil, although they provided considerable geological data. A revitalization of oil exploration began after President Ferdinand E. Marcos enacted a new form of oil exploration contract as one of his early martial law decrees in 1972. Late in the 1970s, a well-respected retired American geologist, Chuck Wilson, offered the hypothesis that the country could well be the place where the next "Elephant field" would be discovered. To be named an Elephant oil field, a discovery must hold 500 million barrels of oil or more. To-date, only ten such fields have been brought into production, four of which are in the United States, with three of the four only recently so named owing to the fresh development of technology that made exploiting oil shale possible. The largest Elephant of them all in the world is the Ghawar Field in Saudi Arabia; it was discovered in 1948 and started production in 1951.

Chuck Wilson's thesis was that the area offshore Palawan was the result of what he called "an overthrust belt," with a continental plate pushing over a sedimentary basin. He called it a stratigraphic trap, which was formed due to lateral and vertical variations in the thickness, texture, porosity, or even lithology of the reservoir rock. To an oil explorer, these are potentially more important than structural traps, as they frequently hold greater quantities of hydrocarbons. He was quite excited and managed to convince several local oil executives, as well as many investors, with the affirmation:

"This is an East Texas."

In short, he was comparing the area offshore the largest westernmost island of the Philippines to the largest oil field in the mainland United States. It created quite a stir at the time. That he was a lone optimist then might have been a warning sign, though many other specialists agreed that there were likely numerous small "reef pinnacles," forms of structural traps, filled with oil. The Philippines could produce oil, but they were seen as unlikely ever to reach self-sufficiency, leave alone net exporter status.

In the late 1970s and 1980s, early successes initially seemed to be validating Wilson's theories. After a practically dry well in the Nido area, to the northwest of Palawan Island, a couple of other wells in the same area were drilled and yielded commercial quantities of oil, reaching at one point a daily output of 40,000 barrels. That production level was unfortunately too optimistic, causing water intrusion into the reservoir and reducing its potential; the phenomenon is called "coning." It occurs when the oil is pumped too aggressively, leading the water that sits below the oil deposit to rise through the layer of oil and thus separate the deposit into two new ones. With vertical drilling the only practical option available at the time, it was determined that it would be too expensive to drill two new wells, one on each side of the original one, to recover what was left.

However, several small fields, all located offshore Northwest Palawan, were subsequently discovered and put into production. Then, in 1989, a relatively large new field was identified, still in offshore Northwest Palawan, with the Camago-1 well, a structure which revealed the presence of oil and a thick layer of natural gas with associated condensates.

In short, the more cautious forecasters had turned out to be correct: the anticipated boom did not eventuate; a few wells produced encouraging amounts of oil; several of them were exploited, but excess enthusiasm on the part of the government as well as the local operators led to exploitation errors which reduced the amount of oil that could be recovered even below subsequently recalibrated expectations. Fortunes were made in the early stages as stock market investors could not get enough of the equity in the four local companies that were the major beneficiaries; much of these were eventually lost when the expected oil gush became little more than a spittle.

Some renewed optimism was warranted ten years later, with the discovery of West Linapacan field in 1990 where production commenced after two years but, repeating by then an unfortunately well-known pattern, it ceased in 1996. Yet, in 1991, the Malampaya gas field was discovered; it eventually became the largest gas discovery in the country, so far. More care was applied to its management, and it only came into commercial production in January 2002; an eleven-year planning and development process. Furthermore, the natural gas from Malampaya provides clean fuel for five power plants in Batangas, some 200 miles from northern Palawan as the crow flies.

Over the years, with expectations appropriately scaled back, exploration and production continued, though at a more modest pace: there was oil both onshore and offshore in the country. Could there be a truly important field? In fact, in 2011, the Philippines were named, alongside Argentina, a new "hot area" for oil exploration. The four major areas of interest that were identified were the Spratly islands, the Sulu Sea, the Celebes Sea, and the Philippines Sea. Analysts claimed that the Philippines was virtually "sitting on a mountain of gold," with untapped hydrocarbon deposits estimated to be worth $26.3 trillion at the time, mostly found in the disputed Spratly chain of islands. Everybody understood that this was more than enough to free the country from the shackles of poverty, and it rekindled memories of Chuck Wilson's predictions. While oil production was still not sufficient to meet the local demand, even more recent estimates put the untapped oil reserves of the South China Sea at 11 billion barrels and 190 trillion cubic feet of natural gas reserves.

This may help explain why China appeared to be trying to appropriate the area. Besides the obvious advantages it offered to control maritime traffic in that crucial part of the world, it could even provide the energy which China had hitherto been importing. Further, China's potentially malevolent intentions were displayed when, despite being a signatory to the UN Convention of the Law of the Sea (UNCLOS), it refused to accept the authority of Permanent Court of Arbitration at The Hague and its verdict in a suit brought by the Philippines against China where the Court sided almost entirely with the Philippines.

According to recent analyses, more than half of the Philippines's total petroleum reserves (five billion barrels of fuel oil equivalent out of nine for the country as a whole) is estimated to occur in the offshore West Palawan and Sulu Sea regions. More precisely, analysts identified five basins which they thought had the most potential; four of them are near Palawan Island: the Northwest Palawan Basin, the Southwest Palawan Basin and, on the east side of the island, the Cuyo Platform and just to the north of it the Mindoro Basin. Further to the east is the Visayan Basin which is often named as the birthplace of oil exploration in the country.

■ ■ ■ ■ ■

The challenges facing the offshore oil exploration industry are well-known and documented. Yet, in the Philippines, they include a dimension which is not always a problem for oil explorers: security. And security here has multiple facets that do not exist, or at least do not exist to the same extent elsewhere. Political issues have so far dominated the debate and are well-understood, as China's claims on the Spratly islands are well-known, though its own demarcation lines would typically exclude the areas around the northwestern tip of Palawan. The recent backing down of China in the case of a Philippine-occupied atoll after imposing a quasi-blockade that provoked strong warnings from Manila and Washington, may represent progress, but may also reflect some tactical posture. Further, the distance between the southern tip of Palawan Island and the northern end of Borneo Island is less than twenty miles. With two of the Malaysian states Sabah and Sarawak on the Island of Borneo, along with the Sultanate of Brunei, all three of them on the northwest side of Kalimantan, the name for Indonesia's territory on Borneo, it is not hard to imagine the claims and counterclaims of Malaysia, Indonesia, Brunei and the Philippines: they have been breeding discontent and tensions that can easily serve as pretexts for ethnic or religious strife, as well as terrorist activities. Finally, an additional danger looms in that geographical area: piracy. It is also well-documented, and though currently limited to crimes against marine traffic, it would not need much of a push to extend to ransoming oil production installations if the opportunity arose. These risks are very real, the closer one gets to Kalimantan.

■ ■ ■ ■ ■

Luis Ramos's holding company had taken advantage of the lull in the enthusiasm for oil exploration to acquire substantial financial and operating interests in the five basins that were identified as offering the best prospects. Thus, he felt that he was in some significant way responsible for addressing the security problems that, in his view, exposed him and related investors to the risk of virtual expropriation, and thus total loss of capital.

Recently, Luis had had the pleasure to learn that one of his wells, east of the Galoc field, but still offshore and around 32 nautical miles from shore seemed to have found what could be a new field . . . Yet, under the limits set by the 1982 United Nations Convention on the Law of the Sea, the first 12 miles constitute territorial waters, while the next twelve define the contiguous zone. In short, with the drilling taking place about 32 miles offshore the northern part of Palawan Island, the field was in international waters. However, these potential reserves were surely well within the 200 miles the Exclusive Economic Zone of the Philippines. Given the field's location, there were minimal reasons for Brunei, Malaysia, or Indonesia to have a real claim on the property, with even less of a case for Vietnam. However, the specter of China was ever present. China on the surface had even less of a claim, but, given its broader actions in the South China Sea in general and the Spratly islands in particular, anything was possible.

Thus, after the initial euphoria associated with the positive exploration results, Luis was now concerned with the issue of developing the field, even though his team had mentioned that it looked potentially quite a bit larger than Malampaya. Luis had met Ehud Shamir, the military attaché of the Israeli Embassy in Manila a few times over lunch or later in the afternoon over a cocktail.

On the day they were sipping a cocktail on the covered terrace of Luis's penthouse and contemplating the wonderful sunset, and after sharing with Ehud the news of the real nature of his latest discovery, Luis turned to the quandary which seemed to box him in:

"I am happy to have some financial exposure, but I am increasingly worried by the financial resources needed to go through exploration as well as pre-production work."

He paused, and noting that Ehud did not seem to follow, added:

"That's where the real money is. Think of it, a drilling rig, whether a jack-up or semi-submersible, will typically range between $100 and $700 million."

"Wow! That is serious money. But that's if you buy it, correct? I always assumed that these were leased."

"Absolutely. But it's still serious money even if you assume that you're just renting the equipment."

"Would you use the same rig for exploration and for production?"

"No. Certainly not. An exploration rig is movable while a production platform is anchored to the sea floor."

Luis paused for a second and added:

"Must be careful how I phrase that. Being fixed to the sea floor is only a small part of the problem. Fact is that the two rigs do different things . . ."

"So, you'll need both."

"Yes, and to make matters worse, a production platform can easily be more expensive than a drilling rig. And you really must buy your production platform if the field has a reasonable life."

Luis paused again, but quickly added:

"Note that clever finance guys can find ways to reduce the cost of ownership with structured finance deals. Anyway, the problem is most acute for a first well. Eventually, when we know more about the deposit, we can envisage having a single platform serving all of them and subsea completions for all the others."

■ ■ ■ ■ ■

A subsea completion is a piece of equipment in which the producing well does not include a vertical conduit from the wellhead back to a fixed access structure. A subsea well typically has a production tree to which a flowline is connected allowing the hydrocarbons to flow to another structure, for instance, a floating production vessel. In short, Luis was referring to a system of pipes, connections and valves that reside on the ocean floor and serve to gather hydrocarbons produced from individually completed wells and direct those hydrocarbons to a common storage and offloading facility.

■ ■ ■ ■ ■

Luis added:

"But the decision to start production is less of a speculation, so it's easier to commit to production expenses."

Seeing that Ehud was not following his barebone logic, Luis explained:

"You would not initiate production if you did not know you had a large enough and accessible enough reservoir, so that production can be commercially viable. The initial exploration wells, we call them wildcat wells, can be successful in as little as 5% to 10% of all cases. After you've drilled another one or two wells, you know a lot more on the nature and potential of the deposit. Can you see the difference?"

"Sure, I do now. Each wildcat well is at best an educated guess, while the production decision rests on hard facts. Correct?"

"Almost. 'Harder' would be better than 'hard.' Not all facts are rock solid, but any assumption is grounded in science and observations. You can always have surprises, good and bad, when evaluating what portion of the reserves you have discovered will be 'recoverable.' You can never hope to extract the last drop of oil in a reservoir, and on average recovery rates range between 20% and 45%, maybe a bit more, if you use secondary or even tertiary recovery techniques. But that's when the cost per recovered barrel rises dramatically."

"Thanks for the crash course. I had no idea . . . So, now, we're talking production for this new well, right?"

"Well, not quite, but getting there. Geology has improved by leaps and bounds over the last thirty to fifty years. We know a lot more than we did when we had any wildcat success in the past. We still need to delineate the field quite a bit more clearly."

▌▌■▌▌

He was not going to get into the gory details of the business, but Luis was explicitly referring to a couple of major developments. The first was the much greater accuracy of seismic work; think of the analogy of images produced by echography and showing babies in the mother's womb. Forty years ago, you were looking at very rough, fuzzy, black, and white images, while now one has much higher quality images which can even be in full color. The second referred to the ability to drill wells that were not necessarily vertical. Directional drilling eventually allowing even horizontal drilling made it possible for oil wells to "follow" the oil or gas deposit and thus make recovery of the hydrocarbon considerably more productive. While the conceptual origin of the process goes back to the 1930s, directional drilling has really been a feature of the last thirty years, as a desire to minimize environmental damage has made the higher cost a secondary consideration. That it has brought about interesting conversations relating to the possible theft of oil cannot be denied; but it only serves as the proof that there always are unintended consequences to any development. The point is that horizontal drilling, for instance, can easily extend deep under the surface into parcels which belong to different owners . . . That's outright theft and it explains why well details are still very closely guarded secrets.

▌▌■▌▌

Ehud was clearly interested in his friend's predicament, but he was getting lost in the details of oil exploration and production. He felt he needed to shift the debate back to the crucial point and thus asked:

"So, in short, Luis, where are we? And how can I help?"

"Do you think it makes sense to agree to the required investments if China could all of a sudden come around and take over the whole of the Spratly Island chain, which, as you know, it had already claimed as its own?"

"Excellent question, my friend. But I don't think I qualify as an expert on that front. Yet, I can think of a few obvious next questions. For instance, the general area has been producing oil since 2008, correct?"

"Not in my contract areas, yet. But others in the area for sure."

"OK. But also, your field, is it not east of all those?"

He paused and added to make sure that Luis got his point:

"And by 'east of these' I mean closer to the Filipino shore than the others . . ."

Luis did not hesitate to reply with a definite:

"Yes."

"And China has not interfered with the others, has it?"

Luis felt he needed to make a key point:

"No. I see where you are going Ehud. You see it could well all be a question of size . . ."

"Hold it. What do you mean by size?"

"Yes. There was very little to gain when the area produced eight thousand barrels per day. 3% of the country's daily production. Peanuts in short. Now, imagine that my discovery is really a game changer for the country."

He paused for a second to let his point sink in and immediately added:

"We may be talking of multiples of that amount. Enough for us to turn from an importer to an exporter of oil. China needs oil. Would not it be a higher incentive for China to meddle? What better way to get some than by grabbing our field if it is as significant as I hope it is?"

After a short pause he added again:

"So, I think the correct answer to your question is not my initial 'no' but more likely 'not yet.'"

Ehud looked pensive for a while, and then blurted out:

"I see. But what can you do about it?"

Luis did not reply immediately. He seemed deep in thoughts for a short while and finally replied:

"All I can say is that we've got to be very careful. Frankly, I see all the Chinese maneuvering in the Spratly islands as totally driven by the resource opportunities?"

"How about sea lanes?"

"That too, but I don't think that's where their main attention really is. Oil and other hydrocarbons, miscellaneous mining, fishing, you name it. That's the 'end game.' As you know, we're not the only ones fighting on that front. Brunei, China, Malaysia, Vietnam, Taiwan, and the Philippines, we're all in it. But truth is, in my view at least, that China is the proverbial bull in the porcelain shop . . ."

Luis paused and added with a wide smile:

"Could not call it the 'Bull in the china shop.' You know?"

Though disappointed that Ehud had not reacted more visibly to his attempt at a joke, noticing only a vague smile on Ehud's face, Luis went straight on. The story does not tell whether Ehud did not notice the joke or simply wanted to keep the conversation moving without unnecessary distraction. Luis continued:

"Now, if the discovery is as important as I hope it is, fingers crossed, there will be oil for quite some time. We could certainly share it with those neighbors who are closest to each specific field. The one thing we can't do is pump oil and gas out too fast. We could ruin the reservoir, though directional drilling, particularly horizontal drilling, ensures that the Nido mistake will not be repeated."

Luis concluded his analysis:

"What I think we need is both official and unofficial. On the official side, we need the key players to continue to defend the small states in the region. Unofficially, though, I would love to see someone like you all help us to create initial defenses that would demonstrate to anyone that attacked the field that the cost could be quite high . . ."

"Wait a minute, Luis. Just a minute. How can Israel help unofficially?"

Ehud paused for a second, and added:

"By the way, I am not even sure how we could help officially? Isn't that more a job for the U.S. or maybe even Japan if you think of regional politico-economic powers?"

"I know. I know. But I was hoping that you might be able to put me in touch with your secret services . . ."

"Our Secret services? *Mossad?*"

"Yes."

"Why? How?"

Luis suddenly looked a bit more confident than earlier as he explained:

"Well, first, I've studied oil and gas exploration in Israel. It seems to me there may well be interesting parallels with us here?"

"Parallels?"

"Yes, you know, offshore deposits, security issues and the like. As a military attaché, you must have ways to connect me with whomever could help us. Whoever dealt with the issue when you were developing your own monster gas field."

"Monster gas field? You mean the Leviathan field in the Levantine Basin of the East Mediterranean Sea?"

"Absolutely. The Leviathan field. That's what I am really thinking of. You must have had to face these issues and it does seem that you've solved the problem."

He paused for a second and then added, somehow shifting to a different point:

"Also, I have heard of missions where Israel was suspected to have played a role, though nothing was ever traced to the country.

Remember, a few years ago, the virus that came from North Korea or China.[3] That's what made me think of *Mossad* as you call it."

Ehud's immediate reaction was that the one thing he would **not** do, however much he viewed Luis as a friend, would be to reveal that he was the senior *Mossad* officer in The Philippines or even that he worked for *Mossad*. At the same time, he knew enough of recent *Mossad* missions to realize that Luis had a point: there might be some room for *Mossad* to help, though the distance with Israel and the lack of a strategic reason to get involved still weighed heavily on his mind. He simply replied:

"Ah! I see. You can easily imagine that this is a tough one. My job really is to liaise with your military and in some ways though less direct with the U.S. military in the area. I've no ground to stand on to start talking of *Mossad* issues in the area . . . Let me talk to Tel Aviv and see how they react. You may not believe it, but I would not know who works with *Mossad* here, and I am not even sure our ambassador knows either."

Luis breathed a visible sigh of relief and with a wry smile replied:

"I'm not surprised that whoever works for *Mossad* in this country is well undercover. Could well be working undercover as a businessman rather than a diplomat. The only thing you tell me that I would not have expected is that the ambassador may not know. But on that point, I assume you're speculating."

"Correct. One thing is for sure, I, myself, don't know."

Ehud paused and asked Luis the obvious question:

"Before I take this any further, can you tell me a bit more specifically what you want me to ask for?"

"I don't know for sure. But given your technological capabilities, would you be able to design and install defense mechanisms on a

---

[3] See "The Shadow Experts" by the same author, published by Barringer Publishing 2021.

production platform? Something which would deter anyone from attacking it? You must have done some of that in the Eastern Mediterranean at the Leviathan field. Or you must at least have considered it."

Ehud did not allow any form of facial expression change and simply asked:

"Sure as heck don't know. Would the defense mechanism be known to the outside or not?"

"I don't know. Maybe it wouldn't. Maybe it could be known. We might even show a demonstration, on some video . . ."

"Can see both positives and negatives. You don't feel the U.S., or your own government can do that?"

"They might, but I think we would be caught in red tape with the U.S., not to mention likely leaks. I know we can't do it in the Philippines."

"Let me see what I can do. I'll get back to you as soon as I can. But we've got to make sure we don't trigger a war with China. You know how they have reacted to various diplomatic overtures with Taiwan, and there's plenty of room for miscalculations here, my friend."

CHAPTER.03

TEL AVIV, ISRAEL

Having just gotten off the phone with Ehud, David laconically said to himself: *all in a day's work, I guess!*

This was the only thing that came to the mind of David Heller, the head of the *Disruption* department of *Mossad*. He was quietly winding down a day which had been routine so far. His group, probably the most discreet within an already very secretive organization, was generally in charge of activities which needed to be carried out in the interest of the state of Israel. They were thus considered within the spirit of Israel's Constitution: defending the country against its enemies. They included assassination of foreign leaders, sabotage of certain installations of which Israel did not approve, internet warfare and the like. His group did not appear on any organization chart—that anyone could procure. In his role, David reported to General Simon Rabinowitz, the overall head of *Mossad*. His group, though secret, was considered by the few people in the know as absolutely crucial. For Israel these were not luxury activities, they directly affected its ability to survive.

David was the ultimate civil servant and a first-class field operative to boot. Prior to assuming his newest functions, he had been the right-hand man of his predecessor, Simon Rabinowitz, and thus had been involved and led several field operations. He was of strong though elegant build, tipping the scales just shy of 190 pounds and stood just this much more than six feet tall. Though he clearly was of an athletic build, he had never allowed himself to cross the line where body building produced almost caricatural features; for instance, his neck was quite visible, despite strong upper body muscle mass. He liked to dress in civilian clothes despite his military rank of colonel and avoided wearing a tie unless absolutely ordered to. That day, he was wearing a nicely tailored light blue shirt, with tan pants. A blue blazer was casually draped onto the back of a chair sitting next to his desk.

After hanging up with Ehud, his first reaction was to call his boss, Simon, and see whether he would have some time for him. Simon immediately invited him to join him in his office, for an evening cup of tea or something else which he liked to call "adult beverages." Simon motioned David to his usual seat on the leather sofa in the corner of his office and said with a broad smile:

"You seem pretty flustered my friend. What can I do for you?"

"Well, I've just been hit with a truly unusual request . . ."

"Pray, tell."

David knew that Simon had enormously enjoyed his stint at the head of the Disruption department and had hesitated to accept the promotion which was going to take him away from its day-to-day activities. Thus, he felt safe with giving him the "long version" though he was careful to start with a headline that ought to grab his attention:

"How about getting involved in the oil business in the Philippines?"

David was quite right. The headline did catch Simon's attention. Simon did not reply immediately, appearing to be deep in thoughts and with a smile though maintaining a serious demeanor asked:

"You aren't serious, are you?"

"I sure am."

He paused and noticed that Simon still looked almost incredulous. He continued:

"Let me give you the short version. Our guy in Manila has befriended a local businessman who is in the oil business among others. His company just struck oil. That's the good news. The bad news is that the deposit is in an area, which is contested by several nations, the most problematic of which is China . . ."

"Now I see. You must be speaking of the Spratly Islands chain or thereabouts."

■ ■ ■ ■ ■

David and Simon went on to discuss the issue in as much depth as possible given the limited amount of information available to them at the time. Though Ehud would probably have been briefed on the topic once or twice, he would not have been expected to know all the details of Israel's own posture with respect to natural gas in general and offshore natural gas fields in particular. That was what Luis had been referring to when he mentioned the Leviathan field. More to the point, the challenges surely did not start with the Leviathan field. The genesis of the challenges went further back. The Mari and Noa gas fields had been discovered as far back as 2000; they fueled an offshore exploration boom in the Levant Basin in the eastern Mediterranean Sea. These fields, which started production in 2004 and were depleted about ten years later, led to the discovery of three much more important ones: the Tamar, Leviathan and Karish fields which began production in 2013, 2020 and 2022 respectively. With total recoverable gas reserves amounting to around 900 billion cubic meters, the discoveries revolutionized Israel's energy sector. Today, Israel produces about 21 billion cubic meters of gas, with almost half of it being exported to Egypt and Jordan.

Interestingly, David and Simon knew that the development of the Leviathan field, the one mentioned by Luis Ramos, had encountered long delays, having been discovered in 2010 and starting production in only 2019. These delays had been caused in large part by circumstances a few of which bore more than a passing resemblance to the situation in the Philippines. With the hydrocarbons flowing from undersea deposits located eighty miles off the shores of Haifa, almost due south of Cyprus, they had to be piped to processing facilities built for the field but located closer to shore. The Leviathan rig was constructed only six miles offshore. From there the gas reaches the mainland at the village of Dor and enters a gas grid that covers the whole country. Though domestic environmental concerns were not expected to play a role in the Philippines, which is eager for more locally sourced energy, the same could not be said for Leviathan: it had been slowed by resident fears that the pipeline could be carcinogenic.

On the other hand, security issues encountered with the three fields and the Leviathan platform specifically were generically similar to the circumstances driving Luis's request for help. While the Tamar platform was located out of sight, the Leviathan platform was positioned much closer. Fears of terrorist interference surely was an important factor. Meanwhile, Turkey's recent moves, though not nearly as aggressive as China's, raised issues because Israel decided to export some of the gas produced at Leviathan, rather than flood the domestic market, unless the current needs for oil could be converted to natural gas. Finally, the advent of Iran's precision-guided missile capability had become an even more serious concern. The attack on Saudi Arabia's Abqaiq installations offered a crystal-clear blueprint of what could be done, though the missiles would likely be routed from the northeast rather than the southeast if it was aimed at Israel's gas producing installation. Thus, Hezbollah, amply supplied with similar missiles by Iran, constituted a risk which was vividly illustrated when a rocket hit Israel just north of where Leviathan gas is coming onshore during one of several Gaza clashes in the prior dozen years.

It was quickly obvious to David and Simon that *Mossad* could not do anything that involved actively and visibly participating in the defense of an oil field abroad, whether it was in international waters off the coast of the Philippines or not. The Israeli Navy did not have the resources to carry out the task. Yet, they concluded that Ehud might get his Filipino contact together with his opposite number at the American Embassy and explore what could or could not be done. The issue of creating defensive capabilities for oil rigs was surely not beyond the realm of the possible, in theory. However, practical considerations, at a minimum how these capabilities would be surreptitiously deployed, were still at best unclear, not to mention how they might be shipped to the Philippines and from there brought on location.

They decided to organize a conference call with Ehud first to make sure they did not miss any detail in their analysis and second to tell him of their conclusions. Ehud took them though both a summary of the history of oil exploration and production in the Philippines and a brief description of the geopolitical tension with respect to the Spratly islands. He concluded that though he could see Luis Ramos De Ayala's point of view, recent history seemed to suggest that his fears might be somewhat overstated. David interrupted:

"You did suggest to me though that it would be great if we could develop some defense mechanism with respect to the drilling platform?"

"I did. I cannot totally discount Luis's concerns. So, my view is that the most discreet help would be to offer defenses for the platform. I don't see what else we can do, frankly."

Simon interjected:

"Neither do I, to be honest."

Simon paused and added for Ehud's benefit:

"Let David and me chew over this one the rest of the day. David will get back to you tomorrow before your lunchtime."

■ ■ ■ ■ ■

David went straight from Simon's office to visit Marvin Goldstein, a veteran of the service. If there was a way to help Luis, he would be the person critical to the execution of any solution they might develop. Marvin had an encyclopedic knowledge of the capabilities of each of the branches of the Israeli Defense Forces and of all that was planned. On the day David went to see him, he was not visiting an Israeli base or near some testing ground; he was in his office, a couple of floors and two buildings away from David's and Simon's offices.

Mossad headquarters were located in the north of Tel Aviv, just about three miles north of Hayarkon Park. The headquarters occupy a modern structure angled to face to the northwest; the complex is made up of seven individual but inter-connected structures, five of which are arranged as the two sides of a right angle. Each of these five towers looks somewhere between square and hexagonal and has a large internal light well which provides natural light to most rooms within. Most of the offices facing the outside and to the northwest have a nice, virtually unobstructed view, across the Glilot Ma'arav Interchange, of the Mediterranean, and of the Herzliya marina, and Marvin's certainly had one of them.

Marvin was all smiles when he greeted David as he was standing at the door of his office. He had a well-documented weakness for technobabble, which people tolerated simply because he was Marvin. The few details which David had given him over the phone were enough to get Marvin quite excited; he surely would have an opportunity to design or at least adapt something calling on advanced technology.

"How are you, David? Please come in . . ."

Marvin's office was just as one would have expected it: messy like the office one always assumed belonged to the proverbial absent-minded professor. He had drawings, blueprints, mock-ups, and detailed models of several of his current works-in-progress. The coffee table in front of his visitors' sofa was covered with technical magazines and papers or articles which he had not yet read or wanted to read again before deciding what to do with them. There were even a few folders on the floor in the general area of his desk. In marked contrast with the chaos which seemed to reign everywhere there were two orchid plants, one white and one purple and pink blooming on the credenza. They had enough sunlight to satisfy their needs for some light and not too much that they might have died. Marvin took care of their weekly watering himself and everyone knew not to tinker with them: they were his and not *Mossad*'s. Once told of Marvin's insistence on watering his plants himself, David imagined him, once a week or so, busy soaking the orchids in water for thirty odd minutes and then lovingly placing them back on their white saucers on the credenza, after having wiped the excess water from the outside of the pots.

"I love your orchids, Marvin."

"Thanks. They represent an area of calm, no, more than that: an area of poetry in this office. Ever heard about Zen?"

He paused for one second seemingly pondering what he had just said and addressing a concern many had mentioning the first time they saw his office immediately added:

"Don't be fooled. The place may look chaotic. Yet, though I know you won't believe me, I can tell you that I know precisely where everything is; which pile and which folder."

David smiled and simply replied:

"That surely would not surprise me."

Then, without engaging in any further chit chat, David suddenly switched to the reason for his visit. He was cautious not to start a conversation on Zen, which he knew very well: as it relates to art, Zen looks for simplicity, asymmetry, austere sublimity, naturalness, freedom from routine, tranquility, and profound grace. He did not want to launch Marvin in some lengthy side-tirade. So, in a casual manner, he asked Marvin:

"Can you imagine a way to defend against terrorist attacks oil exploration or production equipment that may be quite far offshore?"

Marvin surprised David. He did not need to take the time to think before he replied:

"Aren't you aware that we have already had to deal with that problem?"

Incredulous, David could only say:

"Really?"

"Remember, we've had to protect some of our own offshore platforms. We have been using floating production facilities, linked to the wells with flexible pipelines connected to subsea completions. Unless I'm missing something big, the only novelty here would be that none of our platforms are eighty miles offshore."

David motioned that he was generally aware of that though he had not drawn a comparison. Marvin added:

"We quickly decided to link distant deposits by pipeline and maintain the production facilities close to shore. We felt the trouble of an undersea pipeline was well worth it as the closer the platform was to shore, the easier it would be to defend it."

"I appreciate that. Now my question dealt with a Filipino instance. In their case, the mix of oil and natural gas I am told favors oil; while I believe that in the Mediterranean, we've got more gas than oil. Could the Filipinos consider doing the same thing?"

Marvin, as he was wont to do at times then went into excessive detail. David initially tried motioning him to forgo the engineering lesson, but finally let him complete his lecture; he was too far gone:

"Natural gas is more volatile and lighter than crude oil. That would work to the advantage of the Filipinos. A separator used for separating oil from gas is usually under, at most, 100 pounds of pressure. By comparison, the separators used for gas wells are under at least 1,000 pounds of pressure and may have a max test pressure of about 2,000 psi. Yet, they are generally small with a very rugged construction."

He paused to take a sip from his trusted water glass and continued:

"Now there, in the Philippines, from what you told me, they would be separating oil from gas. They'd be operating at a much lower pressure, with potentially lighter equipment."

He paused and immediately added:

"By the way, lighter does not mean smaller or less complicated . . ."

"From your mouth to God's ears . . ."

David paused and then asked:

"Do we have a system to protect the rigs themselves, whether they are fixed or float?"

"Let me give you a qualified yes. I won't tell you it isn't quite complex. In fact, it adds some weight to a rig, but it's doable. Would you seek protection just from the air?"

David looked at Marvin quizzically. Marvin became more specific:

"There are two ways, no, maybe three but two of them are similar, to attack a rig. You can fire a missile at it, that's above ground, or rather that's something which travels through the air. You can also fire a torpedo at it. That's an underwater thing. Finally, you can send divers and have them place explosives on the rig, but that is close to the torpedo problem."

David did not say anything but marveled at the fact that Marvin had been able to describe the three scenarios in such a succinct manner. He asked:

"If I told you I don't know how the attack might materialize, what would you say?"

"Not surprised. We can cover all three, but I must tell you that we're talking of at least two, probably three different systems. It would be complex; and it would be a "first" for us to combine them all in a single package. Yet, I can tell you that we have capabilities to provide each of them already, one way or the other."

Marvin paused. David noticed his right eye twinkling and was ready for the tirade:

"I am simplifying a bit here."

Here it comes, David thought. Yet Marvin only added:

"We already have quite a few items of infrastructure which allow us to do it. I'll spare you the gory details, but just think of the Iron Dome and it'll give you a sense of what I mean."

■ ■ ■ ■ ■

Marvin was referring to Israel's all-weather, air defense system, which was designed, with the help of the U.S., to protect the country against incoming rockets or artillery shells. It had proven its worth in recent times, when it managed to intercept most rockets fired from Gaza or even from Lebanon. Unfortunately, though it might arguably be the world's most advanced missile defense system, it had only been ninety percent accurate, which kept alive the fear that some nuclear-tipped missile might get through.

■ ■ ■ ■ ■

Marvin continued his explanation: "Further, with respect to underwater protection, we are operating within our own territorial waters and if not, we are surely within the contiguous zone. That means we have a lot of freedom regarding what we can do and control over how we do it. Your situation would be quite a bit more complicated: you'd be quite a bit further out at sea."

David hurried to reply:

"I understand, Marvin. Many thanks. This has been super helpful. I think I can use it as a basis to gain a better understanding of the situation over there. Am I correct assuming that everything you told me is pretty much top secret?"

"Absolutely. Need to know only."

CHAPTER.04

MANILA, THE PHILIPPINES AND TEL AVIV, ISRAEL

Ehud Shamir and Luis Ramos De Ayala were calmly waiting on the tarmac for the arrival of Mark Levi, a close associate of David Heller's. They had seen the Gulfstream private jet swoosh down and softly land on the main runway of the Ninoy Aquino International Airport as effortlessly as a crane touching down on a lake shore.

The airport was named after Benigno "Ninoy" Aquino Jr., a former Philippine senator, who was assassinated on Sunday, August 21, 1983, on the tarmac of Manila International Airport as he returned from self-imposed exile. His murder rekindled the opposition to the regime of Ferdinand E. Marcos, who was eventually forced into exile himself, after a campaign of civil resistance against the violence committed by the regime and the suspected rampant electoral fraud. The revolution was nonviolent, and a presidential election was held in 1986. Then, tempers started to run high as the regime declared Ferdinand Marcos the winner and Ninoy Aquino's widow, his sole opponent, the loser, despite evidence that she had truthfully won. In a bit of a surprise move, the military decided to throw its weight behind Mrs. Aquino. Though both Marcos and Mrs. Aquino were concurrently installed as president, Ferdinand Marcos fled the country that same day for Guam, an unincorporated territory of the United States located about 1,400 nautical miles east of Manila. He subsequently moved to and died in Hawaii in 1989. It is ironic to note that the results of the recently long-awaited presidential elections in the Philippines crowned as the country's 17th president Ferdinand "Bongbong" Marcos, Jr., the son of the former dictator, Ferdinand E. Marcos, and this with no suspicion of any electoral fraud.

Mark Levi was greeted by Ehud who introduced him to Luis, as Mike Loeb, at the bottom of the steps of his aircraft. He immediately noted the local attire worn by Luis, a classical *barong Tagalog*, over grey slacks with black shoes. The *barong Tagalog*, the national dress of the Philippines for men, more simply known as *barong*, is an elaborately embroidered long-sleeved formal dress for men; light as a shirt, it is cut and worn somewhat like a jacket. It can both constitute formal or semi-formal attire, always worn untucked over an undershirt with belted trousers. Though it was originally cut as a button-up shirt, new shapes have emerged in the last twenty years which rather than being buttoned from top to bottom, only have buttons down the top half of the shirt. It is traditionally made with sheer textiles woven from banana or pineapple plant fibers, although, increasingly, cheaper materials are also used given the very high cost of pineapple fibers. The newer style would typically be considered less formal than the alternative which, when exceptionally finely embroidered and made of pineapple fiber can be worn in lieu of a tuxedo jacket, though with black tuxedo pants and black patent leather shoes.

After the quick greeting, they walked a few yards to the left of the Gulfstream and climbed aboard the dark blue Bell 206 B-3 Jet Ranger helicopter which Luis owned and enjoyed piloting himself. Though he always had his own private pilot with him, if only in order to bring the aircraft from its hangar to wherever Luis was, be it to the top of the Pacific Towers where he lived, to the top of the building where his head offices were located or any other location, he would take over the controls of the helicopter whenever it was prudent for him to do so. However, he always sat on the left-hand side of the cockpit, leaving the main pilot's right-hand seat to Enrique, his personal pilot. In helicopters, sitting on the right-hand side is most frequent as it allows the pilot to keep their right hand on the aircraft's sensitive cyclic control stick. Luis's caution was often warranted in the Metro-Manila region owing to the intensity of the helicopter traffic crisscrossing the sky over the Filipina capital and its suburbs and to the various landing or takeoff patterns at the international airport. Further, fog is quite common in Manila, except maybe from January to April which constitutes the dry season, and it tends to make flying more challenging, particularly when fog combines with wind.

■ ■ ■ ■ ■

Earlier, David had called Mark to his office. He simply declared:

"Mark, I would like you to be our point man on this potential assignment. Note that I am not using the word 'mission,' because I still don't know whether there can be or even should be a mission."

"Understood, sir. What do you want me to do?"

After providing as detailed a briefing as necessary, David concluded:

"We are being asked for help by this individual, Luis Ramos De Ayala. He is a local contact developed by our man in Manila, Ehud Shamir."

"Met him before. A solid guy, correct?"

"Ah. You mean Ehud. Absolutely. Simon and I feel that there may be a way, maybe even more than one way to help. Yet, as always, helping anyone exposes us to all sorts of leaks. The most critical one would be for people to find out we're involved. But there may also be issues of technology falling into the wrong hands or even our being criticized, no, condemned, for sticking our noses where they don't belong."

David paused and seeing that Mark was totally on board, he came straight to the goal he was looking Mark to reach:

"We need to know whether this is something which we can reasonably undertake. Will it require capabilities which we do not have? If so, where could we find them? And always, above all, what do you think of the people with whom we would be working?"

Mark could not refrain from asking the obvious next question:

"Don't we have someone on the spot? Could he not do the job?"

"We do. I just mentioned his name, Ehud Shamir."

"Sorry, my question was poorly phrased. Why can't he or she do that?"

"It's complicated. Ehud has been cultivating the businessman but has never told him what his real job was; officially he is our military attaché in the Manila Embassy and that's all that his contact, Luis, believe he does. Ehud does not want to run the risk of being 'outed.' We still need him in what we shall simply call his unofficial occupation."

"If I may, sir, does it mean that he does not trust the gentleman, Luis, you called him?"

"Absolutely. I actually asked the question. Ehud's view is that Luis, as that's indeed his name, would probably keep everything quiet. Yet, he told me that the Philippines are not a place where you rely on anyone on the secrecy front. He also reminded me that typically *Mossad* agents do not reveal their true identity except maybe when they are bringing a new local agent in . . ."

"And you want me there?"

"Well, I do, but you shall not be Mark Levi, a senior officer in *Mossad*. You are a consultant whom we have been using on missions where there is a need for us, i.e. *Mossad*, but where we cannot be in the open."

"Isn't that a bit too complicated? Will anyone believe it?"

"Ehud tells me that this setup would work. He concedes that there will be plenty of questions or even rumors. But the absolute key for us is that there will be no smoking guns. In fact, you will be using an official government aircraft, but only because El Al does not fly to Manila. Depending upon what you find and what you think, you may need to return to Manila, or not!"

"I assume you have the appropriate documents as well as a bio for me to learn . . . By the way, what's my name?"

"We used a simple one: Mike Loeb. As you can see, we kept your initials unchanged . . . as usual."

■ ■ ■ ■ ■

Mike, aka Mark, was delighted to have had the opportunity to leave the airport by helicopter when he saw the traffic down below. Though not as congested as Bangkok, in Thailand, Manila developed serious traffic problems over the years: the number of vehicles on the road had grown faster than the number of roads needed to accommodate them. Thus, being able to fly over it rather than slowly crawl through it was a luxury which Mike appreciated at its appropriate worth. The aircraft landed atop one of the highest buildings in Makati, Manila's business district: the Ayala Tower One, in which Luis's offices were located. They quickly stepped away from the helipad to a hallway where they found the building's elevators. Right after the metal door that led to the hallway, Mike was surprised that they all had to subject themselves to the always present security searches which are inevitable in Manila. Luis noticed his surprise and simply said:

"I'm sorry, but this is a crucial need here, given the terrorist risks which are ever present."

He paused for a second and added:

"No exception. Even I have to subject myself to it."

Ehud turned to Mike to tell him something which he had not been able to do over the noise inside the helicopter, though all four of them wore headphones to talk to one another:

"I've booked you for the night. You'll be here at the Peninsula Hotel Makati. It is one of the best hotels around here and has the added benefit of being literally one block away from here . . . We are on Ayala Avenue here and the hotel is at the corner of Ayala Avenue and Makati Avenue."

Laughingly, Luis added:

"And do not answer if anybody knocks on your door at night. I know it's much rarer in hotels like The Peninsula, but, in many hotels in Metro-Manila, you can be sure you'll hear about pretty women, patrolling the hallways, gently knocking at doors hoping to find clients ready to pay for their favors."

He paused and added:

"And at times, they're not even women. They just disguise themselves as women!"

Mike simply smiled and replied:

"I'm a married man with two children . . . Don't have much of a need for these extra-curricular activities."

Luis realized that his joke did not capture the imagination of his guests and quickly switched to another topic. As they stepped out of the elevator which had stopped only a few floors from the top, Mike was surprised by the opulence of the reception area of Luis's holding company's office. He had not been warned that Asian businessmen tended to compete with one another in terms of the overall decoration of their offices, or at least their reception areas, meeting rooms and senior executive offices. Filipinos did not escape that rule and liked to put their best foot forward. They spared little expenses decorating their offices. Here, the entrance door was framed with two large teak statues, had dark hardwood paneling all around and displayed the name of the holding company in large golden letters behind the desk where two receptionists sat. What portion of the walls that was not paneled was dressed in a dark green fabric, offering a nice contrast to the dark red, thick wall-to-wall carpeting. The sitting area was delineated with a large, dark green, Chinese rug with crème designs, and had furniture which though upholstered displayed its deep orange-brown, sculpted rosewood frame.

One of the two ladies behind the receptionists' desk jumped up from her chair when she saw Luis arrive accompanied by his two guests. She wore a long skirt, slit on both sides, made of Chinese or maybe Thai silk. Her top was very sober and suggested that the company's dress code eschewed overly sexy outfits. She ushered all three of them through a large door on the right. Through that door was the Board Area, which comprised three small conference rooms and the boardroom itself, the *piece de resistance*! Opposite the double door leading to the boardroom, another set of double doors would take Luis and his guests into his own office suite. Yet, before taking them there, he wanted to show them the boardroom itself.

It was quite different from any such room that either Ehud or Mike, and quite likely most people as well had ever seen. Rather than having a long table with comfortable armchairs arranged along both sides, the board table itself was semi-circular, with room for people to sit on the straight side of the semi-circle if they were making a presentation. The room was surely more than one-story high, though Ehud and Mike could not understand how that was possible in a high-rise building, with tenants above. The table faced the entrance. A larger-than-life TV screen would rotate down from the ceiling to hang above the door. On the walls on either side of the door, there were four smaller TV sets, two on each side. Mike noticed another door at the back of the room, correctly assuming that it was the sole entrance available when the large TV screen was down. Luis explained:

"My philosophy is that rectangular tables do not make for free-flowing conversations. Typically, one talks to the two neighbors on the same side of the table, and, if one is lucky, one or two across the way. I want people to have direct sight lines to everyone. Further, no position is more prestigious than any other. We all face the screens. Presenters can stand in the middle if they need to, although I discourage it as it can obstruct someone's view of the TV screens."

He paused observing the admiring looks on Ehud's and Mike's faces, and added, in passing:

"Actually, Mike, Ehud can confirm to you that I eat my own cooking; I apply the same principle in my own dining room at home. The table is circular and can seat as many as 16 people. When among ourselves, we have a lazy Susan in the middle, and everyone can serve themselves as a dish is brought around to them. As a matter of fact, every Sunday evening, we have our whole family for an early dinner, and everyone is encouraged, even the youngest, to say a few words. A great learning experience. The round table makes hearing so much easier and conversations more comfortable."

As they were exiting the board room to walk into his office suite, Luis asked if anyone wanted to use the rest rooms. With nobody expressing a need, they entered the cavernous office, which could easily have been sufficient to hold at least five or six large individual executive offices in Israel. Mike made a mental note that the decoration was even more luxurious than in the reception area, as there were a few jade sculptures displayed in individually lit glass cases, together with four very nice paintings, which he believed had to be from the French impressionist epoch. Luis invited them to sit in one of the corners of the office, where comfortable, plush leather furniture awaited them. Cups of teas and glasses of water appeared to the side of each of them, placed on white linen spread on the small individual end tables as well as the central coffee table. Luis politely thanked the lady who had brought everything in and simply asked:

"What can I tell you, Mike?"

"I'm here to try and understand the situation, sir. As you know, I am an independent consultant who does some work for the Israeli government, but also for a number of private businesses."

"What is your specialty?"

"Security. You know this is important in Israel. In reality, for us, it is a matter of survival, not a luxury."

CHAPTER.05

SOMEWHERE IN THE AUSTRIAN ALPS AND TEL AVIV, ISRAEL

"Hello David, so nice to hear your voice . . ."

The female voice on the phone belonged to Countess Renate, founder, and head of The Shadow Experts. That network was as secret as its leader. It consisted of specialists across a wide variety of disciplines who cooperated with and were directed by Countess Renate to defend "good causes." They ranged from micro-biologists to advanced material engineers, to art experts, to cyber engineers, to electronics gurus, and to many other specialties, each as esoteric as the others. All associates knew they were members of the network, but most did not know who the other members were, other than those people with whom they had come to work on one or another assignment. They all knew Renate; most, if not all, had seen her in person or on some video conference call. Yet, no one could claim that he or she had met with her regularly. These specialists were all "part time associates" who came into a team to solve a problem and returned to the shadows when they were no longer needed. Besides enjoying the prestige of being a member of the network, they were all generously rewarded when they participated in a project.

Renate had no board of directors. Her only employees were a handful of individuals who worked for her at the castle, her residence in the Austrian alps. The castle had a completely hidden lair which allowed Renate to remain linked to everyone without anyone knowing where she was. She even had a corporate jet which had been modified to include a vertical take-off and landing capability and could be hidden underground. She could leave or return to the castle without anyone seeing how she had flown in or out, as the castle grounds did not include any visible runway. The handful of employees were the only ones who knew of her twin identities—her real name was Princess Alexandra, a wealthy orphan and distant heir to the Habsburg imperial crown. Her husband, Prince Karl, of Danish royal blood, also morphed into Captain Frederik, her pilot and all-around aide when she became Countess Renate.

David returned the greeting. Always businesslike, he then immediately shifted to the reason for his phone call. Both David and *Mossad* had several opportunities to work with Countess Renate. *Mossad* never doubted its own ability to conduct any form of activity typical of a secret service; in fact, quite a number of members of *Mossad* would unashamedly proclaim that they were at least as good and often better than any other secret service. At the same time, *Mossad* was quick to appreciate that they did not always have ready and almost immediate access to the top minds in several disciplines. They had thus initiated a relationship with Countess Renate and her group, which had so far never failed to succeed. He simply said:

"We may very well find ourselves working together again, Countess."

Uncharacteristically, Renate waited a couple of second to reply:

"That would be great. But wait, you seem unsure. Something's wrong, David. What is it?"

David was not surprised by her reaction. He knew how perceptive she was, and her question made him realize that he was in fact not calling her with the same ultimate goal as usual. Normally, he would call her after having already delved into a mission, planned its execution in some depth and discovered that he needed her services. Here, he readily conceded, he was calling before he really knew whether his team could or even would undertake the mission. He replied to her question taking her through the most recent developments regarding what he called "the Philippines situation." Yet, to make sure that he addressed her concern upfront, he made it clear that the point of his phone call was more to gather information which he might potentially use rather than to request immediate help. More specifically, he argued:

"Simon and I have talked about this, and we are in total agreement. There is no compelling need for Israel to participate in this situation. Our role is to ensure that Israel is free to flourish and thus to fight any obstacle which prevent us from achieving our goal. Here, there would be no direct impact on Israel's security. The only reason we could conceive would be the usual 'it cannot hurt to weaken a potential enemy.' And at this point we are not even sure who the potential enemy is."

"I am sure you're going to expand on this my friend. So far, I am totally confused."

David smiled and went on to explain that he could easily see how the Philippines would benefit from exploiting the hydrocarbons they had potentially discovered. He mentioned that he used the word "potentially" because oil exploration and production there had been characterized as a stop-and-go process, adding:

". . . periods of euphoria followed by periods of disappointment."

He paused and corrected himself:

"I must admit that our sources seem to suggest that the current discovery may truly be significant this time. But forgive my skepticism as this movie has had many reruns and none so far has come up to expectations."

Returning to his general description, he argued that the main issue had to do with the fact that the oil field was in an area which should surely belong to the Philippines, with the potential to share some of the profits with a small handful of neighboring countries. He however conceded that the area was still caught up in a geopolitical squabble, adding:

"The first successful well was drilled in an area which though not within the territorial waters or even their contiguous extension, is still closer to the Philippines and its shores than any other country. As I just indirectly implied, Brunei and Malaysia might have something to say about that, although the well is more than 200 miles from the northern tip of Borneo. This is where you find the two states comprising East Malaysia, Sabah at the very north of Borneo and Sarawak to its southwest. The sultanate of Brunei is sandwiched between the two of them, still on the northwest coast of Borneo."

"I think I know where you're going, David. China is the issue, correct?"

"Absolutely. Excellent deduction. China has become more and more aggressive asserting sovereignty over many islands in the greater China Sea area. By the way, this does not only concern the Spratly Islands in the South China Sea, but also extends to and includes the Senkaku Islands in the East China Sea. These are claimed by both Tokyo and Taipei. With China claiming that Taiwan is part of China, the Chinese feel they also have a claim on the Senkaku islands. A real mess if you don't mind my saying so."

He paused for a short, few seconds and returned to his story:

"Our contact in Manila, the fellow who owns and controls the operations within that service contract is worried about the costs of exploiting the deposit. And here, the key issue is the incremental cost which might be related to security. Now, on the one hand, he knows how expensive this would be and has understood the exploitation would take time, both to create the infrastructure and then to recover the oil and the gas. On the other, he also knows that the Philippines have had experience with the consequences of pumping oil out too fast, destroying reservoirs. So, he is looking for help on two fronts: oil production expertise and security from potential Chinese or Chinese-sponsored attacks."

"Sorry, David, but I can't see why this makes sense. He has his own government and the U.S., doesn't he?"

"Sure does. He is looking for more. Specifically, he's looking for discreet protection for the equipment, and possibly for the field."

"So? Why Israel?"

"Well, as you may or may not know, we have had to deal with somewhat analogous circumstances here in the South-eastern Mediterranean Sea."

"How?"

"Have you ever heard of the Leviathan natural gas field?"

"Have to be honest and say I have not. What's the connection?"

David went on to explain that the Leviathan gas field was a game changer in the energy picture for Israel, adding:

"We needed to think of security issues when we developed it. By the way, it supplies virtually all our natural gas needs and allows us to export some to both Jordan and Egypt."

"I see. I see. But what was the security problem?"

"Distance from our shores and the risk of terrorist attacks from anywhere, Syria, Lebanon, Turkey, you name it."

"Ah! Now, I'm starting to see the connection. What have you all done?"

"Let me simply say at this point that we have developed tools that allow us to locate the 'heavy production equipment' quite a bit closer to shore than the fields themselves. The Leviathan deposit is nearly 80 miles offshore, almost due south of Cyprus. By the way, it covers about the same surface area as that island, if not more."

"Wow. It's massive."

"You said it. That's why it's been called a game changer. Let me explain how we dealt with the problems. We drilled four strategically located production wells and used what the trade calls 'subsea completions' to control the flow of natural gas. These subsea wells were then connected, via two 75-mile-long pipelines, to an offshore platform, six miles offshore the village of Dor. That's where we initially store the gas and feed it into our national pipeline network."

David paused and added:

"The key, as I'm sure you realize, is that the heavy stuff is only six miles from shore, and thus well within our ability to defend it. I am not saying that nobody could mess with the whole setup, but let's simply say that it would be more difficult than if the production platform was 80 or so miles offshore."

"You must have had to protect your subsea installations?"

"Correct. That's the knowledge we bring to the party, protecting the subsea completions, coordinating their operations, ensuring the safety of the two pipelines, and many other ancillary and yet critical activities. Suffice it to say that we designed a system calling upon subsea sensors and drones."

"I know you well enough to be aware that I can't ask for more information. Need to know, correct?"

"Right."

"Well, to me it sounds like you have it down pat. What else would you need that we might be able to provide?"

"Israel per se does not need anything at this point. But the Philippines might. See, the Leviathan field produces natural gas and holds virtually no liquid petroleum. The area in the Philippines, Northwest Palawan Island, where our contact is operating would principally yield crude oil, with some natural gas."

"I'm not sure where that takes you . . ."

David explained that he had talked briefly with one of Israel's top natural gas experts, Frank Meyer, about the issue. The simple conclusion seemed to be that there were significant differences between exploiting a gas field and an oil reservoir. David argued that Frank basically said that he would hesitate to apply the "formula" he had designed for Leviathan without consulting with someone with more experience with crude oil reservoirs.

"Don't need any more, David. I see. In short, you're wondering whether The Shadow Experts could help with a deposit containing more oil than gas?"

"Absolutely, and one which cannot be exploited in a conventional fashion because of location and security risks. But, again, I must stress that there is nothing definite at this point. Your old friend, Mark Levi, remember him?"

"Certainly do . . ."

"Well, he is in Manila as we speak, playing the role of a security consultant and visiting with our local businessman contact. His task is to tell us whether he feels the contact is someone with whom we could deal. If yes, I would need to ask you the question formally. But if no, there is no need to disturb you any further."

Countess Renate thanked David for the extra detail and indicated that she understood that David needed to know whether he could access the appropriate resource before committing to help the Filipino contact, adding:

"If it comes to that."

She paused for a second and concluded:

"I am not sure what it would involve in any sort of detail, as I am sure you already assumed. Yet, I can confirm that I have access to a resource who could surely help with the design of whatever exploitation plan your contact might be interested in. He is a gentleman, now retired, but was involved in many offshore oil production ventures, on the engineering side. I believe he has been working on a new design for an oil/gas separator which allows it to be placed on the sea floor rather than on the drilling or production rig. Now, ostensibly, I would see this in the same vein as our earlier efforts, our joint ventures if I can call them that."

She argued that her network did not have real expertise with respect to ensuring the security of the physical installation, both above and under water, though she mused it might be something for her to think about in the future, adding:

"The question is bound to be asked more and more often."

She was also clear that her resources would surely be capable to help decide how best to exploit the oil deposit. The fact that she kept calling the individual she might introduce a resource led David to wonder whether the gentleman was or was not an associate. Returning to her potential assignment, she added that helping analyze whether the gas can be recovered and sold would be well within her group's capabilities. She asked a last question:

"How about the safety of my resource if we come to that?"

"Excellent question, Countess. At this point, I really don't know anything that would make me believe that the situation within the Manila area requires us worrying, although . . . In the end, who knows? I am not sure I can say the same thing when it comes to Palawan. I know that Abu Sayaff, an Islamic group which had been involved in numerous kidnappings, has been active, principally in the south of Palawan and southward all the way to Northern Borneo. We have not heard about anything to the northwest of the island, but we would certainly need to evaluate the situation in depth before we stuck both feet in the water. That's an issue of coordination with the Filipino government . . ."

"Understood. Clearly, I'll need more specific details if it ever gets to the point where we work together."

"Sounds promising, though you are correct: we need to know a lot more and have much more detailed plans. Thanks Countess."

"Most welcome. Give my best to Simon."

CHAPTER.06

MANILA, THE PHILIPPINES AND TEL AVIV, ISRAEL

Luis and his two guests, Ehud Shamir and Mike Loeb, first went through a very general conversation designed to provide Mike the outline of the "big picture," as Luis described it. He spent time discussing the history of oil exploration and production in the country and the growing challenge he felt the Philippines experienced with China. He then suggested that the three of them went from the sitting area in his office to the round conference table that could be found to the right of the door as one entered the office suite. He explained:

"I have a few maps there. I'd like to show them to you. It'll make everything much simpler."

Mike agreed with a smile, and apologizing for his poor sight, proceeded to don glasses. Luis started with a map of the whole country, adding:

"The Philippines is the world's thirteenth most populous country. It really is an archipelago, consisting of around 7,640 islands that are broadly categorized under three main geographical divisions which we call "island groups" from north to south: Luzon, Visayas, and Mindanao. Mindanao is the region which has given us a bad reputation since the 1960s when the Moro National Liberation Front started to advocate for a 'Moro homeland' through terrorism and the like. Palawan is in the Luzon area and has been relatively calm, except way in the south."

The next map which Luis pulled out was from the Island of Palawan. He said:

"Palawan is the western-most region of the country. If you excluded anything to do with hydrocarbon exploration or production, you'd simply describe it as a pristine underpopulated area. You'd even probably say that a good part of it is firmly stuck in the past: fishing, sustenance agriculture, and a general disregard for things modern, except for those they see on television which is gradually penetrating everywhere."

Ehud interrupted:

"That's probably going to change habits around there. Television and the internet."

Luis nodded with a wry smile and concluded:

"There's quite a bit of tourism; people come here principally looking for beaches and scuba diving. Now, note that it's far from being a single island. In truth, it counts no less than 1,780 islands and islets."

Mark could not resist:

"How many square feet or kilometers, whichever is easiest for you?"

"The whole region has hardly more than 5,600 square miles, 50% again as big as Crete or Cyprus in your part of the world. Yet, it is the largest province in the country in terms of total area. Again, it is known for its great beaches and lagoons and has remained untouched by modern development."

Pointing to the northwest of the main island, which looks like an elongated knife blade, Luis added drawing attention to different points on the map:

"That's where we have been the most successful from the point of view of hydrocarbon development. Here is the Malampaya gas field and a bit further north and west you can see the Galoc field, which is currently in production. It uses what we call an FPSO, which stands for floating production, storage, and offloading. It does not warrant permanent installations because the field is not large enough. So, you have a turret mooring system that floats on the surface and is connected both to the subsea wellheads and to the vessel where the hydrocarbon flow is processed and stored until a large tanker comes and takes delivery."

Pointing just east of the Galoc field, and thus to an area between Galoc and the mainland, he said:

"And here is where the new well we drilled is located. Mike, I'm sure Ehud has mentioned to you that it looks quite exciting."

"He has indeed."

Luis continued:

"A couple of important points. First, being east, we are in shallower waters; Galoc lies in waters that are 800 to 1,200 feet deep, while ours looks like we're rather between 600 and 800. Second, the closer we get to shore, the more we feel protected from foreign intrusions . . ."

Mike asked:

"What kind of reservoir do you have there?"

"Probably the same as in Galoc, turbidite sandstone. The one exciting element is that, based on the various seismic surveys we've conducted, as well as many others that were run before we started, the geological trap seems potentially larger than Galoc. By the way, this is highly confidential. I'm keeping this very close to the vest as I don't want undue pressure from the government or unnecessary attention from anyone."

Mike asked:

"Could that be the trap which Chuck Wilson once thought was going to be found?"

Luis first looked surprised that Mike knew about Chuck Wilson: "How in the world do you know about him?"

Mike explained:

"Ehud briefed me, telling me that this is a big part of the history of the oil industry in this country. So, I went and did my homework. Simple as that."

Luis replied:

"I see. Now back to your question. Again, no word about that to anyone, but I am thinking that it is quite possible, not to say probable that this is what Chuck Wilson had predicted would eventually be discovered."

Mike asked how much work had already been carried out on the field. Luis replied that he had so far frozen all activity ahead of his request to Ehud, arguing that he needed precise budgetary data. Mike then asked how he would go about that plan now. Luis unabashedly made the point that he wanted to keep this one quite confidential, arguing that as a country, the Philippines leaked like a sieve. He still offered a summary of his needs:

"I am looking both for some protection for any installation I may put in place and for some engineering and production assistance from consultants who are in nobody else's pocket."

David found Mark's early report encouraging, at least to the extent that it showed a potentially quite interesting hydrocarbon discovery. He was also impressed by Luis's careful approach to sharing any information or data. Unfortunately, it validated a few of the fears he had originally had that the secrecy which *Mossad* would need to help in this project might not be available.

Originally named Wellhead Drilling, Global Energy is a subsidiary of the Wellhead Group, one of Israel's largest companies. It is involved in the finance and insurance area as well as energy and infrastructure. It has investments in upstream and downstream energy, water desalination and power plants. Global Energy's focus has been the Eastern Mediterranean, where it had initiated the natural gas sector in Israel, and made history with its unprecedented agreements with Egypt, Jordan and the UAE which strengthened peace and increased stability in the Middle East. Global Energy holds 45% of the Leviathan Reservoir, the largest gas reservoir in the Mediterranean.

■ ■ ■ ■ ■

David had fully realized that *Mossad* might, if it came to it, provide some assistance on the security front. At the same time, the critical element, and one which he knew was not within the scope of what *Mossad* could do, related to helping on the technical oil exploration and production front. He also was aware of the fact that Countess Renate's Shadow Experts group might have consultants able to provide insights and even help, but he was pretty sure that they did not have the wherewithal to help with actual operating resources So, his focus turned to who could fill that gap, with the idea that the one thing he would require is for that group or entity to have solid relationships with the Israeli government, principally to manage the risk of leaks about *Mossad*'s role.

His thoughts naturally gravitated toward the group behind Global Energy. He wondered: . . . *might they be prepared to offer a cover for the activities which Mossad and possibly even The Shadow Experts could provide to The Philippines?* His rationale was simple. They had all the experience that one might wish for. Additionally, after all, they had already been prepared to run joint operations with countries like Cyprus or even the United Arab Emirates. The idea of trying to foster a joint venture with a Filipino group might not seem all that crazy, particularly if there were certain government guarantees serving as some backdrop.

He understood he would need to be very careful as the Wellhead Group, which was behind Global Energy, was a public company in Israel and would thus need to make all the appropriate financial disclosures. Yet, the idea that was germinating in his head was that disclosures would only be necessary if the impact on the financial fortunes of Wellhead were deemed material.

David picked up his phone and asked Simon if he had a few minutes for him. Simon was happy to give him fifteen to thirty minutes but said he could not spare more. David rushed to Simon's office and gave a summary of the highlights of his conversation with Mark and asked:

"Do you think we could get Global Energy involved?"

Simon smiled. His protégé's idea was truth be told quite original. It would allow Israel to offer some help and possibly earn some equity in the project all the while leaving *Mossad* and The Shadow Experts to operate behind the scenes. Now, at least two key questions would have to receive satisfactory and positive answers. Would Wellhead be prepared to lend its name to such an endeavor? Would Luis be prepared to share some equity with them?

Simon knew that the man behind Wellhead was Eli Abelman, an Israeli billionaire who first created his wealth on the Israeli real estate, finance, and insurance scenes. He then grew Wellhead into the energy powerhouse it had become, in part as it had been one of the discoverers of the Leviathan natural gas reservoir. Eli had started working in the Israeli Defense Ministry, focusing on a variety of construction projects, primarily on military bases all over the country. Simon was also aware that Eli had divested from a large share of his business interests in the recent past, which led him to assume that he might be ready to help the government in one way or another. Unfortunately, Simon did not have direct access to Eli. Yet he thought: *I'd bet Ariel knows him.*

■ ■ ■ ■ ■

Ariel Landau, the almost legendary former head of *Mossad*, was the one who had groomed Simon to take over from him as he retired. Physically, Ariel had never been of an impressive stature: he was relatively short, and his hairline had receded virtually all the way, leaving but a small crown of black and grey hair arranged in a semi-circle, going from one ear to the other around the back of his head. He wore black-rimmed, round glasses. On the other hand, intellectually, he was a giant. People said that he had one of the most piercing minds. He was noticed almost immediately by his superiors in whatever capacity he was employed. He had an informal nickname within the Israeli Cabinet and within *Mossad* when he was active there: "Steel Trap." This referred to his mind being like a steel trap—nothing escaped. Finally, he was also a fabulous human being, and Simon was humbled that he was able to develop a true friendship with him.

■ ■ ■ ■ ■

Ariel was acquainted with Eli and delighted to make an introduction for Simon. He had decided that the best way to proceed would be for him to invite Eli and Simon for lunch at Manta Ray, a beachfront seafood restaurant located on Alma Beach, less than six miles south of Mossad headquarters near the Glilot Ma'arav Interchange. Though the restaurant is famous for its extensive drink's menu, the three guests chose to stay away from alcohol in the middle of the day. Eli, despite his status as a billionaire, proved to be just as understated as Ariel or Simon, as is so often the case with individuals who do not feel they need to prove anything; they are who they are and are happy and satisfied with that.

Ariel started the conversation with a strong note of caution, telling Eli that the topic they needed to broach with him was top secret. Eli simply replied:

"As you well know, my friend, anything that touches the security of my beloved country is definitely safe with me."

Ariel replied:

"No surprise here. As it turns out, the topic does not relate so much to Israel as to someone who is asking our help. There is no vital Israeli interest at play, though there would immediately be one if we accept the request for help: whatever is done should never be traced to us."

"Ariel, if you don't mind me saying so, you're speaking in riddles."

Ariel conceded the point wholeheartedly and invited Simon to draw a broad picture to bring Eli up to speed as rapidly as possible. Simon skipped several details to which he could always return later and focused only on two main points. First, there seemed to be an interesting parallel between the situation in the Philippines and the Leviathan field; second the principal issue was with security, particularly concerning China's territorial claims on most of the South China Sea. As Simon was pausing to take a sip from his iced coffee, Eli interjected:

"A real can of worms!"

He paused, took a sip of his carbonated water, and added:

"Yet, it could be very interesting. Now, you gentlemen know that I have divested myself of most of my business interests, particularly as it relates to natural gas."

Simon countered:

"I am aware of that; it has been covered in the press, correct?"

With a partially dejected look on his face, Eli replied:

"Correct . . . Unfortunately."

Simon asked:

"Would you mind my brushing for you a picture of what might be a part of the ideal solution from our standpoint, obviously assuming that we do decide to accede to the request from the Filipino businessman?"

"Always prepared to hear but cannot and as you know will not promise more than I can deliver."

Eli listened carefully to the scenario which Simon was painting. He even asked several clarifying questions, taking his cue from Ariel who was also hearing the details of Simon's plan for the first time. As Simon was wrapping up his short presentation, Eli noted:

"The one thing that concerns me here, Simon, is that our experience with Leviathan is almost totally focused on extracting and collecting natural gas. I'm no petroleum engineer, but I know that there are important differences between natural gas and crude oil. Remember that in certain circumstances natural gas is simply flared while the whole production is geared to recovering crude oil."

"This is a very important point, Eli, and I'm glad you confirmed our intuition. I cannot give you all the details at this point because, as you know, we have not made our decision yet. However, we did contact another "friend" of ours who could, if asked, deliver a crude oil engineering resource to complement what we hope we could get through you."

Eli could not resist replying:

"I'm impressed, Simon. Looks like there are quite a number of moving pieces. I must congratulate you . . ."

"I can't accept them, sir. My deputy, David Heller, who would be here with us if he had not had a conflicting appointment, is the one who came up with the plan. My role here is just to help him looking for resources such as you . . ."

CHAPTER.07

MANILA AND PALAWAN, THE PHILIPPINES

As he was discussing the schedule he proposed, Luis surprised Ehud and Mike when he announced that he had planned a field trip for them the next day:

"Today, let me take care of any question you have on the current prospect. Tomorrow, I'd like to leave early to fly you to the Galoc field. It's less than 200 miles from here, so it should take us less than two hours with the helicopter. My plan is to land first at Canimango. It's a village on Culion Island, at the very north end of the Palawan province, less than 5 miles from Galoc. It's growing quite rapidly in part because of the oil exploration and production business. It has both an elementary and a high school. It's a very safe place and I know I can get fuel for the bird. From there, we can fly over to the Galoc installation, and then I'll show you where our own drilling is."

Mike had to ask:

"This is very kind, Luis, but is it really necessary?"

Luis was momentarily taken aback, but he quickly replied:

"Absolutely necessary? Probably not. Obviously, Mike, it's up to you. But I thought that seeing the overall environment would be useful: it's really a place where the two major activities are fishing and tourism. So, it's breathtakingly beautiful. At the same time, it's clearly industrializing thanks to the oil business. I've obtained permission to land on the floating vessel where the Galoc oil is pumped and stored. There you could easily go underwater to see what there is to see."

Noticing the still quizzical look on Mike's face, he added, ostensibly misreading Mike's reservations:

"Oh, and by the way, we have equipment called SNUBA for those who are not trained to use scuba gear. The gas tank floats on the surface, and you have at least 20 feet of hose connecting your mouthpiece to the tanks. That allows you to explore underwater with virtually no risk, as you don't need to think of a decompression halt when you want to swim to the surface if anything goes awry."

Mike smiled and simply replied:

"No need to worry about that, Luis. I'm qualified to use just about any kind of scuba gear."

Luis smiled and concluded:

"I think that this would surely give you the best sense of what we are dealing with. Oh, and by the way, dress quite casually; it will probably be quite hot and humid there, and I'm afraid most of the installations are not air-conditioned, except for sleeping quarters, and even there the equipment is not terribly powerful."

I I ■ I I

The next morning, the weather was particularly clear when Luis, Ehud, and Mike emerged from the elevator lobby at the top of Ayala Tower One. Yet, Mike could not miss the hot and humid air, which surprised him this early in the morning. The blue helicopter was there, fully fueled and ready to go. Luis sat next to Enrique, his pilot, leaving Ehud and Mike to sit right behind them. The second row of seats was elevated about six inches relative to the cockpit, allowing an excellent forward view to both *Mossad* members. They also had side windows to enhance their vistas. They grabbed the headsets that were hanging to their respective right and left; there was a third one, available for anyone sitting in the middle seat which was left empty on this trip. Luis had warned them in the elevator that the noise of the turbine engine that powered the twin-blade helicopter was quite loud, adding:

"As you could tell on your flight from the airport."

He had suggested using the headsets, both to attenuate the noise and to communicate among themselves. As a bonus, the two passengers would be able to hear conversations with air traffic control if it was of any interest.

The helicopter quickly got all the required clearances and Enrique switched the engine on. Luis had not understated anything. The noise was deafening, and all passengers could feel the internal vibrations which are common in all helicopters. Enrique had the controls for the take-off and ceded them to Luis as soon as he had reached 2,500 feet. They started flying in a westerly direction across Manila Bay, remaining below 5,000 feet to avoid interfering with arrivals and departures patterns at Manila airport. Afterwards, Luis climbed to a 15,000 feet cruising altitude as soon as he passed over Fort Drum also known as El Fraile Island in the mouth of Manila Bay. He knew that he still had at least another 5,000 feet of climbing room if it was needed but wanted to balance the goal of being as fuel efficient as reasonable against the desire to be low enough to show as much of the landscape as possible to his guests. He shifted his flying vector, the magnetic heading given to him by air traffic control, to 210 degrees, or southwest south. This would allow them to fly across the southeast end of Lubang Island, clip the northwest corner of Mindoro Island and, later on, coast over Busuanga Island before setting down on Culion Island as planned. In truth, most of the trip was going to take place over water, where there was not much to see. Luis had indicated that he would descend to 8,000 to 10,000 feet over land to allow his guests a better view.

About fifteen minutes before the scheduled landing, the helicopter started to fly over land, the island of Busuanga, which looked sparsely populated: agricultural fields with clumps of trees almost everywhere and a few homes, generally grouped together in small hamlets. Ehud remarked how relatively flat the Island was. Luis confirmed his impression saying that it was the highest point on the heading they were flying and was under 500 feet. Five minutes later, they were surprised to find themselves over an area of water which looked extremely shallow. Luis added that all the water often receded at low tide. As the helicopter started its approach toward Canimango, Mike mentioned how beautiful the sandy beaches seemed to be, particularly when the waters were shallow and turned a turquoise shade of blue. He also noticed a large number of multi-hulled fishing boats either already at sea with fishermen plying their trade in the nearby bay or still moored by, if not on the beach.

Mike added:

"The one thing I find the most surprising is the stunning number of islands which we saw. They seem to come in all shapes and sizes."

Luis smiled, although Mike could not see it as he was behind him, and only replied:

"Think that Palawan has nearly 1,800 of those. Plenty of room for diversity!"

The helicopter gently touched down in the middle of an area to the south of the old village of Canimango. That area, surely the size of at least six football fields, had been cleared and was being developed with a number of smaller bungalows, arranged on a grid, right next to the Canimango National High School. Mike and Ehud marveled at how Luis seemed to have left no detail to chance. The helicopter had not been on the ground for more than a couple of minutes, just enough time for everyone to alight and walk around the back of the aircraft to stretch their legs a bit, when a fuel truck, admittedly a lot smaller than what one might have been used to, arrived and parked next to the copter. Enrique negotiated the fuel quantity he needed and the price he was going to have to pay, and the gentleman started pumping the fuel. Mike noticed that Luis was having a quick chat with Enrique; Luis simply told Mike that he wanted to stop on the way back from the Galoc field as well to make sure he had a full tank before flying back to Manila. With a smile he added:

"I also asked him to bring us some food and beverages. I'm not sure what we'd find on the ship!"

The next leg of the trip took them to the Galoc production site. It proved totally uneventful and almost entirely over water. It took them less than a half hour to get there from Canimango. Mike could discern a boat in the distance; it looked like an oil tanker. However, as the helicopter got closer and closer, he realized that this was no ordinary ship. He could see oil drilling equipment on the main deck and immediately realized that the ship he was seeing was their destination. The helicopter swooped onto the landing pad that was right in front of the living quarters and the bridge of the ship, and gently set down on a well-delineated heliport. As they were disembarking, Luis mentioned that Enrique would stay with the helicopter, though he cautioned:

"Don't be surprised or worried if you hear him take off. The landing platform cannot cater to more than one helicopter at a time. So, he would need to make way for another one if there was a need. Yet, I have checked, and no movement is expected for the couple of hours we are going to be here. So hopefully, Enrique will not need to take off, hover, and land anew."

With his trademark smile, Luis still added:

"But here you never know, my friends. Better safe than sorry."

Mike and Ehud reminded each other of their earlier comment on the details of Luis's organization. His last comment was another piece of evidence to that "file."

As they got off the helicopter, the three men were met by someone who looked like the senior local representative of the group which exploited the field. His orange "uniform" was not soiled with traces of oil, and he did not wear a hard hat as he extended his hand to the group. Luis simply introduced him as Fred and said that he was the man in charge of the oil operations on the ship. Fred then escorted the group on their walking tour of the vessel. Mike pretended to be interested in the various installations and mentally thanked David for having organized a couple of hours of training for him before he left Tel Aviv. He asked:

"From the outside this looks a lot like a supertanker, right?"

Luis replied:

"Mostly right my friend. This ship is a bit smaller than others. So, it's just a large tanker, not a super tanker. Most FPSO vessels are in fact converted supertankers. We need the capacity to store the oil which super tankers obviously have in their massive hulls. You simply add the various production facilities on top and that's about it. For example, you can see, at the stern of the ship, the living quarters and bridge area look virtually unchanged from what you'd expect on a tanker."

Mike asked:

"Hey, what's this structure at the bow of the ship?"

Fred was ready with the answer to the question:

"That's the turret mooring system. It holds the ship steady over the field but allows her to rotate all the way around the mooring point. The captain can thus position the ship in the optimal way for the environmental conditions. Just think of the wind. With the turret near the bow, you want the bow of the ship to point into the wind. It'd be the opposite if you had the turret near the stern."

Mike shifted gears and asked:

"How many people work on the ship?"

Fred was ready for that question as well:

"It varies, as I'm sure you know. Now we have about 80 people, though we could accommodate as many as 120, with a bit of squeezing."

They were shown to a changing room where they could put on the scuba equipment which was provided. Though they had been told that the equipment had already been checked, Mike made it a point to run through its own checklist, ending with his oxygen supply. He thought *better safe than sorry*—a hallmark of his commando training.

The dive was quite interesting as Luis and Fred were escorting Ehud and Mike to the various elements of the installation. They did not dive all the way down to the subsea wellheads as the water was clear enough to observe them from the 100 feet underwater depth limit they had set for themselves. Mike's training with *Shayetet 13*, the Israeli equivalent of Navy Seals, would have allowed him to go as deep as 130-150 feet, but Luis certainly did not have to know that. They were still able to see the flexible risers that brought the crude oil mixed with gas, water and impurities to the FPSO, where the various gases and liquids were separated into their different end uses: the water and impurities are discarded while the crude oil and natural gas are stored.

Here, they could see that the field was operated through three active wells, which, they were told, included sections drilled both vertically and horizontally. This allowed them to access the whole reservoir. To the side, they saw a line which was connected to a large buoy; that was where tankers would come and moor to pump the oil from the FPSO and take it to onshore terminals, usually in Manila. As they were swimming back to the vessel, Mike was surprised to see a large number of tropical fish, of virtually all shades of the rainbow and sizes, from tiny black and white striped damselfish to Moorish idols and butterfly fish, to larger species such as triggerfish and even groupers, which the locals call *lapu-lapu*. Even more important, he saw quite a lot of colorful coral growth on some of the underwater infrastructure, as well as sea anemones in which clown fish in all shades of orange and brown could be seen playing among the otherwise stinging tentacles, taking advantage of the perfect symbiosis they enjoy with them.

When back onboard the FPSO, Mike immediately asked about his last two observations. Fred replied that the coral growth was a wonderful sight, but needed control in certain areas, adding:

"You know, coral reef organisms grow well on steel structures, despite the concerns of certain experts that iron and other limiting nutrients will favor algal or bacterial growth. Corals are an incredibly invasive species I should say. Corals need iron to grow, it facilitates photosynthesis. Coral polyps, which are animals, produce carbon dioxide and water as byproducts of cellular respiration . . ."

He paused for a second and turned to Mike's question about the myriad of tropical fish:

"You know, the waters are reasonably warm here and we tend to throw overboard whatever is biodegradable. That gives the fish nourishment. Plus, since we are super careful with pollutants and the like, they, the fish don't mind the environment. There are a few predators: octopus, sharks and even a few crustaceans, but they tend to not come too close to our installations, particularly with respect to sharks."

Changing the topic completely, Mike noted that the approach that was in use at Galoc was quite interesting, though he asked:

"What's the storage capacity of this vessel?"

Fred replied:

"Here we only have the capacity to store 500,000 barrels. The biggest FPSOs can store twice as much if not more."

Turning to Luis, Mike asked:

"What's the production rate here at present?"

"Less than 20,000 barrels a day I'm told."

"So, you need a tanker to come pick up the crude oil just shy of every other week?"

"I guess that's about right."

"How different would it be if production was quite a bit higher, say twice or even three times?"

Luis replied:

"I see where you're going. You're wondering whether this system with tanker shuttles, if I can call it that, is always better than a pipeline?"

"Precisely. However, I suspect that distance from shore is a crucial element when thinking of pipelines. Also, by the way, would it not be a different answer depending upon the mix of oil and gas?"

Luis retorted:

"I suspect that some permanent installation may well be better in circumstances where the field is considerably more productive or even has a longer expected life than what we have seen around here. There is still the issue of distance from shore, though. One thing is absolutely certain: this system is surely less expensive to put in place. However, this presupposes that there are vessels available, and this is not always true. But we're still subject to plain logic: the front-end costs are higher with a platform, but a platform would be more efficient, particularly over the long term."

Mike followed up with his next concern:

"I can't talk about it right now, Luis, because I would need to do a lot more work. Yet a thought comes to mind: how about some hybrid version?"

"Hybrid?"

"Yes, I mean a combination of pipeline, platform and tanker shuttles."

"You know your stuff, Mike, don't you?"

Mike just smiled.

CHAPTER.08

TEL AVIV, ISRAEL, AND SOMEWHERE IN THE AUSTRIAN ALPS

On his return trip to Tel Aviv, Mark gathered his thoughts and those which Ehud had given him. In short, he was confident in the idea that the mission could work, though he could still see significant issues. Explaining his conclusions to David, he started with the positive elements, focusing on the fact that there was a lot more oil exploration and development along the west coast of Palawan than he had expected. He explained:

"On the return helicopter flight to Canimango, Luis gave us a helicopter tour of the northern end of the Palawan area starting with the Galoc wells where the ship was, which by the way are being developed by a competitor consortium, though Luis has a stake in it as well I'm told."

He paused to drink from his cup of coffee and continued:

"The installations are impressive. However, the output is still small: less than 5% of the crude oil needs of the Philippines, less than 20,000 barrels per day. And no scope to raise it . . ."

Mark added that they had flown all the way to the original Nido field, almost 60 miles south down the coast of Palawan, passing on the way to the east of the Malampaya gas field. There seemed to be, in his view, quite a bit of activity, though he readily conceded that the area was sparsely populated and thus that anything that looked like infrastructure stuck out. After having talked of the positives, he felt he should talk of the couple of items that made him have second thoughts, with respect to the development of Luis's field. He explained:

"First, with so much exploration in the area, and service contracts for hydrocarbon exploration literally all the way up and down the west coast of Palawan, I am amazed that Luis could, in his relatively small service area have stumbled on something as large as he seems to feel it is. Plus, he's concluded that his field could be very big with only one well drilled."

David interrupted:

"Hold it, Mark. Could that be a plain and simple fake?"

"Sure could be. At the same time, I don't see what he has to gain, except maybe some free advice or even exploration consulting. Worse, some short-term fame if he were to publicize it, something he hasn't done so far. Besides, he said he didn't want to go that way. He doesn't strike me as needing that fame. But let me go back to my earlier point: why has he waited so long either to drill or to talk about his results?"

Mark paused again to check his thoughts and then added:

"I'm convinced a major element relates to his fears of Chinese intrusion."

"What do you mean?"

Mark, as he was wont to do, waited a good thirty seconds before he replied, to make sure he had his logic down pat:

"I believe that his fears that the Chinese might come in and effectively grab his discovery are genuine. That is unless the whole thing is a big fake, but, as I just said, I'm willing to set that hypothesis aside. However, to me at least, the question has to be how real these risks are."

"Do you mean that the risk is low in your view?"

Mark again took his time to reply to David's question:

"I cannot comment on the risk in an absolute sense. You know this is binary, about the same as a coin toss: either the Chinese come, or they don't. There's little in between."

Mark paused again as he was getting to his main conclusion. He argued that something made him feel on balance more in favor of the project than against it:

"It is a fact that all the areas currently producing are due west to where he drilled his well. In short, current production is closer to the zone the Chinese claim, the Spratly Islands, than where Luis's new find is located. This would tell me that the Chinese would have to attack or expropriate these before reaching his production area, if it does exist."

David calmly replied that he could see the point, though he could also imagine the opposite scenario. He argued that the rest of the hydrocarbon producing activity in the area is minor and the Chinese might well simply not bother with them. Crucially he added:

"One element I think is worth considering is this: why do we think they would try to capture the operations? That would involve military operations that would be bound to attract a response, first by the Philippines and second by their allies. Why not consider a different approach where disruptive activities, minor or not so minor skirmishes for instance, a sort of blackmail would aim to get Luis to sell them some interest in the project at a low price?"

He paused to drink from his water glass and concluded:

"What about terrorist activities that would exhaust Luis's determination, raise his operating costs and lead him to a point where he would rather partner with them than fight them. Kidnapping anyone? The Chinese always seem to take the long-term view. They would not own the whole thing, but they would have a foot in the door, possibly somewhat more than a foot. Remember the Hong Kong takeover. Initially, there was a legal agreement between China and the United Kingdom and things were allowed to remain pretty much as they were. Then gradually, over almost a half century, China took over and abrogated most of the provisions in the initial agreement. They wanted Hong Kong but took their time to achieve their goal. Reminds me of the frog and water story . . ."

"Frog and water?"

"Yes, you know. Plunge a frog into boiling water and it will jump out in a hurry. Put it in warm water that you heat up gradually and the frog will let itself be cooked and die."

Mark conceded that he could not find a hole in the scenario, adding:

"I should give your idea a lot more thought."

David asked him if he had questioned Luis on the issue of his fears and exploration delays. He replied that he surely did, though he had to be careful not to offend him. He simply summarized Luis's response:

"He says he has known for a while that his service contract had potential as he could read seismic maps just like anyone else. He had decided to wait to do anything until he could see that the Filipino oil industry was developing and attracting the right kind of overseas partners. He also said that the proximity of the Malampaya field and what he saw of the geological structures made him think that his deposit might well have more gas mixed with the oil."

David had interrupted:

"Does that make sense?"

"Yes, sir. Luis told us that until the price of gas rose, natural gas was mostly flared in areas where the exploration work was after crude oil."

Continuing his earlier thrust, Mark concluded:

"Given his other business interests, there is some logic for him to wait for the right moment to proceed. My suspicion is that he wants to drill a second well if only to confirm what he thinks he has. Given the fact that most of the exploration work is done under contract by foreign agents, I suspect that he fears that the results he expects would quickly become public knowledge. So, if I had to guess, I'd say that he's trying to line up his ducks so that he could move quite quickly."

David noted that this did not explain anything with respect to the Chinese threat. Mark replied:

"I know it sounds almost dumb, but I think he fears his hopes might be correct."

"Hold it. You're going to explain that, right?"

"Sure. He dreams of his field being the stratigraphic trap, the Elephant field which Chuck Wilson had hoped to find in the 1970s. Now, if that hope is correct, it changes the situation for everyone, China included. The game might become worth it for them . . . At the same time, it also becomes a major domestic issue for the Philippines. They'd be more likely to want to defend, alone or with allies, something which might change the energy picture in the country."

David smiled and simply replied:

"I suspect you may not have seen the news because it just came out. The Americans have just announced that their 38th annual U.S.–Philippines military exercises will be the largest ever, nearly doubling the amount of personnel that participated last year. I saw that this annual "Balikatan" exercise will have 12,200 troops from the U.S., 5,400 from the Philippines and be joined by over 100 Australians. That compares with less than 9,000 all together last year . . ."

He paused several seconds before concluding:

"I'm not saying that the security issue may have become moot because alliances can be made and unmade. Yet, add to that the deal the U.S. struck with the Philippines according to which the Philippines are giving the U.S. military access to four additional military installations in the country, a few of which will face the South China Sea. That tells me that the cost to China of any direct and visible action in that area has risen substantially. And if that was not enough, the moves by the U.S. to support Taiwan more visibly make me think that China will have its hands full in the Northern China Sea."

"You're right. Didn't know any of this. Why would Luis not have mentioned it? Do you think he missed it?"

Mark paused before continuing. He was doing what David knew him to do whenever he wanted to be sure of himself. He thought for a minute or so and then simply smiled as he answered his own question saying:

"What if Luis was trying to find a partner to help him pay for the development of the field but do it with as little of a reduction in his share as possible? He might argue safety; argue that Israel could help given our experience with Leviathan; and yet not want to let go more than he absolutely needs to."

"That might make sense, but he's barking up the wrong tree . . ."

Mark looked quite surprised at David's assertion. David smiled back and said:

"Let me share a development with you. Have you heard of Eli Abelman?"

"Who hasn't?"

"Well, Simon and Ariel talked to him over lunch . . ."

Seeing Mark questioning look, David interrupted himself and explained:

"I had a prior engagement I couldn't cancel. Plus, we did not want to overwhelm Eli with too many people around the lunch table for a first meeting."

Mark seemed to relax. David continued:

"Anyway, back to my story. Eli would be prepared to create a new subsidiary within his former group with a mandate for that company to help Luis with drilling and production in the new site."

"Wow!"

"But that's not all. I also talked to Countess Renate. She's willing to offer a resource specialized in the planning of the exploitation of an oil field . . . Eli's guys know everything there is to know about gas fields that have some oil, but we believe he would welcome help to exploit a field that has some gas in a field predominantly focused on oil."

"Sounds great. Where do we go from here? Rather what do you want me to do?"

"We follow the plan. Oh, by the way, Mark, Mike Loeb, your alter ego, would need to reveal that he works for Eli's company, if we do get to that point."

■ ■ ■ ■ ■

The next morning, Mark was quietly sitting in his office, writing a shorter version of the report he had given orally the prior day. His phone rang. He picked it up and, as he normally would, simply said:

"Mark Levi, here . . ."

"Ehud here."

"Ehud, what a surprise. What's up?"

"I just talked to Luis. He would like to hire you or someone you would recommend."

"Why?"

"He's decided that he wants to drill a second well in his field and wants to make sure he maximizes the chances of delineating the reservoir."

"Ah. That speeds things up. Let me talk to David and I'll get back to you."

■ ■ ■ ■ ■

"David?"

"Yes Mark . . ."

"We're gonna have to speed up our decision and take action in the Philippines. Ehud just called to tell me that Luis Ramos wants to hire me or someone like me to decide on where to drill the next well."

"Well, you did a marvelous job, my friend. Let me chat with Simon and then invite Eli to lunch with you. We'll use that to plan our next steps."

■ ■ ■ ■ ■

The lunch, including Mark, Eli and David, was considered a great success. Eli agreed that a new company would be formed, to be owned by both Global Energy and himself directly. That new Israeli-incorporated company would provide the logistical expertise which Luis would require. David then knew he still had to place a call to Countess Renate. David had clearly heard Eli's message that Global Energy's specialty was with gas reservoirs when he had said:

"We both know that the problems are different when you are principally producing oil or principally extracting gas. I have heard you mention that the pressures that the oil/gas separator must withstand are quite different, and this is by far not the only issue."

David nodded and replied:

"Absolutely. I have also heard that reservoir delineation does not need to be absolutely as precise when one is dealing with oil."

"That's what I heard too, David. So, in short, Global Energy with need help."

"I believe that I know where to get that help. We have a contact with a global consulting firm which prides itself on remaining at the leading edge of the technologies or disciplines within which they operate."

Eli seemed a bit cynical about the assertion, arguing:

"I have heard that God does not work for anyone in particular my friend."

"I know, I know. Without going into too much detail, let me explain. The group I'm speaking of does not have permanent employees."

Eli could not resist noting:

"Even worse!"

"If the head of the group pretended to know it all, I would agree with you. But her business model is quite different and original. She maintains a number of individuals worldwide under contract, though each of them keeps working in his or her specialty for whomever their current employer is. More to the point, I believe that, in certain cases, she can introduce someone who may not yet be what she calls an associate."

"Quite smart indeed. I think I may have heard of the group, quite a while ago."

■ ■ ■ ■ ■

The gist of David's conversation with Countess Renate focused on the need to bring in the expert to whom she had referred. Mark was in the room as well in case David needed specific details. Countess Renate was delighted to hear the update which David provided and asked:

"Are you ready to pull the trigger?"

"No. Not quite yet."

"Why the wait?"

David explained that with Eli's agreement to help, there was only one last step which had to be completed:

"We need to get the Filipino gentleman to agree to the conditions which should naturally be attached to the help he is asking for."

"Which are . . ."

"First to agree to sell a slice of his ownership of the deposit to the company which Eli will put at his disposal. Second to accept to hire

The Shadow Experts for the assistance which Eli's company cannot provide."

"I see. So, what is your next step?"

David explained that Mark would return to Manila and first reveal his affiliation with Eli's company. He will also lay out what has to be done, including the hiring of an outside resource to supplement the gas knowledge of Eli's company. Countess interrupted to mention one point that could be quite critical:

"The gentleman I plan on introducing to you, Anthony Stacey, resides in the U.K. He worked for most of his career for British Petroleum, though he eventually retired to focus on research and academe. He told me something when I previewed the potential for this assignment which was news to me but could be quite valuable. He has designed and constructed a prototype gas/oil separator which uses the flow of hydrocarbons to generate the power needed for the separator to heat up the mix of oil, gas, and water so that the different boiling points cause them to separate and be channeled through different pipes."

"Very interesting. By the way, am I correct assuming that you cannot tell me whether Anthony is or is not an associate."

"Quite correct. From what you've told me, your Israeli industrialist, Eli, may well have run into Anthony here or there. We certainly don't want to reveal more than what is publicly known: any introduction should be limited to the fact that he teaches at Imperial College in London and conducts his research there as well. We can also say that, prior to that, he was a senior executive at British Petroleum, and was quite active in the early development of the North Sea oil project."

CHAPTER.09

TEL AVIV, ISRAEL AND MANILA, THE PHILIPPINES

Back in Manila, Mike had asked Ehud to organize a meeting with Luis Ramos De Ayala to bring him up to date on the developments which had taken place in Tel Aviv and to begin the new round of "negotiations." They elected to hold the meeting in the Israeli Embassy, *Avecshares Center, 1132 University Parkway,* Bonifacio Global City. The embassy is located on the 10th and 11th floors of the classic twelve-story building within the very luxurious, vast and serene meadows of Fort Bonifacio, Global City, Taguig. The architect imagined a stunning structure with white stone frames surrounding green glass windows. All south-facing offices had a wonderful view of the vast Simon Mann Sport field of the British School in Manila. Crucially for Luis, the building had its own heliport, which would allow him to fly in and fly out without needing to concern himself with Manila automobile traffic. Ehud and Mike had planned an early morning meeting to simplify Luis's schedule, as the Israeli Embassy was to the east of his apartment building, while his office was to the west. He could thus first fly to the embassy and then fly directly to his office. Ehud had booked a room for Mike at the Grand Hyatt, literally less than a half a mile from the embassy. Walking from the hotel to the embassy, despite the early morning hour, gave Mike a renewed sense of what life in the tropics could be: hot and humid, and often quite busy.

Ehud had reserved a conference room facing south. As he walked into the conference room, Mike marveled at the view of the street below. Traffic had already built up, and people seemed to be randomly hurrying along the sidewalks in directions only known to them. When the passersby were far enough away from the embassy, he could clearly discern individuals often carrying an umbrella. However, when he looked straight down, all he could see below was a kaleidoscope of umbrellas. People had seemingly opened them not to protect themselves from the rain, as there were hardly any clouds in the sky, but from the sun which was already quite strong that early in the morning. In the distance, he could see misty humidity rising from the ground, particularly where there were trees and lawns. Oddly, he noted that there seemed to be less of a mist over the Simon Mann Sport field of the British School. He thought, *maybe I need distance to see the accumulation.* Ehud offered a seat with the view to Luis, while he and Mike sat on the other side of the small rectangular table. Mike dove immediately into the meat of the agenda:

"Luis, I hear that you may be ready to explore your discovery in more depth."

He smiled as he realized he had made an unintended pun, though it seemed to escape Luis who simply replied:

"That's correct. As you would say, it's time to fish or cut bait."

Luis paused for a second and added:

"And I am hoping you can help me."

"I would be delighted. Now, before we go any further, I need to 'come clean' so to speak."

Luis was visibly shaken by Mike's comment, though he stayed silent, to allow Mike to expand on his thought. Smiling broadly, Mike said:

"Don't worry, nothing big. Apologies if I startled you with my comment. There is nothing sinister in the situation. I must simply tell you that I work for a company which is a joint venture between Global Energy, one of the top energy companies in Israel and its ultimate owner, an Israeli businessman. The company principally deals with natural gas extraction. As far as its ultimate owner, he will need to remain anonymous for now, although you would for sure eventually meet him."

"Why the anonymity at this point?"

"It's a bit of a complicated matter. First, the gentleman is quite well known in Israel and abroad. Second, he has been gradually withdrawing from his for-profit activities; people know that he desires to become more and more involved in philanthropy. At this point, he prefers for his name no longer to be associated with what you and I might call 'business.' Note that this could change."

Though his face said that the explanation was neither particularly clear nor even convincing, Luis let this one slide by. He asked:

"In what ways is this any of my business?"

"I assume you're talking of my being employed by that joint-venture."

"Absolutely."

Mike replied that it was just a case of full disclosure. He added that there were several possible scenarios regarding how he might help Luis in his oil exploration effort. He mentioned that all of them involved some business relationship. Mike further expanded on the thought, saying that he strongly believed that any and all conflicts of interest or even possible perceived conflicts of interests should always be disclosed. He could see that he had again "lost" Luis and explained:

"Talking of the several ways in which I could help you, the lowest-cost relationship would be for you, Luis, or one of your companies to retain me."

He paused briefly and then immediately added:

"Frankly, there is only a limited amount of help I can provide. As you know, my expertise is in the field of security. I have very little to offer if you want oil production expertise. So, a more efficient and in the long run both more efficient and more profitable alternative would be to shoot for some relationship with the firm which employs me. You'd get me and a whole lot of additional resources."

Luis demonstrated his long business experience, avoiding the details and going straight to the most important matter asking:

"What are they going to ask for?"

Mark immediately smiled. He was aware of the fact that Luis really needed help on the oil production front. He interpreted his last question as an indication that Luis had already made up his mind that whatever help he was going to get would not be for free; it would cost him something. Mark was thus delighted that he was thus willing to discuss some form of compensation immediately. Mike replied:

"I see you're on the ball, my friend."

Luis nodded. Mike took the point further:

"Frankly, actual negotiations are way above my pay grade. I've been told that they would not seek reimbursement of their costs below a certain amount, which I do not know. I guess they would view those as paid-in equity: they would expect to have earned a share of the project with these sunk costs. Does this make any sense or is it a non-starter?"

Luis waited a few seconds and simply replied:

"You never get anything for nothing. That's surely true for them, but it has to be true for me as well."

Mike smiled again thinking: *one heck of a negotiator*. He then added:

"One more thing. They will likely want to bring into the project someone who is a world-reputed expert in oil reservoirs. He would likely need to be compensated as well."

"By whom?"

"To be decided between you and them, but I suspect that the cleanest approach would be to have him compensated through the joint venture you two would form. Again, no need to inject other parties into the project officially."

"What would he do? Why do we need someone like him?"

"Ah. Excellent question. That is something I can address. The Israeli company we've been discussing has a huge amount of expertise in reservoirs which principally contain natural gas, with some crude oil as an extra. However, from what you've told me, here, in the area of your discovery, I believe it's the opposite: more oil than gas. Correct?"

"Absolutely."

"Good. The Israeli company could help, but it would need some external expertise. That expert would surely come in handy with respect to reservoir delineation and production design and management. Makes sense?"

"Guess so."

"The second reason why he could be a welcome addition to the team is somehow interrelated with the question of security. I am told that the gentleman holds a patent on a unique oil/gas separator which can be located under water."

"Many of them do . . . What's new about that?"

"How many of those you know of do not need a continuous external power supply?"

With somewhat of an initially surprised look on his face, Luis eventually replied:

"Ah. I see . . ."

■ ■ ■ ■ ■

Back in Tel Aviv, Mark reported to David and Simon, who had exceptionally joined them, that the project seemed like it could go forward to the extent that Luis had not objected to the two conditions which had been agreed with Eli and Countess Renate at the outset. David however remarked:

"Mark, this seems like excellent news, and yet you do not look satisfied. Am I missing something?"

"You don't miss much, sir, do you?"

David simply smiled. Mike proceeded to discuss a series of meetings he attended with a few oil industry insiders in Manilla after his conversation with Luis. He had taken advantage of being there to get a sense of what the energy landscape looked like, with the help of the commercial attaché of the Israeli Embassy, Moshe Elan. He explained that there were three principal players in the industry, though one could count quite a few more if looking at individuals or companies with smaller stakes. He was thus able to hold informal meetings with the leaders of each of the three main players. David had to ask:

"Sounds just like an idea you might have my friend. But what were you looking for?"

"A couple of things. First, I wanted to get some deeper insight on Luis's reputation. Second, I wanted to gauge the degree of optimism or caution of other industry players as contrasted with Luis's."

Simon cut in:

"Makes sense. And?"

"Well, on the second point, I would argue that Luis may be a bit more conservative in general, but he as well as the other industry leaders have been looking for the giant deposit for almost fifty years now. I don't think they've given that up."

"Isn't this understandable?"

"Sure is, David. Human nature. Potential for wealth creation, though from the financial data which Moshe had provided, I'm not sure that any of them needs a lot more—Luis, least of all. Potential to be 'a savior of the country' with honors and fame. And finally, why not, a real desire to help their country."

Mark paused and added:

"What worries me here is that I am not sure how reasonable any of them have ever been. So, with respect to Luis, the grandiose dreams he discusses on the basis of the results of one exploration well, even if it involved horizontal as well as vertical drilling, seem a bit excessive."

David interjected:

"What's your conclusion on that front?"

"Well, I think we should involve Countess Renate and maybe Eli as quickly as we can. As someone who knows very little on the topic, my guess is that more drilling will most likely be required. In truth, I would have more confidence in the conclusions of either of our friends than in the hopes of Luis."

David interjected:

"Should not be terribly hard, should it?"

"Truthfully, I don't know. But I do have a card up my sleeve."

David noted with a smile:

"I'm sure . . . What is it?"

"I was wearing my special *Mossad* glasses when I looked over the various maps which Luis was showing Ehud and me in his office. I did not want to bother anyone until I knew that we had a chance at a mission being organized, so I did not talk about them, nor did I show them to anyone. But now I would not mind having specialists, on Marvin's team or on Eli's, or maybe even on Countess Renate's, study them before we start in earnest."

He paused and added:

"The reason why I think this is important is that I would not want Eli to start with a misconception."

Simon replied:

"All to your honor my friend. But knowing Eli, I'm sure he would have requested something like that anyway. In fact, he may need more for all I know. Now how did your trade checks on Luis pan out?"

Mike explained that he had introduced himself as an assistant to the managing director of an Israeli company, who had been charged with the job to assess the oil industry in the Philippines, the main players, the potential growth, and related opportunities. He said he should also preface his comments on these meetings with a couple of cautionary notes. First, the people with whom he visited were all competing with one another. Second, they probably talked about their own books. So, he explained that he had been very straight with everyone. He did not try to hide that he had already talked with Luis Ramos De Ayala, nor that he would talk to several other individuals, He even added that, in a couple of instances, he would feel free to make reference to something he had heard, though he would not go as far as providing the real source, adding for each of his "interviews" that he would keep secret anything that would be pointed out to him as confidential.

His biggest surprise concerned Luis's reputation. He seemed to be very well-liked and respected by two of the people he met. However, he did not seem to be appreciated by the third. Everyone gave him credit both for his successes in his non-oil businesses, one of the three individuals even adding:

"He is this close from being viewed as a full-fledged member of the Ayala clan, though he surely did not get in through the front door."

David wondered aloud:

"What do you make of that?"

"I played dumb and asked what the businessman meant. The reply was deceptively simple: his wealth must come close to rival that of the other Ayala branch, though he did not start from the same point. The gentleman even added: 'he worked for his success.' That's the good news. The other side of the coin, the gentleman who did not seem to like him claimed he is viewed at times as having sharp elbows."

Simon asked:

"Jealousy?"

"Quite possibly. Besides, discussing this with Ehud the evening before I left Manila, he made an important point. He said that Manila is not a place where secrets are terribly well-kept. He hinted that he had been hearing rumors that the new find in Luis's service contract might actually be larger than anything that has been seen so far. So, jealousy could very well be at play there. All three of the industry leaders with whom I met have been in the field pretty much since the beginning, in the 1980s at least. Putting myself in their shoes, I could see why they would be upset that the big find, if that's what we're talking about, was made by a late comer."

Thinking aloud a bit more, Mark added:

"Remember, the way those service contracts work, everyone is in bed with everyone else. I'm sure that all three of the companies I saw have a share in Luis's service contract."

David noted:

"A share, maybe, but not a large enough one . . ."

"Grant you that."

David wanted to drive the meeting to a conclusion. He asked:

"So, how do you come out?"

Mark, as was his typical behavior, thought for a short while and then replied:

"I think we need more information on the prospective deposit before we go anywhere. But I believe we're dealing with a solid person. After all, Ehud did a lot of homework on Luis and said he seems quite straight. Now, with respect to the project, I think we should move on two fronts. First, we might try and start what might look like negotiations between Eli's company and Luis on the one hand. On the other hand, we might invite Countess Renate to see what she can dig up on her side. I would have no problem sharing the pictures of the various maps with here."

He paused, as if to check his logic, and concluded:

"I don't know whether Eli will or will not need to talk to Luis to form an opinion of the deposit. Maybe that's our first next step. That will dictate whether we must introduce Luis in the project immediately or have a few days or weeks."

David had to inquire:

"By the way, I'm guessing there's a fuse to that . . ."

"Exactly. Luis wants to start drilling a second well soon. So, I think we should feel under some time pressure. On the other hand, you have taught me never to allow pressure to force a decision I'm not ready to make."

Simon smiled when David simply replied:

"You learned your lesson well. But you should know you have the original master here; he's the one who taught it to me."

Never one to miss an opportunity, Simon simply replied:

"Not to forget our friend and master Ariel Landau . . ."

CHAPTER.10

TEL AVIV, ISRAEL, MANILA, THE PHILIPPINES, AND SOMEWHERE IN THE AUSTRIAN ALPS.

Suddenly, Luis's cell phone, which he always kept near him, even when sleeping, rang:

"Am I speaking to Luis Ramos De Ayala? Eli Abelman here . . ."

■ ■ ■ ■ ■

Mark, David, and Eli had gotten together after Mark's internal debriefing. They agreed that the next step had to be for Eli to establish contact with Luis. They agreed that this could be done over the telephone if travel was somehow too difficult, time-consuming, or both. The point of the call would be to ascertain whether a deal was truly feasible. Eli had asked his engineers to look at the pictures which Mark had brought back from Manila. Somewhat predictably, the message he received in return was hedged. The Global Energy team recognized the likelihood that there was something "there" if only because, among the pictures, was a set which showed the results of the first exploratory well. There was no question that the well had struck oil. At the same time, they told Eli that the potential deposit was one of the first two sandstone deposits in the area. Though that was still decent if not good news, it was totally evident that the reservoir was thus quite different from the Leviathan structure. The engineering team therefore argued that they would need quite a bit more information to refine their analysis.

Mark and Eli agreed that Mike would send an email to Luis introducing Eli Abelman and telling him that Eli would like to have an initial conversation. Luis wholeheartedly agreed to take the call whenever it came.

■ ■ ■ ■ ■

"Mr. Abelman. A pleasure to hear your voice. Mike Loeb had told me that you might call."

Luis had taken the time to google Eli Abelman and thus to discover his status as a well-known Israeli billionaire. Though Eli had always been careful to protect as much of his privacy as he could, there are pieces of data that are bound to make it onto the Internet, if only because of the web of public corporate interests he had, at least until recently.

"Please, call me Eli. It'll make our conversation that much less formal."

"Thanks. Please call me Luis. So, what can I do for you?"

Eli explained that he was contacted by Mike Loeb, a senior executive in one of the companies he used to own:

"Mike is telling me that there may be an opportunity for us to work together. Is that correct?"

"Certainly is. How much do you know about our project?"

Eli did not lie and said:

"Not as much as I would like. Do you think the two of us could meet, either here in Tel Aviv or in Manila and spend a bit more time together? This would help me get a more precise sense of what is known and what is not, and where common interests between us might exist."

"I would be happy to fly to Tel Aviv to see you. It would be a first for me."

"Never been in Israel?"

"In truth, no. Might be an opportunity to spend an extra couple of days visiting the Christian holy sites. You know, the main religion here in the Philippines is Catholicism."

"Can certainly help you with that. Would you be able to have sufficient data with you so that our conversation would be based on facts?"

"I'd suggest we work from computer files which I would certainly be able to access remotely, through my laptop."

"Sounds excellent. Is there a date that works best for you? I still maintain an office in town. May I suggest that we book a room for you at the Drisco Hotel on Auerbach Street? It's certainly one of the best around here and quite convenient to the center of town."

■ ■ ■ ■ ■

Luis' commercial flight landed at Ben Gurion airport, which struck a marked contrast with Ninoy Aquino in Manila. Everything seemed clean, crisp, and working in as efficient a manner as feasible. Yet, he noticed that there was a sense that security was a major concern to one and all, though security in Israel did not involve quite as many armed soldiers patrolling the corridors as in Manila. After clearing customs with his wife, Luis was surprised to see someone right opposite the door through which they emerged into the public section of the terminal. That someone wore a hotel uniform and held a computer tablet in his hands, and the tablet had Luis's name written on it. He approached the individual who introduced himself as a driver sent by the Driscoll Hotel, as confirmed by lettering on his jacket, lettering which Luis could only partially read as most of it was in Hebrew. He said he was to drive him and his wife to the hotel. Luis was even more surprised when reaching the hotel in Tel

Aviv that the driver told him that the transfer from the airport had already been paid.

The next morning, he found another car with a driver waiting, to drive him to Eli's offices. He picked up two other contrasts with his Filipino experience. First, there was no visible security checking cars as they came to park near the front door of the building that housed Eli's offices. Second, the office suite which Eli occupied was elegant but definitively understated. Additionally, Eli did not wear a tie though he did have a jacket on. He had been warned that Luis would probably be somewhat formal for a first face-to-face meeting. Eli welcomed Luis and, in a typical Israeli fashion, he quickly removed his jacket and draped it on the back of a chair, inviting Luis to do the same. His blue open-collar dress shirt looked quite comfortable, and carried his initials, in Hebrew, on the left-hand side, below his heart. After having offered Luis a morning coffee, Eli proceeded to dive directly into the oil project. Luis thought that Eli was definitely all business, though his demeanor throughout the couple of hours they spent together for the initial rundown was quite friendly. Eli shook Luis's hand saying:

"This was certainly a very useful couple of hours. I hope you won't mind if I spent a few hours with members of my team to get their thoughts. The car will take you back to your hotel. I'd like to invite you and your wife to lunch, nothing fancy. There'll be a driver to pick you two up. Then, the two of us can regroup for another session, while the driver takes your wife wherever she wishes."

"What a wonderfully kind offer."

Later in the afternoon after quite a bit more detailed conversation, Eli shook Luis's hand again and said:

"As agreed, we have organized a car and a driver to take you tomorrow morning to Jerusalem. You can spend the day visiting the Holy Sites, while I spend more time with my own people. We could meet again the day after tomorrow to discuss next steps . . ."

"Sounds perfect. I spoke with our Cardinal Archbishop in Manila, and he kindly provided an introduction for me to the Patriarchate of Jerusalem. They have prepared a whole day of visits of the sites which Christians consider holy as well as a few meetings with local architectural and community specialists. I'm sure my wife and I shall be quite tired when we return."

■ ■ ■ ■ ■

The following day, Eli welcomed Luis back to his office. Luis thanked Eli for his hospitality, expressing surprise and gratitude at the fact that his hotel expenses, as well as the cost of the car and driver for the round trip to Jerusalem, were all paid for. Eli simply replied:

"You paid for the longest and more expensive part of the trip . . ."

They moved to the sitting area of Eli's office, with Eli motioning to Luis to use the sofa. Eli then surprised Luis when he declared:

"I hope you will not mind, but I invited Mike Loeb to join us. Just like me, he is no great expert in the hydrocarbon exploration and production world, but he would be our point man if we go ahead. I'd like him to hear and participate in this conversation."

Luis was happy to oblige and stood up as Mike stepped into the room. Luis asked:

"Did my friend Ehud know that you were more of an executive than a petroleum safety engineering consulting expert?"

Mike simply replied:

"He knew that I worked on safety issues in the petroleum industry. I never represented myself as a petroleum engineer, though I must have absorbed some of the discipline working around so many first-class experts."

Eli took back control of the conversation to share with Luis his current conclusions. He started with congratulations as it did seem as though the first well was somewhat of a gusher. He asked in passing whether they had initially planned to drill vertically as well as horizontally, to which Luis replied, somewhat predictably:

"We had provided for the possibility but would surely not have drilled horizontally if we had found nothing or even if the flow and downhole pressures had not been as encouraging as they were."

Eli nodded. He moved to the challenging part of what he needed to communicate to Luis. He looked straight at him when he said:

"We would be happy to consider working together, Luis, but at this point I fear that we do not have all the information we need to ascertain how big the opportunity is."

"What would you need?"

"In an ideal world, we certainly would prefer knowing the results of drilling a second well far enough away from the first to be able better to infer the potential size of the reservoir. I do appreciate that this may take some time. So maybe an option would be for me to commission an independent expert with more experience with oil reservoirs than my people. Would that be acceptable to you and, more importantly, would he be able to have access to all the information you have?"

Luis did not hesitate:

"He would have to sign a 'do not disclose' agreement, but otherwise I don't see any real problem."

He paused and added:

"How much of a delay would this create?"

"My friend, your guess is as good as mine. But I would assume that you did not come to your own conclusion without some help from a consultant. Correct?"

"Absolutely. This includes the people who ran all the wireline tests and determined the depth and the direction of the horizontal drilling."

"Good. I think we could do a couple of things. First, we might organize a zoom conference call which would have the independent expert, your people, Mike, you and me, the last three of us primarily in listening mode, though nobody would be muted. That should help us determine what next steps our expert would need to carry out to help you and me get a better sense of what the reservoir may hold. Then, let's regroup. Am I making sense?"

"Sure are. When can we do this?"

"Give me a couple of days. Let's talk on the phone when you are back in Manila and decide on a time and date."

■ ■ ■ ■ ■

"Countess Renate? David here."

"David, how nice to hear your voice."

"Countess, I must tell you that I am not alone here. Let me turn my camera on so that you can see the two gentlemen who are seating with me. To my left, you'll have no trouble recognizing Mark Levi, though I should say that for this mission outside of Israel, he is Mike Loeb. To my right, let me introduce Eli Abelman. He has had a prestigious career around the world with a particular focus on oil . . ."

Countess Renate interrupted:

"I know of Mr. Abelman . . ."

"Countess, please, call me Eli."

"Happy to. Thank you."

David turned to the meat of the conference call. He described the conversations which Eli had had with Luis Ramos De Ayala, adding:

"You know, the Filipino oil entrepreneur we discussed a week ago or so . . ."

"Remember that conversation well."

"Let me have Eli himself tell you where he is, though in short, we think we are going to need your help. Particularly the help of the oil expert you mentioned to me—Anthony Stacey I believe."

"Excellent memory, David. So, Eli, how can we be of help?"

Eli summarized the quandary. He explained that he understood why it might make sense for David and his team to help Luis, if it was a way to strengthen the position of the Philippines vis-à-vis China, adding:

"I know that the U.S. is making substantial efforts on that front as well, with their joint exercises and the use of additional bases."

He then conceded that the reservoir which Luis and his group seem to have discovered surely looked quite interesting, though he had to caution everyone:

"Don't get me wrong. It could very well be the Elephant field of which it seems like every Filipino has dreamt of since the late 1970s. At the same time, based on what we really know, it could also be a much more modest find. I have been told that a couple of fields which had been touted as great discoveries at the time went dry after less than five years. In reality, I'm told that small reef reservoirs can produce great flows and yet contain only limited quantities of recoverable oil. The bottom line is that we should know more before we start spending serious money, and, by the way, we will spend serious money if the field is what it is hoped to be."

Countess Renate asked:

"What would you need from our expert?"

"Before we get to that, could you give me a sketch of his bio and his expertise?"

Countess Renate immediately agreed, though she said that she could not disclose more than what she felt was necessary, adding:

"I would prefer he did it himself as and when . . ."

"Understood."

Renate said that Anthony, who did not like to be called Tony, had had an impressive career working for British Petroleum, starting as a low-level petroleum engineer. More for the sake of David and Mark than for Eli's, she reminded them that petroleum engineers are one of the most well-paid oil and gas jobs. Not only do they have to devise methods to extract oil and gas in an efficient, safe, environmentally acceptable, and cost-effective manner but beyond strategic issues, they are also faced with unique challenges daily, as they may have to figure out solutions under incredibly tight deadlines and massive pressures.

Returning to Anthony Stacey, she said that he could easily have risen into the top management ranks if he had wanted it. Yet, he was and still is the kind of professional who likes the technical aspect of the job and surely did not want to get promoted beyond it. She said that administrative management was clearly not something he enjoyed, adding:

"He likes to get his hands dirty."

Continuing, Countess Renate said that he was thus eventually promoted to become the top petroleum engineer, though that did not prevent him, as he put it, dabbling in research from time to time. That led him, according to Countess Renate, to devise an algorithm which gave his reservoir analyses more precision than before. She added:

"Today, we would call it 'artificial intelligence', but the term had not been coined or at least put into common use then."

She offered a comment that Anthony had, since retirement, developed and patented a system which allowed subsea completions to comprise an oil/gas separator that used the pressure making the oil flow out of the reservoir to generate the power needed for the heating element that leads the gas to separate from the oil, as it boils at a lower temperature. Countess Renate concluded her short introduction:

"I have already shared with him a few key elements of the issue after David first called me, and I can say that he is willing and able to help on this mission."

Eli could not resist asking:

"How long have you known Anthony Countess?"

"Quite a number of years. I was first introduced to him by a friend who had been impressed by Anthony's original ideas whether one discussed oil exploration or production."

"Is he a member of The Shadow Experts?"

"Eli, this is something which I cannot discuss. A few people talk of the group as if it was a known entity. I cannot confirm or deny that it is. In many ways, does it even matter? What I can say, however, is that I have been working with a few individuals who agreed to help me serve one or several clients that needed their expertise. A few of these individuals have worked with me on so many missions that one could come to the view that we are a formally created group. Whether that group includes all these people or solely a small nucleus is somewhat of an academic issue, wouldn't you say?"

Without letting Eli reply to her somewhat rhetorical question, she continued:

"Others, however, have only helped me a small number of times. Whether they have the same or a different status is also somewhat of a moot point. Wouldn't you agree?"

Eli simply smiled and replied:

"I understand what you mean. David tells me that you, personally, have helped him and *Mossad* more broadly address and resolve several issues in the past, that you are highly efficient and totally trustworthy. That's good enough for me. So, let me go back to your earlier question: what you could do to help me . . ."

Eli paused to drink from the glass of water on his right, returned it to the side table and rattled off:

"First, I would like to have him look at the reservoir with the data that we have and tell me what he thinks. I want to have a much higher level of certainty that we are not talking of the small reef reservoirs people have found in the Philippines in the past, but something verifiably different."

Countess Renate interrupted:

"Makes all the sense in the world, Eli."

Eli did not miss a beat and went on with the discussion of his needs:

"Second, assuming that the information is sufficient to go forward, but also insufficient to be fully convinced, I would like him to help me collect the additional information needed; by the way, the operator of the field tells me that he is prepared to drill a second well. So, I would like Anthony to opine on whether another well is needed and if yes where it should be drilled. Third, assuming that the reservoir warrants it, I would like his views as to how to exploit it. Finally, I hear that there might be safety issues in the Philippines, particularly if the field is substantial. So, I would like Anthony to advise us as to how best to structure production to minimize the risks of sabotage or expropriation."

Countess let go of a polite whistle and said:

"What a menu! Yet, I fully understand your concerns. Let me do this. Could we organize a zoom call including Dr. Stacey, and decide then what the best next steps should be?"

CHAPTER.11

MANILA, THE PHILIPPINES AND TOKYO, JAPAN

Armand Duchemin was probably the most senior researcher and a professor at the prestigious French 'Institut Pasteur.' In the relatively recent past, having demonstrated to his peers a surprising business acumen, he had also been invited to join the institute's board of directors, though he professed to have little to no interest in management issues. He had been one of the earliest associates to join Countess Renate and her group, The Shadow Experts. He had been a key player in the resolution of a thorny issue involving a plot to spread a deadly disease though the use of a modified virus throughout the world a few years earlier.

Dr. Duchemin was not really surprised by Countess Renate's call about the mysterious fishermen's deaths in the Philippines. After all, it seemed almost like a problem custom-made for her services with his help. His first reaction, though, was to suggest that his friend and colleague Koichi Oshima, one of the leaders at the National Institute of Infectious Diseases in Japan would be at least as good a candidate as he for the mission. The Japanese Institute was in the Toyama district of Tokyo in Japan. Dr. Oshima would thus only have a five-hour flight between Tokyo and Manila, rather than the more than eighteen hours it would take Dr. Duchemin to fly from Paris, not counting the time spent on the ground somewhere along the way. Countess Renate, however, had no difficulty convincing him that he should be the one in charge of the mission, repeating the rationale which Mark had given her. Armand still insisted that Dr. Oshima would need to be involved, if only because it would be considerably easier for him to "commute" back and forth between Tokyo and Manila if they were able to collect samples that could be analyzed.

■ ■ ■ ■ ■

As previously agreed, Dr. Duchemin was invited to the Philippines by the country's Secretary of Health. Armand's reputation in the world of virology was virtually second to none. Additionally, from the point of view of the Secretary of Health, the idea that they could just invite him to come and look at the fishermen's deaths puzzle was too good to pass. In normal circumstances indeed, rather than having the offer of a visit presented to him on a silver plate, the Secretary of Health would have had to go through diplomatic channels and possibly even the World Health Organization to have such an eminent expert come to Manila. They offered to fly him first class at their own expense, using Emirates, their airline partner for the national Filipino carrier, Philippines Airlines, as there was no flight between Paris and Manila on the national airline. Dr. Duchemin was told that, once in the country, he would be accompanied throughout his trip by an official of the Department of Health, who could help him deal with the Tagalog language. Armand had on his side asked to have Ehud Shamir from the Israeli Embassy with him as well, if only to have a second pair of ears to verify translations.

Ehud was there to welcome him as came out of the customs and immigration area at Ninoy Aquino Airport. He had made sure, with Emirates' help, that Armand would be shepherded by Emirates personnel through the various formalities he would have to submit himself to, thus sparing him any unpleasant experience and ensuring that the whole process did not last too long. Emirates was additionally always careful, and this time was no exception, to have the luggage of their first-class passengers retrieved as a matter of top priority and brought to them by Emirates staff rather than left to the local luggage handlers. Ehud had never met Armand before yet had no difficulty recognizing him. He wore a light-colored linen tropical suit, with a white open-neck shirt and a straw hat, ostensibly to protect himself from the sun. Ehud actually quickly noticed Armand's shoes which combined cream-colored knitted fabric with brown suede leather and a thin rubber sole. Armand noticed that Ehud was looking at his shoes and simply said:

"You can't believe how comfortable they are. After all, they're just simple loafers, but the fabric allows your feet to breathe better than suede leather, and the rubber sole makes them more usable in wet climates than when it is made of leather."

Ehud simply nodded. He then told Armand that he would drop him at the hotel, asking whether he would like to have a simple dinner with him early in the evening. Armand thanked him but replied that he would rather rest for the balance of the afternoon, and after a simple dinner, possibly in his room, try to have a good night's rest, adding:

"I have a couple of very effective sleeping pills which do not leave me partially sluggish the following morning. Would you like to meet for breakfast?"

"Happy to, but do not feel obligated. I was told by colleagues in Tel Aviv that you did not enjoy this terribly American custom."

"I'm impressed. They are correct. Let's meet after breakfast. How should I plan on going to visit with the Secretary of Health?"

"I will be taking you there and will meet you in the lobby at 8:00 a.m. I'll have a chauffeur take us there. He'll wait for us and take us to the embassy when we are through. I'm sorry for the early departure, but Manila traffic is at times unpredictable."

Though Ehud has his helicopter pilot license, and the embassy had its own helicopter, he believed that it would be easier and less ostentatious for him to use a car to escort Armand. He paused for a second and added, switching topics almost as an afterthought:

"By the way, people in the Philippines more often than not go by their nicknames, rather than their full or official name. The Secretary of Health, Andres Ruizon goes by 'Bambi.' I know it can surprise but trust me that's how he likes to be called."

■ ■ ■ ■ ■

Though nicknames for people of the political standing of the Secretary of Health may seem odd to people steeped in western customs, it is in effect quite frequent across most layers of Filipino society. The use of nicknames is deeply ingrained in the Filipino culture. It is quite frequent for Filipinos not to use their legal first name in their day-to-day lives. These nicknames often find their origins in English, using words which may be chosen because they relate to certain themes, such as countries, car trademarks or popular brand names. In some cases, the meaning of these words may sound peculiar as a nickname to a native English-speaker; for instance, one recalls here a minister whose first name was Benjamin, and whose nickname was "Benhur!"

■ ■ ■ ■ ■

The next morning, Ehud was there as promised. Armand climbed into the black Mercedes limousine while the embassy driver, in uniform, shut the right door behind him. The chauffeur immediately informed Ehud that current traffic conditions meant that they should arrive about 10 minutes early, at 8:50 a.m. They drove in a generally northerly direction, principally using major axes. That gave Armand plenty of opportunities to see jeepneys as well as *habal-habal*, these local taxis built on motorbikes, bicycles, or older imported cars to which carriages had been attached. They weave into and out of the various mostly informal lanes, as if the other cars or buses on the road were legally obliged to let them through. Armand jokingly asked how many deaths they caused on an average day. Ehud simply smiled. After crossing the Pasig River not far from the *Malacañang* palace, the official residence of the country's President, and driving near the Minor Basilica of San Sebastian, they arrived at their destination, a low-rise building surrounded by several others comprising both a couple of hospitals and various offices. They were stopped at the entrance of the driveway to the Office of the Secretary by security services which inspected both the trunk of the Mercedes and, using mirrors attached to long poles, looked under the car to ensure that no bomb was attached. They cursorily looked at the visitors' identification papers and were suitably impressed when they saw Ehud's diplomatic credentials. Once in the building, they were ushered directly into Bambi's suite of offices.

Armand's meeting with Bambi allowed him to find out firsthand the official version of the events, though he had already been extensively briefed first by Countess Renate and second by Mark Levi. Though he initially found it hard calling the Secretary of Health Bambi as requested, a gentle prompting by Bambi got him comfortable enough:

"So, Bambi, what can you tell me?"

"My instructions are quite clear: there is no secret for you. We would just ask you not to discuss in public whatever you learn."

"Totally understood. Thanks for your confidence, by the way. So, the victims are all fishermen, correct?"

"Well, if you had asked me that question yesterday, I would have replied yes. However, we've just had a new development."

"And?"

Bambi initially seemed to ignore Armand's question and yet quickly veered and started telling the story of a couple of tourists who seemed to have contracted the same disease. He explained that they had simply sailed from MacLambay Island, which lies half a mile to the north of the biggest of the two twin islands.

He added:

"We don't know a lot quite yet. But we assume that they sailed to the largest beach among the two islands. That would be the one on the northeast side of North Twin. Assuming that the waters are not too shallow, that is that the tide is not at its lowest, sailboats, even if they have a small auxiliary outboard engine, can usually navigate directly through the reef."

He paused for a second and conceded:

"In point of fact, I don't know where they beached their boat."

Armand interrupted:

"Should it be hard to find out?"

"No. Not at all. It's just a case of getting all the details. The highest point on North Twin Island is a mere 35 feet above sea level. You can easily walk across the whole island in fifteen minutes or less, lengthwise. In short, they could have beached the boat pretty much anywhere. Logic would have it that it should either be near the northeast beach or in between the two islands, as that would offer the most protection from currents."

"Any idea when you expect to find out?"

"Soon, I hope. As a matter of fact, I was just about to ask."

Bambi picked up his phone and spoke to his assistant in Tagalog. Given his last statement, Armand guessed that he was asking her to find out the answer to his question. Within less than five minutes, Bambi's phone rang. He picked it up, smiled and only said: "*Salamat po*" which means thank you in Tagalog. Turning to Armand he said:

"The boat was at the west end of the north island . . . Makes sense if what they were looking for was a good protection from currents and ease of dragging the boat far enough on the beach to avoid it being drawn back into the sea by the tide."

Armand asked:

"Aside from these two people, all the victims are fishermen?"

"Yes. But wait. It's even a bit quirkier than that. Galoc fishermen typically ply two zones. The first is between these twin islands and MacLambay Island to their north; the other is southwest of the twin islands. I'm told that depending on the time of day when they set out, and more importantly on the tides, they choose one or the other. Well, believe it or not, only those who went east seemed to have been exposed to the bug. No case has been reported by fishermen who went to the west of either island, in deeper water."

He added:

"The surprising thing is that the boat of the two Spaniards was anchored closer to the west than to the east."

"What do you make of that?"

"I'm not sure in the case of the Spaniards, but for the fishermen it seems to be clear: the contamination agent was east of the islands as well. Now, for the Spaniards, you said that the island is small?"

"Absolutely. After all, North Twin Island is not even 1,500 feet in length."

"Could they simply have walked to from the west to the east side? Isn't that where you said the best beach was?"

"Indeed. They could also have gone swimming there as it is good snorkeling as well."

Armand had to ask:

"Does it make sense to conclude that the contaminant was on the east side?"

"Depends on what you believe may be causing the epidemic. If it is a bird flu like infection and is carried by birds, I can't think of why the source would seem to be so precisely located. Birds fly across the whole island and most probably across both all the time."

"Now what if there is only one sick bird?"

Bambi asked right back:

"That could do it. I'll grant you that. But, in your experience, is that a reasonable assumption?"

"Well, typically, unless you're talking of solitary birds, infections tend to spread to the flock that lives or travels together. But let's not go too far here: do we know it's a virus borne by a bird?"

Bambi displayed an embarrassed smile as he replied:

"No, we don't. Yet, other than birds, there aren't many terrestrial animals on these islands. Plus, whatever species there is would typically not travel to and from them. One exception might be turtles, as the islands in the area are so close to each other that a turtle could easily swim across to the other island."

"Yet, they typically come back to the same spot to lay their eggs."

"Absolutely. Other than that, you have plenty of varieties of fish and dolphins."

Armand persisted in his questioning:

"How about rodents using fishing or tourist boats to hop from one island to the next?"

"Excellent point. Nobody has mentioned that so far. That's definitely something for us to look into."

"Anyway, in short, we do not know what caused the first case?"

"I hate to admit to it, but I'm afraid you're correct, Armand."

Armand wanted to go back to the issue of the difference between the eastern and western zones of the twin islands. He asked:

"Out of the blue, from where do the prevailing winds blow?"

"Typically, west to east."

Bambi seemed surprised by his own reply and after thinking but a few seconds added:

"Wait. This is it."

He could see Armand nodding as he continued:

"The contamination agent could have been spread by the wind. Assume the agent was found anywhere on the island even to its far west. There would be no wind to carry it westward. That would be why no one has yet been found sick that sailed west of the island . . ."

Armand smiled broadly as he said:

"Quite possible. We'd simply have to assume that the virus is airborne . . ."

Bambi was now fully engaged in the intellectual game:

"Or spread in an airborne manner: mosquitos, for instance."

Armand looked as if he was getting increasingly interested in their dialog. He replied:

"Absolutely. Let me turn to a completely different question. How were the various samples collected."

Bambi conceded:

"We always follow the standard protocols recommended by the World Health Organization. But I've got to be honest. You'll probably be disappointed when you find out the details."

Armand interrupted:

"How far along the potential contagion chain would you typically go?"

"Truth is that we should follow it as far as it goes. However, reality does not always correspond to the rules. You must understand that we are talking of poor to very poor communities. The first couple of cases came to us after the patients had died. Yet, at that point, we still did not know what the cause was. So, we did not test direct relatives, unless they already had symptoms."

"And later?"

"Well, the problem has been with the spreading of the epidemic. So, I worry that we still do not have as adequately broad testing procedures as we should."

"Interesting. How many cases so far?"

Bambi hesitated and then replied:

"Well let's see. We've had five death and a dozen reported cases."

"How many people live in close proximity?"

"I don't really know. Hundreds, but surely not thousands."

Armand slightly changed tack:

"Back to your tourists. Where are they now?"

"In isolation in Puerto Princesa. They were transferred to the hospital there via helicopter. Interestingly, the young couple seems to be reacting more slowly or maybe less dramatically to the virus."

"Any idea why?"

"I'm told that they may have some immunity because of vaccines which they have received. They are from Spain, Bilbao to be specific, and their embassy is in the loop. I know that the medical director of the hospital has talked to the Spanish Ambassador, who apparently had a way to get their vaccination records."

"Very interesting. By the way, any chance that's related to their presence on the west coast of the island?"

"Possible. I've been told they had gone snorkeling. The waters off to the northeast of the island are much more scenic. Many more types of corals, sea anemones or tropical fish. Everything you can think of, from blue tangs to clown fish, to parrot fish, to multiple types of damselfish or angel fish, and many others."

"Point taken; must be truly beautiful."

"Breathtaking at times."

Armand wanted to bring the conversation back to his principal concern. He asked:

"Also, did you keep data on people who did not seem infected and yet could have been?"

Bambi was surprised and asked:

"Why are you asking this?"

Armand explained that the thought had been suggested by Bambi's comments with respect to the two tourists, though he immediately added:

"We always do this now because experience taught us that people that could have been infected and did not fall sick often have antibodies which others don't have. This allows us more speed, both identifying the offending virus and finding a possible cure via the antibodies."

Bambi briefly looked down as if from embarrassment and conceded:

"I do not believe we did. Now how long do these antibodies live in healthy people?"

Taking an almost professorial demeanor, as he occasionally did, Armand answered:

"Could last forever, but most frequently from a few months to several years. It's just like the efficacy of a vaccine. After all, a vaccine is nothing more than an effort to make the body create the antibodies needed to fight the virus, except that the viruses are often "neutralized" so that we don't infect healthy people. Now, certain vaccines are kind of once in a lifetime and done, while others require boosters every so often. For Covid-19, for instance, we've been recommending a booster every six months for the people most at risk."

"I understand. Thanks for the crash course . . . Anything else?"

Armand thought several seconds and then quite carefully broached a completely new topic:

"Yes. One important subject matter. Though I totally understand that you might have delegated that to another government department, I wonder whether you can tell me anything on any investigation that was carried out on the islands themselves."

"Ah! Armand, what a wonderful question. Truth is that we decided not to expose police officers to whatever the cause of the disease was until we had a better sense of what was behind the sickness."

"I can easily appreciate why, Bambi, but doesn't waiting too long increase the risk that any physical evidence, if there was any in the first place, might be corrupted or even lost?"

Bambi conceded the point noting that the government had identified that risk and taken measures to palliate it. The decision had been made to send a small team of a half a dozen military investigators, who were dropped by military helicopter and were picked up by the same helicopter later on, adding:

"We wanted to shield the local environment as much as we could from the disruption brought by the helicopter blades. So, the helicopters hovered about fifty feet above ground and the guys, who were all dressed in protective clothing, rappelled down."

"And?"

"Mixed results. On the negative side, they did not see any footprint on the beach, but that's not a surprise . . ."

Seeing Armand's quizzical look, Bambi added:

"The tide's movements would typically wipe out anything that's not deep enough."

Armand nodded. Bambi continued:

"On the positive side, beyond the beach, they picked up footprints on the sandy and gravelly ground of South Twin Island. Now, they could belong to anyone, local or tourist. Yet, whoever walked there was wearing some footwear and did not go very far, maybe fifty feet at most."

He paused again and before Armand could react added:

"Most tourists would be barefoot. So, we thought these footprints would be suspect."

"Now isn't that interesting. Where were they?"

"On the west side of the island."

"Did they go in one direction or both ways?"

"From what I heard, the footprints were coming from and returning to the beach."

"Bingo."

Bambi looked stumped, but Ehud saw that Armand's mind had been working faster than that of the secretary. He quickly explained that he could construct a scenario which had some third party, still to be identified, drop something on the west side of South Twin Island, and then leave right away. The footprints on the beach would have been wiped out by the tide, but the sea level did not rise high enough to penetrate the bush behind the beach. He concluded:

"Now imagine that whatever was dropped was infectious in one way or another, could that be carried by the wind or by mosquitos carried by the wind to the east side of both islands?"

"Armand, you should be a detective, not a virologist . . ."

"Virology is at times a bit like detective work . . ."

"Point taken."

Bambi paused and then added:

"But we haven't found anything. Should whatever they dropped have left traces?"

Armand replied:

"Should have. Nothing on the beach and in the bushes behind the beach?"

"Neither place; nothing anywhere. Now, in truth, I am told that the team could not walk much into the bush other than following the path which previous travelers had traced?"

"You mean they couldn't because of their protective clothing?"

"Yes. It's not a question of weight. It's mostly because movements are partially impeded and the glass in front of the eyes creates some distortion. They didn't want to take the risk that the protective clothing might be partially ripped by some thorn they had not seen."

Mischievously, Armand asked:

"Could it be then that the right formulation should not be 'they haven't found anything' but rather 'they have not found anything **yet,**' my friend?"

The Institut Pasteur maintains a wide system of thirty-three associated organizations located around the world. Of those, nine are strewn around the Asia-Pacific region: New Caledonia, South Korea, the countries that made up Indochina (Cambodia, Laos, and Vietnam), Thailand, and China. The system's mission is to contribute to the prevention and the fight against infectious diseases worldwide. It focuses on research, public health issues, education, and training as well as the development of solutions and transfers of technology.

Early in the mission, Armand had decided, following the strong advice of Countess Renate and David Heller, that he would not get in touch with any of the regional Pasteur offices. The rationale was deceptively simple: with at least some measure of suspicion that China directly or through proxies for its secret services, it was more prudent not to let anyone know that he was working on the issue. This was all the easier as the sickness and its consequences had been kept under wrap by the Philippines authorities.

Armand still decided to call his good friend Dr. Oshima, with whom he had worked in the past and whom he had introduced to Countess Renate as a potential associate for The Shadow Experts. He had talked to him before leaving Paris, as he knew he would eventually need his help. At this point, he wanted to make sure he kept him in the loop. Upon hearing that Armand was on the phone, Oshima-San exclaimed:

"Armand-San good to hear your voice . . . How has the trip been so far?"

"On the whole, I'm rather optimistic."

"Really. But didn't you tell me earlier that there had been a few deaths? That's serious, right?"

Armand conceded the point but proceeded to suggest at least a couple of interesting developments. The first one on which he focused was the case of the two Spanish tourists. The fact that they had exhibited a few of the symptoms, including high fever, but no marked deterioration after they were moved to the hospital in Puerto Princesa gave him hope. He added:

"They, the Filipinos, seem to think that there may be some residual immunity from other flu vaccines . . ."

"Quite possible. Very interesting, very interesting. Do you agree with them?"

Armand replied that he did for at least two reasons. The first, which he was quick to credit Mark Levi, was totally consistent with the "attack" being potentially the first salvo in a bigger conflict, suggesting:

"Whoever did that may have just wanted to send a warning. You do not need to kill or infect a whole bunch of innocent people to achieve your goal. Taking this further, assuming that there is some local complicity, would they want to hurt natives? They have succeeded since the Filipinos agreed to have us involved."

He paused and pointed to the reality of the climate in the area. Assuming that the virus was introduced through contaminated mosquitos, you must assume that viral concentration would decline gradually as time passes and winds blow the mosquitos away. Further female mosquitos may live thirty to forty days, but the males die much more quickly. So, he was assuming that the initial contamination, applied as it was to a very sparsely populated area, would be bound to wane quickly, unless the virus could also be carried by mammals on the island.

Turning to the second reason why he was hopeful, Armand mentioned the fact that there did not seem to have been any new case for at least two days. This might serve as further support for his assumption that the first "attack" had been just that, a warning, involving some weak contaminant. Ominously, though, he added:

"Now, since we know that nothing is likely to change on the Filipino oil development front, there is a serious risk of another attack. Given my rationale so far, you'd have to believe they would try to make it more dangerous, however they do it."

"What do you make of that?"

"I think you and I should work to come up with antibodies as quickly as we can."

"And to do that we must first identify the virus, if we are really speaking of a virus, and second find people who developed antibodies which we could reproduce in the laboratory."

"Couldn't have said it better myself, Oshima-San."

CHAPTER.12

TEL AVIV, ISRAEL AND MANILA, THE PHILIPPINES

Anthony Stacey landed at Manila airport following a very comfortable flight on Singapore Airlines. It required him to spend just about an hour at Singapore's Changi International Airport, but, as someone used to international travel in general and travel in Asia in particular, Anthony knew that a stopover in Singapore would never be painful. Changi airport is almost always ranked as one of the top one or two airports in the world, and surely seems to deserve its rank.

After arriving at Terminal 3 in Manila, Anthony, who was wearing light but elegant clothing, walked from the gate to the quarantine desk which was but a formality and then through passport control. From there he went downstairs, bypassed luggage claim as he was traveling quite light with cabin luggage only and proceeded through customs. This was also relatively easy for first and business class passengers, not because they received special treatment, but because they had disembarked first and thus did not have much of a waiting line before custom officers cleared them. Ehud Shamir and Mike Loeb were right through the glass door behind the custom officers' station to collect him when he reached the arrival hall. As he met his two local contacts, he could not resist saying:

"I am always surprised when I land in the Philippines, or Indonesia for that matter; I can't get over all the gold Rolexes or equivalent fancy watches worn by customs officers . . ."

Ehud replied:

"I know what you mean. It either reminds you of the flourishing trade in counterfeit goods or makes you wonder about corruption . . ."

Anthony deadpanned:

"Exactly. Or both. Neither inspires too much confidence. However, it is what it is and there no way any one of us will change it."

Ehud added:

"Glad you knew to dress lightly. This is surely not the rainy season yet, but the heat and humidity can still be hard to bear if you aren't dressed for it. I remember, I once heard someone say that people here dress more for the weather than to abide by fashion rules . . ."

Anthony smiled and simply nodded as they walked straight out of the terminal, to the curb where a car and driver from the Israeli Embassy was awaiting them. Anthony could not resist the quip:

"Seems it's always easier for official vehicles to park illegally here . . ."

Ehud only smiled. As he was settling into the car, Anthony remarked:

"Thank God for the air-conditioning, though I must confess that I often find that it is set too low in many instances in this part of the world."

Ehud immediately enquired:

"Is it too cold for you in here?"

"No, you've got it just about right."

Though the trip from the airport to the Peninsula Hotel in Makati was barely more than five miles through Epifanio de Los Santos, Mike who was seated next to Anthony used the fifteen odd minutes to brief him on where they were in the process:

"The key at this point is for us to firm up the opinion which you had preliminarily reached when we discussed the mission on Zoom."

"You mean my preliminary view that this may well be quite a profitable deposit? Fully understood. When am I meeting with Luis Ramos De Ayala?"

"We booked a meeting at 9:00 a.m. tomorrow morning. We'll pick you up and drive you there. We decided to give you the full afternoon to rest since it's hardly past 2:30 p.m. now. Would you like to have dinner tonight or maybe just a drink?"

"Dinner would be fine provided it's not too complicated. After having taken a short sleep first, I'll go for a swim this afternoon. I must keep myself awake so that I get a full night's sleep tonight."

As a frequent traveler across time zones, Anthony knew that the best way to adapt to time zones as painlessly as possible was to get a couple hours of sleep when he first arrived at the hotel. Then he would get up and pick up his day at the correct local time. Today, as he alluded to in the car, he would probably spend a half-hour or so in the gym and swim for about as long a time. He could then go back to his room, take a shower, and get himself ready for an early dinner with Mike and Ehud. He knew very well that all hotels, including the most sophisticated throughout the region, Singapore excepted, offered in-room massage services; however, he also knew that these services easily slipped into sexual activity which he did not want to enjoy. Though there were certainly moral reasons behind his choice, the most important concern for him was the spread of sexually transmitted diseases, something he had no intention of bringing back home to London.

Anthony was not really surprised when Ehud told him at dinner that the meeting the next morning would be at Luis's offices. Ehud only had to add:

"That's where all the data that you might want are . . ."

The one surprise was when Mike and Ehud met him in the lobby of the hotel the next morning. Rather than escorting him outside, ostensibly to climb in a chauffeur-driven car, they went toward the elevator of the Makati Tower of the hotel, and pressed the button indicating they were going to the helipad, which was available from 8:00 a.m. to 5:00 p.m. Ehud explained that Luis had sent his helicopter to fly them the short distance to his office, adding:

"Helicopter flights are frequent around here. Just look at the traffic and you'll understand. That way nobody who might wish to follow you will be able to . . ."

"Hate to tell you guys that I'm unsure how good the stratagem is."

Ehud and Mike looked surprised. Anthony added:

"Most people will probably not even know who I am; they won't bother. As for the few who might know me, they'll be able to see that I am going up to the helipad; just stand in front of the elevator and you'll see which floor I am going to . . . Then they can follow the helicopter, if as you say Luis's office is that close."

Mike interrupted and said with a broad smile:

"Can't fault your logic, but we've kind of anticipated that."

He paused for a second to let his statement sink in and continued without giving Anthony a chance to react:

"I hate to say that, but we have taken two important precautions. First, the helicopter is not here yet, and won't be for at least a good ten to fifteen minutes. Second, we are not going to the helipad . . ."

"Hold it. You pressed on the button, didn't you?"

"Did indeed. But I also pushed on floor 7. That's where we'll get off."

"What will we do there?"

"Nothing. We'll step out of the first elevator, call another and take that one to the helipad."

Anthony could only congratulate the team:

"I can vouch for the fact that you all know what you're doing. Any other curveballs?"

"Who knows?"

Mike simply noted that the ideal scenario would be for an unrelated helicopter to land on the helipad before theirs came, adding:

"Anybody looking at this would reasonably believe that the person who went to the helipad on our first elevator ride will take that helicopter. That's the one they would follow, if they were going to follow you."

"And what if none comes?"

"Well, we just have to hope that they'll lose patience and will stop watching when Luis's helicopter comes in in fifteen minutes. In the meantime, the three of us will get to enjoy a nice cup of coffee while we wait . . ."

Anthony added:

"I assume we're not walking the short distance is also for security reasons."

"Absolutely. It'd be too easy for someone to follow us."

Luckily, another helicopter landed, and soon thereafter took off before Luis's aircraft arrived. Anthony reflected:

"That was one heck of a short stop!"

Mike smiled:

"We might as well tell you now. This helicopter came from the Israeli Embassy and waited up there until the pilot got a radio message from Luis's pilot."

"You mean this was a setup?"

Ehud beat Mike to the punch:

"You bet."

"Got to repeat what I said a few minutes ago. You guys are real pros. Sorry I even doubted for a second."

The short flight to Luis's office was totally uneventful. It took less than five minutes. Luis was at the heliport at Ayala Tower when the helicopter landed, having received a radio message from Enrique when he took off from the Peninsula. As usual, he looked quite dapper with a light-green colored *barong* with darker green embroidery and beige pants. He greeted Anthony and his two escorts warmly and took them directly to his office suite. Anthony was surely impressed by the decoration, though, in fairness, he had already had several opportunities to visit senior executive offices in Southeast Asia. He was used to some of the ostentation.

Anthony spent the whole morning with Luis and his top petroleum engineer, Angelo DeSousa. Luis said that he had had a long working relationship with Angelo, explaining:

"We go way back. He was a star student in the high school and college where he studied. Though he was originally a poor orphan from the countryside, as we say, he had been adopted by a family of Indian origin, ergo the name DeSousa, which is not common in the Philippines. They had been posted from Manila to Mindanao for a brief period. They took Angelo with them when they returned to Manila and provided him with as good an education as he could handle."

Angelo appeared originally a bit embarrassed, though he started to smile when Luis concluded:

"It seems that there was nothing that the faculty could throw at him and which he could not handle. I hired him straight out of engineering school, and he has been my right-hand man on petroleum issues ever since."

Ehud and Mike had introduced Anthony as a top-flight petroleum engineer and Luis very quickly noticed that Angelo's behavior was changing. While he was initially posturing to some extent, probably trying to impress Luis's guests, he quickly assumed the demeanor of a pupil in front of his master, very much as one would have expected him to behave in most of Asia. Anthony must have noticed the evolution. In fact, in some ways, he fully welcomed it. On the surface, he was sure that it was giving him all the credibility he needed to get straight answers from both Angelo and Luis. At the same time, he wanted to flatter, however discreetly, Angelo so that he kept the trust of his own employer and felt some gratitude toward his new advisor.

The ploy seemed to work well, as Ehud mentioned in Mike's ear:

"Interesting. No more bullshit and bravado. Looks a lot more fact-based . . ."

"Totally agree. I was initially worried of a potential conflict. But Anthony is a real pro. He knows how to get people to collaborate with him."

Mike paused and added:

"Must have come from all his corporate experience. You don't rise up in the ranks unless you know how to manage egos around you."

Ehud replied:

"Part of the local culture too. I'll explain later . . ."

Their initial conversations involved the physical description of the so-far only well into the new structure. Anthony noted that it was a rare occurrence, in his experience at least, for a first well to be evolved into the more complex set-up which they now had: a vertical well, plus two horizontal extensions. Luis replied that he was responsible for the decision:

"My first concern was to avoid telegraphing to others that we might have made an important find."

Angelo added:

"Indeed. It quickly became obvious, based on downhole pressures and on the height of the oil column that this could be quite big."

He paused but seeing Luis's approving nod he almost immediately added:

"Based on our geological work, we had solid indications that the two directions we chose for the horizontal wells were the most potentially rewarding. Obviously, we could have plugged the well after finishing our tests and moved the drilling rig, a jack-up here given the relatively shallow waters, to another spot."

■ ■ ■ ■ ■

Offshore oil exploration typically requires the use of one of three varieties of drilling rigs, the key determinant of which equipment should be used being the depth of the water on the drilling site. For exploration in relatively shallow waters, jack-up rigs usually offer the best alternative. They consist of a buoyant hull to which a number of legs, most often three, are fitted. These legs, when in the up position, allow the rig to float on its hull and still carry all attached machinery. It can thus be towed to the drilling site, or, however quite rarely, to move on its own power. Once onsite, the legs are lowered until they reach the sea floor, raising the hull above water, thus increasing the weight borne by the legs. When the drilling site is in waters that run deeper than 400 feet, a semi-submersible rig is used; the legs of a jack-up would have to be much too long. It looks just like a jack-up rig, minus the legs. The semi-submersible rig remains partially buoyant during the drilling process, though it is partially submerged to provide the required weight and thus stability. They can operate in waters as deep as 12,000 feet. For deeper waters still, one must turn to a drillship which is larger than a semi-submersible rig, but also less stable.

■ ■ ■ ■ ■

Luis interrupted:

"I knew that I could not control the news that the well struck oil. Too many eyes, too many people . . . Now, imagine that we then moved to another well in the vicinity. People would have started to speculate and who knows what that would have done."

Angelo resumed telling the story:

"Extending the original hole with two horizontal wells would be quite a bit more discreet."

Anthony had to ask:

"How did you know how far you would drive the horizontal well? That has implications for the size of the drill bit and other elements, correct?"

Angelo was smack in his area of expertise and enjoyed the dialog. He replied:

"Sure does. But I knew that we could extend the first horizontal drill-hole at least 1,000 feet, and possibly twice as much."

He then explained that, with the continuous testing which can now be carried out while drilling, he could see changes in the oil pressure in the reservoir and thus make an educated guess as to whether or not he was running close to the end of the field. He simply added:

"We didn't reach the end of the deposit with the first horizontal well. So, we drilled another one in the opposite direction, with the same parameters. And guess what?"

"Tell me!"

"Well, we didn't reach a point when pressure fell either . . ."

Anthony asked:

"How far did you extend the horizontal drilling?"

"We stopped at 1,400 feet in both directions. My guess is that we could extend the wells at least 600 feet each, maybe more. We can always go back if needed."

Anthony noted that this was excellent news, though he remarked that given the work to date it might be smarter to attack the deposit with one or two additional wells. Angelo nodded vigorously. Anthony cynically added:

"Haven't you guys only postponed the inevitable?"

Neither Luis nor Angelo seemed to follow. Anthony clarified his thought:

"You said you didn't want people to know how big the discovery was. Aren't they bound to know now?"

Luis smiled and replied:

"True. True, but now we also know a lot more ourselves and I hope that nobody has all the details of what we actually did."

Anthony casually asked what security measures they applied to their custody of data. Angelo's confidence seemed to decline somewhat as he honestly came back:

"Truth be known, it's not nearly as good as we would like it to be. Thank God, nobody has all the pieces. Also, so far at least, we have managed to keep this out of the press. But Luis keeps reminding me that some of the ownership of the project is in the public's hands."

Luis interrupted Angelo to complete the point:

"My group's stock is quoted on the Makati Stock Exchange, and the stocks of several of our partners are as well. We have a duty to inform investors if there is any material information."

He paused for a second, smiled and added mischievously:

"However, for as long as no one with any knowledge of the find trades in the stock, nobody can be accused of insider trading. Plus, I can say with a straight face that I don't want to share information which might be neither complete not fully checked. After all, this is plain truth. Isn't this the reason you are here?"

Anthony nodded, but immediately threw some cold-water on the argument:

"I get this Luis. But, as you know, my role here is to help my client determine whether this is a venture in which he should get involved. So, one way or another, there is going to be some transaction and thus some valuation of the asset."

Luis grimaced as Anthony's point was valid and reminded him that he would have to accept at least one new partner in the venture.

■ ■ ■ ■ ■

After lunch, during which the group suspended their detailed conversations, Luis remained with Ehud and Mike, while Anthony went to work with Angelo. Ehud and Mike focused on the topic of the joint venture which would need to be established. They clearly said that they were not in a position to negotiate or even to make any specific offer, but still wanted to share with Luis what Mike had generally gathered from his conversations in Tel Aviv. The point was that Eli would be willing to participate in the venture, bringing in both money and resources on two conditions. First, all safety considerations would be addressed and managed by *Mossad* however they elected to carry out the mission. Mike told a little white lie as he added:

"I will play a liaison role on this, but I will not be in control. Not sure I love it, but I'm not given a choice."

He then mentioned that Eli would need to have some financial participation in the success of the venture. To Mike, who wanted to be as neutral on this as possible, the key contribution which Eli would make was his ability to operate in adverse geopolitical conditions. Luis motioned that he fully understood what Mike meant and conceded that he knew he would have to negotiate something that made sense. Ehud jokingly added:

"Eli is already a very wealthy man. I doubt that his goal is to make another fortune. If anything, he has been divesting of it, so that he may focus on philanthropy."

Luis dejectedly replied:

"Good to know. But it's clear that this project would not be undertaken for philanthropic reasons, right?"

■ ■ ■ ■ ■

Anthony's time with Angelo was spent gathering all the data that he needed to run his proprietary software. Over the years, he had developed something which Countess Renate had already told David and his colleagues might well be called "artificial intelligence" today since the label is so gratuitously applied. His software used all the data he had been able to accumulate to predict reservoir size and potential recovery rates based on a series of standard measurements that are acquired during the exploratory drilling process, together with geological data which seismic surveys and their more recent 3D versions could provide. Traditionally, reservoirs were "sized" based on geological data together with whatever the experience of petroleum engineers had accumulated. Using "big data principles and processes," Anthony was able to create an algorithm which could substantially improve the combination of experimental data and human experience.

With his software installed in "the Cloud" with cyber security protection devised for him by Wong Hai Chock, an associate from The Shadow Experts living in Singapore, Anthony was able to run a simplified version of his algorithm based on a subset of the data provided by Angelo.

When they rejoined Luis, Ehud and Mike, nobody could miss the smile on Angelo's face. He had ostensibly been wowed by Anthony's work and loved the preliminary conclusions they had reached. Anthony did not want to let the suspense continue and simply stated:

"Luis, I do think you may really well have found an Elephant!"

He let that sink in. Luis and Angelo were incredulously beaming. Anthony then added:

"I'll have to do some more detailed work, but I believe first you have located a stratigraphic trap of quite significant dimensions. Second, I would not be surprised if you needed another couple of wells at most to be able to exploit the field, though, as you well know, needs to drill may further arise simply because of flukes or developments during production."

He paused and then added a small qualifier:

"By the way, I am assuming that each of these three wells would comprise one or two horizontal dimensions as well."

Luis nodded, though, always the practical businessman, he immediately asked:

"Where should we drill the next well?"

Anthony's face became a bit more severe as he replied:

"Luis, it's not as simple as it seems. I will be happy to work on this with Angelo as I know he can bring in a lot of local knowledge. But we have quite a bit of work ahead of us before we can pinpoint the ideal location of the next well."

Angelo was beaming, while Anthony continued:

"There are quite a few additional analyses I must carry out."

Anthony could clearly see that Luis was disappointed. He nevertheless added:

"My strong advice to you is to avoid rushing things. From what I know of the Leviathan field in Israel, there may well be a number of common features between it and your discovery. Thus, whichever way production is designed, and I am speaking here of well location, I suspect that a lot can be designed while you're doing additional drilling: said differently, I view additional drilling as confirmation rather than a precondition to starting the work."

Luis was starting to smile again. Turning to Mike he asked:

"What are our next steps there, with respect to the Israel connection?"

CHAPTER.13

TEL AVIV, ISRAEL AND MANILA, THE PHILIPPINES

Back in Tel Aviv after his initial investigation, Anthony Stacey reported his findings to Eli Abelman. Though surely used to traffic, as London's can seem deadly slow at times, he noted that Tel Aviv certainly had its own issues with cars double parked in narrow streets and blocking traffic or trucks unloading their goods at the wrong time of day. At least, in contrast to New York or New Delhi, the use of car horns was usually kept under control.

The conclusions which Anthony had reached immediately convinced Eli that he needed to have another direct conversation with Luis. To him, Anthony's report was sufficiently enticing that the project represented a reasonable, if calculated risk. In an ideal world, he surely would have liked to have more detailed information on the deposit in order to be able to make more robust estimates of the potential cash flow to be drawn from the venture. On the other hand, he knew very well that smart, and at times a bit lucky, money was often only rewarded when one can "see the potential" while others don't yet.

Though, in normal circumstances, he would have preferred to conduct that conversation face to face, he felt that the earlier opportunity he had had to meet Luis in person, when Luis had joined him in Tel Aviv, made a zoom call quite sufficient, at least as the next step. Assuming that an agreement could eventually be struck, he knew very well that they would have to meet in person again, probably in Manila, to sign whatever document was eventually negotiated. He made a "conference appointment" with Luis and called him at the agreed upon time:

"Luis, Eli here."

As always, Luis appeared smiling and delighted to have the opportunity to confer with Eli. He replied:

"Great to talk to you, Eli. I hope you have heard the good news of Anthony's assessment. What should our next step be, my friend?"

"You're correct. I've read Anthony's initial report and though short both in terms of words and in the real detail, it's clear that his visit there was pretty good, right?"

"I don't know what his report said, as, understandably, I did not get a formal copy."

Eli nodded, effectively conceding that Luis could not have received the report. He went on to offer his read of Anthony's conclusions to ensure that they were both on the same wavelength. Luis thanked him and suggested that, to him, all the advice he was getting seemed to argue that there were good reasons to drill at least one, probably two more wells, to delineate the reservoir more precisely. Luis added:

"It seems to me that he believes this could be a very big find . . ."

"That's the gist of what I heard, though his report was not as strong in his conclusion as an optimist might have expected."

With a clearly worried tone of voice, Luis replied:

"Really? What did he say?"

Eli did not want to dash Luis's hopes too dramatically but given what he was about to suggest, he did not either want to speculate more than needed. He replied that the results of the first well had clearly been quite encouraging, even more so as the two horizontal extensions saw downhole pressures maintained and the overall flow rising. He added that Anthony had judged that the geological structure in which the reservoir appeared to be had the potential to hold considerably more hydrocarbons. Luis replied:

"To me this is all good news. Do you have any doubts?"

Eli cautioned Luis:

"That is where we both need to be quite careful. There is excellent potential, but at this point we are only talking of potential. Anthony reminded me of the earlier predictions, way back in the 1980s, that Nido could be a huge field. In the end, it was clear that dreams had taken over where reality should have stayed in control. The same could be said about Matinloc. Neither you nor I want to repeat that mistake."

Eli paused for a few seconds, to drink from a glass of water that was on his desk to his right. Luis remained silent though in his mind he was thinking that the tools used to measure and assess the potential of oil deposits had considerably improved over nearly a half century. Eli finally added:

"Further, as the suggestion I'm about to make could require certain official disclosures, we sure as heck don't want people to start going crazy and speculate."

"I understand, Eli. But you must appreciate that this has the potential to make a huge difference for the Philippines . . ."

"Don't get me wrong. I do. I certainly do. Remember, the Leviathan gas field in the Eastern Mediterranean Sea did change things for Israel. I was smack in the middle of that. In some ways, you could say that I've already seen the movie."

"True. Sorry. But I haven't and am quite excited."

"Don't be sorry. Your reaction is totally natural. The news is wonderful. The key is that you don't want to attract attention too early. You want to play the whole thing close to the vest, and to project only some measure of optimism. Let people be surprised if the results of the next couple of wells meet your hopes and mine by the way."

"You're right. I totally agree. So, what's up?"

"Well, in short, I'm ready to consider doing business with you."

"Great news. On what terms?"

"Forgive me if I'm too direct, but, at my age, you don't want to waste time beating around the bush. It's been a while since I stopped buying green bananas."

"A man after my own heart."

"Doesn't surprise me."

Eli paused again to let what he had just said sink in and then completed his thought:

"I would like to offer to create an oil exploration and production company, which would be a joint venture between you and my group. At this point, I would plan on having your contribution to the venture to be a material percentage ownership of the deposit. On my side, we would provide both operational expertise, call it sweat equity if you will, and more importantly the financing for the next couple of wells. If everything goes according to plan, I might even offer to pay for some or most of the production infrastructure, as a means of raising my own personal share of the equity in the venture."

"This sounds very interesting Eli, but I have financial resources which I can also bring to bear."

Luis paused and could see Eli's interest being piqued. He continued:

"So, I'd like to be sure I don't dilute my ownership too much; I'd like to say that I would prefer not to dilute my own ownership any more than I have to. Let me ask you: would you accept that a smaller share of the deposit be placed in the venture, if I also contribute some additional cash?"

"Can't see why we couldn't go in that direction. Makes a lot of sense. At the same time, I'm sure you'll understand that I would still want to have significant upside potential. This is only worth my time if it is an unusually high potential return venture. You understand my position, too, don't you?"

Before letting Luis reply, he reminded him:

"You know that I have been divesting many if not most of my business interests to focus on philanthropy. So, you've triggered what may be one of my last entrepreneurial enterprises; that's good. But it must be worth my while, not just for me but really for my foundation and future generations. Maybe some warrant to buy some additional equity at a later date . . ."

Luis nodded that he understood, though a sharp negotiator such as Eli could clearly see that it was not exactly the message which Luis wanted to hear. Eli shifted gears and asked:

"Now, on a different note, what kind of disclosure requirements do you have to make to the local financial authorities? I assume that the deposit is owned by a company listed on the Makati Stock Exchange, correct?"

"Yes, correct. My lawyers tell me that, for as long as there is no additional news on the drilling front, we probably do not need to disclose anything more, though we will eventually have to say something . . ."

"I get it. After all, the amount of cash which I personally or you and I together put into the venture will in practice put a value on the deposit. However, I do not see how it could affect the other owners of the deposit in anything other than a positive way. Right?"

"Absolutely. I think it will add value to the deposit if only because we would clearly be saying it's commercial."

"Right on. Come to think of it, the only new news, if we can call it a development, is the report Anthony wrote. It's not public yet, but our deal would implicitly recognize that some new information had led us to where we are. Since I paid for it, I'd like to have a share of that value added as well. Fair?"

"Totally fair. Listen, Eli. We are both gentlemen. Here's what I think we should do. Could we have your financial people and legal counsel meet with mine to work out the outline of some reasonable deal? I suspect you will want Anthony to be involved as well. Let them advise us on what regulatory requirements we must satisfy. Let them come up with some structure and we can then meet, you and I, to agree on the specific terms and values and sign on the dotted line."

"Totally agree. I suspect we both strive to be whiter than white! I've always believed that no surprise can be a good surprise."

■ ■ ■ ■ ■

Though the weather in Tel Aviv can be hot, Eli could not fail to notice the late afternoon hot and humid air at the Ninoy Aquino International Airport. Even at around five in the afternoon, the air outside of air-conditioned facilities felt sticky, sultry and even muggy. As he stepped out of his Dassault Falcon 8X, the top of the line offering in the aircraft maker's corporate jet range, Eli was quickly reminded that he had landed timewise near the start of the rainy season, which runs from June to September. The jet had no difficulties covering the nearly 4,800 nautical mile distance given both its official 6,500-mile range and the fact that it only carried one passenger, plus the flight crew and a cabin attendant. With the flight having lasted almost ten hours, Eli had taken the opportunity to rest. The aft of the plane's vast cabin could be made into a bedroom, with a second bathroom for privacy. The first bathroom was just behind the cockpit, and could be used by everyone on the plane, crew included.

The Israeli Embassy had sent a chauffeured stretched Hummer H2 limousine to pick up Eli as he stepped down from the aircraft. Though a simple Cadillac might have sufficed, Ehud had feared that sitting three abreast in the back, or having either Mike or himself sitting in front next to the chauffeur would not have been optimal. Unfortunately, most limousine users in Manila preferred a stretched

Hummer to a stretched Cadillac, which was therefore quite hard to find. Ehud had also arranged for customs and immigration personnel to be available on the tarmac so that Eli Abelman would not need to transit through the terminal, a courtesy which was often extended to diplomatic personnel and their guests. Ehud and Mark almost simultaneously got out of the Hummer and greeted Eli. The flight attendant helped the chauffeur load Eli's luggage in the trunk of the beast. Less than fifteen minutes after the aircraft had touched down, the car was leaving the airport and driving Eli to the suite which had been reserved for him at the Makati Peninsula Hotel.

There too, all registration formalities had been pre-arranged for Eli. A guest relations officer took him to his suite and had him sign the various papers up there. A bellhop soon came with his luggage, while a maid was ready to unpack his belongings and hang them in the closet. A few minutes later, Eli joined Ehud and Mike in the Old Manila, the best restaurant at the Makati Hotel. Eli had made it clear that he was not looking for anything fancy and would only like a relatively light dinner. Ehud still had selected the Old Manila restaurant on the ground floor as he had been able to arrange with the chef for a Kosher menu to be made available, if Eli desired a meat course. Otherwise, starters such as salads and main dishes such as fish courses would satisfy his needs, provided the fish had gills and scales and there was no shellfish along with it. A bottle of Kosher wine had been brought from the Embassy to ensure that Eli's desire to maintain his Kosher routine would be met, if it was a requirement.

After a few pleasantries while they were enjoying a local cocktail, a Gin Pom (Gin and Pomelo juice) for Mike and Eli and a Myth (coconut rum, pandan and lychees) for Ehud, the men quickly came to the main point. Ehud and Mike needed to verify with Eli that the schedule that had been set for the next 36 hours was what Eli wanted. Mike first asked:

"Are you truly satisfied with the agreement Eli?"

"Absolutely. The structure that has been negotiated fits perfectly within my group and I hear that there were no necessary additional disclosures needed. I'm told that between our cash infusion, which initially is in the form of a letter of credit, and Luis's actual cash contribution we will have plenty of liquidity to finance the work that needs to be done."

Mike interrupted:

"Talking of disclosures, they will come once the agreement is signed. I can't wait to see what the paper gain will be then?"

Eli smiled and only replied:

"Bound to happen. Speculators always come in at that point. Remember, however, that you only hear of those who have been successful. Yet, for any successful bet by some speculator I am sure there are at least five others who lost all their money; and you hardly ever hear of them. The real payoff, the only meaningful lasting gain, will come after we drill the next two wells. The paper profits will melt like ice cream in the sun if we do not hit oil in sufficient quantities."

Mike nodded:

"Understood."

And then Mike immediately moved to the next topic:

"By the way, we had an important meeting with Anthony and one of your own engineers yesterday. The two locations for the next wells have been identified."

After a short pause he added:

"Obviously the location of the third well can easily change depending upon the results of the second . . ."

He continued explaining that the whole project had been designed so that the actual vertical holes would be as close to the expected east end of the deposit as feasible. This would eventually save on underwater infrastructure, if, as firmly hoped, the deposit could be exploited following the model which Eli's group had designed for the Leviathan structure. He added that the logic, as he understood it, was to locate production equipment as close to shore as possible, in areas which could not possibly be disputed territory."

Eli simply replied:

"I hate to tell you this, but I doubt that the Chinese, if they are really going to try and get ahold of the reserves, would worry too much about these niceties. Just see how they have dealt with Hong Kong, abrogating an agreement they had with the U.K. as and when it served their purpose. I fear they'll do the same at some point with respect to Taiwan. The Philippines might well be next. However, let's be honest; what do I know? I'm just an old roughneck!"

"Roughneck?"

"Yes, Mike. That's how oil drillers are called!"

All three had a good laugh and Mike came straight back:

"You're being too humble, Eli. But I see your point. Nevertheless, the conversations in which I participated clearly suggested that the closer the production platform was to shore, the more challenging it would make China's claims."

Eli replied:

"I can see this. I've heard that assuming they strike the kind of oil they hope they will start producing with an FPSO, you know a floating production infrastructure. While pumping oil, they'll discreetly build an underwater infrastructure such as the one we have with Leviathan. One day, the FPSO ship will depart from the location, and no one will have to know anything more. The oil will keep flowing, but it will initially travel underwater until it reaches the production platform nearer the shore. I have full confidence in my team, and Anthony seems to be a first-class addition. At least, that's what my people tell me."

He paused to drink from his white wine glass and laughed:

"I don't want to be rude, but this Corton Charlemagne is definitely better than the Kosher wine which they first served. You know, my household only broadly follows Kosher principles, no pork or pork products and that's about it. We view the rules more as guides reflecting important society and health concerns way back when they were developed rather than as appropriate directions for today."

He paused smiling and totally switching topics then asked:

"The formal signature is confirmed for tomorrow right after lunch, correct?"

Ehud replied:

"Absolutely. We understand that you asked for an hour or so with Luis first to go through every detail."

"That's correct. One of the things I have learned over the years is that I hate surprises; and most other people would agree, except those who try to squeeze something out of you without you noticing. These are the crooks, and I avoid them like the plague. So, going over the agreement with him with both sets of lawyers and financial experts in attendance should ensure that there are none. Both he and I can ask any question we want."

He paused and humbly added:

"You know, I'm starting behind the eight ball. It's already embarrassing to know that we have two of my former group's three corporate jets here! The team needed one to get here earlier in the week and I needed the other. To make things worse, they both are the largest we have, since the third would not have flown the full distance without refueling! That's not the image I like to project. Thankfully we are in Asia and ostentation is not frowned upon as it might be in Western Europe or Israel for that matter."

Ehud and Mike simply smiled.

CHAPTER.14

MANILA AND PALAWAN, THE PHILIPPINES

Luckily, the Israeli-Filipino consortium had no difficulty finding a drilling rig when they decided to start their second exploratory well. There were at least two that could do the trick in Singapore where they were undergoing maintenance. It took just under ten days for the rig they chose to be towed from Singapore directly to the area where Anthony had suggested the well should be located. The water depth was barely 210 feet, and the rig had all the equipment which would be needed, both for the initial vertical hole and eventually for the two directional horizontal sections if they were required. The team fully anticipated the oil deposit, if as expected it did extend that far from the initial hole, to start around 6,000 feet below sea floor level, in a turbidite sandstone reservoir.

The drilling results exceeded all expectations. Not only was the oil-bearing sandstone layer even thicker than anticipated, but the horizontal wells proved that the reservoir extended even further than they thought.

Spontaneously, when he received the news in his office where he was with Mike and Ehud, Luis declared:

"Let's name this the Wilson field."

Seeing that his Israeli friends did not seem to follow, he added:

"Chuck Wilson was the geologist who first thought that we could find a great oil field in this area of the Philippines, forty years ago or so. So far, people thought he had been proven wrong and that he was but an old dreamer. Moreover, I'd say that he hadn't been proven right yet. We just did."

He asked his assistant to get a bottle of champagne and immediately toasted to the major oil find with Anthony, Angelo and his two Israeli friends. They were joined by Larry Edelstein, Eli's right-hand man on hydrocarbon issues. While Eli was delighted to rely on Anthony and his in-depth knowledge for input and recommendations, he wanted to have his man on the job; after all, Larry had CEO responsibilities for hydrocarbon decisions in Eli's group and the progress report Eli had been receiving through the drilling process quickly convinced him that he needed his own eyes and ears very near ground zero. Larry arrived after the vertical part of the second well had struck oil. He had participated in the decision to drill horizontally, though he had let Anthony recommend the parameters of the drilling.

Larry surprised the group when he injected a serious note of caution into the otherwise optimistic proceedings:

"Friends don't get me wrong. I don't want to be a spoilsport, and I am enjoying the Champagne; I don't know anything which you don't know, but experience suggests that we should probably be careful celebrating before we have the results of the third and hopefully final exploration well."

He paused, surveying the room, and noticing the surprised look on all faces except those of Anthony, Ehud and Mike. He sipped some of his champagne and continued:

"I know it is not my decision alone, but if it were mine, I would not name the field quite yet. The moment you bring back good old Chuck Wilson's name, you're going to ignite a speculative fever which not only might not help but could truly hurt."

Mike immediately saw the smarts behind Larry's suggestion. He not only agreed with it, but felt it was what sheer prudence dictated. The issue of the sudden severe flu-like symptoms in the area a few months earlier made him want to manage that as well. However, he could not be too obvious for fear of revealing that his real specialty was in the secret service world and not with hydrocarbons, even if he was officially presented as a security specialist in the field of hydrocarbons. Mike simply said:

"I totally agree with you Larry. However, I would still push back slightly on your point."

He could see Larry sit up straighter in his chair, and continued:

"I remain quite concerned by the issue of the dead or sick fishermen or tourists."

The whole room immediately started paying more attention then:

"As Mr. external security here, I've been thinking as soon as I heard about this flu onset. What if this was but a first salvo orchestrated by China?"

He paused, let the point sink among a somewhat stunned audience and added:

"I know. I know. It's still only a hypothesis that China was behind the short-lived epidemic, and we don't want to go too far down that path. Yet, you have to accept that the timing looks incredibly coincidental. We heard the first rumor of the problem when the first well struck oil while it was still in its vertical phase. So, if you stick with my theory, China should become quite interested if there was a real oil deposit. The first well would have been perfectly consistent with the smaller fields which were discovered earlier. The second well suggests that the theory needs review. If you also agree that China would rather not attack a field visibly, then doesn't it strike you that the most natural thing for them to do is to try to wreak havoc in the area and trigger nationalistic tensions. That would allow them to see whether we either will slow down our drilling activity or might become interested in some offer to purchase some or all the deposit from the consortium. By the way, Luis, have you recently received any unsolicited offer?"

"Not yet. Great question though. I see where you're going."

Mike continued:

"OK. That may come later. So, I would argue that we need to show that we are moving further forward on the drilling front **and** at the same time to demonstrate that we are still going forward toward production. If they're after the field in one way or another, that's bound to trigger another skirmish; again, that's valid only if my theory holds. Who knows?"

Larry interjected:

"I see your point, Mike. If I may paraphrase you to make sure I understand fully, you're arguing that there should be some news, just to serve as bait in case whoever triggered the last skirmish as you call it. But let's not disclose too much as we're probably not prepared to deal with anything more serious. Am I about right?"

"Better than that, mate. You're right on."

Mike then offered a strategy which he said ought to be seen as supporting progress while not giving the whole game away:

"One option would be to say little, keep drilling and leave it at that. To me that's unrealistic. Any leakage of real data is bound to shoot our credibility down the drain and could even, but I'm no lawyer, have regulatory disclosure implications."

He noticed Luis nodding his approbation and went on:

"The alternative would be to be cautious in our interpretation of the results of the second well and indicate that it fits with our program to drill a third confirmation well. We would however add that we are beginning to plan for production from the first well and announce that we will use an FPSO vessel for that."

His main recommendation was that there was no need to hype the project. In his view, whoever was thinking of acting against the consortium should interpret the plan as a clear indication that the field offers serious enough potential to start production. Anything more was unnecessary and could be detrimental. Turning to Anthony he asked:

"Is it fair to say that launching production this early would be an unusual sign?"

Anthony first cleared his throat and then replied:

"Sure would to some extent. Yet, it would not be totally unusual. I see your point. It would say that the results of the first and the second exploratory wells are enough to convince us that we have a viable oil field but would also indicate that we still do not have a solid handle as to how large or small it might in the end prove to be. So that bit is in total alignment with your scenario."

He paused to make sure in his own mind that he was not missing anything big and then added:

"But it would not telegraph what we have really found. If I may interject here, I would like to spend some time with Angelo, Anthony and you, Mike, to look again at our computations and confirm that the location for the third well is truly optimal. Somewhere in the back of my head, something says that I may prefer to move a bit further away from the other two."

Luis was smiling broadly as he said:

"Gentlemen, you must understand that I'm living a dream here. I fully realize that I may have been a bit overoptimistic based on what very limited data I had, when I jumped the gun and said I wanted to name this the Wilson Field. Mike and Anthony are correct. Does anybody disagree with their suggestion? Larry, do you feel that Eli needs to be in on the decision?"

"Thanks for thinking of Eli, but I know he trusts us. I will report to him our plan and he can always then ask for us to reconsider. However, in the who-knows-how-many years I have worked with him, it would be totally out of character for him to second guess a decision such as this one. Remember, the real dollars and cents are not so much in exploration but in planning and organizing production."

■ ■ ■ ■ ■

While the group did follow Mike's, Anthony's and Larry's recommendation, the news somehow leaked out that the second well had yielded better than expected results. Anthony, Mike and Ehud had wanted to discuss the leak issue over an after-dinner drink and had wanted to go to the Salon de Ning, the night club lounge in the Peninsula Hotel; it was designed in an art-deco style to remind patrons of the glamorous world of Madame Ning, of vintage 1930s in Shanghai. Unfortunately, they learned it had been indefinitely closed, most probably for redecoration purposes. So, they elected to wind down at The Bar, whose ambience was reminiscent of the dimly lit bars of La Antigua Cabana in Cuba. They were surprised that they were able to find a sofa in a quiet corner where they could chat without needing to speak louder than with a normal voice. As they were beginning their discussion of the leak and its implications, Mike noted:

"Finally, an architect or decorator who understood the need for certain patrons to have some local calm and quiet."

Anthony was the most upset of the three by the fact that the news of the drilling results had leaked. Mike worked to calm him down:

"Let's be fair. There was a leak. Someone said more than they were supposed to. But first didn't we anticipate that it would happen? Frankly, I view this as a blessing in disguise actually. Whoever is stalking this operation is bound to make a move soon."

Anthony had to argue:

"I can understand your optimism, Mike. My real worry is what happens in the second phase."

"Second phase?"

"Yes, Ehud. When we begin to build an underwater infrastructure to exploit the deposit. It's supposed to remain secret. That's why we have the FPSO vessel as a decoy for the production from the original well."

Anthony paused and sipped some of his A'Bunadh single malt scotch, suitably brought down from its 60% alcohol level to the optimal 35% above which too much alcohol anesthetizes the tongue and prevents one from truly enjoying it. He swirled it in his mouth, enjoying the aromas and the flavors to the full. Then suddenly he shifted his stance:

"Guys, we must do something about that."

Mike interjected:

"I don't know if you have something in mind, but I've got a couple of thoughts."

Anthony conceded that he had not really thought of the problem as he viewed Mike as the real specialist. Ehud immediately asked Mike to expand on his thoughts. Mike proceeded to call upon the well-worn tricks which he had learned through his career at *Mossad,* of which both Ehud and Anthony were aware. He started with a simple premise:

"Disinformation always works best."

It was now Ehud's turn to wonder:

"What do you mean?"

"Simple . . ."

Mike explained the principle of the action he was prepared to put in place, prefacing it with the note that only four people could be in the loop. Beside the three of them, the only other person who would know of the operation would be Larry Edelstein. He added:

"We cannot run the risk that Eli finds out something crazy and gets mad."

Anthony calmly noted:

"Hold the thought. The only two people you're obviously excluding are Angelo and Luis himself. Are you really having doubts on them—on both, including Luis?"

Mike cooly and deliberately said:

"Don't disagree, but it's a bit more than that. There are other suspects, starting with people on the drilling rig, but right now I don't know who they are or better yet how to reach them. So, I would first direct my attention towards Angelo. If there is no leak from him within a couple of days, then we must shift to Luis."

Anthony was not through with his objections:

"What do you hope to achieve with Angelo?"

Mike went through a scenario which could end in one of two ways. The first would be that the news would be "in the market" soon thereafter. That would mean that Angelo was the leaker. The second would be that the news would not spread until the details they were going to announce seemed to require a change in the drilling activity. Looking straight at Anthony, Mike asked:

"Is that feasible?"

"Sure is, provided you don't allow it to last too long. My first thought if what you have in mind happened would be to ask for the drilling to stop so that I could verify something . . . If asked, I don't need to explain why I'm asking."

"Great. If there is a leak, it would have to come from the rig. Now I don't know how we deal with it, but there must be ways to tap into cellphone or Wi-Fi traffic."

Anthony cut in:

"How do you do that?"

Mike simply smiled replying that he knew Countess Renate had a resource in Singapore who could take care of any sort of network penetration. Anthony remained stone-faced. Mike noted that it might mean that Anthony did not know Wong Hai Chong or did not want to confirm any relationship with him. He might not know Hai Chock if he, Anthony, was just an acquaintance of Countess Renate but not a member of The Shadow Experts. However, his reaction might simply confirm that operating procedures within the group were to avoid disclosing anything that people did not need to know. Anthony knew Hai Chock: he was the person who built the cyber security systems installed on Anthony's computer. Though he could not truly be sure, Mike correctly concluded that it probably was the second explanation that made the most sense: nobody needed to know that Anthony knew Hai Chock. Anthony was still not finished; returning to the flow of questions he asked:

"And what if we have no leak there?"

Mike deadpanned"

"Well, I can think of only two explanations. Either somehow the leaker has figured our trick out or the leaks come from elsewhere. If that's the case, Luis would have to be one of the most obvious suspects."

Mike had stopped and suddenly started shaking his head. Rhetorically he asked:

"Now for a brand-new twist: assume that Angelo is not the source of the leak. Rather than jumping directly to the conclusion that Luis has to be the leaker, what if it came from someone in whom Luis might be confiding too much? In other words, what if Luis was the leaker, but an unintentional leaker?"

"His family?"

"Could be, but that's not where I'm going, Ehud. I would rather suspect that Luis is sharing progress notes with the government for whatever reason, most probably not nefarious in any way. The leak, however, would come from there, directly from the official with whom he is sharing or with someone who works in the official's office."

Anthony quipped:

"You should write spy novels, Mike."

Mike had a hearty laugh but then became profoundly serious as he simply said:

"I've studied the history of oil drilling in the Philippines in some detail, though I only looked at published documents, the Internet in other words. Well, one thing jumps out: the Nido field would have been much more successful if political pressures had not forced the consortium to produce more oil than they should have. I've read that peak production was 40,000 barrels per day, when more conservative estimates thought oil should have been produced at less than half, and maybe even less than a quarter of that rate. Bottom line: political pressures existed then and could easily exist today. We know they can be powerful. Couldn't we imagine that someone may be trying to hitch his financial or political wagon or both onto Luis's discovery?"

Anthony could not resist:

"That's frightening. Producing at such a high rate, at Nido. They must have "coned" the well . . ."

"That's exactly what I read happened. The water table below the oil deposit started rising too fast where oil was being pumped and soon enough it reached the top of the oil layer, separating what had been one reservoir into two smaller ones. Without directional drilling available then, they were in deep trouble. Lots of lost opportunity, and quite a bit of egg on peoples' faces!"

CHAPTER.15

MANILA AND PALAWAN, THE PHILIPPINES

Still focusing on the last case of viral contamination, Mark and Ehud were having a quiet meeting at the Israeli Embassy to discuss how the suspected virus had been introduced around the Twin islands and by whom. Mark started the conversation with a straightforward observation:

"There seems to be no urgency on the part of any government official in Manila with respect to investigating the question. I get it when they say they don't want to subject any official to any contamination risk or don't want to frighten the population. Yet, they appear mostly concerned with consequences. They feel they have done their first and only run-through; they found nothing worth reporting and therefore feel under no compulsion to do anything more."

Ehud did not need to ponder the point. He was clearly in total agreement with his colleague and friend. He initially suggested that *Mossad* in Israel had useful pieces of equipment with quite a few of them being accessible by the Embassy.

Mark asked:

"Readily available?"

"Absolutely. In fact, we have a few of these things in our local 'bag of tricks' right here in Manila, principally monitoring equipment, cameras, mikes, and the like. The rest we know of and have been told we can call on it when needed. They're at most a plane ride away."

"With that, we could go take a look at the Twin Islands ourselves. What's stopping us from acting immediately? What's the issue?"

Ehud replied that the real problem was exactly the question that was raised by the Filipinos. How could anyone plant the equipment without risking contamination? Mark conceded that the issue was definitely serious, though suddenly he exclaimed:

"Wait a second. Wait a darn second. Assume we are correct assuming that the virus is transmitted by mosquitos. Then we should be able to cover all skin surfaces, don a gas mask and get the thing done with only minimal risk, correct?"

"True. But what if the contamination vector is different? For instance, birds or rats?"

"I don't think it changes much of anything. Would any of them attack us?

"Don't know, but remember that rabid animals attack while they would never do it when they are not sick . . . What if there is something like that at play there?"

"Let's have a quick chat with Dr. Duchemin and see what he thinks. After all, we have a couple of important data points. First, we believe that the virus concentration in the area has been decreasing."

Ehud interrupted:

"How can we be sure?"

"That's a question for Dr. Duchemin, but there hasn't been any new case reported in the last couple of weeks. The second data point is that other flu vaccines seem to be providing at least some protection. Remember, the case of the two Spanish tourists. So, I'd like to know if I'm correct assuming that the risk of catching the disease we are running is lower than it might have been. Additionally, I'd like to know if as I believe I am protected by the vaccines I got."

Mark paused to double check his logic and satisfied with it concluded:

"I'd be ready to volunteer for the mission of placing the monitoring devices you all have here."

Ehud was all in:

"Subject to Dr. Duchemin agreeing, I'm ready to join you on the mission.

■ ■ ■ ■ ■

Dr. Duchemin could not be as categorical as Mark or Ehud expected or at least hoped him to be. After all, what scientist would be categorical with as much uncertainty around the facts as was available at that time? However, he gave them enough reassurances to allow them to plan their mission. He simply said:

"Gentlemen, I don't see anything that would seriously threaten individuals who are well protected. After all, that's what we routinely do in virology labs. The one thing I would suggest you do is for whoever is involved to get a general anti-flu booster. We suspect that this is what helped the Spanish tourists. I'm sure I can find what we need here or get it from Tokyo within 24 hours or less."

Ehud and Mark decided to take advantage of the fact that the Israeli Embassy in Manila had a helicopter on a long-term lease. Moreover, as a *bona fide* military attaché at the embassy, Ehud had access to the helicopter and was licensed to fly it himself: he did not need to use the official embassy pilot. The point of the mission he and Mike had sketched was to install up to six motion-activated cameras with night vision and equipped with data transmission capabilities, tuned into the local mobile phone network in place on Palawan. They could thus monitor the islands and their immediate vicinity from the quiet comfort of the Embassy in Manila.

They loaded an inflatable dingy into the helicopter. Mark planned to use it to get ashore if the helicopter could not find a spot where it could safely land without running the risk of leaving too obvious traces that might lead the terrorists to look for another spot.

Mark and Ehud first noted that based on the images they could get of the two islands, they could not reasonably carry out the mission without a third person helping them. Ehud, who did not want to expose or jeopardize any of his local resources, placed a quick call to Tel Aviv to request some help. David Heller was delighted to send a *Katsa,* the Hebrew acronym for "intelligence officer" on a military jet. Though Mark had not worked directly with Nathan Heimer, the intelligence officer who was sent, he knew of him. He was particularly aware of the fact that Nathan, who preferred to be called Nate, had worked in *Shayetet 13*, an Israeli elite commando unit. He was thus quite familiar with the work he would need to do to help Mark and would have received all the training he needed to carry out the required tasks.

The three of them, Nate, Mark, and Ehud had planned the mission to involve two phases. The first would require a low altitude fly-over of both islands to identify where best to locate the cameras. They readily conceded that they could have dispensed with that phase using a drone; yet, they felt better knowing that they were looking at the site with their own eyes rather than through images. The second would have Mark work to place the cameras while Ehud either hovered over the area or stayed with the helicopter if he had been able to find a landing spot. Nate's job would be to remain in the helicopter, help Mark carry out his mission and guide Ehud if needed so that he could stay right above where Mark was.

The first phase proved to be relatively easy, with one notable exception. There were two spots on North Twin Island, where it seemed possible to install the cameras so that they could obtain the right pictures from as far away from the island as possible and yet not be immediately visible by a terrorist coming ashore, provided the terrorist came ashore at night. One was on the east side, at the back of the large beach and the other also at the back of a smaller beach on the west side. Mark would thus place two cameras on the larger island, all hidden in the bushes at the back of the beaches. Ehud figured that he would rather hover over both sites rather than land, though landing on the large beach on the east side of the island would be very straightforward. He noted however:

"I'm not sure I want to run the risk of taking in any potentially contaminated air. Having said that, I can hover so close to the beach that you would only need to jump at most a couple of feet to get on the ground. I could do an "almost touch and go" to pick you back up, where I never actually land though I am so close that it's as if I had, though, again, I'd prefer not to come any closer to the ground than a couple of feet."

They had a short conversation wondering whether the proposed strategy would really shield them from taking in potentially contaminated air and in the end decided that the risk was small enough that they could stick with that plan. The smaller island, South Twin Island, proved to be a bit more challenging. There was a similar beach area, though quite a bit smaller than on the other island; the back of the beach was no more than 50 feet from the water at high tide. Ehud still felt comfortable he could handle it, provided the weather was relatively calm. The real challenge was at the other end, the west end of the island. The coastline was simply pure rocks, with a few square feet here or there where one could locate a camera; however, there was absolutely no hope of being able to land or hover super close to the ground. Ehud would have to let Mark drop the inflatable dingy first, with Nate standing at the door. Once Mark had rappelled into the dingy, which auto inflated as soon as it hit water, Nate would use the same rope and pulley system to lower all the material they needed. Picking Mike up would simply involve taking the same steps, in reverse order. The dingy would be deflated inside the helicopter, using an electric pump to expedite the process. The team agreed that Mark would use three cameras on the smaller island, one at the back of the eastern beach and one each on the north and south sides of the western promontory.

■ ■ ◼ ■ ■

Once the cameras were in place, the next step in the operation required Mark to get into the disinformation business. It was time for him to implement the plan which he had hatched with Anthony, Ehud and Larry earlier. The opportunity for their initial attempt arose naturally as the four of them, with Mark well ensconced under his Mike Loeb identity, were discussing recent progress in the drilling of the third and final exploratory well with Angelo around the table with them. Larry casually asked Anthony:

"Anything important to report?"

"At this point, not a lot, though I've just seen something somewhat unusual."

Anthony could see that Angelo was suddenly paying more attention when he added:

"I don't fully understand why, but we are about 1,500 feet away from the depth at which we hope to start to run into the oil-bearing sandstone layer. And yet we have already picked up small oil flows."

Angelo immediately asked:

"How come?"

"Well, I can only think of three possibilities. One, the oil-bearing rock layer is thicker than we anticipated. Two, the oil-bearing rock simply tilts up at some point though its thickness remains the same. Three, the oil readings we get are minor leaks which accumulated over time."

Angelo was surprised:

"If it's the first, the find could be even bigger than we thought. Right?"

"Absolutely. But at this point let's not jump to conclusions. The other two alternatives do not lead us to the same outcome at all. After all, that's why we're drilling this third well. We wanted to check the parameters of the deposit. It's not unusual for oil-bearing layers to tilt, particularly in the case of stratigraphic traps."

"Shouldn't I still inform Luis immediately."

Laconically, Anthony simply replied:

"Personally. I wouldn't. A couple more days and we should be at the start of our target depth, since we're drilling at a rate of 700 to 750 feet per day. I wouldn't want to create false hopes."

The group could clearly see that Angelo did not like the decision, though he only allowed his feelings to come out through his body language. Mike bluntly asked him why he seemed uncomfortable to which he replied that he hated operating without keeping Luis always in the loop. Conceding that the feeling was totally understandable and honorable, Anthony then suggested a compromise:

"Why don't we stay put at present, wait to see what happens in the next 6 to 12 hours and then decide whether we should accelerate the drilling. With the equipment which we have, particularly with the huge engines that are on the rig, we can drive the rotary bit somewhat faster. The pumps that circulate the mud or air down the center of the drill stem can still clean out the hole continuously at those higher speeds."

■ ■ ■ ■ ■

Drilling mud is the name given to drilling fluids that operators add to oil wellbores to facilitate the drilling processes. The drilling mud helps to suspend rock cuttings, control well pressure, stabilize exposed rocks, and provide buoyancy.

■ ■ ■ ■ ■

Angelo's face lit up. He felt the compromise was worth it. As soon as the meeting was adjourned, Mike congratulated Anthony for his thought, adding:

"This will make it easier for us to order a visible change to drilling procedures if we don't hear of any news leak in the hours ahead."

Anthony simply smiled.

■ ■ ■ ■ ■

With Countess Renate's benediction, Anthony then liaised with Wong Hai Chong in Singapore, asking him what needed to happen for him to intercept any phone call that might come from the rig. Hai Chock rapidly provided simple instructions which could be implemented with the purchase of one small router that could be surreptitiously sneaked onto the drilling rig by Anthony as he was doing his daily check of operations. He added that Anthony should be able to buy the router in Manila, though, if needed, he could always airfreight one to him. Anthony did find the required equipment in Manila, and the trap was thus set with two or three hours to spare, which the team thought was a good thing as, so far, there had been no detectable leak from Angelo.

While on the rig, Anthony positioned the router near the staff quarters in the cabin. He had decided that installing his communication equipment too close to the drilling operations would generate too much background noise. He hesitated to place it next to one of the three vertical steel legs, which are also called chords. He worried that, assuming that the leaker, if there was one, might want to be outside of the cabin to make the phone call, which would naturally lead him to walk toward one of these chords. Unfortunately, not knowing which leg the leaker would choose, Anthony went for simplicity.

As he was reading the wireline reports continuously produced by the drilling activity, he called the foreman and asked him to speed up the drilling to as close to 1,000 feet per day as possible. He simply explained:

"We might be lucky and get to the oil-bearing rock sooner than expected."

He flew the company's helicopter back to Manila and joined Ehud, Mike and Larry for a drink at The Bar.

■ ■ ■ ■ ■

By the next morning, the activity in the equity shares of the consortium had not seemed to pick up. Simultaneously, Wong Hai Chock was able to confirm that none of the conversations he had intercepted seemed to focus on the news, cautioning his friends:

"Bahasa Malay and Filipino Tagalog are distantly related Malayo-Polynesian languages. But I've been told that they are not mutually intelligible. Fortunately, I love the Philippines and have been there on holidays frequently. I've picked up enough Tagalog to understand roughly what these guys were saying, except for one or two who had an unusual accent."

In the absence of any visible leak, Anthony, with his usual British phlegm, simply announced:

"We must ask Angelo to inform Luis . . ."

CHAPTER.16

Ehud had decided to place an unauthorized telephone tap on Luis's phone lines; it covered the office's land lines and his own cell phone. Though this was surely not a legally acceptable move in the Philippines, it was still pretty much a typical tool of the spying trade. He absolutely wanted to get a better sense of who was connecting with whom when new developments on the oil field were disclosed to a small group. Mark had cleared the decision with David Heller in Tel Aviv who had agreed on the strict condition that the tap would not be in effect for more than 48 hours. The next morning activity in the stocks of the consortium companies picked up significantly, with one paper going as far as touting the "news" that the deposit could be twice as large as expected. More ominously, the article was entitled: "Chuck Wilson Vindicated?"

Mike remarked:

"Well, I guess we know where the leaker is?"

Ehud could only agree:

"True, though we don't know who he or she is?"

"That's true, but at least we know it isn't Luis, which is a big relief. He only discussed the news with his contact at the Department of Energy, the Secretary's Chief of Staff."

Ehud added:

"Correct Mike, but the one thing that surprises me is that Luis's contact is as high as he is in the hierarchy there. You'd think that he would be super careful with his direct line to the secretary . . ."

Laconically Mike observed:

"Could surely be. But the seniority of his contact would suggest that he is currying political favors rather than financial rewards. That's why we must continue to be very careful. It could well be that though he has a direct link to the secretary, he yet elected to call a more junior employee. It's none of our business, but I'd love to know whether there are flows from Luis's bank account to that of the chief of staff or some other employee . . ."

He added:

"And I pray that the leaker is not the minister himself."

Ehud interjected:

"Unlikely. He may well be a party to some insider trading if that's what we're looking at, but I can't believe he'd be so obvious. These guys are pros. I believe they are not corrupt themselves, but if they are they know better than to be so obvious about it."

Ehud continued:

"In most financial places we'd have no trouble trying to find out. But here I would not want to touch this one with a ten-foot pole. Calling the secretary is out of the question: what if he is in on the deal? Calling his Chief of Staff is equally dicey. I guess we're better off letting sleeping dogs lie."

Mike simply concluded:

"I know. Couldn't agree with you more, though I think David should know, and I suspect he will want Simon and Eli to know as well."

■ ■ ■ ■ ■

Earlier in the day, Ehud had not finished his first cup of coffee at the office when his phone rang:

"Ehud, this is Luis."

"How are you, Luis? What can I do for you?"

"Did you read the headline in Business World?"

"Got to be honest. I don't read business news until I have read issues closer to my mission."

"The headline says: 'Chuck Wilson Vindicated?'"

"Holy mackerel! Can't believe it. Still these darn leaks."

"I know. I know. We must trace them. But the highest priority must be to deal with the consequences."

Ehud remained pensive for a fraction of a second. He was asking himself whether the lack of urgency Luis seemed to have in finding the source of the leak was an indication that Luis was in it in one way or another, directly or indirectly. At the same time, he mentally conceded that Luis's reaction was exactly what a typical businessman would have in the circumstances. He let go of that thought which occupied rent-free space in his brain and returned to the crux of the mission. Ehud knew that *Mossad* had done that tracing work already and had concluded that Luis's own phone call to his contact at the Department of Energy was most likely the source, not because there was any proof, but simply since they could not identify any other. Yet now was not the moment to have the needed confrontation. So, he calmly replied:

"Well, someone's let the cat out of the bag. Whether the news is even true or not is still unknown. I know that Anthony has not determined yet whether the deposit is larger or smaller than originally delineated. Let's just deal with the consequences as you said."

"What are you thinking of?"

Ehud did not blink an eyelid as he simply said:

"Whatever has happened in the stock market, maybe I should say whatever is happening, is a done deal."

Luis continued:

"The real important stuff for us must be first to make sure that nothing is said that could be considered a misleading statement by some corporate insider or anything that could be interpreted as stock price manipulation . . ."

Ehud could hear the tone of Luis's voice changing a bit. He thought: *Could it be that he had initially not fully appreciated the consequences of his actions? Now he sees them and is panicking. Did he do this just to help a friend and now realizes that the friend could point the finger toward him? Is he being played?* He decided to try and calm him as the last thing anyone needed then was one of the key players starting to "lose it." He continued:

"I think we should quickly talk to Anthony to get a sense of where we really are in terms of the drilling."

Luis immediately agreed, though he asked:

"Do you want me in the meeting?"

Ehud made the executive decision that Luis was not needed, though he promised that he would inform him immediately if there was something worth reporting. Ehud could hear a bit of disappointment in Luis's voice, but Luis still agreed.

■ ■ ■ ■ ■

The next morning, Ehud made it a priority to review the status of the five cameras that had been placed on the two Twin Islands. While he had diligently looked for any signal they might have sent since they had been placed on location, he was a bit more excited this morning, thinking: *after all, the news of the better-than-expected results on the oil front leaked twenty-four hours ago.* He was initially disappointed to see that there had not been any activity.

The cameras had two important features. The first, which was quite common, was their being motion-activated. They would not film unless there was some noticeable motion in their field of vision. A software program which many would describe as basic artificial intelligence allowed them to differentiate between the movement of a leaf which would not trigger them and of a human or larger animal which would. The second which was less common though increasingly available was their auto zoom. As soon as a camera detected any motion lasting more than a fraction of a second, it would automatically zoom onto the area where the motion was. Then it would work to keep the entirety of whatever it was that moved into full focus and follow it if it moved further. There had thus been a few "misfires" as he called them, when a camera started recording, for instance because a stronger than usual wind misled the camera into thinking that something was moving, when it simply was some random branch movement. Another time, a camera had zoomed on a small mouse that crossed its field of vision.

Twenty-four hours later, as he was again going through the tapes, Ehud had every reason to be excited. There **had** been movement on the western end of South Twin Island. The recording clearly showed a fishing boat approaching in the dark of the night, with only a small light at the bow of the vessel, to help the occupants steer their boat. He assumed that the movements of that small light was what must have triggered the cameras and got it to zoom on the boat. There seemed to be two people on board. Once the bow of the boat was close enough to shore, one of the individuals stepped out of the craft and started to climb on the rocky shore. Now that he was moving, the camera had focused on him and followed his movements. The man's features, as Ehud was pretty sure he was a man, were hard to discern as his skin seemed quite dark against a dark background and he wore a hat that hid some of his face . . . He appeared to be very careful as he probably could not see terribly much, despite the full moon, relatively cloudless sky and the light maneuvered from the boat by his comrade. Eventually, when he arrived at a flat spot near the top of the rocks, he swung a bag he had been carrying on his back. In full, zoomed-in view of the camera which Mike had hidden not more than two to three feet away from where the man stood, though in a bush, he picked up what seemed to be an earthenware container. He placed it delicately on the ground, checked that he was happy with its placement and retraced his steps toward the boat. The one element which attracted Ehud's attention was the care with which the man was handling the container. He thought that it had to be because he was worried that he might drop it. Ehud thought, *he's not wearing protective clothing; I wonder what this means. Does he know of the deadly contents? If yes, does he know that the contents are not deadly until something else happens? Could it be a different trap this time, one which does not involve a virus?*

Ehud noted that everything which the man had done fit perfectly with the original scenario painted when Ehud learned of the trace of steps on the shore, other than the absence of protection gear for the terrorist.

The camera continued to follow the man, and thanks to its auto zoom, remained centered on him as the boat sailed away. It was a fishing boat, which Ehud recognized as a kind of *bangka*, the generic name of various native watercrafts in the Philippines: a small double-outrigger dugout canoe used in rivers and shallow coastal waters. Looking more carefully, Ehud determined that the boat was a *bigiw*, a *bangka* used in the Palawan, Mindanao, and Visayas regions of the Philippines. It was a bit bigger than the others as it had to allow sailing in the coastal region of the sea. They take their names "needlefish" which is the English translation of *bigiw* from their knife-like bow.

Ehud was about to stop his review of the tapes when he realized that another camera had been activated as well. That one, at the back of the western beach of North Twin Island, provided pretty much the same scene, except that the man did not have to climb on rocks. The shallow waters at the beach allowed him and his associate to beach their *bigiw*, the same outrigger sailboat, native to the islands of the region, as in the earlier tape. *Did that mean that there was only one two-man team of terrorists, or did they simply use the same equipment and tactics?* Ehud was clearly leaning toward the hypothesis that there was only one terrorist team. Having beached the boat made the disembarking and reembarking considerably simpler, as the two men came ashore. Though they did not have to walk on rocks but rather on the fine sand so loved by tourists, they were both quite careful as they carried their containers, two this time, one each, as close to the start of the vegetation at the back of the beach as they could. The wide angle of the camera still allowed it to film the scene. Unfortunately, as the camera was not remote controlled and as the containers once on the ground were not moving, it kept focusing on the men returning to and climbing back into the boat. It depicted them first paddling away before they adjusted the small sail and were eventually lost in the dark of the night.

■ ■ ■ ■ ■

Ehud immediately called Mike and Nate who were sitting in an office near his:

"Looks like we've had a new virus delivery. Or at least a delivery of something . . ."

They both rushed to Ehud's office, and he showed them the relevant parts of the two tapes. They did not need to spend any time discussing the issue. Mike spoke first:

"Let's get the helicopter as fast as we can. While you do this, let me talk to Dr. Duchemin in Paris to tell him about what we saw and ask for any advice on how we should proceed. I want to know whether we should just collect samples of whatever is in the containers or rather attempt to retrieve the whole shebang."

The conversation with Dr. Duchemin lasted a bit longer than Mike initially expected because in their excitement, the three agents had not discussed a crucial element. Dr. Duchemin had initially simply asked:

"How do we think the mosquitos, if that's what these contain, are released?"

Mike remained quite pensive for a few seconds until Dr. Duchemin came up with a possible answer. He explained to Mike that certain forms of paper had been developed which could dissolve when wet. Matter-of-factly he said:

"That's why we call it water-soluble paper."

He added:

"I've read about a variety that dissolves in 30 seconds, but it's probably still a bit of an exception. Anyway, whether it's that fast or not, you'd have to have an external source of water that hit the paper leading it to dissolve, opening whatever floodgate for anything that's inside."

Mike reacted to Armand's point with surprise and gratitude:

"Thanks. This makes a lot of sense. Would dew be enough to dissolve the paper or do you need actual rain?"

"Don't really know. It would depend on where the dew point is and thus on the amount of dew that is deposited. But, in the end, you're at the start of the rainy season, correct?"

"Absolutely. So, you're right. It doesn't matter much; dew or rain, we're bound to get some liquid humidity daily."

Mike paused and added:

"Any recommendations as to how we should proceed? As you know, we're helicoptering out to the twin islands in an hour or so? What protective clothing is necessary?"

"I would be very, very careful, Mike. Try and get medical grade protective clothing, wear masks and gloves and breathe through an oxygen mask."

"Oxygen mask? Would an aerosol, filtering mask not be enough?"

"Could be. More than that: It should be. But you're never too careful. You won't need a lot of oxygen if the operation takes as little time as I would expect. So, any tank you will require won't be bulky or cumbersome."

I I ∎ I I

Mike, Ehud, and Nate managed to organize their trip to the twin islands even more quickly than anticipated. All the various items which Armand had suggested they took along were readily available at the embassy, except for one: a tool to create imperfect vacuum in and seal plastic bags. They really did not have the time to look for one, so they decided to take a simple clothes iron, which though imperfect would still do the trick. They had also agreed that this time all three of them would wear protective clothing, though they would dispense with masks, at least on the way out. While Ehud was running his pre-departure checklist, Mike and Nate worked to secure a hermetic ice box to the outside of the helicopter.

Unfortunately, the helicopter leased by the Israeli Embassy had retractable landing gear, which allowed it to fly faster. Not having the extended landing gear to which to secure the icebox made matters a bit more complicated. In the end they found a couple of hooks which could easily serve as anchors to which the icebox could be attached. This kind of operation is often known as "sling-loading" and well enough known that it is considered safe and efficient. The embassy's helicopter was fitted with a couple of large hooks supported by a frame with pulleys at the corners. This would help dampen the tendency of the load to swing around in flight. This would require them to lower the icebox to the ground when they had retrieved the containers, place them into the icebox, and then re-attach the box to its anchors. Jokingly, Ehud noted:

"Could easily have decided to keep the landing gear down for the whole flight. But this allows us to have our cake, speed, and eat it too in that we can sling-load the cargo."

They had decided to start with the south island as it would surely be the most difficult to access. Mike, fully clothed up with an oxygen mask connected to a small external tank, rappelled down to the inflatable dingy which had already been lowered just off the rocky coast of the island. He motioned to Nate that he was going to look for the container, as agreed. The team had fitted itself with small three-way radio microphones and earphones which allowed some oral communication. However, the presence of the oxygen mask made whatever Mike was saying harder than usual to understand.

Nate saw Mike deliberately climb the rocky western face of South Twin Island. He did not go straight in the direction of the place where they had seen the man put down the container. Rather, he went for the camera he had earlier installed and replaced its battery so that it could keep on operating for a while. He did the same thing for the other two cameras, although every step of the way to them he kept swearing at the hindrance which the suit was to his forward progress. He then moved toward the container and made a wide arc with his right hand above his head to tell his partners that he had located it. He observed that it basically was a flat-bottomed, earthenware bowl. He first touched it carefully with the tip of his gloved fingers and thus verified that the whole still looked reasonably solid. He was very happy to note that it still held together very well. Getting even closer he carefully inspected the top of the container though he did not touch it. He was especially looking to see whether the top, which he assumed was made of water-soluble paper as predicted by Armand, was still in one place. He was thinking: *is there a hole anywhere?* It seemed intact. He grabbed a double-layer plastic bag that he had taken along as per Dr. Duchemin's instructions. Unfortunately, with his gloved hands less precise than when they were bare, he pulled too hard on the top of the bag, where the plastic zipper was. Though he was not absolutely sure that he had in fact ripped some of the bag, he preferred to place that bag back in his right pocket and to retrieve another one. He thought: . . . *sure glad Armand had suggested we take a few spare bags.*

This time, being as cautious as he could, he slid the bag carefully over the top of the container, being extra careful not to touch its sides. He motioned the container slowly but deliberately into the bag, preferring to not hurry rather than waste another bag. Once his fingers felt like they had reached the ground below the container, he knew he was almost finished. The next and final steps would be to slide the plastic bag under the flat bottom of the container without damaging it. He gently leaned it to the right, in effect transferring the weight of the container to the bag still resting on the ground; that way no part of the container was directly touching the ground any longer. Once he had slid one side of the plastic bag under the container, he started to pull on both sides of the bag, allowing the container to glide gently all the way down to the bottom of the plastic bag, although maintaining it as vertically as he could as he thought: *whatever liquid is in there, if any, should not leak out.* Mike breathed a huge sigh of relief when he managed to bring the two sides of the plastic bag together without seemingly in any way interfering with the integrity of the container. He zipped the plastic bag partially closed, proceeded to expel as much air as he could to create some sort of substantially incomplete vacuum and zipped the bag totally shut. He then slipped that bag into another, which he also zipped shut.

Carefully retracing his steps down the rocky slope, he seized the rope which Nate was dangling for him from the helicopter. All three of the men had decided that there was no point taking the risk of climbing into the dingy, just so that the helicopter could be lower near to the sea surface. As it was now, Mike would need to be reeled up a few extra feet, but that was well worth not running the risk of falling while getting into the dingy. He handed the plastic bag to Nate who had already heated the clothes iron. Nate carefully used a small air blower to blow some air into the bag and then sealed the external bag an inch below the zipper thus ensuring double protection against whatever was in the container to escape. They decided that they would keep the bag inside the helicopter for the time being, as the double layer of plastic ought to provide incremental protection. They lifted the dingy back up into the cabin though they kept it substantially inflated as they knew they were going to use it again soon. They then flew in the direction of the western beach on North Twin Island.

Ehud suddenly said:

"Look, we are definitely at low tide. Let me land this bird on the beach, it will make your job easier, Mike."

Mike disagreed:

"I don't think I would do this. First, we still have the problem of potentially taking contaminated air into the helicopter. Second, we have no idea what the wind from the blades might do to the containers. Better to keep to the earlier plan: forget the dingy, drop me a few feet above the beach."

Just as he had done when first getting to South Twin Island, Mike rappelled down to the western beach on North Twin Island, though, this time there was no need for the dingy, which Nate promptly deflated so that it used less space inside the helicopter. Mike first went to change the batteries of the two cameras he had placed on the island. Once that chore was complete, he repeated the steps he had followed on South Twin Island and thus collected the two containers which the terrorists had placed at either ends of the western beach. Once the two bags he had collected were conditioned and heat sealed by Nate, the group carried out their final step.

Mike had kept the two plastic bags he had used for the containers he had just collected. Nate lowered the last of the three sealed plastic bags. He then lowered the icebox so that Mike could open it, place the three bags into it and close it tight again. At that point, Ehud landed the helicopter on the beach, as nobody worried anymore about damage that could be done by the turbulence caused by the helicopter blades or by contaminated air since all were wearing oxygen masks. Nate jumped off the cabin of the helicopter and helped Mike secure the ice box back to its two hooks outside of the cabin. They then both climbed back into the cabin for the flight back to Manila. Though they kept their protective clothing on, they chose to dispense with the need for an external oxygen supply wearing aerosol, N95 masks instead. It certainly made it much more convenient for Ehud in his conversations, however limited, with air traffic control.

CHAPTER.17

MANILA AND PALAWAN, THE PHILIPPINES, TEL AVIV ISRAEL, AND SOMEWHERE IN THE AUSTRIAN ALPS

Dr. Duchemin and Oshima-San landed in Manila, from almost opposite directions, as Armand flew in from Paris, while Oshima-San only travelled from Tokyo. Mike had elected to let them relax and even have dinner by themselves, hopefully followed by a restful night in their respective hotel rooms, The following day, Mike, and Nate picked them up after breakfast and drove them to the Israeli Embassy. Ehud, who had organized a conference room, greeted them. Mike could not resist a quip:

"Ehud, next time, please send a helicopter. Traffic was really heavy this morning!"

Ehud nodded smiling, adding:

"I should have, though I have to confess that fitting five people in our helicopter including the pilot is a bit tight, particularly in the back!"

The group's primary objective was to debrief "operation recovery" as they called it. They surely did not intend on spending too much time on details of how the mission was carried out. The professors knew that the containers had been retrieved and that no one seemed to have gotten hurt or contaminated, though that could not be categorically declared given potential incubation times. That was really all they needed. Mike and Ehud were more interested in what the professors would tell them. Armand was quite congratulatory on the work which the three *Katsas* had done.

Yet, he quickly turned to the examination of the "evidence" which the men had brought back. Displaying the care which a veteran virologist would have learned through experience, Armand started with a verification that the plastic bags were truly airtight. He wanted to be sure that there could not possibly have been any leak from any of the three containers; at first blush, the seals must have been strong given that none of the three agents appeared to have suffered. Yet, one is never too careful. He asked for a large bowl filled with water. Though initially surprised, the men immediately understood what Armand was doing when he carefully immersed each of the three bags under the water pressing lightly on all sides though not compressing the containers themselves. No tell-tale air bubble appeared, confirming that whatever was in the containers when they were retrieved was still there with whatever air was left. Casually he asked how they had heat sealed the bags.

Mike simply replied:

"With a clothes iron, what else?"

Armand laughed and asked:

"A clothes iron?"

Matter-of-factly Mike answered:

"This seemed like a good idea at the time . . ."

Everyone had a good, short laugh. Armand decided not to punch a hole in the bags into which some air had been pumped. He explained his decision to the three agents. They did not have the required equipment at the Embassy to capture that air: it could have been contaminated if a hole had somehow been made in the bag which directly held the container. He added:

"Oshima-San and I will use our own resources to carry out that operation in a well-protected environment. I can still inspect the containers further as they are."

So, returning to his inspection of the contents of the bags but without opening them yet, Armand noted that the structure of each container was slowly crumbling. The group got closer to the table on which the bag was, as Armand explained what he thought was happening:

"Mike, do you remember what we discussed when we were on the phone before your recovery?"

Without leaving Mike the time to respond to a question which might well have been purely rhetorical, he continued:

"I can confirm that the hypothesis which we jointly developed now seems right on the mark."

Armand argued that it seemed that the containers were truly made of tightly packed sand, probably from regional beaches to avoid anyone discovering suspect sand when inspecting the area, and equally importantly to ensure that no one could trace the sand they had used to their own location. The terrorists had kept the sand humid enough that it all stuck together. He added:

"A few bursts of water mist every ten minutes or so is plenty to ensure that the sand does not dry out too much. The only challenge was to ensure that the mist was directed at the body of the containers and avoided their paper covers. That and making sure that no pressure is exerted from the outside should ensure that the contents stay inside the containers. Mind you, I would not be surprised if a closer analysis doesn't reveal some sort of binding agent . . ."

"Binding agent?"

"Yes Mike, a sort of a natural glue . . ."

Turning to the top of the containers, which he was still observing through the double plastic layers, Armand noted that it seemed to be made of paper, casually adding:

"Bet you it's water-soluble."

Mike interrupted:

"Just as we discussed. Dew or rain would dissolve the paper and free up the mosquitos inside?"

Armand matter-of-factly replied:

"Exactly, my friend, if that's what they contain. Now I don't know how they kept the paper glued to the sand mixture, but any sugary solution, or even molasses, a viscous substance produced when refining sugar cane in this part of the world, would surely do the trick."

Armand paused for a short while, thinking, and then blurted out:

"Wait, come to think of it, the binding agent to which I just referred to keep the sand together . . . Could very well be molasses as well, if that's what they use to keep the paper on top."

Seeing a quizzical look on Mike's face, Armand added:

"Mixing some molasses would reinforce the compressed sand structure; should allow the container to stay together longer."

Mike smiled, indicating that he had understood. However, he was not finished with his questions, asking:

"By the way, what you just described explains something which had troubled me for a while."

Armand could not stop himself interrupting:

"What?"

"How could the terrorists, if I can call them that, bring the mosquitos onshore the last time and the Filipino rangers did not see anything left over? Assume they would have used a glass container, or anything that doesn't self-destruct; someone ought to have found whatever remains there were. With these, the containers eventually dry out, disintegrate and mix with the surrounding sand."

"You're absolutely right. Quite frankly this is also why it was key for you all to go retrieve them as quickly as you did. If you had waited too long, the paper would have dissolved enough for the trap to be set."

"And for the mosquitoes to have flown away!"

"Absolutely, Nate."

Armand then concluded his explanations suggesting that his and Oshima-San's analysis would probably find some chemical gelatinous growth medium at the bottom of the containers. It would probably be shown to be rich in viruses and potentially attractive food for female mosquitos, since they were the only ones who could sting. He then added, almost as an afterthought:

"By the way, I worry less about the containers breaking down than about dew of rain dissolving the top and releasing the mosquitos. The longer you waited, the more of a chance there was that the mosquitos would be released, as Nate just guessed . . ."

Mike thanked Armand, but added:

"The real key for which credit goes to the whole team was the idea of placing the cameras on site. Without the films we couldn't have known that the terrorists were at it again."

Shifting gears, he noted:

"The one thing I still wonder about is whether they used the same number of containers the last time."

Dr. Duchemin cynically added:

"And whether they are using the same virus . . ."

■ ■ ■ ■ ■

Mike and Ehud first organized a conference call with David Heller in Tel Aviv and Countess Renate in Austria to brief them on the developments, prefacing the presentation with a comment from Ehud:

"I approved private jet transportation for both professors to Tokyo so that they could work as quickly as possible on the viruses which we captured. They also took along with them the cultures they had been able to get from the prior attack and in particular from the two Spanish tourists. By the way, they thankfully appear to be well on their way to full recovery. They should soon be able to fly to the Galoc area and get their boat back."

David could only reply:

"Wouldn't have done it better. Well done."

Their main topic of conversation turned quickly to what should be the next step. It did seem to Mike and Ehud at least that someone was trying to deter exploitation of the deposit or trying to force themselves into the consortium's equity. Mike noted:

"It does seem that the two virus attacks, if I can call them that ..."

David jokingly interrupted:

"How else would you call them, my friend? Sorry to have cut you off mid-sentence."

"No problem, each attack seemed to follow quite closely on the release of good news on the viability of the field."

They agreed that nothing would likely happen for a few days unless the terrorists somehow had a way of monitoring the sites where they dropped the containers from a distance. Yet, at some point, there was bound to be some surprise that no one had fallen sick. Mike concluded setting out what he believed was the key question:

"So, for me at least there is an important decision that should be made: when should we inform Luis of this last operation?"

He offered his view that one could wait several days to the extent that the drilling of the third well should soon hit oil. Some news was bound to leak and simultaneously there would be reports that the drilling was proceeding as normal. He however added:

"The next step will have to be to bring together the petroleum team to agree to the design of the production process."

Mike, however, noted that production would thus be unlikely to start for at least another four weeks, if one is optimistic, owing to the preparatory design work that had been done as soon as the second well yielded oil. He added:

"Yet, both Eli and Luis ought to be aware of the earlier attacks. They should surely know that we expect that these might well persist if not get even more aggressive as production nears."

Countess Renate supported Mike's view arguing:

"It's going to raise the cost of production if they do need some serious defense system."

David asked:

"And what about the Filipino Government? It's their country. We can't keep operating below the radar for too long. After all, let's be honest: Israel has no direct interest in this, other than the theory that anything which does not strengthen our enemies cannot be bad for us."

Countess Renate added the simple thought:

"Mike, I don't think you can wait too long. I would quickly bring Luis and Eli into the loop, even the part that's been confidential so far, without necessarily telling them anything that they do not need to know. At that point, the government is bound to be brought into the loop. Can't imagine Luis not sharing whatever you tell him with the Secretary of Defense, at least. Now, then, whether your team, David, or mine remains involved is entirely up in the air."

She paused for a second and corrected herself:

"Except obviously with respect to the virus bit. Beside the fact that intentionally placing pathogenic agents for the purpose of infecting people is illegal under any law of any country I know about; it has to be exposed. That means that more work needs to be done to figure what the virus is or what they are if there are more than one and where does it or do they come from."

Mike budded in:

"Yes, totally agree Countess. If I may let me take this one step further."

Mike explained that his related concern is that the Chinese are somehow using a local terrorist proxy. In his words:

"We cannot be absolutely sure, but I would be very surprised if the men we saw depositing the containers on the tape were Chinese. They looked like local people, and their mode of transportation confirmed it. I would bet that they're Filipinos, or at the very least from the region defined to include the Philippines, Indonesia, and Malaysia."

David Heller closed the debate with a simple statement:

"My friends, this is above my pay grade. You're talking multiple international dimensions, none of which is a direct threat to Israel. Simon needs to be in the loop, and I suspect he will want the Prime Minister if not the War Cabinet to be involved in and discuss this. I'll grant everyone that there is a 'project dimension' which is well within our purview. But there is a geopolitical element which surely isn't."

Nobody disagreed.

■ ■ ■ ■ ■

With the drilling of the third well completed and its results analyzed, the whole group was nothing short of ecstatic. The deposit was most likely at least 50% again as large as originally expected and its production would eventually not only serve all the needs of the Philippines, but also allow it to export hydrocarbons. Anthony had called a meeting that included Angelo and Larry as key participants, while Mike joined as warranted by his cover. Anthony started the conversation addressing Larry:

"I am convinced that we can reproduce quite a bit of what you did at the Leviathan field in the Levant Basin of the Eastern Mediterranean Sea."

Larry interrupted:

"Can you quickly outline the key elements for Angelo and Mike?

"Sure."

Anthony prefaced his answer with an important comment:

"This is quite big, by the way. It took seven months to design the whole set up for Leviathan. But here, I suspect we can shave at least half of it. We have the original experience and we have been planning for something similar for several weeks now. But we must realize that this is likely to be what I would call an industrial-scale project: it will take time and money; quite a lot of both as it turns out."

Angelo chimed in:

"Big indeed."

■ ■ ■ ■ ■

Anthony explained that the concept behind the Leviathan setup was based on a single production platform located close to Israeli shores, while the field itself, though still almost 100 miles offshore Haifa, was still in Israel's Exclusive Economic Zone. Yet, because the waters are almost 5,000 feet deep there and the areas somewhat disputed by certain neighbors, Israel elected to create an underwater pipeline running almost 80 miles to the platform, and then a second of about the same length. The consortium needed the two pipelines because there are four wells which are connected via a subsea manifold and the two pipelines to the offshore platform where all processing of the gas takes place.

■ ■ ■ ■ ■

Angelo had to ask:

"Can you replicate the Leviathan setup here?"

Anthony was blunt:

"Unfortunately, not. It must be modified, though the concept can be used. The Leviathan field is a gas field with some oil mixed in. Here, we have a field with two of the three wells are mostly oil with some gas, while the third is a bit of a mix, still leaning heavily on oil rather than gas."

Larry asked what that meant. Anthony replied that it made the project a bit more complicated though he said he had a simple solution in mind. He argued that the field should be brought into production in stages. The first well, which happened to be the furthest away from shore should be put into production immediately using a standard subsea completion and an FPSO vessel on the surface. He added:

"The amount of gas is so small that it is better to flare it than to try to collect it separately."

He paused for a quick second and added:

"Come to think of it, it might make sense to collect the gas if there is enough gas in one of the other wells to combine their respective output. But we're not there yet. Not by a mile."

Returning to the rest of the project, he suggested "officially" delaying production of the other two wells, so the project could be studied in more depth. He did note that nobody would be expecting such a project to come on stream in less than a few years. He added, however:

"We should be building an undersea pipeline linking the first and second wells. Again, officially, this will be done to allow both to produce through the FPSO used for the first well."

He paused and concluded:

"For the third well, we should not be worried about disclosing that it contains more gas than the other two. We can argue that, for it, we need a more robust infrastructure and make the point that it would eventually be linked to a platform constructed closer to shore. The key to the whole thing is that, eventually, all three wells will be linked, and they will all produce through the platform located closer to shore. Not to put too fine a point on it, I patented an oil/gas separator which could come quite handy . . ."

Angelo had to ask:

"Can you say anything about it?"

"Let me simply say for the time being that I realized that the pressure with which the oil and gas mix comes out of the well represented a great source of potential energy which was typically ignored or wasted by the industry. I found a way to use it. At this point, I would rather not go into further detail . . ."

CHAPTER.18

David's intuition had proven absolutely correct. The moment he approached him with his concerns on the ongoing Filipino operations, Simon felt that the prime minister and at least certain members of the cabinet ought to be brought into the loop. The various individuals got together in Jerusalem, in the cabinet room next to the office of the prime minister to save time. David and Simon flew in by helicopter from Tel Aviv. The prime minister's office was located in Jerusalem, in the government center on the same hill as the *Knesset*, dominating a part of Jerusalem's skyline. The Cabinet Room was quite large and could seat not only all the ministers, but about twice as many people again, on chairs arranged along three of the four walls. The long, rectangular table was made of light-colored wood, with inserts of brown leather. The armchairs for the people seated at the table were upholstered in the same leather as used for the table and had chromed, flat metallic frames.

To say that the discussions which ensued were tense would be the understatement of the century. As could be expected, the debate was centered on why should Israel be involved in such a distant project. Additionally, distance here related to geographical terms as well as Israel's political interests. In the end, some consensus emerged that Israel could maintain some activity, though a *sine qua non* condition for its continued help was that there should be some official, though not necessarily publicized, agreement between the governments of the Philippines and Israel. The decision recognized, as David had suggested, that there were two projects which overlapped somewhat though surely not totally.

On the one hand, the oil exploration and production project could be described as warranting Israel's interest at least on the basis of the involvement of Eli Abelman through an Israeli company. It looked like a perfectly reasonable commercial enterprise. The similarities between the new Filipino field, which had been officially named the Wilson Deposit after the success of the third well, in honor of Chuck Wilson the Palawan hydrocarbon pioneer, and the Leviathan deposit in the Levantine Basin, justified the joint venture. Additionally, at least conceptually, the two fields shared another important feature: both were sizable enough to change the energy picture for both countries. That Israeli involvement was technical in nature and fully disclosed, though one could call it "indirect, as the Government of Israel had no role, other than the normal consular function of protection Israeli citizens and their interests abroad. Though *Mossad* and The Shadow Experts were involved in the delivery of the global oil expertise, *Mossad*'s role was secret and related to the initial steps to be taken with respect to the security of the production infrastructure.

The second project had a definite geopolitical dimension to it. The increasingly frequent harassment of Filipino navy vessels by the assertive Chinese navy was seen as a prelude to potentially even more consequential operations. Clearly, China wanted to develop a complete hegemony on naval operations in the China Sea which they defined as going all the way down to the Island of Borneo and thus to Indonesia, Brunei, and Malaysia, all south of The Philippines. The territorial claim which had already been made and had been boosted by the seizure and fortification of several strategic islands, had quite a logical extension when it came to any natural resource which could be exploited within the area, which was additionally quite broadly defined. The subject of their attention was not limited to the Philippines but also included countries which might have been considered their friends, such as Vietnam. The Chinese behavior in Hong Kong and more recently around the island of Taiwan only reinforced any fears that anyone rationally could have.

That second project however, in everyone's opinion, was not something in which Israel would want or even could afford to be involved in a visible manner. Any activity to which Israel might contribute had to be such that it could be argued as an advisory service provided by Israel to the Philippines and yet executed by the Philippines. Other countries, starting with the United States, would absolutely have to be in the loop and at least consulted and informed. Israel knew it already had its share of natural enemies in the Middle East and certainly did not want to make any additional ones.

■ ■ ■ ■ ■

Upon returning to Tel Aviv, David called a conference with Simon, Countess Renate and Mark, whom he viewed as his leader in the field with respect to both projects. After having summarized the official position which Simon and he had adopted as a result of the meetings with senior Israeli officials, David asked Countess Renate and Mark whether it compromised their actions in any way. Countess Renate replied that, from her point of view, she was only focused on what they all agreed to call the "first project," and thus not involved with the "second project." More specifically she argued:

"Any security work which Anthony has carried out so far, falls squarely in the exploitation and production part of the project.

Additionally, let's not forget that he is doing that work under the name of his own consultancy based in the U.K. and that his company's official client eventually is Eli Abelman."

Mark interjected:

"I see that and can't fault your logic. However, how about the work carried out by Drs. Duchemin and Oshima?"

"Excellent question, but not a problem either. As senior virologists in their official lives, they were invited by the Secretary of Health of the Philippines. Thus, though it is not germane to the main project in a literal sense, the key role of the Department of Health makes it a non-issue in my view as well. That they are involved in The Shadow Experts remains unknown and absolutely ought to stay that way."

Simon asked a hypothetical question:

"Countess, when and how would their roles, the two professors' or Anthony's become suspicious or questionable from the point of view of China?"

"Another great question. I believe that for as long as China operates in a covert manner, say though proxies, we are OK. Reading a recent CIA report, I came to two conclusions. First, the main terrorist groups operating in the Philippines appear to belong to various ISIS East Asia factions, with the notable exception of rogue elements of the Moro Islamic Liberation Front (MILF). Second, none of them has been reported in the vicinity to Palawan, except again for a few Moro members at the very south of the island."

She paused and concluded:

"So, to me at least, it seems that China is not officially in the loop. What could change? Well, the answer is almost obvious: China becomes officially involved, though the use of official Chinese resources which are either announced—and I couldn't see why the Chinese would take that step, other than as a means of intimidation— or unannounced but brought into the open because someone is captured. I should add that at that point I think that all hell breaks loose."

David noted in passing that the links between local terrorists and the broader ISIS group would potentially serve as a useful cover for Israel. Simon immediately replied that the point was totally valid, though the real question would have to be whether anyone would be stupid enough to claim a link to ISIS. David agreed, though he added:

"My real worry is the potential for China, directly or indirectly becoming involved in a way with formal enemies of Israel."

Simon replied:

"My friend, I'll grant the point without argument, though, frankly, haven't we at least once or twice found a link between ISIS and Iran, and then between Iran and China."[4]

David could only nod his agreement. Mark was still concerned and asked what would happen in a scenario where some attack was orchestrated against the production infrastructure at some future point and was thwarted through defensive weapons provided by Israel. David conceded that the worry was real, though he quickly argued that the risks were reduced by a couple of key elements: the most important point related to the fact that the weapons might be supplied by Israel but would not be directly operated by Israeli agents. Mark interrupted:

"You'd be arguing that we supplied a defense system and not any manpower, correct?"

"Correct and by the way this would generally be true. You guys aren't going to stay there forever."

David continued with his earlier logic. He shifted to the second fact that could implicate Israel, as he called it. He argued that it was unlikely to come out:

---

4   See from the same author, "Below the Surface," Barringer Publishing 2022, and "Glitter and Smoke," Barringer Publishing 2023.

"For this to become an issue, someone would have to admit to having approached the oil production installation to be able to claim that they had been attacked. Say a mini submarine had been destroyed by some automatically triggered torpedo. Even if China was behind that attack, how willing would they be to admit to such an attack? They'd have to admit that they had sent a mini submarine into Filipino territorial waters. Couldn't that be seen as a formal act of war?"

Mark replied that he accepted the point, though he argued that China might describe any mini submarine activity as a part of a general observation mission, adding:

"Imagine them saying that they were monitoring that the production activity was not damaging the environment. They might even appear to be heroes to the ecologists around the world."

David conceded the limitations on his point, though he still maintained that worrying about the environment is not a valid reason to violate territorial sovereignty, be it below or above water. Mark nodded. David then turned to his third point, which he argued took them back to the first one:

"How would anyone be able to point to Israel other than through the argument that the Philippines did not have the skills or the knowledge to build these defense mechanisms? Wouldn't the obvious reply be that Israel might have sold the technology, but the Philippines exploited it on their own? How different is that from the first point I made?"

Mark agreed that the logic was compelling. After all, he conceded that Israel was known as a high-tech country and could thus very well be viewed as a provider of sophisticated systems, be they defensive or offensive. After all, they were already known as a premiere supplier of drones, for both peaceful and military purposes. A few more questions and answers fused right and left, until Simon offered in summary a simple list of the next steps that the team should consider.

His main conclusion was that the most urgent step was to bring the government of the Philippines formally and completely into the loop. They had to be aware of and even to authorize any step along the way. He added:

"I don't mean that we need to disclose the crucial parts of the various technologies or the real functions of our people currently on the ground there. I mean that nothing can be deployed without them being aware. I should add that this requirement also means that our government must also be aware, both the prime minister and the defense minister. Countess, is that OK with you?"

"Just fine, Simon. In short, my group remains in the shadows . . ."

She paused to allow herself a quick smile and added:

"And we must make sure that we always keep in mind who our client is. We will keep David and his team in the loop, but our clients are either Mr. Abelman or the Government of the Philippines. No one else. And in fact, with respect to contacts with the Government of The Philippines, the relationship is not with The Shadow Experts but with two highly regarded virologists."

David nodded and concluded:

"Though this will create some potential frictions and delays, I think the arrangement is workable. Now, Simon, can I leave with you the coordination between our government and that of the Philippines?"

"Clearly in my territory. I'll make sure you're well briefed on anything that comes up."

■ ■ ■ ■ ■

Luis was surely not delighted when Angelo reported the production plan sketched by Anthony to him. He immediately zeroed in on the fact that the apparent delay before going to full production would likely affect the price of his company's stock negatively. He had been thrilled when the news came out that he had decided that the oil field would be named after Chuck Wilson. He was sure that every market participant would remember the predictions which Chuck had made. The additional fact that the announcement mentioned the words "stratigraphic trap" would bring the memories of the late 70s and early 80s back to everybody's mind. Predictably the stock of consortium members had jumped by anywhere from 50% to 75% when the news came out, depending upon the share of the deposit owned by each member. Similarly, the reaction of the government had been ecstatic as it had immediately drawn the conclusion that energy independence for the country was around the corner.

Now, having to walk some of the enthusiasm back was not something which Luis was prepared to entertain. Angelo therefore suggested that Larry, Anthony, and Mike be invited to join them to allow Anthony to discuss his rationale and Larry to talk of the financial implications, particularly on the likely investments that would be needed in the short term.

Somehow that meeting, which still lasted more than a couple of hours in the semi-circular board room of Luis's holding company, managed to convince Luis that the proposal was the only strategy that made sense. Though the simplest, the most compelling rationale was that all other successful hydrocarbon deposits in the country had taken time to develop, while earlier rushes caused some loss of recoverable reserves. Starting with financial issues, Larry outlined what the cost would be for everything to be funded at once. The number was a big surprise for Luis who, in fairness to him, was accustomed to smaller scale projects. Anthony then discussed the basic problem of logistics. He asked:

"How do we procure the pipes and all other elements to construct the pipelines, as here too as we did in Leviathan, we will need two pipelines? How do we start pumping from three wells before we have the production platform in place? Where do we get three FPSOs in this current market environment, particularly since one of them would need to be able to handle storage of both crude oil and natural gas?"

Luis nodded but still asked:

"Why do you want to appear to downplay the likely size of the development?"

Mike chimed in:

"Remember Luis, at the very beginning, you had asked me to help with security issues. Correct?"

Luis nodded and Mike explained that the security strategy that they had designed involved a form of deception or disinformation. He noted that there would most likely be spies here and there to monitor what the consortium was doing. He added in passing that there should be extreme care devoted to the selection of the people working on the project, stating point blank:

"They cannot ever get a sense of the whole picture. If they do, the whole thing could go up in flames."

He paused for a second and whimsically, though at the same time quite seriously, added:

"And I mean this literally!"

The room fell eerily silent for a few seconds at the realization of what Mike had just said. Returning to his main explanation, Mike reminded Luis that the point was to make people believe that some form of production optimization was being conducted. He even added:

"According to Anthony, we may as a matter of fact be drilling one or two additional wells, slowly, near the ones already in place. We want people to focus on our drilling activity and not on what else we will be doing."

Luis had to ask:

"But what **will you** be doing?"

"Building the pipelines and assembling the production platform near the shore. You will probably also need to build some shore infrastructure, probably on Galoc island. When the platform is installed, we will have to shuttle personnel from shore to it when their rotations are over, and they can take a deserved rest. We'll probably need at least a heliport if not a short airport runway to transport them to and from wherever you need to take them. Manila?"

Luis replied:

"Not sure. Many of these workers are now in this general vicinity."

"Good, so we may not need a proper runway. Helicopter facilities might be enough."

Mike paused again and summarized the plan:

"So we visibly start production at Wilson 1, the first well. Bring it into production and use an FPSO, with, most likely, a weekly or bi-weekly tanker shuttle to carry the hydrocarbons from the production site. By the way, that may be another need: where will you base your onshore stockage?"

Luis motioned that he had not yet considered that though he added:

"There are existing facilities in the Nido area."

"Excellent. It will probably take a full year before the undersea infrastructure is built for Wilson 2 and Wilson 3 to enter production."

Anthony jumped in:

"And for Wilson 3, we will probably need to separate oil and gas at the wellhead as it is unclear where the gas might be stored. It'd be great if you could do here what has been done in Israel: build some onshore infrastructure to pipe the gas to some local network."

Luis interrupted:

"Don't go too fast on this one. I have a hunch that the most economical solution will be to build a local electric generation power plant using gas. This will improve the lives of local people . . . However, I know that there are already five gas-powered power plants in Batangas, three of which have been there for almost 20 years. So, an interim solution might be to get the gas to them. Pipeline or shipment by boat? Let's mark this as an important work-in-progress, but I don't think we are close to thinking of something like a liquid natural gas project . . ."

Anthony replied:

"You know better. But remember, you may eventually find the deposit producing more than can be used locally. You really don't want to flare that quantity of gas. It'd be one heck of a waste."

Luis was by then fully back to his own optimistic and joyful self. He added that he needed to bring the government into the planning process. He noted:

"I need to meet with Eli and Larry soon to decide what we plan on doing and what we need to ask from the government."

Larry smiled and simply replied:

"Goes without saying. We need both of you to agree on the financial implications of the project. Thankfully, even with the cost of the subsea completion and daily rate for the FPSO, Wilson 1 could be cash-flow positive within twelve months. But the others . . ."

CHAPTER.19

PALAWAN, THE PHILIPPINES, TOKYO, JAPAN, TEL AVIV, ISRAEL, AND SOMEWHERE IN THE AUSTRIAN ALPS

Though as trained researchers, Armand Duchemin and Oshima-San would never feel that they had done enough work on virtually any subjects, they had agreed that they should jointly brief Countess Renate, David Heller and his team, before Armand returned to Paris. The zoom conference call had been organized to bring the key players up to speed on the work which the two professors had done with the team at the National Institute of Infectious Diseases in Tokyo. Their goal had been to analyze the pathogen recovered on the two small islands, a pathogen which they suspected was a virus. Countess Renate and David immediately noticed that Armand looked quite gloomy on the screen. They started fearing the worst, even before he had begun to talk, even more so as his colleague, Oshima-San did not look any more cheerful. Armand's first sentence told it all:

"Oshima-San and I must tell you that the news is not good."

David and Countess Renate imperceptibly shifted just a bit forward and straighter in their respective chairs, now sitting on the proverbial edge of their seats.

The speed with which the three-person *Katsa* group formed by Mark, Ehud and Nate had been able to grab the containers before they had released any of the contaminated mosquitos had given Armand and Oshima-San a huge head start. Notably, it had freed them from time constraints which would otherwise have potentially compromised the accuracy of their analysis. As things stood, with a high likelihood that no one had been infected this time around, they did not need to scramble to find some treatment and could focus on identifying the virus and, if possible, link it to other known variants.

Armand's initial headline had shifted expectations, and the group was surprised when he did not delve immediately into the conclusions directly affecting the virus, its potential treatment and a possible immunization. Rather, he added with a worried look:

"These guys are not amateurs. They are professionals."

Though David and Countess Renate were burning to ask a question, they both refrained from doing so to allow Armand to develop his thoughts. He proceeded to discuss the way the various containers had been configured and how they were supposed to work. His initial point was no news to anyone as it simply reiterated something they all knew or at least assumed: the containers were made of sand with some binding agent, which, as expected, did turn out to be molasses. The container top was, as initially assumed, made of water-soluble paper, glued to the edges at the top of the container with the same molasses. The next couple of points however were stunners:

"We retrieved both viruses and mosquito eggs from the compound at the bottom of the containers. Remember, viruses require a growth medium containing living cells. Without a host cell to which to attach, a virus dies. The growth compound was a semi-solid medium, some kind of gel-like substance, which as we expected was a sort of pure agar to which nutrients had been added: nutrient agar, plate count agar and trypticase soy agar. The surprise was finding mosquito eggs."

He paused and explained that though mosquitos have a short lifespan, mosquito eggs can survive months until they find themselves immersed in water. He noted in passing that this was the very reason why mosquitos tended to appear as soon as water had accumulated, for instance after a rain shower:

"The eggs lie dormant on the dry surface, whatever it is, a leaf, a blade of grass, anything really. They come to life as soon as they find themselves in water. You don't need a lot of water for them to hatch."

Returning to his earlier flow, Armand said that the eggs typically would quicky hatch and the larvae be fully grown not more than four or five days later. By then, they will have changed their shape and entered their pupal stage which lasts one or two days. The pupal skin eventually splits at the water's surface and the adults emerge, with the females soon ready to bite.

Always somewhat impatient, Mark asked what this meant. Armand replied that Oshima-San and he believe they were now able to understand the nature of the attack planned and executed by the terrorists. That in turn allowed them to understand the process they therefore followed. Oshima-San explained:

"We believe that the containers are shipped to the terrorists a few days before they are meant to be placed so that viruses and mosquitos can be released. We assume that the gel-like growth medium allows the virus to keep developing, but that the mosquito eggs remain dormant, as they need water to develop. We found a trace of molasses on the semi-soluble paper at the top of each of the containers, near the side. Initially, we had simply assumed that it was part of the way the containers were closed."

He paused and let Armand continue:

"However, the fact that there was that "molasses overflow" if I can call it that way on each and every container and roughly in the same spot near the side told us that there was a method to the madness. And there is: we assume that some water is poured into the containers before they are transported to the place where they are to be deposited. The water is meant to allow the eggs to hatch. The extra molasses we found on the paper on top of the container must represent the terrorists' way of closing the hole so that nothing escapes, mosquitoes or virus, until the containers are where they should be. So, mosquitoes develop but remain stuck in the container. Eventually, water in the form of rain or dew dissolves the paper cap and all hell can break loose."

David whistled his admiration but still asked:

"Would the terrorists not be worried that the hole they create is not properly sealed?"

Armand replied that it was a perfectly valid question, though, cynically, he added it probably was one which the terrorists did not ask. He also made it clear that the hole through which the water was poured into the containers was pre-made, with a papier-mâché capsule which was sealed into the hole with molasses, adding:

"Not rocket science and no hard manipulation. You can guess that the masters knew that they were dealing with people who have had no relevant training."

He paused for a second and cynically added:

"Plus, I suspect the masters, which we assume are Chinese, but that is not an established fact as of yet, probably do not care too much about the well-being of the local terrorists."

Mark nodded, though he cautioned:

"That's the thing that worries me. The people we have seen on our cameras are not the real thing, the masters. They're probably expendable soldiers. The real issue has to relate to the masters, and what Armand and Oshima-San are saying tells me that the masters are not on a one-off deal here. It's part of a plan of action. We must find out as much as we can about who's behind this."

Everybody agreed. Realizing that the conversation had drifted away from the virus and its effects Armand asked:

"Are we ready to discuss our findings with respect to the viruses?"

Seeing unanimous agreement, he first noted that all containers seemed to hold the same agent, in highly comparable concentrations. He added:

"We focused principally on the virus that was still present in the growth media at the bottom of the containers. Thanks to Mark, Ehud and Nate, we had lots of excellent material. And because they acted so rapidly, there were only mosquito larvae and eggs; very few adult mosquitoes, except those that had developed after the terrorists had poured the initial amount of water into the containers."

He paused ostensibly to sip from a cup of green tea to his right and let Oshima-San explain what the team had been doing. In his own typically Japanese, calm, and humble manner, Oshima-San noted that they had first focused on any difference that might have existed between the new virus and the one that had contaminated the few fishermen and the two Spanish tourists. He reminded the group that, with respect to the first contamination, they could only collect the first viruses from people who had been infected, as there was no growth gelatin which they could exploit. His conclusion surprised no one:

"We believe they're one and the same."

He paused and immediately followed up with the observation that their efforts could only be focused on the nature of the virus and not on differences in the virus concentration between the first and second attack. With a wink, he explained that they could not test the virus concentration in the first attack, adding:

"However, with respect to the second attack, with three almost perfectly intact containers, let me add that both Armand-San and I believe that the concentration this time was almost as high as scientifically possible. Whoever is involved is not kidding."

Armand interrupted to add:

"If it's a warning, they're surely not trying to hide much."

He went on to explain that knowing more about the virus concentration in the growth medium, and to a certain extent in the mosquitos, would have been quite an interesting piece of data:

"Assume that the concentration had risen between the two operations, and you could conclude that the second attack was intended to inflict more damage. Conversely, assume everything was the same and it would be reasonable to conclude that there was no intention on the part of the foe to escalate the attack."

Armand paused and immediately added:

"What this means though is that the first attack was already quite serious. We're lucky that there were not any more casualties."

David interrupted:

"Armand, Oshima-San, is it possible that whoever deposited the containers was taking them from a "stock of containers" they had given previously?"

Oshima-San immediately replied:

"Nothing is impossible, David-San. As Armand-San explained, the mosquito eggs could stay "alive" for an extended period. The problem here would be with the viruses. They would continue to develop for as long as there were enough living cells to which they could attach in the growth gelatin . . ."

David had to ask:

"Living cells?"

"Remember, viruses cannot survive without attaching to a living cell. So, here, the terrorists placed amoebas in the growth gel."

David was increasingly lost. He interrupted Oshima-San to ask:

"Amoebas?"

"Sorry, David. I should explain myself better. Amoebas are a type of cell or unicellular organism with the ability to alter its shape, primarily by extending and retracting pseudopods. To feed, an amoeba stretches out the pseudopod, surrounds a piece of food, and pulls it into the rest of its own body."

Anticipating David's next question, Armand immediately interrupted his colleague and added:

"Don't get hung up on terminology. The amoebas here feed on the nutrients in the growth gelatin. Taking one step back, remember viruses were initially cultured, probably in a laboratory, using living cells, probably some variant on hen eggs. They were then transferred onto the agar plate infused with nutrients and amoebas; then they were allowed to keep developing. So, for as long as the amoebas have the nutrients they need, they grow; once they don't have enough nutrients, they die. So, the viruses stay alive for as long as amoebas are alive. There is a fine time frame within which the culture can be kept, though you can even prolong that time frame by using low temperature or even freezing. But we're not talking of easy manipulations."

Oshima-San took over and concluded his reply to David's initial question as to whether there could be a stock of containers somewhere in the Philippines:

"No, the most likely scenario has to be that the three containers which were placed and which your team recovered were a new batch that had been delivered to those who placed the containers on the islands. Now, the one thing we don't know is whether the masters deliver fully operational containers or simply the viruses, growth medium, and amoebas with the terrorists charged with manufacturing the containers. Irrespective of who does what to whom, I would guess that the delivery to the terrorists would not take place much more than a couple of days before they are deployed."

Returning to their research and focusing now on their findings with respect to the viruses, Oshima-San surprised all the group except Armand who had been in on the research. He simply said:

"We believe that the virus in the second attack looks like a coronavirus, though it had obviously been manipulated."

Armand interrupted and added:

"By the way, as you know, we had kept samples of the viruses which had been used by the Middle Eastern terrorists a few years ago.[5] We immediately wondered whether they had similar characteristics. In short, we found that any family resemblance to those was at best distant. The virus which the terrorists place on the islands is of the same family as Covid-19, while the earlier virus in the Middle East wasn't."

Countess Renate asked:

"Covid-19? You better believe I remember it, but what does that mean?"

Armand replied that it was both good news and bad news. The good news was that the whole scientific community had developed significant experience with Covid-19 and thus probably had tools to combat it. The bad news, he argued, was that they were probably looking at yet another mutation, which could complicate matters. He observed:

"We do not know what would happen if this new strain was to combine with one of the earlier ones. Theoretically at least, it could increase the potency of the prior strains . . . Remember, as we said earlier, viruses need host cells to survive; so, they tend to trade off some of their potency as they mutate to increase their ability to attach to host cells. That's why you have seen the severity of Covid-19 decrease over time . . ."

"That and the vaccines or drugs . . ."

Armand replied:

"Certainly, Mark. I'm oversimplifying to make a point. Now, you can easily imagine that the biologists responsible for this new strain took mutated viruses and worked to give them additional potency. Sounds complicated, but it is a pretty standard procedure. We already

---

[5] See "The Shadow Experts" by the same author, published by Barringer Publishing 2021.

knew we had problems with the various vaccines that were developed. Now, we must conclude that the new strain will require significant modifications to both vaccines and treatment."

Mark was not through with his line of inquiry. He asked whether the relationship which the professors had found between the new virus strain and Covid-19 could explain why the Spanish tourist couple did not suffer as much as the locals. Laconically, he added:

"We know they had received at least one dose of anti-Covid vaccine."

Armand smiled and simply replied:

"There you go! Seems quite probable, but you know that in this field nothing is ever certain until you have all the facts . . . Which we don't."

David immediately noted that this was terrible news, explaining:

"Clearly, if anybody placed the new virus on the Twin Islands has any connection with whoever was involved with the original Covid-19, I'm ready to bet that it must mean that such a someone has already developed further mutations of the original strain and could well decide to use it."

He paused slightly for effect and ominously added:

"What if this one was just a trial run?"

Realizing that his question, however rhetorical it was, surely did not seem precise enough, he added:

"By 'this' I mean what we are witnessing here in Palawan."

Armand and Oshima-San both exhaled noisily, quickly making the point that this was exactly what they worried about. Oshima-San added:

"Note however that it would not make a lot of sense not to use their latest strain. Why wait to use it later?"

He paused for a second and added with a visibly worried look:

"Now the real nightmare scenario would be if they did have a more powerful strain and if their activity here on Palawan was a testing ground ahead of a more devastating attack elsewhere in the world."

Taking over from his colleague, Armand explained that they had been quite concerned that Covid-19 may have opened the first serious instance of truly biological warfare on a global scale. This recent incident clearly indicates that whoever is behind it is ready to use biological weapons. David interrupted:

"Now, going back to the virus which originated in the Middle East, we know that there was some Chinese and North Korean dimension. Here, we have been surmising that there could be a Chinese connection. Does that fit with your findings?"

Armand and Oshima-San looked at each other and seemed to nod in complete agreement. Armand replied:

"Absolutely, but nothing is obvious. As I said earlier, we believe that this new virus is closer to the Covid-19 virus than to the one we found originating in the Middle East. However, it's fair to remember that we also know there was a Chinese connection in the Covid-19 virus."

Oshima-San interrupted:

"I want to emphasize that we are not totally sure that Covid-19 was "manufactured" in China. It is still scientifically possible that it developed on its own, as was proclaimed early on. What this new virus tells us however is that the chances are rising that Covid-19 was intentionally developed. This new one is a variant on the first one and it shows that the first one could surely be manipulated; remember, we call this 'gain of function research.' The step between this belief and the suggestion that Covid-19 was a modified virus that might be otherwise occurring naturally is quite small."

David thanked the scientists but immediately asked the key question:

"What are the medical implications of your discovery?"

Armand replied that they had concluded that additional work had to be done on whatever treatment had been developed with respect to Covid-19. He further explained that this involved both preventative and curative measures. He added:

"As I just said a short while ago, combining something with the old strain could create an agent that can be simultaneously more powerful and more contagious . . ."

Countess Renate had to ask:

"Does this mean that you have to start from scratch in terms of both vaccines and medicines?"

Oshima-San tilted his head slightly to the left and seemed to breathe in through clenched teeth. Renate and Armand who were quite familiar with Japanese customs understood that he wanted to suggest that the question was excellent and not easy to answer. He simply said:

"Not so simple. Some basic work is still useful; however, we aren't really sure how much will need to be redone."

Though quite interested in the current line of discussion, David offered a new direction which he summarized.

"We don't want whoever created the virus to know that we know . . ."

Armand was the first to pick up on the point, realizing that anything that told the creators of the virus that it had been intercepted, analyzed, and identified would set the stage for a more rapid development of yet another, probably deadlier variant. He noted however that the scenario which they had so far brushed made it clear that developing virus-based biological weapons seemed a well-established activity, concluding:

"I don't want to be a prophet of doom, but we have to assume that research is ongoing. So, we probably should not lose so much time if the news that we have identified the virus came out."

He paused for a second and added:

"It's really a difficult ethical question. On the one hand, we should marshal all possible resources to develop a treatment and a vaccine against that new variant. On the other we don't want to create panic and to tell the terrorists and their masters that we have pierced their secret."

David readily conceded the point, although he felt that the crux of the problem lay elsewhere:

"To me, keeping the work which you two professors carried out secret is key to giving us a chance to identify where this new virus comes from. Assume that the adversary, whoever he is, finds out what you two gentlemen and your teams have done, and you can be pretty sure that the foe will keep his head low until they have a usable weapon. And that may mean a more deadly virus. So, my vote would be to stick to our current strategy. Anyone disagree?"

After reaching unanimous agreement on David's point, the group concluded that a key element now was to bring the Philippines government into the loop without saying too much. They knew that they needed help to track whoever was placing these viral containers and that only the Filipino army and police forces could do the key work.

■ ■ ■ ■ ■

When it was clear that the call was nearly over, David thanked Oshima-San, Armand and Countess Renate and immediately invited Mark and Ehud to stay on the line. His main instruction was to look for entries into the Philippines from Vietnam or Thailand. He added that he was not disagreeing with the need to bring the Filipinos into the loop as they had just all elected, though he argued that there were ways that certain discrete inquiries could be made which did not need full disclosure of the whys and wherefores. He explained:

"Remember that in the last virus attack which we were collectively able to foil, we found connections in China and North Korea in particular. Thus, if the same or a similar connection were to be found here, the fact that North Korea does not have an embassy in the Philippines but has resident diplomats in Hanoi and Bangkok would mean that the virus would have been brought from or at least through there."

Mark immediately replied:

"Excellent idea, sir. By the way, though there is a Chinese Embassy in Manila, I cannot believe that they would conduct their biological work locally. So, we'll add China to the list of countries from which travelers should be monitored."

David nodded adding:

"But it's quite far, better to focus on departure points that are closer."

Mark concluded:

"Plus, I assume that these entries ought to have been quite recent given the timeline the professors discussed."

"Quite right, Mark. I should also add that I am not terribly hopeful that your search will be fruitful, as there are many ways the viruses could have been brought into Palawan."

Mark conceded the point and thought that it was more practical to think the containers would have come in by sea or by air, in unofficial vessels. With a wry smile, he added:

"As you just said, the problem is distances. The closest major Vietnamese city to Palawan probably is Ho Chi Min City. However, it's more than 800 nautical miles away . . . All over water. Can't believe that a small plane would attempt that. On the other hand, Puerto Princesa has an international airport with 15 gates. That is probably where we should concentrate, though you could also assume that the virus is smuggled by boat from Sabah, East Malaysia. Kota Kinabalu has significant aircraft traffic and the distance by boat or by plane from there to Palawan is totally manageable."

Ehud asked:

"What about a Chinese submarine transferring the containers to some local agent while still at sea?"

David thought for a minute and replied:

"Can't rule anything out, but I can't believe the Chinese would do anything that could be traced back to them so simply. Playing the odd harassing game in international waters is one thing, carrying out openly a blatant act of biological war is a totally different kettle of fish."

He paused to check his logic and added:

"No. Imagine the number of possibly loose tongues . . . Things would be so bad they would have to escalate from there. No going back."

Mark reinforced the point:

"Agreed. Plus, I know that submarines have freezers, but would anyone want to bring potentially lethal contaminants in such close quarters? Makes more sense to think in terms of an air transshipment. The question is how and where."

Ehud nodded and concluded:

"I guess we know where to start . . . And it's going to involve airports . . ."

CHAPTER.20

When David casually suggested to Ehud that he needed to brief his local boss, Aaron Meyer, the Israeli Ambassador to the Philippines, Ehud smiled broadly, saying:

"Glad you're mentioning it, David, as I was about to ask for your opinion."

Standard operating procedures do not require *Mossad* operatives to keep the local diplomatic leadership abreast of their activities. Certain elements tend always to be disclosed, while others almost never are. However, this time, it was clear that there were too many points of possible contacts between various elements of the project and the responsibilities of Filipino political leaders. Though David was not Ehud's "boss," he clearly was a senior *Mossad* figure and, in the context of this mission, was the senior *Mossad* officer. It was thus natural for Ehud to ask David for instructions. In this case, David wanted Ehud to move ahead to make sure that all the proverbial ducks were properly lined up. Above all, he felt he needed to ensure that there would not be a serious surprise which would jeopardize bilateral relationships.

Accordingly, when Ehud had requested a meeting with Aaron, he suggested that their conversation should include David Heller, the Head of Mossad's Disruption Department in Tel Aviv, who would be joining by video conference. The meeting was set for 2:00 p.m., Manila time, which corresponded to 9:00 a.m. in Tel Aviv. David joked that all parties would be drinking coffee; for him it would be morning coffee, while the Manila contingent would be having their after-lunch cup of coffee.

Ehud opened the conversation with a brief history of his current mission, starting with the request for help from Luis Ramos. David and Ehud had agreed that they would place the focus of their conversation on health issues, as the initial request they would make would be for Aaron to contact the local Secretary of Health. Ehud recalled that he had needed to contact the Spanish Ambassador because of the two Spanish tourists having been contaminated in Palawan. Aaron's body language showed some degree of displeasure at not having been informed at the time. His behavior was easily understandable as he would have thought that it was his responsibility to deal with the Manila diplomatic corps. David sensing that an issue was brewing, as he had been totally briefed, explained that the contact was not made by *Mossad* but by the Secretary of Health, Andres "Bambi" Ruizon. Aaron needed further clarification and asked:

"How was the secretary first contacted?"

Ehud sheepishly replied:

"I had to contact his right-hand man when Luis informed me of the problem with the Spanish tourists. At the time, I did not think the matter would go much further. Then, after Colonel Heller had secured the participation of one of the top virologists in the world, a Director of the French Institut Pasteur, I needed to talk to him again, suggesting that we might need to involve the Secretary of Health himself."

Realizing that Ehud was walking on eggshells, David interrupted again and added:

"We happen to know very well someone who can secure the services of such super high-qualified people. At that stage of the process, we did not know that this would become much more serious. I organized a sting operation from here, in Tel Aviv, and Simon Rabinowitz, the Head of *Mossad*, as well as Moshe Shamir, our Defense Minister, were in the loop."

Aaron seemed to calm down quite a bit, realizing that David was both fully covering Ehud's actions and discreetly pulling rank over him. David let Ehud continue the briefing, in particular mentioning that a second potential source of infection had been identified, isolated and neutralized. He concluded with the dramatic news which had been conveyed by Armand Duchemin and Oshima-San: the virus that has been intentionally placed in the vicinity of Galoc island was a variant on the Covid-19 theme. Aaron figuratively jumped up from his chair and repeated:

"Covid-19?"

David replied as calmly as he knew how:

"I'm afraid so, Aaron."

Aaron came back with another implicit question as he simply said one word:

"Chinese?"

David decided to reply in a more complete though less categorical manner given the number of unknowns still in the air:

"Well, let's first concede that this is more a suspicion than a fact. However, we have top-secret information that pointed to China and North Korea in an earlier incident which I still can't comment on, as, despite being a few years old, it is still very tightly classified. However, I believe it is generally accepted around the world that the Covid-19 virus was born in China, near or in Wuhan specifically. I should add that no one really knows whether the virus occurred naturally or was 'manufactured' in the laboratory."

He paused to let Aaron absorb the information and concluded:

"At this point, we have no way of pointing to one party or another with respect to the current problem, though I personally suspect that China would not act directly and in the open anyway. So, I'm ready to bet that even if China is involved, we will find that there are other players in the chain. But the similarities between this and previous incidents would make me lean in the direction of suspecting the same actors are somehow in the play."

"I must congratulate you on the use of diplomatic language. I couldn't have done better myself. So, between us, you're suspecting North Korea again somehow working with China?"

David smiled and did not hesitate:

"They're the most logical culprit. North Korea working **for** China, but there may be others . . . Who knows?"

Aaron had by then completely shed any form of resentment at having been kept out of the loop. He was now back in his official role having realized the crucial nature of the work which *Mossad* had done. He asked:

"Any relationship with all the oil exploration work that's going on in that area?"

David replied:

"Nothing that we can directly point to, but circumstantial evidence would suggest a link. Logic as well, I should add. After all, the initial contamination and the second attempt to contaminate further both took place very close to where the drilling was taking place. Moreover, the timing of the second attack coincided with the unofficial news of the start of the exploitation of the new field developed by the Ramos-led consortium, which has been renamed the "Wilson field" in honor of the famous geologist. He's the guy who initially predicted that there were large quantities of oil in the country."

Aaron looked quite pensive and said nothing for a good minute or so. He finally surprised David and Ehud:

"What I am about to tell you is still totally secret and though it comes from the highest levels of local government it is still not official. I received the information in confidence, and we cannot make official use of it."

Aaron could clearly see that David and Ehud were now all ears. It may have been his way of scoring some points with his colleagues: diplomats also have important roles! He explained that there were indications that certain religious tensions were beginning to arise in Palawan. He reminded Ehud and David that there were three major indigenous tribes on the Palawan archipelago and noted that they kept practicing certain animist rites, though officially the bulk of the Palawan population were Christians. He paused and seemed to correct himself:

"However, before going any further, I should add that most Muslims live in parts of Mindanao, Palawan, and the Sulu Archipelago—an area known as Bangsamoro or the Moro region. Moreover, we all know that Mindanao rather than Palawan is their traditional territory."

He paused again to sip some coffee and kept going, explaining that Muslims in Palawan have traditionally been concentrated in the south of the island, though recent analyses argue that they may have gradually migrated north. He added that estimates were now suggesting that one inhabitant of Palawan in ten is Muslim, practicing the Sunni form of the religion. To him, it meant that with such a rising percentage of the population practicing Islam, it must have spread throughout the island.

Continuing, Aaron brought up the touchy subject of the Moro rebellion which covered the better part of the prior 150 years, noting that an agreement was finally reached that led to the creation of the Autonomous Region in Muslim Mindanao. David asked:

"So that is kind of a closed chapter, right?"

"Well, not really my friend. I don't want to turn philosophical or political on you, but history teaches us that wars with revolutionaries are never over, or at least hardly ever over. Wars are paused with treaties, though the real goal of the revolutionaries remains. Call the lull generated by these treaties a time for regrouping, reorganizing forces, or refilling depleted ammunition inventories, whatever you will, but most often it is a time for preparing the next attack. Depending on the circumstances, that lull can last a few days, a few weeks, or months, or even years. So, in this instance, I was surely not surprised by the fact that there have been continuous skirmishes, and, but this is again top-secret, neither was the government. Now add to that the fact that the region happens to be the area where the bulk of mineral extraction happens in the Philippines . . ."

David interrupted:

"Mineral?"

"Yes, Mindanao has huge mineral resources, including lead, zinc, iron ore, copper, chromite, magnetite, and gold. Note that gold mined in Mindanao accounts for nearly half of the national gold reserves. Having said that, the largest current gold extraction project is on Masbate Island, which is part of Visayas and not Mindanao. So, things can change; however, do people change as well? Maybe, but more slowly would be my guess."

David immediately bounced on the insight:

"And you're saying that the treaty with the Moros mandates that a part of that wealth has to be paid back to the autonomous region?"

Seeing Aaron nod, he paused for a second to check his thoughts and added:

"Hmmm. What are the odds that some similar development could be brewing in Palawan if the oil deposits are anywhere near what some people think? And are the terrorists regrouping in Palawan because of the shift of gold mining to Masbate?"

Aaron simply said:

"Your guess is as good as mine. But revolutions need funds and mineral resources are a terrific way 'to earn' the funds needed to pay for arms and people . . ."

■ ■ ■ ■ ■

Meanwhile, negotiations between Eli, Luis, Anthony, and Larry had come to a conclusion, and significant progress had been made toward the future full exploitation of the Wilson field. Their first order of business had been to choose a location for their "home base." Ideally, it had to be accessible via the air, preferably by planes, but certainly via helicopter. It also had to have direct access to a harbor so that ships needed to ferry people and equipment would have a convenient place to dock.

Realistically, they had observed that there were only two airports which made sense, with a third serving as extra safety. Puerto Princesa was probably the best alternative as it was unquestionably the largest airport on Palawan. However, the distance separating it from the area of the oilfield made it all the more impractical as the town of Puerto Princesa itself was on the east side of Palawan while the oilfield was on the west side. Add to this the problem of the capacity of the airport, and it made sense to consider at least one alternative. Thus, they agreed that it would serve as a backup solution, reinforced by all the civil and medical infrastructure which the regional capital could provide. This left them with two solutions, neither of which was truly ideal.

El Nido, the main resort center on Palawan, had been inhabited by humans since early 2680 BC, if not much earlier. Some people argue that the first inhabitants date back up to 22,000 years ago, which appeared to be confirmed by fossils and burial sites, dating back to the Late Neolithic Age. Further, it comprises several nice resort locations, including high-end accommodations alongside the less expensive options which certain tourists naturally require. It has been named several times by travel publications as having the best island beaches in the world because of its white sand, turquoise waters, vibrant coral reefs, and stunning limestone cliffs. It offered a good airport, located on the west side of the island, and with numerous infrastructural amenities, not a surprising observation as it has served as a base for several of the oil exploration and production activities in the past. Its main shortcoming was that it was a place where it would be hard to remain discreet, let alone anonymous, and, to a similar extent as Puerto Princessa, it could quickly be overwhelmed if activities at the Wilson Field picked up dramatically.

The island of Busuanga, to the north presented its share of potential advantages. First, it had a commercial airport, Francisco Reyes, located in the middle of the island, in the eponymous town of Busuanga. It was a much less frequented area, though Coron, the major town located on the east side of the island, was as a matter of fact well-developed and had a harbor which provided access to cruise ships. Additionally, it had a buoyant tourist trade because of its magnificent dive sites, where one can find wrecks from the Japanese Navy. Further, Coron is often viewed as better value than the better-known El Nido for all tourists except those looking for top of the line resort amenities. In the long term, it would likely be the best solution, though its major shortcoming in the short term was that the harbor was to the south of Busuanga Island and would thus require a longer time at sea if trying to reach the oilfield by boat—which would be necessary to bring the drilling and production crews onto and out of the production site.

Angelo, who was naturally given local operating responsibilities under the general guidance of Anthony from a technical standpoint and Larry for financial matters, had elected to split the apple. While he would be building a base in Coron, he would initially have people and equipment transit through El Nido. Besides, thinking of the longer term he bought office space in Coron for himself and storage hangar space at Busuanga airport. He had justified the decision to Luis on the grounds that he could always reach the oilfield via helicopter.

The other major decision which the group had made was to start production formally from the first well. However, it had intentionally elected to limit the actual output to avoid attracting more attention than desired, at least during that initial phase of the development of the field. They understandably wanted to generate some operating cashflow, if only to cover their fixed costs, but they did not want people to talk too much. Mike, always the cynic, had whispered in Ehud's ear that trying to be discreet made a lot of sense, though choosing to name the field formally after Chuck Wilson surely did not help.

As originally anticipated, they had selected the relatively lowest cost production system alternative, though they incorporated an important wrinkle. They elected to use an FPSO vessel anchored on site to house most of the production facilities, together with all the oil workers. They also chose to use the location as a test site for Anthony's recent invention. The well had only a limited natural gas flow, though the team knew very well that further development might lead to a greater share of natural gas in the hydrocarbons produced. In normal circumstances, they would have simply placed a subsea completion structure on the ocean floor and separated crude oil from natural gas on the FPSO vessel which would be anchored there. The limited quantity of natural gas produced would be flared and the oil produced would be stored in tanks which would be regularly emptied by tankers shuttling between the well and an ultimate refinery. That was exactly the way the other wells in the same general area had been exploited. The subsea completion would also allow them, in due course if needed, to drill additional wells in the immediate vicinity and connect them to the production tree of the first well.

Anthony's contraption could, in his view, have significant implications elsewhere in the Wilson field. As he explained the genesis of his patented setup, Anthony noted that, as it comes out of the ground, the crude oil mix comprises both crude oil, but also natural gas and water, among others. Separating crude oil from natural gas typically involves heating the combined flow and taking advantage of the different boiling points to collect the gas at the top of the column while the oil is recovered at the bottom. Normally, the separation takes place on the FPSO vessel or on the oil production platform and the heat which is needed is generated on board the ship or the platform as well. Anthony's invention was based on the reality that oil in the underground reservoir is under pressure, just as everything around it is. He was the first to realize that he could capture that pressure as the oil emerges from the reservoir and transform it into electricity which could in turn provide the heat needed by an underwater oil/gas separator. His simple but quite elegant solution involved placing a few webbed wheels, set on needle bearings, within the pipe that collected the oil, just at the point where the pipe is connected to the subsea completion. The rotation of these wheels, caused by the oil flowing through them under pressure, could then be used to generate the electrical power needed to heat the combined hydrocarbon mix.

Though in the first well the sophistication of the solution was surely unnecessary, he argued and managed to convince others that it would be a useful test bed for his idea. It would only introduce one unnecessary complexity: rather than one pipe exiting the subsea completion, there would be two, one for the oil and the other for the gas. The oil would then be pumped onto the vessel, while the gas would be directed up to a flare located a few hundred yards from the vessel's anchorage. Later on, when the time came to exploit the two other main production sites of the Wilson field, separating the gas from the oil would still allow each of the two hydrocarbons to be pumped to different locations, though both locations would be exploited financially: both oil and gas would be sold. Actually, the plan provided for a fixed production platform as close to shore as possible and an electric power plant which would eventually be connected to the grid in the region, including the power plants fed by the Malampaya gas field and located on Batangas.

The subsea completion to which Anthony's contraption had been attached had taken a full six months to be manufactured and delivered to the site. The consortium had been particularly careful to hide its activities as much as possible, with the first well to serve as a decoy while the other two were worked on quietly. The official news release had mentioned 10,000 barrels per day as the target production rate, though it said that it could be raised if everything worked according to plan. This made sure that the Wilson field was not viewed in the same light as Nido or Matinloc in the last quarter of the 20th century.

CHAPTER.21

PALAWAN AND MANILA, THE PHILIPPINES

Unfortunately, however much care had been taken to avoid telling too much and igniting passions, the press, as well as the rumor mill one should add, hyped the news of the start of production at Wilson 1. Predictably, it had two consequences, one being welcomed by most investors, while the other raised a few caution flags. The first, not surprisingly, saw sharp increases in the stock prices of the companies involved in the Wilson consortium. Some spill-over effect extended to the whole of the oil sector, though there was no material link between several of the companies whose share prices rose and the deposit. Several speculators might well still eventually get their fingers burned.

The second was quite a bit more serious and caused disruption. It started with reports that indigenous terrorists had tried to kidnap a handful of oil workers near the hangar which the consortium maintained at the Francisco Reyes airport to store goods before they were transported to the production site. As planned by Angelo, though the bulk of the employees working on the project were located on the drill site and in El Nido, a handful worked at the airport and an even smaller number in Coron Town. They were a part of the first groups that worked to develop an operational base on Busuanga island.

The men at Francisco Reyes subsequently explained that they were saved by their quick reaction to an unexpected event. They heard the roar of the engine of a truck coming closer and closer. They went to the door of the hangar to see what it was. As soon as they saw a pick-up truck racing in the general direction of the hangar, they went into emergency action mode. A couple of men closed the main door while the other two went and locked all other accesses, the front door next to the main entry, the back door and the three windows. In effect they had barricaded themselves in the building. The terrorists tried to find a way in but were unsuccessful. They then attempted to start a fire in front of the main door.

With the benefit of hindsight, that was a bad idea from the point of view of the terrorists. The men saw them starting the fire from the inside of the hangar through a window and immediately activated their fire alarm. It took less than a minute for the airport firefighters to arrive, as their station was literally two buildings down from the hangar. The sound of the alarm and the response they heard from the fire station were enough to lead the terrorists to rush out and escape into the neighboring countryside. They dropped a few leaflets saying that they were affiliated with the Moro National Liberation Front and accusing the government and the corporate sector of pillaging the area's natural resources and stealing them from their rightful indigenous owners. Once safe and the hangar doors re-opened, the foreman on the site called Angelo to let him know what had happened and ask for instructions.

Luis had called Ehud as soon as he had heard from Angelo DeSousa. Though Angelo was creating his own operational base in Coron, he also occasionally worked from El Nido, where the consortium employed more workers, at least temporarily. That day, he was actually in El Nido and after having reported the incident to Luis he took a helicopter to fly straight back to Francisco Reyes Airport. He was able to see that there was no material damage to the hangar or the equipment in it, other than minimal fire and smoke stains to the outside of the building; a quick pressure wash would easily take care of it. At the same time, Angelo could attest to the fact that the men were all quite shaken. Terrorism was something people talked about in the past tense, and it was thus quite a shock to witness it firsthand.

■ ■ ■ ■ ■

Ehud could not miss the fact that Luis was partially flustered when he and Mike walked into his office at Ayala Tower. Luis had reserved his first call for Ehud who immediately called Mike Loeb and rushed with him to Luis's help:

Ehud asked:

"What happened? You look terrible, Luis . . ."

Luis tried to be as matter of fact as he could, though both Ehud and Mike would likely argue that he was not successful attempting to play the "all is almost alright" businessman. He said:

"Moro terrorists just tried to kidnap some of our people at the airport in Busuanga."

Ehud could not restrain himself and blurted out:

"WHAT? Come again!"

"Well, my friend, a truckload of terrorists just tried to kidnap the four employees we keep at the Francisco Reyes Airport. Clearly, it must mean the terrorists are against our project. But why us? Others have produced oil here before . . . First the viruses and now that. What's next?"

Mike could clearly see that it was going to take some effort to get the kind of information they needed out of Luis. He was emotional and appeared to be switching topics back and forth. So, he decided to try to calm him and ask:

"Thank God, the men are safe. What do we know for a fact, Luis?"

Luis was about to repeat his earlier statement when Ehud added a different question. Mike initially appeared surprised, but a smile was appearing and widening on his face as Ehud spoke:

"Please, give us all the details you have. To you, something may appear trivial, but to us it might actually be quite useful."

Luis went back to the conversation he had had with Angelo and tried to repeat faithfully every aspect he could remember. Mike asked:

"We've never been to that airport. Can you describe the place in a bit more detail? Just to help us visualize the scene a bit better . . ."

Luis prefaced his comments with a caveat stating that he had not been there more than once or twice, though he said that he would try his best. Yet, he almost immediately added that he still knew the geography rather well as he was required to approve the plans that were drawn up to build the hangar that had been attacked.

Mike asked:

"How long ago did you build it?"

"It's been operational for less than a year. We decided to build it when the results of the first well were positive."

"Was that not risky? What if the second well had been dry?"

"We thought of that, Mike. It's not a purpose-built hangar, but rather a hangar that could have multiple uses. We could always have sold it if we did not have a use for it . . ."

Luis went on to describe the whole surroundings of the airport: a lot of agricultural fields cultivated by the local people, principally to grow vegetables and to pasture sheep and more rarely cattle. The sole runway ran virtually perfectly in an east-west direction, with the two resulting runways marked 9 and 27, to denote their compass readings of 90 and 270 degrees, respectively, 90 degrees for east and 270 degrees for west. There was nothing north of the runway, just fields, with a fence separating the airport's land from the fields. He mentioned in passing that it looked as if the local government was building another runway with almost the same heading less than two thousand feet further west, tough smiling he added:

"Come to think of it, that may be an old runway which they may be rehabilitating . . . Should find out, just for information."

Continuing to describe the airport, Luis said that the new terminal, quite modern with a partially rounded roof was to the south of the runway, just behind the tarmac which provided parking for up to five jets or at least large commercial passenger planes. He added:

"To the east of the terminal, there are a couple of buildings, one of which is the fire station. We built our hangar to the east of these two buildings, adding some tarmac to its right. On the other side of the terminal, you can find a large hangar where smaller, general aviation planes can be stored."

He paused and mentioned that hangar protection was useful for small planes particularly at the height of the monsoon, when rain often comes down in sheets. Continuing his description, he said:

"Further south of the terminal, you'll find a semi-circular, U-shaped driveway for passenger pick-up and drop-off and a few houses. That's about it."

Mike who had been sketching a map as Luis was speaking, thanked him saying:

"That's very helpful."

Placing his simple map in front of Luis he first asked:

"Looks familiar?"

"Not bad. Not bad. I'm not sure the scale is perfect, but it's close enough."

Pointing to his makeshift map, Mike then asked:

"Where did the terrorists come from?"

Luis explained that there was a fence, pointing to its general location on Mike's sketch, that ran along the side of the runway, about 70-75 yards north of it. He said that the terrorists managed to cut into the fence without triggering any alarm, adding with a wry smile:

"I'm not sure they even have an alarm!"

Mike offered an encouraging smile. Going back to the terrorists, Luis mentioned that once through the fence, they drove first through a stretch of land that acts as a buffer from the perimeter, then across the runway and the taxiway, and finally across the tarmac in front of the hangar. Mike asked:

"Shouldn't other people have seen them?"

"Sure should but didn't. Or if they did, they didn't choose to do anything about it. My guess is that they were doing something else, as it was in the early evening and there were no planes on the tarmac."

"Nor any that were expected I bet . . ."

Luis replied:

"Probably right, Ehud. Probably."

Mike kept asking for more detail, all the while making sure that he did not seem to be pointing the finger to anyone:

"You said that there were three structures on the right of the terminal, looking toward the north. Correct?"

"Absolutely."

"Which one of the two to the left of your hangar is the fire station?"

"The one closest to the terminal."

"So, there is one building separating the fire station from your hangar?"

"That's it."

"Do you know what's in it?"

"Nope. I think it's just another hangar. So, there could be virtually anything in it."

He paused for a second and added:

"Come to think of it, I believe that there are offices above the hangar. I seem to remember a row of windows above the main floor. You don't put rows of windows in a hangar, and you don't construct hangars with a second floor around here."

Mike kept pushing as gently as he could, but he wanted to have as much information as possible:

"How did the terrorists flee?"

"I'm not sure because our people could not see; they had locked themselves in our hangar, and there's only a small window to the right of the main door and another two at the very back on the east side. There is a smaller door to the left of the main door; it's used for people to access the building when the main door is not up. But that small door does not have a window. So, the right window is it, unless you talk of the windows on the east side of the hangar, facing the tarmac we created. But these would be facing away from the action."

He paused for a second and returned to the question of how the terrorists managed to leave the airport:

"The one thing we know is that they did not leave the way they came in. Our guys would have seen them. They must have sped in front of the terminal and taken the road that separates the terminal from the hangar for small planes, and then veered onto the main road."

"How far is that?"

"Less than six hundred feet, I'd guess."

Mike kept on with his questions:

"Wonder why they did not flee the way they came?"

Luis replied that he surely did not know, though he offered what he called a wild guess:

"I asked Angelo the same question. He told me that the terrain north of the airport is not really good even with a 4x4 vehicle. His guess is that the terrorists wanted to reach a regular, sealed road as quickly as they could. Once on a paved road, they could easily disappear into the landscape."

Mike appeared deep in thought when he finally asked his next question:

"One thing I don't understand. If the terrorists are Moro-related as their pamphlets said, they would be Muslim, wouldn't they?"

Without giving Luis the time to reply, he added:

"I thought the area was mostly Christian, correct?"

Luis simply nodded. Mike asked his next question:

"I assume that the airport is usually pretty deserted, correct?"

"Yes. Though there's usually some police presence."

"Where were they?"

"Excellent question. We do not know that yet. "

Mike was not ready to let go. He asked Luis how the terrorists could drive first 600 feet in front of terminal facilities and then all the way to the road and escape in a place that was still supposed to be under some police protection. Luis could only shake his head and reply:

"Mike, I know. It doesn't make any more sense to me than to you. Plus, as we both just established, if the vehicle they had could ride through one mile of cultivated fields and then through the airport fence, why didn't they use the same escape route? They would have been going away from the terminal rather than in front of it. As I said earlier, my guess is that they sought access to a major road, but who knows?"

"Any chance that there were local complicities?"

"Everything is possible. But we hadn't heard of any Muslim activity in this area. The closest building outside of the airport to the north is a Presbyterian church and there is a Catholic church about two miles away. No mosque that I know of. So far, we haven't heard of any Moro sympathy in the area."

Mike replied that someone trying to create mischief might have encouraged terrorists from a different part of Palawan to move north. He recommended to Luis not to do anything at this point, adding that he and the rest of the team had to reconvene and look at the whole safety issue in somewhat more depth. He even offered:

"We already knew that we couldn't let the virus go further without having conversations with the government. This attack only increases the urgency of that meeting. We cannot deal with this without close cooperation with the government . . ."

Luis exhaled visibly, indicating that he did not relish the idea of having the government stick their nose in what he saw as his affairs but only added:

"Make sure you remain quite discreet. We don't want any of this to get into any of the daily papers."

■ ■ ■ ■ ■

Once off the conference call with David Heller, Israeli Ambassador Aaron Meyer was in his office with Ehud Shamir and Mike Loeb. He could not help asking the obvious next question:

"Do you think we could be seeing something involving China in the upper Palawan region?"

Ehud looked straight at Mike as he felt caught in a bit of a trap. On the one hand, as the Embassy's military attaché, he owed the ambassador his best intelligence. On the other hand, he could not disclose information which might endanger the operations currently carried out by *Mossad*. Mike simply batted his eyelids, suggesting to Ehud that he understood his predicament and trusted him to reply as best he could. Ehud decided to deal with the incipient conflict with a bit of a *pirouette*; rather than provide an answer to Aaron's question, he asked him a related question:

"What do you mean by something?"

Aaron understood why Ehud had answered the way he had and took a different tack. He offered a scenario which was starting to germinate in his head and, if confirmed as realistic, would require him to speak to Fernando Solano, the Secretary of National Defense. He started with the assumption that terrorists somehow linked to the Moro National Liberation Front were behind the biological attacks.

He could not point to the source of the virus but said obvious suspects could be regional third parties with whom China was known to cooperate, which placed North Korea at the top of the list. He added the idea that the goal of the Chinese would be to impede or at least slow the development of oil and gas production, assuming that the Wilson deposit was truly a game changer. He even mentioned that the Philippines government had recently taken the unusual step of placing buoys at the limit of its economic exclusion zone around the Spratly Islands to signify to the Chinese that they could not intimidate the country into abandoning its claims to its own territory. The irony of having an island already occupied by the Chinese within the territory marked by the buoys did not escape anyone!

Aaron continued the development of his scenario, arguing that the Chinese might be promising some share in the profits from the oil to the Moros. Thus, the Chinese would be using the Moros to interfere with the oil exploration and production efforts. At that point, he was assuming that there was only a limited amount of activity that could be carried out offshore, if only because no one would believe that the local terrorists would have the capability of projecting force there. Yet, there was plenty that could be done in the interim, as substantial onshore infrastructure would need to be built. Actions could range from discouraging employees from working on the site, disrupting supplies, kidnapping foreign as well as local contractors or even sabotaging installations that were already built. In short, the idea would be to make any financial investment in the area more expensive and riskier.

Mike and Ehud both conceded that the scenario had a number of totally believable elements, though they also noted that the hypothetical use of the Moros would allow the Chinese to maintain some "official distance" and offer them plausible deniability. They suggested that an important next step involved meeting with the appropriate government officials and request quiet, behind-the-scenes help to identify the key facts and formulate a full plan of action. Mike added:

"Without a few key facts, I don't see how anything one can do. Cannot confront the Chinese. Cannot interfere in any visible military fashion."

He paused to let his point sink in and then smiled as he said:

"However, if we are correct assuming that the Chinese not only use the Moros but also some other nation such as North Korea, there is quite a bit that can be done covertly . . ."

Ehud nodded, indicating that he had fully understood what Mike had suggested.

CHAPTER.22

TEL AVIV, ISRAEL, PALAWAN AND MANILA, THE PHILIPPINES

Before letting Aaron Meyer, the Israeli Ambassador to the Philippines meet with government officials, David and his team needed to make a couple of important changes. Their principal worry was to ensure that neither Ehud nor Mark Levi would be outed as *Mossad* agents, though, in the case of Ehud, Aaron was now fully aware of his double role. They immediately agreed that Nathan Heimer, who had helped them retrieve the virus containers deposited on the Twin Islands, should be introduced to Aaron as a Tel-Aviv-based *Mossad* operative, while Ehud and Mark would keep playing their current roles. Nate had been involved with enough of the mission to have been briefed on all key operating details. Additionally, the immediate proximity of Ehud and Mike to help would make the effort as smooth as it could be.

Aaron Meyer had requested a meeting with Fernando Solano, the Secretary of National Defense, in Quezon City, an eastern suburb of Manila, and more specifically in Camp General Emilio Aguinaldo. As he drove to Fernando Solano's office, Aaron's car passed by the camp's golf course which he observed was in perfect condition, not a surprise as the climate helped and there had to be plenty of labor available. Upon being ushered into the secretary's office, he was warmly greeted. Aaron had decided that he would be alone for this first visit, both because it would surely follow more closely the typical diplomatic protocol and as it would avoid divulging more than he should: he had been well-briefed but could still always and quite plausibly argue that he did not know all the details. To say that Fernando Solano was surprised by the contents of Aaron's revelations would be the understatement of the century. A better phrase might be that he seemed crestfallen.

Fernando readily conceded that he had heard rumors of a virus infection on Palawan, in fact from Bambi Ruizon, the Secretary of Health, at a weekly meeting of government ministers. Yet, at that time, Bambi elected to keep his source confidential and within a couple of weeks had been able to dispel any remaining fears. The Spanish tourists had returned to MacLambay Island where they were able to return the boat they had rented and had then flown home to Bilbao. No new case had been diagnosed and those who were sick had recovered. In some ways, Bambi had been able to "declare victory" and move on.

The idea that there had been not one but two separate viral attacks and that an attempt had been made to kidnap employees of the Wilson consortium hit the Secretary of Defense like a ton of bricks. Though Aaron had been very careful not to use any inflammatory language and to couch the hypotheses in the most uncertain light possible, Fernando was stung by the possibility that China or one of its "client countries" as he said might be behind the attacks and further be in some cahoots with some branch of the Moro National Liberation Front.

Aaron provided as many hard facts as he could, though names were always withheld for everyone's safety, which eventually led Fernando to ask directly what he or the Philippines Government could do. Fernando had prefaced his last statement mentioning the various steps recently taken by the country to communicate to China in no uncertain terms that there were clear limits to how much they could insert themselves into the politics of the South China Sea in general and the Spratly Islands in particular. Aaron dutifully congratulated him and his government for their courage and pledged that he would offer all possible support as and when needed.

Turning to the current challenge, Aaron asked Fernando for help trace the people who placed the viral containers. He had already told the minister that there were dark but still quite usable videos of the placement of the second set of containers. He added that his team's analysis of the various probabilities suggested that the most likely source of supply of viral containers for the terrorists had to involve airports. He noted however:

"There are many ways that the virus containers could come into the country . . ."

Fernando interrupted:

"You are rejecting the hypothesis that the virus is already here, onshore, possibly even in Palawan?"

"You never know, but the odds do not look good. I'm told this is a serious virus and I cannot believe that the Chinese, if they are the ones behind the scheme, would give up control over those kinds of biological samples."

Fernando nodded as Aaron continued:

"Thus, we believe that it must be brought in each time there is a specific mission. As an aside, I should add that the second batch of viruses seemed about as concentrated as possible. Now, I've been told that this could simply be the result of a longer delay between the moment the viruses were released in the air . . ."

He paused for a short while, as if debating something in his own mind. Then moving slightly forward in his seat, he said:

"What I am going to tell you is absolutely top-secret."

Fernando nodded and smiled as Aaron shared a crucial piece of information:

"A few years ago, I'm told that our secret services were able to foil what could have been a devastating worldwide viral attack. It was driven by Middle Eastern terrorists. However, I am again told that our secret services were able to infiltrate the network and neutralize the virus, which been placed in a number of distinct locations."

"In the Philippines?"

"I'm not privy to these details, but I believe the principal targets were in Israel, Europe and the U.S., plus a few Middle Eastern countries. The point that is germane to our conversation today is that the terrorists were never given more than three containers at a time. Our people tell me that this is what makes them strongly suspect that the containers are delivered prior to each attack."

"I see. How do you think they, the terrorists, are managing that?"

"That frankly we don't know. I'm told we know that the containers, or at least all that is needed to fill them in if they are manufactured locally, could come onshore via sea or via air. For reasons I have been told I did not need to know down to the ultimate detail, it seems that our team tends to discount the sea route; I'm told it has to do with the fragility of the cargo and the fact that private yachts or even cabin cruisers would roll quite a bit in the waters around here. Plus, the distances are so big."

Fernando seemed to follow and asked:

"What do you want to do next?"

"We would like to have permission to go inspect the landing and departure records of all airports in the Palawan area . . ."

Fernando immediately replied:

"There aren't too many. Puerto Princesa, El Nido, Francisco Reyes and Cesar Lim Rodriguez, in Taytay. And of those, only Puerto Princesa is classified as an international airport."

He paused and added with a wink:

"Not that I mean that terrorists would not be ready to break the law. But Puerto Princesa would be the best place to start, though I guess that terrorists might have landed first in Puerto Princesa and then flown onto one of the other three, maybe with a smaller airplane, or even a helicopter."

"Very interesting hypothesis. Would you be willing to contact whoever is responsible for airport management and ask him to provide clearance for our agents?"

"Wow. How many agents are you talking about?"

"Not to worry. At this point, we only have one person who can do the work. He is normally based in Tel Aviv. But there may be a need for more at some point unless you want to take the project over yourself."

The Secretary looked pensive for a short while. He then surprised Aaron:

"I have been told that an Israeli group is helping Luis Ramos in his endeavor. I even heard that at least a couple of people from that group have been in Manila on and off for the last year. These people would not be secret service agents by any chance, would they?"

Aaron smiled and simply replied:

"You're asking the wrong person. Our secret services do not disclose much to us diplomats, unless there is a need, as in this instance, for official bilateral government-to-government contact. I'll take this further. I would bet quite heavily that one of my attachés has to be a front for the secret services. Yet I don't know who he or she is . . ."

"And you don't mind it?"

"Who said that? I do mind, but I understand that this is required for both the individual's safety and those of all the embassy personnel. So, I play by the rules, those I like and those I like less."

"You're amazingly stoic, Aaron. Still, will you be able to let us know who is doing the investigation in our airports?"

Aaron looked pensive for brief seconds. Then he replied:

"I don't know. If you believe that it is absolutely critical, there may be a way to tell you, but I think that it would be best if the authorization to investigate was drafted in my name and I entrusted one of my people with the role to investigate. I am not sure we need the person who collects the information to be a trained secret agent and it might be best that way. Come to think of it, I could nominate my military attaché, Ehud Shamir. He's as straight as they come, knows the country well, speaks the language . . ."

"A secret agent?"

Aaron replied with a broad smile:

"Of all the people around me, he's probably the last one I would pick to be a *Mossad* agent. But again, who knows?"

■ ■ ■ ■ ■

In the end, as had originally been agreed among the *Mossad* trio, Nate Heimer got the nod. Everyone was grateful to Aaron Meyer for having conducted the meeting with Fernando Solano the way he did, including the off-the-cuff mention that Ehud might be the chosen individual. However, the consensus was that Ehud could play a much more useful and effective role if he stayed in the shadows, while given Mark's seniority in the agency it was simply out of the question for him to operate in the open.

Nate's first visit was not, as one might have expected, to Puerto Princesa, but rather to Francisco Reyes airport in Coron. He had discussed his choice with Ehud and Mark at length, and they had even thought that David ought to be in the loop. The rationale that won the day was that nobody, least of all Nate, knew a lot about what they should be asking. Marvin Goldstein, the technology wunderkind of *Mossad*, had obviously arranged for him all the training that was necessary. He had made sure that the training would be in Tel Aviv just to make sure that the most sophisticated techniques could be shown to Nate. He had even taken him to Bar Yehuda Airfield, which has the distinction of being the lowest airport in the world, standing 1,240 feet below sea level. It is a small desert airfield located in the southern Judean desert west of the Dead Sea and is mainly used as an alternate airport and for charters and sightseeing flights. Marvin had chosen it as he assumed that Nate needed to see an airport with relatively simple installations and low traffic, along with Ben Gurion in Tel Aviv which would stand at the opposite end of the sophistication scale.

Ehud accompanied Nate on his visit to Francisco Reyes airport, which they had reached by flying a twin-turboprop Beechcraft Super King Air 350 directly from Manila. Ehud was officially on the mission as Nate's pilot and interpreter, as Aaron had intimated to Fernando Solano might be the case. David, Mark and Aaron had agreed that the cover was absolutely reasonable: Nate was not fluent in Tagalog and thus needed some escort. With Ehud used to flying planes in the Filipino airspace, he was an even better choice, though Nate had his pilot's license; Ehud seemed custom designed for the task. The plane was not the fastest plane available, but it was considered the one best suited to the mission. Its take-off runway needs were met by all the airports he was scheduled to reach, and it was large enough for the mission, though Ehud noted that he might have to rent a single propeller plane for Taytay.

Nate and Ehud were now ready to start their investigation, hoping that they would be able to get sufficient information. Plus, with any luck, this might be the place where they would find the trace of the terrorists they were looking for.

■ ■ ■ ■ ■

Meanwhile, at the Wilson oil field, things were proceeding apace. Production from Well 1 had started and was on target. The engineers had even chosen, discreetly, to boost production for a couple of days, by releasing a choke that controls well flow. Though well short of the real production capacity, the engineers wanted to get a sense of whether their plan as currently designed was working as expected. The doubling of production for two days was totally uneventful. One would have had to be a trained engineer to notice first that the gas flare seemed to be somewhat more forceful than usual and second that the FPSO vessel had called for a tanker to take delivery of fuel sooner than would have normally been anticipated.

A couple of weeks later, Mike found himself with Anthony and Luis in Manila, though Angelo had not been able to join as he was still onsite. Anthony told Luis that he was delighted with the experiment, and that the project was less than a couple of days away from connecting Well 2 to the production infrastructure. Luis was visibly happy though he asked:

"What about the construction of the near-shore production platform?"

Anthony replied that progress was steady and that the work was on schedule. He reminded Luis that the platform was intended to be "prefabricated."

"Prefabricated?"

"Yes, without going into too many details, let me just say that all the major parts are being built in Singapore. When completed, they will be brought by ship to the site and assembled here. To be more specific, they will be first pre-assembled onshore in Manila and then finally towed to its desired offshore location here."

"Why by ship for Singapore to Manila? Why not by plane?"

Anthony deadpanned:

"One day versus ten days seems a lot, but it isn't. Ten times the cost seems a lot to pay for such a small gain . . ."

Luis simply nodded. Returning to the Wilson field, Anthony, however, observed that the well, Wilson 2, would initially be linked to the production facilities of Well 1. Luis asked why and Anthony replied that he wanted to be sure that everything had been fully tested. He was about to continue when Mike jumped up:

"Hold it guys. My watch just buzzed me. The cameras on Twin Islands. They broadcasted something a few minutes ago."

He went straight into the feed and appeared downright upset:

"You won't believe it, but we had visitors again. It looks like they placed something, maybe other containers. Whatever it is, it looks bigger than the last time."

Luis was beside himself:

"Why? Why now?"

Mike looked him straight in the eyes and simply said:

"Guess what. We just completed a test that showed Well 1 could produce more. Luis, I hate to say it, but I believe that we have a mole somewhere."

He paused and added:

"It looks as if something happens on the terrorist front each time there is positive news on the development of production. It's beginning to look as if there are way too many coincidences."

He paused again and much more seriously said:

"We've got to find the mole. But in the meanwhile, we need to mount an expedition similar to what we did the last time to retrieve the containers."

With his eyes looking straight at Luis he added:

"And to do that without anyone knowing about it, other than you."

CHAPTER.23

As soon as he saw that new containers had been placed on the Twin Islands, Mark had decided that it would be best first to go and see what they actually were. He explained to David why he was asking for additional resources:

"I can't believe that the enemy would be so naïve and stupid to repeat the same tactic a third time. I worry that they cooked up something different. Hopefully, we will be able to detect what it is from the air before we have to go onsite."

A brief phone call from Aaron Meyer to Fernando Solano allowed David and his crew to bring into the Philippines a couple of small drones and two pilots. Within a day, the Filipino permission obtained, two Orbiter Trojan, Israeli-made reconnaissance drones were loaded in an unmarked aircraft Lockheed C-130 Hercules cargo plane, which landed in Manila the next day. People on the ground were not terribly surprised as the sight of Hercules cargo planes was not unusual there, given the immediate proximity of the headquarters of the Philippine Air Force to Ninoy Aquino International Airport.

The Trojan looks like a small aircraft with a couple of vertical rudders below its short and stubby fuselage. Its wingspan is barely more than 13 feet and its maximum take-off weight is under 100 pounds. Its two key capabilities for the mission Mark had in mind were first that it can take off and land vertically, as it is equipped with four small helicopter-type rotors located on either sides of the nose and the tail of the central fuselage. It can also hover which would allow the operator to get quite detailed photographic evidence, even more so as the drone is equipped with state-of-the art electronic equipment. Its only weakness is that its battery power provides it with the ability to stay aloft for only about two and half hours, and to travel no more than 100 miles.

Though Mark and Ehud had asked for two drones and two pilots, they had no intention, originally at least, to deploy them both. They just wanted to have a drone in reserve and for the two pilots to be able to cooperate on the one drone that would be deployed. Quickly, they had come to the decision to fly the drone to its destination, while they would travel by helicopter if not alongside, at least on the same route. The 100-mile maximum range forced them to accept that they would have to make at least two stops before reaching their destination. They could have chosen to have the Hercules aircraft bring the drones directly to Francisco Reyes, but decided against it as it would be too "visible" in their opinion. As Mark had said:

"The less people know, the better, even if it makes our jobs a bit harder."

They would need to fly from Manila to Batangas on Luzon Island, the island where Manila is located, then from Batangas to Sablayan on Mindoro Island and then from Sablayan to Francisco Reyes Airport at Busuanga. They had asked for spare batteries so that, at each stop, they would quickly replace the used drone battery with a new one and fly it onto the next definition. The batteries, though relatively heavy, would not be a challenge for the helicopter, which would also carry a battery charger to ensure that the team always had sufficient reserve power for the drone. Mark disliked the need for the two additional stops and, possibly for staying a short while in Busuanga, arguing:

"The more places we stop and the longer we stay, the more chances people will figure out what we are doing or at least ask questions we'd rather not be asked. Plus, these advanced drones are not known to be available to many countries. Guess what? Every finger would be pointed to Israel. Yet, flying into Francesco Reyes with a big cargo plane is inviting even more attention."

Prompted by Mark, Ehud called Luis to tell him that they were going to conduct their investigation the next day. Luis apologized that he could not be with them, as he and Angelo were meeting with Larry and Anthony for an oil production update which they were told might well take the whole day. Ehud simply smiled, thinking, *thank you Larry and Anthony! Mission accomplished.*

■ ■ ■ ■ ■

The helicopter which would be flown by Ehud and carry Mark and the two drone pilots would also carry an additional passenger: Armand Duchemin. Conversations including Countess Renate, Armand himself as well as Mark and David had led to the conclusion that one should be very careful with these new containers. Everybody agreed that it would make little sense for the terrorists to keep repeating the same action over and over, more so as Countess Renate had observed:

"They must have realized that their last attack produced absolutely nothing. That must have them wondering what happened . . ."

Armand had added:

"Totally true. We have seen some glimpse of a pattern. The first attack may have used a lower virus concentration than the second. Though, again, remember that this is a view we inferred from the impact the first had on people, but it is not data-based. It would be perfectly logical, even if evil, to think that the next attack will represent some further escalation."

When queried as to what kind of escalation was possible, Armand initially demurred, and then offered two possible alternatives. The contaminated solution in his view could not have a higher virus concentration, but it could have some additional virus alongside the first. He conceded that there were theoretical instances where one virus would effectively block the other, but he added that most often two viral strains could co-exist. Matter-of-factly, he added, stressing the "and":

"Remember, there were people who were simultaneously infected with an influenza virus **and** with Covid 19 . . ."

Mark interrupted:

"You said you could think of two alternatives, correct?"

Armand conceded and added that the second alternative was a variant on the first. He explained that the second strain might be intended to create a separate infection in the same target, or potentially to target a different genus. Seeing that the word "genus" did not convey an immediate meaning to Mark and Ehud at least, he added:

"Could imagine that they might also want to infect say some animal."

He paused and after a short while declared:

"I know that fish can carry viruses, but my first guess would be to assume that the target genus might well be birds. Plus, I'm not sure how they could get viruses into fish by depositing something on land, unless it is within the amplitude of the tide. Even then, it is really difficult for me to imagine the transmission mechanism. On the other hand, it's easy to imagine birds drinking infected water."

He paused again and simply argued:

"I believe I should go along with you, if only to see what the containers look like and where and how they are placed."

Jokingly, Mark asked:

"Have you ever rappelled from a helicopter?"

Armand did not look particularly fussed and simply replied:

"There's got to be a first time for everything, Mark."

■ ■ ■ ■ ■

Early the next morning, before the sun had appeared on the horizon, the five men boarded the helicopter. One of the two drone pilots had already launched his drone toward the first intermediate target, after having verified that the command pod of the second pilot was also set to the same frequency. He checked that he could control the drone from inside the helicopter and was delighted to observe that it was not a problem: no interference with any of the helicopter electronics. With its higher speed, the helicopter arrived in Batangas before the drone, which had been flying at 18,000 feet, while the helicopter remained at 15,000 feet, though it could have climbed up to 25,000 feet if needed. With the higher than usual take-off weight, Ehud had preferred to avoid climbing too high. As soon as the helicopter landed at the Sampaguita Farm Heliport, a couple of miles east of the center of the city of Batangas, the drone pilot disembarked first to get ready to have the drone hover and then hopefully execute a perfect vertical landing. Mark and the other pilot prepared the little material that was needed for the battery exchange: the spare battery and a Phillips screwdriver. Meanwhile Ehud and Armand remained aboard, ready for take-off, as they had initially taken enough fuel not to need any more yet, and as the drone pilots had sent their aircraft on its way. Mark joined them quickly to minimize the number of people on the ground when the drone would land.

The men could see the drone arrive and were again surprised at how small it looked unless they were standing next to it. The pilot brought it to a virtual standstill about twenty feet above ground and executed a flawless vertical landing; Mike observed that the drone had landed with the weightless attitude of a wader bird. While the first pilot went to disconnect the battery that had provided the energy for the drone to get there, the second pilot brought and installed the second, fully charged battery.

The battery exchange over and the drone sent on its way, the two pilots climbed back into the helicopter, ready for the next leg of the trip, which should take another hour at most. Through the Ambassador and Fernando Solano, Ehud had obtained permission to land at the Siburan Training Camp just outside and to the south of Sablayan. He had felt that the use of a government military facility would help him fuel up to ensure that the helicopter always had all it needed to execute any maneuver. In particular, he understood the next stage would be the Francisco Reyes Airport in Busuanga, and that prudence suggested that they should assume there were terrorists in the area, given the earlier attack on Luis Ramos's Hangar. This was the reason Mark had initially considered nixing that location and looking for another. On the other hand, Ehud had argued:

"There are several flights and several of them with helicopter every day on Busuanga. I accept that the drone would look special, but remember, it is small, and nobody should be expecting it. Even Luis does not know what we are doing. The only thing he knows is that we are dealing with the Twin Island issues as he calls it."

He paused for an instant and concluded:

"Unless the leak we worry about comes straight out of the ministry of Defense, I cannot imagine why terrorists would be watching the airport 24/7."

Mark conceded the point and agreed, if only because there was no way to be certain that any other location would be better, while it was sure that their landing on a small helipad closer to the islands would surely attract even more attention.

The battery exchange at Siburan went like clockwork and the last leg of the flight was totally uneventful as well. Once they had exchanged the battery at Francisco Reyes, the five men boarded the helicopter after the drone pilot had sent the Orbiter Trojan on its way to the largest of the two Twin Islands, the north island.

■ ■ ■ ■ ■

Meanwhile in Manila, as anticipated, Luis was being briefed on developments on the Wilson field. Anthony spoke first and made two main points. The first was that the connection of Well 2 to the subsea completion of Well 1 had taken place, thus doubling the daily production at the site. Looking at Angelo for confirmation, he added:

"This really means that we will need to transfer the oil to a tanker about every third day. The storage capacity of the FPSO is around 50,000 barrels, Angelo, correct?"

"Absolutely. Note that this will require us to organize a tanker shuttle."

He saw that he was losing Larry and thus added:

"Say that the tanker has to sail about 200 nautical miles to Manila. That would take a full day. So, we need a two-boat shuttle: it should provide us with the exact capacity to operate continuously."

Luis was smiling, but still asked:

"Anthony, is that the maximum production rate?"

"Heck No! We could quite likely double it with little or no effort."

Seeing the quizzical look which came on Luis's face, Anthony added:

"Remember, we do not want to draw more attention than necessary. It's already going to be a big enough change for the field to need a two-tanker shuttle to manage our current flow. I would rather keep production at that level and continue to work on the subsea completion for Well 3, leaving aside the management of the construction and installation of the production platform near the Galoc shores."

Angelo was not convinced and asked:

"I know we made that decision earlier, but do we really need to remain discreet as you say. The extent of our work is now hard for anyone to miss. The announcement of the start of production at Well 2 was already noticed by the Makati Stock Exchange. What else do we expect?"

Looking at Larry, Anthony conceded that Angelo's point was valid. Yet, he added:

"Some of what we're doing at Well 3 and around it is top-secret as you know. This is what is costing so much more than usual. The last thing we need is for people to start talking and for the terrorists which we know are active there to get excited."

Luis bumbled and asked:

"When will the defenses be operational?"

Anthony looked at Luis and his eyes conveyed a clear message: *why did you need to say that? Only you, Larry, Ehud, and Mike know. Did you need Angelo to know as well?* He refrained from saying anything when Luis, realizing he had goofed, tried to correct his mistake:

"By 'defenses' I mean the normal precautions you always take . . . We're not doing anything special, are we?"

Though this was not enough, the cat being now out of the bag, Anthony behaved as if it was not and replied:

"As you know, the main challenge is that all the risers, or rather most of the risers we use for the oil to flow from the well heads to wherever it is collected need to be safely anchored in a few places. Currents can become quite violent when typhoons strike, and we need to be prepared. That takes time and effort, although, Thank God, we are dealing with relatively shallow waters."

■ ■ ■ ■ ■

The point which was supposed to remain secret was that Marvin Goldstein had designed and provided an underwater defense system which would have the capacity to shoot mini torpedoes or plain underwater missiles at any target that came too close to a key production element. The system comprised underwater sensors, both photographic and sonar-related, which first warned that something was approaching and, when close enough, used artificial intelligence recognition software to determine whether the intruder was a large fish, a torpedo, a mini submarine, or the hull of a ship. Once that determination was made, the system would fire a mini torpedo or a missile which was designed to harm or maim, but not to destroy completely.

The system was quite complex as it had to be able to operate in all dimensions, up, down and sideways, in short, very much like a radar which one would find at an airport for instance. Though not the easiest, that part was not the most complex, as the sonar which was charged with that role was simply rotating a full 360 degrees around a vertical axis which could also be tilted. The complexity came from both the need for analytic power which required electricity and for shooting power that could also work in all directions. Anthony's invention proved crucial in terms of providing the needed electricity, except for the part of the system which protected the near-shore platform which had its own electrical generators. Using torpedoes with homing features also helped considerably. However, the firing tubes needed to be moved to at least some extent which required some movable and automatically activated metallic infrastructure.

CHAPTER.24

PALAWAN AND MANILA, THE PHILIPPINES

Ehud Shamir, who had served in the Israeli Air Force before joining *Mossad*, brought the King Air 350 to a gentle stop after a perfect landing at the northeastern end of the single runway of El Nido Airport. His approach over the sea had been quite scenic reminding Nate who was seating to Ehud's right of many landings in tourist paradises, which in a way El Nido was. Ehud had stopped just short of a tarmac area to his left and exited the "active runway" to take the lone taxiway and then park the plane in front of what was officially called "the departure lounge," a 230-feet long structure, with two dormers in the roof at either ends, facing both the tarmac and on the other side the countryside.

■ ■ ■ ■ ■

Earlier, Ehud and Nate had discussed the order in which they would check the various airports' log systems. Though it might have been logical to start with the largest airport, they had decided to order their visits by proximity to the oil field and increasing operational complexity. Thus, they would first fly to Francisco Reyes in Busuanga, then to El Nido, to Cesar Lim Rodriguez Airport in Taytay and complete their work at Puerto Princessa.

■ ■ ■ ■ ■

Ehud and Nate repeated the steps which he had followed when they had visited the Francisco Reyes Airport in Busuanga. They walked to the second floor of the terminal, reaching a room where "airport operations" were located. The official letter asking the local manager to extend them all courtesies they requested proved to be the perfect opener, as it had already confirmed its worth in Busuanga.

Once he had the written log of all aircraft movements, Nate started the tedious process of looking through the list seeking anything which might appear suspicious. The logs typically provided the tail number of the aircraft, its point of origin and the destination as stated on the flight plan when the plane took off again. Here, as had been the case in Busuanga where the search had proven futile, Nate was hampered by the obvious fact that he did not know what he was looking for. So it was not a case of searching for something specific. He was also taking pictures of every page to make sure that he could return to any one of them later.

■ ■ ■ ■ ■

In their earlier preparatory discussions, Nate and Ehud had worked together with a map of the South China Sea. They were looking at the various distances from different cities from which the terrorists could fly to one of the four airports on Palawan Island. They had drawn a few rough circles helping them mark broad distances from various points to each of the airports on Palawan. Since they were here looking for flights which might have come from China or North Korea, their two principal suspect countries at the time, they had focused on distances from various points in either country. Though most points in China were closer than any point in North

Korea, Ehud was somehow convinced that any flight coming officially directly from China was unlikely. The risk for China being found out was just too great. At the same time, a flight from Pyongyang was a solid 2,000 nautical miles, and thus did not seem terribly likely either! Not to mention the undeniable fact that aircraft flying from North Korea to the Philippines would never be legions.

Their first break in the search occurred as they were studying the map and thinking of all permutations they could imagine. Ehud suddenly exclaimed:

"Wait a minute. We know that China has built military bases on at least three reefs in the Spratly Islands in the South China Sea."

Rushing to an internet connection, Ehud quickly identified the three reefs by their names: Fiery Cross, Mischief, and Subi. More to the point, the Pentagon map at which they were looking showed that these three islands were surrounded by others where Chinese outposts were already located, though they did not have airfields. Nate cynically added:

"Yet!"

Ehud continued:

"What if the Chinese had chosen to have a plane transit through one of these airfields. Fiery Cross is hardly more than 450 miles and it's the furthest one. Subi is about 350 miles and Mischief Reef barely more than 250 miles, each time depending upon where you land on Palawan."

Nate added:

"This adds at least one degree of complexity to our challenge. Why assume that they would fly a plane? Why couldn't they fly a helicopter, which they surely could from Mischief Reef. They might even than dispense with an official airfield . . ."

Ehud simply replied:

"That would make it next to impossible for us to track them. But something tells me that though possible it isn't the most likely course."

"Why?"

"Well, we don't know how dangerous the packages are when they are flown into the Philippines, or even when they left the place they were prepared. So, though I know helicopters all have a separate small cargo hold, the space is usually very limited and would be shared with any luggage the crew would have."

He paused for a second to check his logic and concluded:

"The cargo holds of many planes, particularly private jets and even private turboprops, do not have that problem. The crew and the passengers could keep their personal stuff in the plane, while the dangerous containers are kept, by themselves, in the hold. First, there is no air communication between the hold and the cabin. Second, the crew would know that nobody touches the hold before it has been thoroughly cleansed, most likely after they've flown back to base, wherever that is."

Nate conceded the point and simply asked:

"So, what are we looking for?"

"My initial guess would be to look for any plane whose flight originated any place in the Spratly Islands as well as any direct flight from China or North Korea."

"That surely narrows the list, but what if they were cleverer than that?"

"We should keep an eye open for other places. There are many islands, but thankfully, not too many offer runways on which you could land a plane with a totally separate hold: I guess we're talking private jets, as well as only a few of the largest twin turbo prop planes."

▌▌▆▌▌

Even with the narrowed list of possible airfields, Nate and Ehud were no luckier in El Nido than they had been in Busuanga at Francisco Reyes Airport. Nate did find more landings from planes which might fit the bill in terms of engines or cargo hold capacity, but none from any of the three suspect Spratly reefs. They immediately flew to Cesar Lim Rodriguez Airport in Taytay, about 15 miles to the southwest of El Nido. Nate joked:

"It would have been almost as fast to drive it . . ."

Ehud deadpanned:

"Not sure given the local roads."

Arriving at the airport, Nate noticed that work was being done to expand the terminal, as well as the area where the lone runway was. Upon querying the local manager, the men found out that the facility was named after Taytay native Cesar Lim Rodriguez, a former judge who donated part of his property for the airport. He learned it was owned by the Province of Palawan which wanted to make it into a competitor to Puerto Princesa, 150 miles further south. They quickly concluded that they were not going to find anything in Taytay. They both knew that Puerto Princesa was the logical choice initially, but they still agreed that the order in which they investigated the four airports was still logical. As Nate noted:

"Any movement in Puerto Princesa is bound to be visible and officially detected."

After arriving at Puerto Princesa International Airport Ehud agreed though he noted that it might have allowed the terrorist to "hide in plain view" as their aircraft was only one of many. Nate remarked that this was the first airport they visited whose terminal facilities really looked like those they were used to in other countries. He was mesmerized by the pillars supporting sections of the ceiling of the terminal; they looked a bit like wooden fans and were set in reflecting pools. Analyzing the activity at Puerto Princesa on any of the days which they were considering, took them more time because of the number of flights. However, it did not prove much more successful, and Nate was surely starting to experience the tedium of the process. Yet, one aircraft movement attracted his attention.

■ ■ ■ ■ ■

One of the filters which Ehud and Nate used when looking for the proverbial needle in the haystack was the date of the aircraft movement. Though nobody really knew when the first attack had taken place, the team had been able to draw up a window which covered not more than two weeks. This was a lot more than for either of the next two attacks, for which there was an actual date when the containers arrived on the Twin Islands. Thus, allowing for at most a couple of days in transit, Nate's search was limited to a small number of days. The most tedious part of the effort involved looking at the aircraft tail number, assuming it was not forged, and finding out what aircraft type it covered.

■ ■ ■ ■ ■

Nate was initially disappointed when he did not find any flight that met the list of potential origins that Ehud and he had drawn up. However, suddenly, Nate's mood changed. He called out to Ehud and told him that he believed he was in luck. He had just found a plane which had landed two days before the second attack, at Puerto Princesa, flying in from Woody Island. For some reason, not knowing where Woody Island was, rather than simply forgetting about it, he chose to investigate it further: it was in the Paracel archipelago. That is when he discovered that China had, since 1974, occupied all the Paracel Islands which belonged to Vietnam. Chinese troops simply seized a Vietnamese garrison and occupied the western island. More importantly, China built a strong military complex there comprising both an artificial harbor and an airfield with a runway able to accommodate most airplanes.

Nate's luck continued when he found out that the people who had arrived on the jet had immediately chartered a twin turbo prop and flown into Francisco Reyes in Busuanga. He hit his forehead with the palm of his hand and turning to Ehud said:

"Why didn't we not flag that one?"

"You mean Woody Island?"

"Absolutely."

Ehud conceded that it was one option which they had not considered. Helping Nate regain his calm, he further added that there were a few internal flights which he could have flagged and did not because domestic flights within Palawan would surely not have appeared suspect.

They immediately called Mark to report on their findings. Mark was obviously delighted, but still wondered what happened to the first and the latest attacks. He could not believe, as he and Ehud had agreed, that the terrorists would bring a supply of virus all at one time, if only because Professor Duchemin had concluded with his colleague Oshima-San that the second wave seemed quite concentrated and thus potentially quite dangerous. Further, if they had, it would have had to occur before the first attack, not before the second. Matter-of-factly, Mark said:

"This is great work you two, but we're gonna have to expand the list of possible airports beyond Palawan. The new thing we learned is that the containers don't have to be flown from overseas to their ultimate destination."

Nate immediately replied:

"Understood. The key is that any domestic flight into the three Palawan airports we're monitoring, since we've given up on Taytay, is potentially suspected. Back to the drawing board, Mindoro here I come . . ."

He paused and added:

"Hey, Mark. Ehud and I have agreed that I can operate solo now. I have my wings and can thus dispense with a pilot. We've also noted that most of the time there's someone in each of these airports which speaks enough English for us to manage to communicate. However, I'll still need the Israeli Embassy to provide an interpreter. My knowledge of Tagalog is too weak, and I would hate to get stuck on a language issue."

Mark simply smiled, thinking: *the plan is working, but they had to discover it by themselves. That will free up Ehud to conduct other work.*

■ ■ ■ ■ ■

While each previous time, the five men had boarded the helicopter as soon as the drone had been sent onto its next destination from Francisco Reyes, they elected to remain on the ground, though in the helicopter and ready to take off. They had not forgotten the terrorist attack on the hangar and wanted to be ready to fly away at a moment's notice. That included having the engine operate at idle so that a take-off would not have to wait until the turbine had been started. Even further, Ehud had organized for the nose of the helicopter to face to the north which was where the terrorists last came from.

The controls which the drone pilot was using comprised both the unit that controlled the aircraft's movements and a laptop screen on which the various images the sensors on the drone were capturing. The drone pilot was seated in the middle seat on the back bench of the helicopter with Mark and Armand Duchemin on either side. The other drone pilot was seated in front on the first officer's seat, next to Ehud. The drone was arriving near the southernmost of the Twin Islands when the pilot turned to Mark:

"Where should I be going?"

Mark replied with a short list of the locations of the three cameras which had been placed on the Island, suggesting that the one furthest to the west was the camera that had picked up some movement. The drone was aimed in its direction while the pilot was simultaneously executing a sharp descent which placed the drone no more than fifty feet above ground. The pilot, Chaim, was now in a search mode somewhere between a normal flight and a hover. While he was not keeping the drone still above a certain point, he was guiding it so that it would move sideways quite slowly allowing Mark in particular to observe the ground. Mark was the one who had gone onto the island to retrieve the last set of containers and he was therefore as familiar with the ground as anyone on the helicopter.

Suddenly Mark said:

"Hold it right there. This must be it."

Turning to Professor Duchemin who was watching the screen of the first pilot next to him he added:

"But wait a minute. This is surely not the same container as the last time."

Armand conceded:

"Certainly not. It's in fact quite a bit larger. Chaim, is there a way we can get closer?"

"The altimeter tells me I can descend a further forty feet, but I would not want to get much lower than half that. The island is fifteen feet above sea level. I'd like to maintain some room to maneuver. You don't want a sudden lull in the wind to create trouble."

Mark suggested:

"Can we try another twenty feet down?"

Chaim simply replied:

"Sure."

Armand observed:

"There is no question this is different. If you look carefully in the northwest corner, if I can talk of a corner in an oval vessel, maybe the northwest quadrant, you can see something shining in the sun. I have absolutely no idea what it could be."

Mike asked:

"Does this mean we don't try to retrieve it now?"

"What kind of protective equipment do you have?"

"Whatever you asked us to take along . . ."

Armand concluded:

"Let's change into these protective clothes here, as discreetly as possible, and let's fly there. Chaim, while we do this, can you look for something similar in the other locations on both the southern and the northern island please?"

Mark interrupted:

"The only other camera that seems to show something is the one that is also on the western side, but on the northern island. I would do a quick reconnaissance flight over the other three cameras, but at this point my two main targets are this one and the other on Northern Twin Island."

Chaim replied:

"No problem. We're on it."

Armand added:

"Just as a precaution, could we ask my colleague Oshima-San to fly in from Japan with as much of his field material as possible. With any luck he can catch a flight and be in Manila this evening. I would rather not waste any time. I must admit that I am truly worried."

He paused for a second and unexpectedly asked:

"Chaim, by the way, can your sensors detect explosives at a distance?"

CHAPTER.25

PALAWAN AND MANILA, THE PHILIPPINES

Mark was waking up from the prior day expedition when his room phone rang. Anthony was on the line and seemed quite anxious to meet him. Mark immediately invited him to join him in The Lobby, the hotel's coffee house, for breakfast.

Anthony did not waste any time after shaking Mike's hand:

"We may have a problem . . ."

"What?"

"Well, Luis made mention of the defenses we were planning at a meeting yesterday."

"Who was with you?"

"Larry, Angelo and Luis of course."

Mark thought for a second and said:

"Not good. Not good at all. Are you telling me that you do not trust someone in particular?"

Anthony swallowed a mouthful of his plain, light, buttery French croissant and simply replied:

"The only person in the group I would totally trust is Larry. But since we have been concerned as to who might be leaking, we have to be concerned that either Luis or Angelo may not be 100% straight."

Anthony paused and added:

"I know that Luis would seem above that, but I have to keep him on the suspect list. Now, with respect to Angelo, I can't think of why he would do this given his purported relationship with Luis, but who knows?"

Mark made a face and reminded Anthony that this was now partially water under the bridge:

"Remember, we went through these paces a few months ago, and we satisfied ourselves that we could not point to either Angelo or Luis. We concluded that either of them might be talking to someone whom they believed was trustworthy but was not."

"I know. I know. However, what if our trap was too obvious then? After all, the leaks have continued whenever there was important news, right?"

Mark could only concede that the problem remained and that the issue of the whole production set-up being defended by sophisticated equipment had to remain totally secret. He and Anthony then agreed that they needed to set up another trap. This would require them to execute a couple of maneuvers without informing anyone and then to announce that they were going to install something important at some specific date. Mark concluded:

"Nothing is foolproof, but I think this should allow us to test the waters. Assuming that we have some measure of success on that, our next step will be to verify our results with another similar maneuver."

■ ■ ■ ■ ■

Nate Heimer expanded his search to three airports on Mindoro Island. Luck was with him as, instructed by his experience on Palawan, he went straight to the largest airport first, leaving the smaller targets for later. San Jose Airport, which used to be known as McGuire field, seemed as it turned out the most logical. First, it was clearly the closest to the action, if action was defined as the drilling site. Though all three possible airports, San Jose, Mamburao, and Lubang serve the Eastern parts of Mindoro Island, San Jose is considerably closer to the Galoc area, with the other two airports being respectively 75 and 100 miles to the north-northwest. Second, its runway exceeds 6,000 feet while those of the other two airports are only around 4,000 feet. Finally, it is fully equipped to deal with regular traffic, including aircraft as large as most single aisle jets such as Airbus 320 or Boeing 737 series.

The manager of San Jose airport was as impressed as those of the other airports Nate had already visited by the official letter Nate showed her. She immediately gave him access to the documents he requested. As he was going through the list of aircraft movements around the dates which might have worked for the first attack, he was initially disappointed that he did not see any incoming plane stating its origin as being Woody Island, though he knew that this was the airport with the longest runway in the South China Sea. However, he found a flight which he immediately flagged as it was coming in from a military airport on Mischief Reef, one of the three Spratly Islands occupied and developed as a military base by the Chinese. Noting that it could fit with the first attack, he took down the specifics of the flight and immediately looked for any aircraft movement that could have coincided with the third attack. That was when he found another flight from Woody Island. Nate was thinking that the Chinese or whoever had been involved surely had not been very careful, at least at the outset. Indeed, while the airport on Woody Island serves for both civilian and military purposes, the airports on any of the three Spratly reefs are strictly military. The first attack had used San Jose.

As he was reporting his findings to Ehud and Mark, the trio was quick to point out that the choice of "departure" airport was very telling. Mark suggested:

"The first attack, if you all remember, was before there was any direct link between Luis's operations and Israel. Thus, one could imagine that the Chinese did not think they needed to be particularly careful. The choice of Mischief Reef makes sense to the extent that it is the closest to the Philippines. Why did they then choose to land in San Jose rather than in Puerto Princesa is less clear."

Ehud observed:

"Not so odd my friend, if you note that the distance between Puerto Princesa and Busuanga is at least two and a half times longer than between Busuanga and San Jose."

Mark immediately came back:

"That does it. They, the Chinese, were looking for convenience. They wanted an intermediate stop somewhere in the South China Sea so that whether the plane came from China or North Korea, the actual origin would not appear anywhere."

Ehud added:

"They might even have used military aircraft or at least military pilots . . ."

"Right. Once it appeared that there might be some form of Israeli involvement, and here I hope no one is talking of *Mossad* involvement, it became considerably more important to muddy the waters. That's when Woody Island came into play, as an alternative to Mischief Reef."

Nate added:

"And they mixed their landing spots choosing Puerto Princesa once and San Jose the other time. As you know, I found out in San Jose that the occupants of the jet that landed there before the third attack did exactly what they had done out of Puerto Princesa for the second: they boarded a smaller plane with a flight plan indicating Francisco Reyes airport as their final destination."

"And as you told us they promptly returned from these trips and flew the jet back to Woody Island!"

Nate confirmed:

"Exactly Mark. Now the one thing I have not had the time to verify yet is whether the planes that landed in Busuanga from San Jose and Puerto Princesa were logged into the aircraft movement log of Francisco Reyes and if yes what their origins and return destinations were. I will ask my interpreter to make a call to the chap I met there."

Ehud interrupted:

"Why don't you let me do it myself? The fewer people in the loop the better."

■ ■ ■ ■ ■

Meanwhile, on Southern Twin Island, the team had returned after having brought the drones back to Francisco Reyes Airport. The two drone pilots had elected to remain there, with all their equipment. They had decided that they had to be ready to send the drone aloft at the first sign of any possible intrusion by terrorists on the airport premises. Mark had rented for them a local 4x4 truck in which they had placed their paraphernalia. This would allow them to drive around and be as inconspicuous as possible. The plan was that the SUV would remain parked close enough to the tarmac so that the pilots could see anyone approaching. If that happened, they would immediately have the drone take off, which was simpler with its electrical power source, as the motor would engage without delay. Chaim would then control it, placing it in a holding pattern, while his colleague, Adam, would drive.

Mark and Armand, with Ehud as their pilot, had elected to deal with the container on Southern Twin Island first, as their earlier survey had shown that there were only two such containers this time. They both had put on the most complete protection outfits they could in two stages: the overall first when they were still at Francisco Reyes Airport; and the last few steps, the overcoat, the hood, and the up-to-knee shoe covers just before they would exit the helicopter. Ehud would only wear protection so that all areas of his skin were covered, and he breathed oxygen from the onboard tank.

Armand climbed down first, as he surely needed Mark's help, hanging from the helicopter's side, which Ehud would keep hovering. Mark joined Armand as soon as Armand was safely on the ground. The Trojan drone had helped dispel the fear that there could be any explosives within the container. Armand then touched with a metal stick the area of the container which he had seen shine in the sun. He was surprised to note that it was a piece of plastic that seemed to cover the inside of the container then. Speaking in his microphone, he said:

"Just as we expected. I bet you the plastic is there to cover the mix of sand and molasses to ensure that it does not disintegrate too quickly when water hits it. See, here, we already have a real water accumulation, which is not surprising during the rainy season. I'm sure most of the mosquitoes are gone, but there's got to be a whole lot of virus here in the solution still in the container."

"Do we stick with the plan in terms of how we remove the container?"

"Absolutely. It looks similar to the previous ones, though larger and oval rather than circular."

Armand proceeded to pump out as much of the liquid that was inside the container as possible and save it in an air-tight bottle which they had brought. He then invited Mark to help him try and lift the container to see if they could move it over a sheet of plastic they had placed right next to it without breaking it apart. Fortunately, the structure was still strong enough that the whole slid onto the plastic without any hiccups. They then covered the container with another plastic sheet. Armand took out what looked like a large, battery-operated vacuum-sealer. This allowed him first to seal the package on three of its sides, transforming it into a plastic bag with an open top. Sliding the last side, the top, into the slot in the vacuum-sealer, he pumped as much air out as he could without causing any structural damage to the container and reserved the air he was pumping in a separate pocket to be able to analyze it later. He then applied heat to seal the last of the four sides. Mark noted:

"Looks great. Rests comfortably on its flat bottom."

"Thanks, the probability of any contagious material leaking out of this, or the bottle is extremely low."

Mark helped Armand attach the package to a harness he had brought with him as he rappelled down from the helicopter. Once the package was attached, Armand paused for a second and added:

"Now, let me spray antiseptic liquid to the outside of both packages. Also, I need to spray the same antiseptic on you and will ask you to do the same for me. That should minimize the risk that we contaminate Ehud as we climb back into the helicopter."

Mark then climbed straight back into the helicopter using the cord that had been kept dangling while Ehud was hovering. Once inside the helicopter, he hoisted the harness and placed the package into a box which they had prepared while at Francisco Reyes. He copiously sprayed its inside with antiseptic and then hoisted the bottle into which water had been pumped and the container into which the air that was inside the container was aspirated. He placed both into the same box and, after having again sprayed more antiseptic, he closed it up tightly. Mark then hoisted Armand's equipment and helped him climb back into the helicopter. Mark used the hoist to lift Armand as he was not sure whether Armand could handle the physical strain of climbing by himself on a dangling rope.

They moved straight to the second container location, on Northern Twin Island. Finding a set-up which looked exactly like the one they had just seen on Southern Twin Island; they simply repeated the exact same steps. They then flew back to Francisco Reyes, and, after having contacted the drone pilots to verify that the coast was clear, landed there. The two drones' pilots quickly slipped into the protective clothing they needed to wear to ensure that no contagion could possibly take place among them. They then climbed into the helicopter after they had launched the drone on its return voyage, which would include the same stops they had used on their way in. Several minutes after takeoff, Ehud noted through his microphone:

"I will not only need to get some fuel at Siburan Training Camp. I'll need to refill our oxygen reserves."

■ ■ ■ ■ ■

Laten on, in Manila, Armand confirmed with Mark their earlier agreement that he should immediately bring Bambi Ruizon into the loop. Understandably, when told, the secretary of health was definitely upset that another attack had taken place, but very effusive in his thanks to Armand and Oshima-San for having taken the bull by the horns. He accepted the request that the news be kept to the fewest members of government officials possible. Though they were all humanly concerned that they should avoid creating panic in the general population, they were even more worried that the terrorists would learn that their containers had been found and in effect neutralized.

Bambi provided them with access to a laboratory where Oshima-San could install the equipment he had brought along with him from Japan. Still with a focus on the need for secrecy, Armand was about to turn down Bambi's offer as he was afraid that somebody would be bound to discover something. Bambi replied:

"Not to worry, Professor, I will make sure that the laboratory where you and Oshima-San will conduct your tests will be locked and that only you have a key to it. I will argue your tests are carried out for a project under my direct control and will insist that I will not tolerate any leak."

"Thank you very much. By the way, your excuse happens to be generally true, isn't it?"

"You're too kind Professor Duchemin."

Oshima-San and Armand proceeded to conduct a battery of preliminary tests first on the liquid that was pumped out of both containers. They were looking for one or several viruses, most likely along with amoebas, and for unhatched mosquito eggs. They also conducted tests on the air which they had aspirated out of the containers before they vacuum-sealed the plastic bags in which they carried it back to Manila.

Neither scientist liked what they found. They decided to call Mark and Ehud as soon as the results were conclusive enough. Armand announced:

"Gentlemen, the good news is that there was no trace of the prior virus in these samples."

Ehud interrupted:

"No trace? That's good news indeed."

Armand's voice did not display any sign of levity when he replied:

"Don't jump to a conclusion my friend. That's good news, but I'm afraid there is bad news as well. Furthermore, I would argue that the news overall is surely not good."

He paused for a second and ominously added:

"We found another virus. The enemy seems to be adopting a new tactic, and it's certainly not welcome!"

CHAPTER.26

PALAWAN AND MANILA, THE PHILIPPINES

Mike called Angelo on the phone:

"Angelo. I just talked to Anthony. He tells me that the first piece of the underwater security system will arrive the day after tomorrow. Everything will take place underwater, sufficiently far away from the increasingly well-developed skeleton of the platform or the FPSO for anyone to know. Yet, you might want Luis to be aware of that. Anthony told me that though the piece is quite important, an outsider would not be able to determine what it is. So, the idea is that he should know, though Anthony believes it would be better for Luis not to get a tour until there is more to see."

■ ■ ■ ■ ■

Meanwhile, the drilling platform that was intended to be placed near the shore of Galoc island had been delivered to Manila harbor in what they called a completely knocked down (CKD) form. All the various components, whether they be technical or structural, were constructed and put together to make sure that everything would function correctly. They were then totally disassembled for the structural parts and only partially for the technical equipment and shipped to Manila harbor. The structure would then be put together, effectively reassembled, there in Manila. It would then be towed out to sea to the desired destination, about 10 miles offshore from the west coast of Galoc Island in northern Palawan. It would then be anchored down to the sea bottom, in this case using precast concrete boxes which were directly anchored down.

■ ■ ■ ■ ■

Earlier in the month, Luis had been invited to come and witness the arrival of the drilling platform. The team had asked him not to make too big a deal about it, as they still felt that there was work to do on the security front. Yet, the fact that the platform was now unquestionably still within the territorial waters of the Philippines was a very important day for both Luis and the Philippines.

Work still had to be done, the most important but not necessarily most visible of which was the anchoring of the platform to the seafloor. Massive concrete blocks had been poured onshore and dropped one by one into the water. The challenge was now to install the impressive screws into the pre-drilled holes in the concrete blocks to secure the platform to the blocks. Initially, a few cables were also positioned around the platform to provide additional support. Serious architectural stress analyses would then be performed to ensure that the original concrete blocks were absorbing all or at least the vast bulk of the load, at which point the cables might or might not be removed.

The work that had still to be done around the platform principally concerned all the different connections between the various risers coming from the field and the equipment which was going to be on the platform, separating the oil from water and impurities, for instance. Initially, both the oil and the gas that would flow to the platform would be stored on it and transferred to tankers that could be moored to it, though the plan was that eventually the gas would surely be piped onshore where one of two things would be done: either a gas-powered electric generation plant would be constructed, or a pipeline would bring the gas to Batangas, at the very south of Luzon Island, where all gas-powered electrical generators already were. Luis had decided that he would prefer not to get involved in the downstream activities, focusing solely on the extraction and commercialization of the hydrocarbons.

The security and defense systems which Marvin Goldstein had designed with the help of Larry Edelstein and Anthony Stacey comprised several key elements which had three main goals. First, detect and if possible identify any underwater threat around the three subsea completions and the platform itself. These involved the use of underwater sensors, both sonar and photographic together with a central computer processing unit located on the platform and able to transmit any relevant information to a control center away from the installation, initially in Manila, but eventually to be located nearer to the platform on Galoc Island.

The second goal involved the surveillance of the waters around the whole of the installations, with a specific focus on the various risers, those bringing the hydrocarbons out, together with their interconnections. This task was entrusted to a couple of self-controlled underwater drones equipped with the same sonar and photographic equipment as those installed around space principally delineated by the three subsea completions and the platform. Marvin had created underwater boundaries using sonar installations at various points along the periphery of the field. They were meant to mimic the installations which one often found for private pool cleaning or automatic lawn mowers. As an example, an automatic pool cleaning apparatus moves randomly within all the sides and the bottom of the pool and changes direction as soon as it hits either a wall or the water surface. In the same way, the two drones would move randomly within the space delineated by Marvin and would bounce off the virtual sides of the space. Marvin had to have two drones rather than one because they were going to use electricity as their power source. They would typically be parked in a recharging bay built on the platform, but under water, when their battery capacity fell below 25%, at which point the other drone which would be fully charged would take over the random patrolling. Again, all signals would be sent to the common control center.

The third goal dealt with defense and involved the mini torpedo installations, located in three strategic places which would be signaled by the control center to fire when an intrusion had been detected, the nature of the intrusion verified, and the decision made to respond.

The delivery to which Anthony referred concerned the second system: the two drones. A couple of weeks earlier, the various sensors were installed which would help both monitor the area from fixed locations and provide the limits to the field which would ensure that the self-propelled underwater drones would remain within the area they were supposed to patrol randomly and automatically. Their first reaction when bumping into anything within the area was programmed for them to move up, down or sideways, the choice being equally randomly selected. On the other hand, when they reached the outer perimeter defined by the sonar beams, their program had them "bounce" in the same way light would when it encounters a mirror.

It is important to note that Anthony and Larry had organized the delivery and installation of the first system without any fanfare and without informing anyone, other than Mark and Ehud. Even Luis had not been made aware of it, and neither was Angelo. The circumstances were virtually ideal. They had used the delivery and anchoring of the platform to have divers install everything else. The most difficult challenge had been for them to dive with sufficient electrical cable to link the various installations to the electricity generator on Anthony's prototype subsea completion. The control center for the system had temporarily been set up in the Israeli Embassy, actually in Ehud's office, using the various communication connections which had to be available on the platform, radio, wi-fi and satellite.

■ ■ ▓ ■ ■

Mark and Ehud had engineered an amazingly simple trap, though it required another of these contraptions for which Marvin was famous. Their idea was that if there was a leak somewhere between Luis and Angelo about the delivery of new equipment, the "other side" would first send something to observe what it was. Everyone on the team was quite convinced that there was only a very small chance that the enemy would send someone. Thus, the odds were against an above surface vessel being sent by the Chinese or their local allies. This would be much too obvious. Plus, a small craft such as a *bigiw* would not provide sufficient stability for any serious underwater inspection to take place.

So, the logical alternative was for the enemy to send one or several manned or unmanned submarine drones to take pictures of what was being installed. Mark initially asked Chaim and Adam whether the Orbiter Trojan drones could detect underwater movements. Their reply was that they should in most circumstances, but they pointed to the real concern that they would need to patrol a large area, constantly, which would require the use of two drones as one could not stay along longer than two and a half hours. So, they would need to establish a base, most likely at Francisco Reyes, and were not terribly anxious to be there by themselves without any backup. Mark hit his forehead with his hand and said:

"Obviously. We would need more people and we don't have them. So, we will need to use our late warning systems,"

He was referring to the undersea sensors. The plan was not complicated though it was going to be tedious, particularly if nothing happened early on. A question which kept swirling around was:

"When will we know they outfoxed us or that the leak which we thought existed was not where we expected it?"

They still decided that Nate would fly a helicopter, dropping Mark off on the new drilling platform and himself afterwards to the FPSO, where the helicopter would temporarily be parked. Ehud would stay in his office monitoring the command center. They hesitated having Ehud and the Embassy technicians rejig the communication lines so that the hardwired system in Manila could rebroadcast to a laptop somewhere on Palawan. They quickly decided against it on the grounds that they did not want to miss any opportunity because of some communication malfunction, or even the possible anticipation by the enemy: they might find a way to scramble the communication . . .

Both Mark and Nate would be on radio standby while Ehud remained in his office. Immediately upon landing on their respective platforms, Mark and Nate would don scuba gear and plunge with an elongated piece of equipment along with them. That piece of equipment would be a dual mini torpedo launcher, which would be temporarily fixed to the platform, sufficiently below sea level to be effective, but not necessarily near the ocean floor. Once contacted by Ehud indicating a possible intrusion, the one nearest to the intruder would trigger his mini torpedo, using an electric connection provided by a cable attached to the launcher at one end and provisionally attached to the deck of the platform or the FPSO. This would prevent them having to redon their scuba gear and control the launchers from below the surface.

■ ■ ■ ■ ■

As soon as Nate came back from his airport tour, as he called it, he and Ehud requested a meeting with Fernando Solano, the Minister of Defense of The Philippines. They gave him chapter and verse as to their discoveries and offered the theory they had developed. In

274 | ANDREW B. LOUIS

their opinion, the ultimate origin of the viruses was still unknown, though they tended to think it was more likely than not coming from outside of China, simply because sending the packages directly from a Chinese laboratory would be just too scandalous if ever discovered. Fernando let them continue though he briefly interrupted:

"I may have a different view on that, but I need to hear more to make sure . . ."

Nate continued and argued that the cargo however one wanted to call it was brought into a Chinese military base somewhere not too far from Palawan. He noted that the two origins he had been able to confirm were Mischief Reef in the Spratly Island and Woody Island which is a *part of the Amphitrite Group in the eastern Paracel Islands* and is approximately equidistant from Hainan and the Vietnam coast. Fernando interrupted again:

"Do you think Vietnam has something to do with this whole thing?"

Nate replied that he understood where the question came from, as the Paracel Islands were captured from Vietnam by China. Yet, he said that he could not imagine how Vietnam would be involved noting that the airport on Woody Island was both civilian and military, suggesting that China was careful to stay at or close to military installations as long as it possibly could. Returning to his flow, Nate then went on to suggest that once the packages had been brought onto Palawan or close enough since one of the packages ended up in Mindoro, a local flight would bring them to their eventual destination. Fernando asked again:

"Why do you think they need some non-Chinese courier?"

Nate replied that it was all a case of not being caught red-handed. Fernando elected to take a different view, arguing that a different theory would be that China was assuring the full logistics until they got to the penultimate flight, leaving the contact, and thus the last flight, to some emissary, possibly from North Korea. Ehud immediately liked the idea, noting that the planes that landed in Puerto Princesa and in San Jose were both registered and chartered in Hong Kong. Nate interrupted:

"Given the distance between Wuhan, the notoriously infamous lab during the Covid-19 pandemic, and Hong Kong on the one hand or Pyongyang on the other, it is not hard to imagine that bypassing the Pyongyang stop would be welcome by everyone."

Ehud added:

"Would not be hard to conclude that the North Korean agents, if they are involved, would be revealed as employed by the North Korean Consulate in Hong Kong . . . And one or several of them might actually be spies operating within North Korea for the benefit of China."

Nate concluded:

"And this would mean that China would never lose control of the biological weapon."

"You said that the planes were chartered in Hong Kong."

"That's true Fernando, but they could easily have been chartered by the Chinese or the South Korean military, couldn't they?"

The story was beginning to take shape, although all three of them realized that their theory was dependent upon a number of assumptions, several of which were not obvious. Ehud asked Fernando whether it would be possible for a good part of the airport surveillance to be taken over by the Filipino Army. Specifically, he suggested that all incoming flights should be monitored, particularly looking for origins in the Spratly or Paracel Islands. His idea was that some mechanism should be put in place so that such flights might be allowed to continue on and to land without challenge, upon which time the passengers and crew would be intercepted by Filipino officials. He added:

"I can't believe they would be traveling on their diplomatic passports . . ."

Fernando came right back:

"Even if they did, we could surely have them wait for a couple of hours while we inspect the plane."

"What if they claimed diplomatic immunity for the plane as well?"

"Well, Ehud, that's when we need to be creative and conduct an inspection without it being called an inspection. Didn't you tell me that your two scientists thought that the biological material ought to be in the cargo hold?"

"Absolutely."

"Well, we can always peek, can't we? Just for health and security purposes obviously. More to the point, just for **their** own health and security purposes."

CHAPTER.27

PALAWAN AND MANILA, THE PHILIPPINES

Professor Duchemin and Oshima-San had called Mike, Ehud, and Nate to join them in the laboratory which Bambi Ruizon, the Health Secretary, had provided them and where they would test both the gel-like liquid and the air that had been collected from the two new containers. As a courtesy, they had also invited Bambi Ruizon to join them for this presentation of their first conclusions. The laboratory looked somewhat like a classroom, with three levels of seats with attached desks looking down to a large marble slab at the front, the desk which a professor would have used. Right behind the desk area, one could see sophisticated equipment behind a glass partition, which was the space where the experiments had been conducted. Oshima-San and Armand sat down behind the desk, while their four guests took place in the wooden seats on the front row of the small amphitheater.

Their first order of business for Armand and Oshima-San was to thank the Health Minister and congratulate him on the quality of the material which was put at their disposal. They added that they were able to do most of what either of them could have done at home, since Oshima-San had brought along with him the samples to which results would be compared. They then immediately dove into the meat of their findings, which as they had warned in their opening statement were not good. Armand started the presentation:

"Friends, though we have not found any trace of the virus which had been present in the last two attacks, we feel that what we did find is more serious. Let me give it to you straight at first and offer explanations afterwards: we found a modified Avian influenza Type A virus."

The room was immediately totally silent as the four guests were sharply focused on every word that came out of Armand's mouth. Though they had a general knowledge of what the bird flu might be, Armand thought he should start with a brief explanation of what Avian influenza really was. He reminded those who might have forgotten that it is a disease caused by an infection with bird flu type A viruses. He added that these viruses typically spread among wild aquatic birds worldwide, eventually infecting domestic poultry, wild birds, and even certain land-animal species. He emphasized that the virus rarely spread to humans, though when it did there were a wide variety of outcomes, from minor discomfort to death. Seeing that his audience seemed to relax a bit at the news, he repeated the point he had made earlier, this time in a somewhat ominous tone of voice:

"Unfortunately, gentlemen, as I said a minute ago, the virus which we found was not the same as the well-known original. We are virtually sure that it has been engineered."

Amid strong facial reactions from "the audience," Oshima-San took over:

"The virus in the liquid we collected seems able to infect humans. By the way, this is not and cannot be described as a normal mutation. This is definitely an attempt to redirect a nasty virus and target it at an extended group of potential victims."

He paused for a second and continued:

"Said differently, we believe that the virus has been genetically altered in what, in virology, we call a 'gain of function.' Now, normally, this gain of function research is designed to acquire a better understanding of current or future pandemics. In those instances, researchers work to get a head start on a virus, for example to develop a vaccine or treatments before the virus naturally develops. However, I don't need to tell you, and the Covid-19 pandemic provided ample opportunity to discuss the issue, that there are times when gain of function refers to research which could enable a pathogen, here a virus, to gain power, replicate more quickly or in general to cause more harm in humans. Armand-San and I believe that this is what we are looking at: a variant of the Avian influenza Type A virus designed to infect humans."

He was about to continue his presentation when Bambi interrupted to ask:

"Is there a treatment or a vaccine against the bird flu virus?

Given the preeminent role of Institut Pasteur in vaccine development, Armand took over and replied:

"The easy answer is yes, sir. But, as is often the case, things are not as easy as they seem. Let me explain. I don't want to bore you with gory and unnecessary details, but you need perspective. Two strains of avian flu have been of greater concern. A(H5N1) appeared in 1996 and was first picked up in Southern China and Hong Kong. It was not terribly well-adapted to humans, as transmission was difficult and human-to-human transmission quite rare. However, when it occurred, the human disease it caused was severe. Unfortunately, it did spread and caused the largest outbreaks in wild and farmed birds ever observed in Europe. The other, A(H7N9), is more recent, having been first found in China in 2013. It was the first time that a low pathogenic avian influence virus was found to cause severe illness and death in humans. Let me simply add that this new virus, we call it a subtype, developed into a highly pathogenic form which also causes human infections."

Mark interrupted Armand's professorial flow:

"Sorry to interrupt, Professor Duchemin, but where are we with respect to vaccines and treatment?"

"You're right to bring me back on point. Sorry, but once a professor, always a professor. The news is good. At least two vaccines have been developed to deal with these strains, and they have proven successful, when used both with poultry and with humans. In fact, A(H7N9) has not been observed since 2019. Additionally, several treatments based on anti-viral drugs have been used with success."

The room was just starting to breathe more easily when Oshima-San came back with the really bad news:

"Though we need more work to be absolutely certain, Armand-San and I believe that we are looking at some genetic modification of A(H7N9). In other words, someone has taken a virus which was known to be transmissible to humans, albeit not always easily, and modified it so that it can be more readily transmitted all the while retaining its lethal power."

Nate could not contain himself:

"But this is criminal!"

Oshima-San replied with an air of unfortunate impotence:

"I cannot disagree with you, Nate-San."

Returning to his earlier flow, Oshima-San continued:

"Our real problem at this time is that we really don't know whether our current treatments and vaccines would be effective against this new strain. We need more time and more tests."

He paused and tilting his head slightly to the right and aspiring air through clenched teeth he added:

"Our assumption should be that the new strain would resist to these treatments or vaccines, if only because whoever developed it would have to have known how the drugs operated and thus have closed that avenue."

Mark asked:

"What can we do then?"

Armand matter-of-factly replied:

"Start the research immediately on this new type. I need to be careful controlling my normal tendency to be an optimist, but we have, no, more broadly, collectively the scientific community has quite a lot of experience with the original virus. I suspect that we will not need to reinvent the wheel. However, in the meantime, we must put in place the most stringent precautions, starting with educating people about the risk."

Bambi interrupted:

"You're going to create a panic, Professor . . ."

"We could, I'll grant you that Mr. Minister. But we don't have to. After all, people have heard of that flu, particularly in Asia since it was more widespread here than in certain other places. Nobody needs to say anything about the variant engineered by the terrorists."

Bambi nodded and calmed down. Mark came back, looking at Bambi:

"It seems to me that we need to pass the baton."

A bit flustered, Bambi replied:

"What do you mean?"

"Well, Mr. Minister, it seems to me that the time has come and gone for our efforts to-date. I believe that we should let your government take over the control and the management of the various activities."

Seeing Bambi twitch in his chair, Mark immediately added:

"Obviously, speaking for the professors, I am sure that everything they have could be made available to you, but my guess is that we need a much sharper policing of borders particularly in the Palawan/Mindoro area. We also need to find a way to root out the

Moro terrorists which seem to have penetrated the territory around Busuanga and maybe even Coron island."

■ ■ ■ ■ ■

Meanwhile, back at the Wilson site, Nate and Mark had taken their respective positions on the two drilling platforms offshore Galoc Island. They both had underwater scooters to speed up their movements if they needed to get into the water. They were linked by satellite phone to Ehud, who, in his office at the Israeli embassy in Manila, was monitoring the signals coming from the first set of defensive infrastructure installed by *Mossad*, unbeknownst to Luis or Angelo or hopefully anyone else not on the small Israeli team. Though they allowed themselves some time to rest, as they had both been provided guest cabins, Mark and Nate were on pins and needles, as the key question was: will anyone attempt anything?

The first sign that something was not totally normal hit Ehud's monitoring device as the sun was setting on Manila Bay. The instruments that had been placed below the surface near the Wilson 3 subsea completion showed a glare in the distance. Although no feature of the intruder was at all visible, Ehud still immediately informed Mark and Nate that there was a potential intrusion coming. He simply said:

"Seems to me to be a light and the Sonar is detecting some mass in that same direction."

Calmly, Mark who was closest to the action if it came to it replied, mostly to Nate's intention:

"I'm on it. Let's allow it to keep coming."

He paused and added:

"Actually, my guess is that nobody will try anything dramatic at this point, if only because they still don't know what they're looking at."

Everybody agreed. Less than five minutes later, Ehud came back:

"It's definitely getting closer. I still can't see the full outline of it, but, to me, it looks like a submarine."

Mark asked:

"What kind of submarine? The sea is much too shallow here to allow a submarine to operate."

Ehud replied:

"That's most probably true for a normal submarine. But what about a small submarine? We know both the Chinese and the Russian have built a few of those. Come to think of it, it could even be an underwater drone; it would have no difficulty navigating these waters."

Nate reacted:

"This is serious. We can't let them take too many pictures, though in truth the only thing they would see is that there are underwater sensors. And even in that case, they are well hidden, aren't they?"

Mark interrupted:

"Agreed, Nate. But still. Ehud, which way is the submarine going?"

"Looks like it is moving in the general direction of your platform, Mark. I am not a betting man, but it would not surprise me if a similar piece of equipment had not already inspected the FPSO set up. Probably before we installed the sensor infrastructure. It's been around for long enough: they'd have had plenty of time."

He stopped for a short second and asked:

"Mark, are we still convinced that this is just an inspection mission?"

Mark replied that he did not see why he should change his mind yet, though he argued:

"Let's remain ready for anything. I don't want to shoot at it right away, but, Ehud, are you sure you could pick it up if the submarine was to drop anything, say a small depth charge, next to a part of our setup?"

"Don't worry. I have it on visual. By the way, it is a small submarine, couldn't have more than a two-man crew. Could also be a drone though. Can't see yet if it has any window."

Ehud suddenly said, his voice a good ten decibels higher:

"Hold it guys. It looks like it has stopped. It is near the area where the riser from Wilson 3 is connected to the one from Wilson 2. What in the world is it doing there? Mark, these risers are not operational yet, are they?"

"No, they're not. They are intended for the time when all production from the three wells goes to the platform on which I'm sitting. They wouldn't want to create an ecological disaster. Wait a tick. If they're after it and know that would not trigger an ecological problem, it must mean that they know they're near a non-operational part of the installation. Now, by the way, how would they know that this is not operational yet? Who told them? Anything more, Ehud?"

Ehud did not reply immediately, but then suddenly said:

"Looks to me as if they are dropping something on the bottom. Can't tell what it is, but it can't be anything good, unless it's their own way of monitoring our activities."

Mark simply replied:

"Let's still hold our fire. I would rather they didn't know the defense capabilities we have. Our torpedoes could easily go after the mini sub, but what would we gain? Ehud, can you see clearly if it is a manned submarine or a drone?"

"With the sharper images I am getting now, my guess is that it is a drone; can't see any glass surface through which humans could see. By the way it makes sense, why would they take the risk of humans being captured at this point."

"Agreed. But what that means is that the stuff the drone dropped could be anything. Could even simply be a mine which we might trigger if we come too close to it."

CHAPTER.28

PALAWAN AND MANILA, THE PHILIPPINES

Mike Loeb decided that he needed to know more about the potential leaker of information, the mole as he called him. This time, the fact that an "enemy inspection" of their new production installations had taken place right on cue left virtually no doubt. The only two potential suspects had to be either Luis or Angelo. It was time for him to find out, so that *Mossad* and Eli Abelman could take the necessary measures.

However, he quickly realized that he could not do anything himself. What grounds could he possibly have as an executive of Eli's company to ask a private detective for information on two Filipino citizens, one of whom was a well-known billionaire? He called a meeting with Ehud and Larry at the Israeli embassy after having checked his intuition and his logic with his boss in Tel Aviv, David Heller. David had agreed that he had to tackle that issue however unpleasant the implications might be, particularly if the leaker was Luis.

Larry was the first to speak:

"As you both know, I did my normal due diligence on Luis Ramos De Ayala when we were about to sign our joint venture agreement. At that time, I did not find anything that seemed to raise any flag."

Mark asked:

"Would you be in a position where you might share these findings with us?"

"Can't see why not, though I would first want to get Eli's agreement."

He paused for a second and asked:

"What would you be interested in?"

Mark had a short laugh and replied:

"The whole lot . . . At this point, I can't think of anything, but let's play this along among the three of us. What could be a red flag?"

Ehud answered first venturing that any financial difficulty, though currently hidden, might have put him under pressure. Larry conceded that a scenario such as this might make sense, though he immediately added:

"The Wilson field discovery pretty much rules this out, doesn't it? It's bound to enhance his financial position, right?"

Mark agreed that the logic held, though he painted a scenario where it would break down:

"Imagine that he made a bet against the field ever being as successful as it turned out to be. It would have been logical for him to try to unload some of the financial costs onto someone else, who would be a better victim than Eli? Now, assume further that he had made his bet by shorting stocks in the listed members of his consortium. He would be bleeding badly now and would need help to cover his bet."

Larry could not help himself:

"Quite a vivid imagination if you allow me to give an opinion, Mark. However, I must tell you that it does not look like we have our answer. I know that the Philippines just allowed short selling and our conversations with Luis substantially predate that official announcement. So either he could not do it legally and didn't or he did it illegally and behind the scenes . . ."

Mark would not give up so easily:

"What if he had been selling stock to the Chinese?"

"What stock?"

"It would have to be stock in his company as he could not be selling shares he did not have."

Larry thought briefly and simply concluded:

"I'm prepared to grant you that this is remotely possible. However, for my money, I'd look for something more convincing."

Ehud asked:

"Do we know if Luis has ever had or still has any business deal with the Chinese? Something they could hold over his head to blackmail him. Something like we'll ruin you if you don't cooperate . . ."

Larry replied that he did not find any trace of such a deal when he carried out his due diligence. Ehud pushed back and wondered whether he was in some way indebted to the Chinese. Again, Larry said that if such a loan existed, it had not been disclosed. Ehud pushed further arguing that being indebted could mean anything, including some non-financial issue. Mark came into the dialog and suggested that some background check should be carried out on Luis, arguing:

"As always guys we don't know what we don't know. Ehud is there a way in the Philippines to have someone do that checking without it leaking all over the place?"

"The embassy has someone whom we use. I never used him in my *Mossad* capacity but have asked for a few background checks on certain individuals. We couldn't use him without Aaron Meyer knowing, but that shouldn't be a problem. That's neither expensive nor sensitive; Aaron delegates these decisions to his attachés."

Mark concluded that Ehud ought to move ahead with that background check and asked whether it could also include Angelo in the same mandate, adding:

"I don't know what we'll find, but at least we will have done everything we could."

■ ■ ■ ■ ■

Meanwhile, at the Wilson Field site, Mark and Nate were very carefully monitoring the movement of the mini submarine. Nate suddenly interjected:

"Hey, I've got a thought. The special anti-fire and anti-explosion blankets that are routinely stored on production platforms, you know when a fire starts at a wellhead . . ."

"Yes, so?"

"Couldn't we use one here?"

"Great idea, Nate, you're thinking of finding a way of depositing one on whatever the submarine dropped off."

"Exactly."

Mark seemed to go back on his initial reaction when he said:

"Hold it. If it's a mine, how do we know that it won't explode as bringing the blanket there creates currents?"

Nate realized immediately that Mark's caution was warranted. Yet, he replied:

"I know it could be expensive if we are wrong, but couldn't we use the two underwater drones?"

"Which ones?"

"Those which we use to monitor the field and were just brought in?"

Though Nate could surely not see it, Mark was smiling as he said:

"Hey, not bad; not bad. You might have the solution. Let me call Marvin Goldstein on the satellite phone and find out what we would need to do. I'll let you know as soon as I hear from him. He's going to hate me since it is quite late in his evening now. But we can't wait."

Within less than thirty minutes, Mark was back in communication with Nate:

"Marvin was chuckling as I was talking. He thought it was a great idea. He took me through the steps that needed to be taken to change the drones' function and to set them back to their automatic mode once we were done."

Mark went up onto the platform to the small cabinet where secondary controls for the drones were located. He sent one of the drones to Nate after having asked him to tie an anti-explosion blanket to the drone. The second drone was then charging its battery, but Mark decided that it had enough power already to carry out the mission. Once Nate told him the first drone was ready to bring the blanket to him, Mark called it back and brought it to the platform. He had elected to make the trip with the drone skimming underneath the surface rather than further down to minimize drag. He attached the other end of the blanket to the second drone and proceeded carefully to pilot them both toward the package which the mini submarine had dropped. He positioned the two drones, a few centimeters at a time, until he was sure that the blanket would cover the package when it was dropped. They both had jerry-rigged the attachment so that a short burst of electrical energy would release the clip.

Two short bursts of energy later, Mark saw the blanket gently float downward. *Hope there are no currents which could jeopardize the mission* was all he could think. He was greatly relieved when he noticed that the blanket was now on the package and that there had not been any explosion. He called Nate to tell him that he was bringing the drones back to the platform where he sat and asked him to join him, using his underwater scooter. Nate agreed though he asked:

"What's up?"

"Remember when you said that we should check that our theory is correct?"

"What?"

"Yes. You suggested that we should drop something heavy as close to on top of the package now below the blanket as we could . . ."

"I remember now. If the package somehow contains any explosives, the stuff we drop on it should trigger an explosion and it should be far enough from either of us. Don't know how well the drones would fare."

Mark deadpanned:

"It's a lot easier to replace them than to replace us."

Nate still had another question:

"How are we going to carry that heavy load? The drones do not have any attachment that allows them to carry a parcel."

Smiling though Nate could not see it, Mark replied:

"I know. I know. That's why you will not swim back to your platform but will come to join me. We will bring the two drones here together; we'll place something in between or rather on top of them. We'll pilot them as close together as we can back to the place right above where the package and the blanket are, and we'll drop that something by moving the drones away from each other."

Nate conceded that the idea was great and simply added:

"That'll be the point at which we'll risk losing the drones . . ."

"I suspect we can mitigate the impact by bringing them closer to the surface so that if anything explodes, they will be far enough away given the role that the blanket should play."

"Agree, but we don't want to be too high as currents might make us miss our target."

"I see we're on the same wavelength my friend."

■ ■ ■ ■ ■

Ehud had another conversation to brief Ambassador Meyer. His goal was to prepare the ambassador for another meeting with Fernando Solano. Aaron was greeted warmly when he entered Fernando Solano's office:

"What will you require this time, my friend?"

Aaron prefaced his reply with a brief outline of the developments on the drilling site, in particular as far as the mini submarine intrusion was concerned. He was delighted to report that "his people" had been able to retrieve the package dropped by the mini submarine and that it was not anything directly dangerous, something that could explode. Rather, it was just a box containing several sensors which would inform its "masters" as to what was happening on the site. Fernando congratulated Aaron but chided him for having carried out the operation on his own, adding:

"There was a lot of danger in the mission. We could have helped you and avoided many of the risks which you people took."

Aaron did not know how Mark and Nate had operated, as Ehud had not felt it necessary to bring him into the loop with respect to the "hidden security precautions." Staying focused on what he thought were the needs which could be met by Filipino resources, he replied:

"Thanks for the offer, but I guess our people did not want to bother you. Now, in terms of what we now need near the Wilson site, I think we have to add some protection. We need maritime as well as ground surveillance. We need maritime surface surveillance around the field, probably with some visible Coast Guard presence, obviously within the country's territorial waters. I also think that we will need some protection for the hangar at Francisco Reyes and in the general area including Galoc island."

Fernando came back with a crucial question:

"What do you worry most about?"

Aaron smiled and jokingly initially replied:

"Do you have an hour?"

Fernando smiled broadly. Then returning to his serious self, Aaron rattled off the three main risks:

"My biggest concern relates to sabotage of the infrastructure because it would hurt the field considerably and could lead to an ecologic catastrophe. As I understand it, the consortium is in the process of installing primary underwater defenses, but one must guard against both punctual acts of sabotage and some more serious attack, say an arial drone or a missile, or both."

He paused for a second and continued:

"Next, we must worry about the safety of all personnel. As you know, people live on the FPSO and will eventually be on the platform as well, but they must rotate in and out at regular intervals. This would be when they would be exposed to kidnaping or worse. Finally, we must ensure operational safety within the whole area."

"What do you mean?"

"Well, I am talking of safety at the airport which is bound to become more active. I am talking of safety on the site where the gas-powered electric generator might be built. I am talking of the villages where new permanent residents are bound to make a home."

Fernando smiled and said to Aaron that he admired the extent to which he and his people had thought the project through. Aaron smiled back and simply said:

"We try our best."

Fernando replied:

"And your best is plenty, my friend."

CHAPTER.29

PALAWAN AND MANILA, THE PHILIPPINES

While Aaron was in his meeting with Fernando Solano, Mark and Nate had elected to return to their positions on their respective platforms in the Wilson Field. Ehud was himself in his office monitoring the various sensors which the team had put in place.

▌▌■▌▌

Later the prior evening, Mark, Nate and Ehud had gotten together for a quiet dinner to discuss their next steps. They quickly agreed on the need to have Aaron Meyer go ask for official help with a visit to the Secretary of Defense Fernando Solano. The other decision they made was that they should maintain as close as reasonable a surveillance of the oil production site. As Mark explained:

"After all, what we now know was that a sensor box dropped by the enemy is no longer there. Thus, whatever information those who placed the box were expecting, is not forthcoming. My guess is that they will wonder why. They might also immediately try something else."

He paused briefly and added:

"Or at least want to go and find out what happened to their package."

Ehud agreed yet asked:

"What do you think they can do?"

Mark candidly admitted that he did not know. He was visibly thinking when he blurted out:

"What would we do in their place? How about assuming that the box is malfunctioning? What options do they have then? They can go retrieve it and inspect it in the mini submarine if it is manned or in whatever mothership there is, if it is a drone submarine."

Nate cut in:

"I see where you're going. If they follow your logic, they will discover that the box is no longer there. They will not know that we went and picked it up once we saw that it had not exploded after we dropped that boulder on top of it. So?"

"Two options. First, they could assume that it had been moved by currents and they would look around the whole place. Second, they could assume that it has been discovered and they might try something nastier."

Ehud could not resist:

"Nastier? What do you mean?"

Mark was ready with an answer:

"I would assume that they would not simply replace the box. If I were they, I would either place another box with some photographic component to see what is happening to it, or I might booby trap it so that whoever tries to retrieve it the same way they picked up the first would blow themselves up."

Ehud concluded:

"Nastier indeed."

Mark and Nate flew to the Wilson field by helicopter, with Mark taking his station on the platform and Nate on the FPSO, both in full scuba gear and with their underwater scooters at the ready. In a repeat of their last experience, the mini submarine was announced by Ehud several minutes before it reached the scene. Mark reminded Nate that they should still hold their fire, if only to see what the enemy is doing. He still told Nate to swim in the direction of the spot where the last package was dropped, but to make sure that the scooter's forward lights were not on. If they were on, he should stay out of the likely field of vision of whoever was following the progress of the submarine. He asked:

"Can you follow your progress on the GPS screen on the scooter?"

"Sure. I'll dim it to minimal luminosity for safety. To be safe, I'll follow the riser. We both know that it ends up very near the spot the submarine should be looking for. We don't want the mini submarine to see me."

"Good. Make sure you also have a torpedo launcher. You never know."

The submarine had by then slowed down considerably, as if it was looking for something. Mark assumed, correctly as it turned out, that since the box was surely not emitting any signal, the submarine would soon find out that the box was no longer there. Whatever credit the enemy earlier gave to the notion that something had malfunctioned inside the box had by then gone out the window. That was when, in Mark's calculations, the submarine would start to look around the original drop spot, hoping to find the box if it had drifted or debris. Finding neither except for what looked like a larger than usual piece of rock, the mini submarine would retrace its steps. With the sequence of events unfolding eerily and exactly as Mark had anticipated, Nate powered his scooter to the surface and asked Mark for instructions. Mark asked him for his thoughts, and he simply said that he could not believe that this was it. Mark offered:

"Exactly my thoughts as well."

He paused and added:

"My guess is that it has gone back to the host submarine. The key is what is it that it'll come back with?"

"Agreed. I'm going to tread water around here for a while. Mark, by the way, did you switch on your stopwatch when Ehud said the mini sub was returning to the mothership?"

"Sure have. Mind you, it's gonna be hard to determine how far the host sub is since we don't know how fast the drone goes and how long it would take for it to load whatever it will be bringing back."

"Can't debate that, but it should still give us a few insights. Assume it is going at maximum speed of 15 knots and that it should not take more than five minutes to load whatever they want it to drop here."

"Sounds reasonable, Nate. But these numbers must be seen as within a wide range. Correct? Let me ask Ehud how far from here a full-size submarine would have to stop because of depth issues."

Within seconds, Mark was back on the mike with Nate:

"Ehud says assuming that the submarine needs at least 150 feet of water to navigate comfortably, it could be anywhere. The water depth around here is apparently between 150 and 250 feet."

Ehud came back on the line:

"Mini submarine back in the area."

Nate immediately replied:

"Am going back underwater . . . with the scooter and all lights out."

Mark did not feel he needed to reply. He just waited at the surface so that he could still communicate with Ehud. He did not have to wait long before Ehud announced:

"The mini sub is in the vicinity of the earlier drop."

Mark sent a sonar signal to Nate asking him to fire a mini torpedo at the drone. At the same time, he asked Ehud:

"Can you tell me the vector I should use to launch another torpedo at the mother ship. Based on the time it took the mini sub to do the roundtrip I guess the mothership is less than 4 miles away."

"285 degrees."

Mark positioned the torpedo launcher that was attached to his platform so that it could fire in the appropriate direction and fired. He did not expect the torpedo to sink the submarine host, but it should create enough of a shock that the sub would feel it and likely elect to move away. He still added with a mischievous note to Ehud:

"Unless it chooses to torpedo the platform."

▪▪▪▪▪

Days later, Mark and Nate found themselves in Ehud's office. The point of their meeting was a review of the first findings of the private detective whom Ehud had hired to learn more about Luis and Angelo. Ehud did not seem terribly satisfied as he started his briefing:

"Friends, we haven't really made much progress. I hate to say it, but so far both individuals look totally clean."

Mark was surprised that they could not get a bit more detail on Luis:

"With all that is publicly available on him, I hoped that your detective would be able to give you more information . . ."

"Well, yes and no. As you can imagine, I had done my share of digging before I elected to develop Luis as a contact. Remember, at that time there was no oil exploration project, other than the semi-successes that had been widely reported by the Press. So, I was looking to Luis for his contact within the government and the leading businessmen circles."

"Nothing stood out then I presume?"

"Absolutely, Nate. He looked quite clean, even though, somehow, in the back of my mind, I was wondering about his need to keep the "De Ayala" name."

Nate interjected again:

"After all, he was already quite a successful businessman, though he did not quite have the wealth or the clout of the other branch. Why would he not be proud of his own achievement?"

Ehud replied that one of the particularly important traits of Filipino business culture was the combination of pride and modesty. He took this further:

"Filipino culture frowns on people who focus too much on individuality; they call it '*pakikipag-kapwa tao.*' This extends into what they call '*nakakahiya,*' which has people toe the line for fear of being different in a negative way. Finally, you have '*utang ng loob,*' which leads Filipinos at times to view favors as something which can extend down several generations. In short, a bit like certain Europeans, they value lineage and do not boast of their success. Take it a step further and you'd get the classic case of the man who has been successful but claims that the wealth that he has was in truth built by his parents."

Mark took exception to the point:

"How does that fit with the conspicuous consumption of which you see quite a bit?"

"Grant you that one. The point is that Filipino culture does not look down on success, it only tends to look down on success which seems to be claimed as one's sole responsibility, if I am making sense."

Mark conceded that the point though subtle was valid and paraphrased his colleague's insight:

"So, what you're saying is that Luis may have kept the 'De Ayala' in his name as an act of modesty allowing others to attribute some of his success to his lineage."

"Precisely."

"So where does that leave us?"

Ehud replied that there did not seem to be any ghost in Luis's closet. He said that his detective had found the odd minor issue, a couple of stories about extra-marital affairs many years ago, but again stated that this was not anything unusual in the region. He added that Luis seemed to have connections with the government, though he never seemed to be too heavily leaning to one side or the other of the political spectrum. Mark asked:

"Is there anything else we can hope to find?"

"The only avenue would be in his relationships with less senior members of officialdom."

"Less senior?"

"Yes Nate. It looks as if anything he has done with people at the minister level is above board . . ."

Nate cynically interjected:

"Or done carefully enough that no one will ever find out . . ."

Ehud conceded:

"Possible."

He then added:

"However, corruption here tends to involve people below the most senior level. They're the ones who make policy in the sense that their recommendations are usually accepted by the top echelon; I guess I'm talking of the difference between career government officials and political appointees."

Mark asked whether the detective had found any such contacts. Ehud immediately conceded that he had found several, adding:

"I would have expected him to find them. Remember, this is how certain things are done here."

"Anything more we can learn?"

"Not from the detective, Mark. I think that our next step on that front is to have a frank discussion with Luis."

"One on one?"

"Probably. He thinks you are employed by Eli and does not know about Nate."

Shifting gears Mark asked:

"And how about Angelo?"

Ehud shifted in his chair and looked seemingly embarrassed. Mark asked what the problem was. Ehud then blurted out:

"At this point, nothing. Absolutely nothing. You'd have to have a mind prone to conspiracy theories to develop anything. Moreover, you'd have to go back to the time quite soon after his birth. He was born on Mindanao, was orphaned quickly but we don't know how or exactly when. He was adopted by a couple from Manila who had been posted there. They brought him afterwards to Metro-Manila where they had returned. Great schooling and highly visible loyalty to both his adoptive parents and to Luis."

Nate asked:

"But why do you say that what you just told us could be the basis for a conspiracy theory?"

"Mindanao has been a hotbed of Moro nationalist activities."

Nate laughed and said:

"I see. The fact that he was born there would mean that he never totally forgot his past. And that somehow maintains some contact."

Mark added:

"Possible, Didn't forget his past, or equally likely went back looking for it at some point and . . ."

■ ■ ■ ■ ■

Back at the oil production side, Mark and Nate could not verify whether the second torpedo had caused serious damage to the submarine they believed was of Chinese origin. Yet they clearly heard a sound that convinced them that the torpedo had exploded. As they had regrouped on the platform closest to shore, Mark said:

"Clearly the torpedo hit something. Now whether it hit the submarine, or some anti-torpedo defense launched by the submarine we'll never know."

Nate nodded and suggested that they should first keep watching with their infra-red binoculars for a submarine breaching the surface of the sea in the distance and ask Ehud to be on the lookout for its movements if it should stay underwater. Mark agreed and added:

"I'm training the defensive system of the platform in case they decided to send a torpedo our way."

Nate agreed and noted that the network of sensors they had placed throughout the field would give them ample notice, adding:

"And we're not lacking in firepower!"

CHAPTER.30

PALAWAN AND MANILA, THE PHILIPPINES

Luis was initially quite surprised by Ehud's phone call:

"Why do you need to see me so quickly?"

"I can't discuss it on the phone, Luis, but trust me it is quite important."

Luis agreed to have lunch at the Manila Club that same day. Initially, Luis was not really sure that he wanted the meeting to take place in a public place. But the setup of the Fairways Grill was such that he eventually agreed: the tables were somewhat further apart than in many other locations, and, at this time of the year, during the rainy season, the club was not overly crowded.

"What can I do for you, my friend?"

"Well, Luis, I need to talk to you because my colleagues and I have come to the conclusion that there is a mole in your organization . . ."

"Wait a minute Ehud, wait a minute. A mole? That's a big word. Someone is spying on us?"

"Yes. A mole. Each time there has been any new news with respect to activity at the Wilson oilfield, some terrorist act has taken place."

Luis looked noticeably uncomfortable, but did not say anything, just encouraging Ehud with the look on his face to keep going. Ehud added:

"I must tell you something which will not make you happy, but, please, hear me out as it was done in order to help you."

Luis grimaced but still managed to keep calm. Ehud had decided when he prepared for this meeting with the help of Mark and Nate, that they had to come as clean as possible. Adopting his best diplomatic habits, Ehud explained to Luis that there had been a few actions that had taken place, at the field, of which he, Luis, had not been made aware. That did it, without raising his voice too much he still exclaimed:

"How could you do that?"

Calmly, Ehud replied:

"Please, hear me out."

He could see that Luis was grudgingly going to let him carry on and so told him that the coincident advent of terrorist attacks each time something favorable occurred in the field quickly became too much for them. Bringing Mark into the picture, he even added:

"Mike was getting quite concerned that the security of the project might well be impossible to ensure if that particular issue was not resolved."

Luis asked:

"Why did he not tell me about it?"

"In truth, he broached the topic with Eli Abelman and Larry Edelstein. He works for them, you know?"

"Guess so, but it does not feel good to learn that I was not in the loop. I own the thing, don't I?"

Ehud decided at that point to play one of the few jokers he had in his hand. He said:

"Luis, play along with me on this for a second. Let's assume that everybody knew that the mole so to speak could not be you. Why would you do this? Damaging your own project and what you've told me was your dream would make no sense? Agreed?"

"Sure."

Luis who had by then gotten a bit more into the game still noted:

"What if I was subjected to some blackmail?"

"We thought of that but decided that we would only deal with it if everything else failed. Between us, I can tell you that we had agreed that if it came to that we would come to you and ask you point blank. After all, there are ways to deal with blackmailers . . ."

For the first time, Luis smiled and then said:

"So, keep going with what you called your game."

"Don't mind if I do. If you were not the mole, it had to be someone close enough to you to be aware of what was going on . . ."

"Angelo?"

"Well, he does fit the bill. However, he is not the only possible suspect."

"Who else?"

"Is there someone in any of the various ministries with whom you shared some of the progress?"

Luis' look became somber as this was surely not a question he had contemplated. Yet, now well-aware of the Filipino culture which emphasizes kindness and relationships, he was realizing that he might have been his own worst enemy. He conceded:

"I did share a few details with at least someone who has been my contact at the Department of Energy. He is quite close to the secretary, and he has helped me smooth out a few rough surfaces, if you see what I mean."

Ehud looking straight in Luis's eyes said:

"He's got to be a suspect too . . ."

Luis's face displayed total surprise and suddenly turned quite worried as he said:

"Oh My! What can we do now?"

Ehud pretended to think, though he already knew exactly what he was going to say next. Suddenly he blurted:

"Do you suppose we could get permission to place a tap on the phones of these two individuals?"

Luis seemed even more lost. He knew very well that telephone taps are illegal unless approved by the Secretary of the Interior and Local Government Miguel Santagio. He explained his predicament:

"Miguel Santagio, the Interior Secretary, is very close to Benjamin Duarte, the Secretary of Energy. Now I am sure that Miguel would have no difficulty with the tap on Angelo. But asking him to place a tap on the chief of staff of one of his friends and allies in the cabinet is a different story. Do you see the problem?"

"Sure do, my friend; sure do."

Ehud kept up the pretense that he was thinking of the issue for the first time and then came back with "a thought:"

"Do you know of any reason the Chief of Staff of the Energy Secretary would want to support local terrorists or a foreign country?"

Luis was again blindsided. He asked Ehud why he was asking the question. Ehud simply explained that there were only three reasons why someone would serve as a mole, kidding:

"We call that person a mole, but years ago we might have used words like spy or traitor."

Seeing that Luis was not reacting to his quip he proceeded to list the three reasons one might become a mole: religious or ideological beliefs, ethnic or related convictions, or simply blackmail . . ."

"Blackmail?"

"A girlfriend that is not supposed to be known about, gambling debts, some past shady act that's coming back to bite you . . . You see?"

Luis only replied that he could not think of anything with respect to the first two categories, though he immediately added:

"Your first example could just as easily fall into the blackmail category, my friend."

"OK. Agreed. So?"

"I wouldn't know where to start to try and uncover any attempt to blackmail Ignacio Bantag."

"Ignacio Bantag?"

"Sorry. He's Ben's chief of staff."

"I assume you mean Benjamin Duarte when you say 'Ben,' correct?"

"Absolutely. You know our tendency to use nicknames."

Ehud shifted gears:

"How about Angelo?"

"He's like a son to me, though I know he still maintains excellent relations with his adoptive parents."

"Anything special in his past?"

"Nothing to note."

Luis paused for a second and blurted out:

"Hold it. He was born in Mindanao of native parents."

He quickly corrected himself:

"But that's more than 40 years ago. No, forget it—can't be."

■ ■ ■ ■ ■

Luis remained adamantly opposed to the idea of bringing the Secretary of the Interior into the loop, even though they had known each other when Miguel served as Chairman of the Metropolitan Manila Development Authority. At that point, Ehud simply said:

"I'll report our conversation to Mike Loeb and see what he says the consequences are from a security standpoint . . ."

Luis asked:

"Is there a way it can be done without anyone knowing here in Manila?"

"I assume that by 'it' you mean the phone lines being tapped, correct?"

With a bit of a sheepish look on his face, Luis replied a simple: "Yes."

"Unfortunately, as you know, I'm only a humble military attaché. So, frankly I wouldn't know how it could be done. At the same time, I have strong suspicions that this is routine work for secret agents. Rather than approaching Mike who, I'm sure wouldn't know either, let me talk to Tel Aviv."

"Thank you. Whatever they tell you, I don't want to be in the loop if they agree to do it."

"Sounds perfectly reasonable."

■ ■ ■ ■ ■

The following week, the usual monthly meeting of the main characters involved in the Wilson Field was being held in the Board Room in Luis's offices. Attending were Luis, Larry Edelstein representing Eli, Anthony Stacey representing the advanced oil technology operations, Mike Loeb representing field security, Angelo DeSousa Luis's right-hand man, and Ehud representing the Israeli Embassy. The mood in the Board Room was quite cheerful. By then all three wells had entered production, though at a reduced level as all the shore infrastructure was still not fully operational.

Luis asked:

"Angelo, when can we hope to reach normal production capacity?"

Angelo looked a bit surprised as he believed that Luis had always been in loop when production level decisions had been made. He elected to deflect the question saying:

"This is really a question for Anthony."

Anthony did not hesitate to reply, though he provided more information than the strict answer Luis was seeking. He prefaced his reply with a comment on the fact that he preferred for production not to be pushed up too quickly, in his words:

"At least as long as the Coast Guard protection is not in place."

Everyone noticed that Angelo looked totally surprised. He had not been a party to any of these conversations. He blurted out:

"What Coast Guard protection?"

Mike took over and replied that the Israeli Ambassador, speaking on behalf of Eli Abelman had requested visible protection around the Wilson field as a condition for bringing the third well into "full" production. He added:

"The Secretary of Defense was quite willing to oblige, as the request was smartly couched in terms that covered the security of the whole area. He committed to create a port near Galoc, very much in the same way as the Port of San Fernando was created at El Nido, although the hydrocarbon wealth that is now apparent will likely justify having some permanent Coast Guard presence to monitor the whole area in the not-too-distant future. In the meantime, we expect a Coast Guard cutter to be anchored or at least cruising in the vicinity of the Wilson field."

Mike paused and added, as an afterthought:

"And he has committed to have any flight coming in from suspect overseas locations inspected upon landing at any airport in the Palawan and southern Mindoro area."

Angelo smiled an awkward smile and mumbled:

"What a great piece of news. This is fabulous. I knew that you were going to help create defenses for the platform, but this is a lot better, than I would have ever hoped for."

Mike smiled.

■ ■ ■ ■ ■

A week later, Ehud was having lunch again with Luis at the Fairways Grill, but this time, Luis had called Ehud to discuss an issue with him. As the opening chit chat was lasting longer than normal, Ehud told Luis that the news he had was not good. Luis looked quite surprised. Ehud explained to Luis that somehow some phone taps had been put in place. Luis grunted but did not say anything more. Ehud kept going:

"I hate to say that, but neither Ignacio nor Angelo placed or received any suspicious phone call."

He paused and added:

"I was told by Tel Aviv that there was no activity near the sites when the virus had been deposited the first time. You know? The Twin Islands."

"That's great news Ehud."

Ehud in turn asked Luis:

"What is it that you wanted to discuss?"

"Well, I think your news is great, but mine is downright worrisome. Unfortunately, we noticed activity in both El Nido and at Francisco Reyes Airport. Somehow, someone knew of both the offices or hangar space we maintain and a couple of so-called 'last notices' were nailed to our doors."

"Last notices?"

"Yes. Propaganda papers which were couched in clearly threatening terms. No room for misinterpretation. We were told as I just said in no uncertain terms that we should negotiate with the Moro Liberation Front as soon as possible."

"About what?"

"They want a piece of the action . . ."

Ehud startled Luis with his next statement:

"Hold it right here, my friend. Do you notice the timing again? Less than a week after the news of the Coast Guard protection is shared with a few more people, including Angelo, a security issue crops up. Did you share anything with Ignacio?"

Luis could not hide his profound anguish:

310 | ANDREW B. LOUIS

"It's Angelo . . . Correct?"

"I don't know my friend. I really don't know. We didn't pick up any suspect activity on his phone. So, question: how was he able to pass the message onto anyone without using his phone?"

"Email?"

"Sorry, wasn't supposed to tell you that, but both your office network and his personal Gmail account were bugged as well."

Luis was about to let out steam, when he realized how pointless the reaction would be. Sheepishly he asked:

"Any email traffic?"

"Nope!"

CHAPTER.31

Armand Duchemin opened the meeting with a strong sentence:

"Gentlemen, I must tell you that we came unfortunately very close to a full catastrophe."

Armand Duchemin and his Japanese colleague Koichi Oshima had agreed to give a last briefing on the outcome of their research into the viral attacks. Though various parties had surely heard bits and pieces of their conclusions as the two scientists proceeded along their analyses, everyone had agreed that it would be great to hold a final, almost "plenary" session to ensure that everyone was on the same page.

In truth, the idea had come from Mark and David Heller who had discussed this earlier. While their concern was surely that everyone had all the available information, they had also decided that bringing the matter to a close as well as expanding the circle of those who were aware of what was done and how serious it was, might be a way of flushing out the mole which they still had not identified. They were still concerned that there would be risks for both Luis and, to some extent the Philippines, for as long as the mole had not been unmasked. He could continue to leak selected data or insight to terrorists who could then disturb the production of oil and gas and even threaten the installations which both Luis and the Filipino government had created to exploit the Wilson bonanza.

Luis had thus invited the Secretary of Health, The Secretary of Defense, Angelo DeSousa, Aaron Meyer and Ehud Shamir, as well as Mike Loeb, Larry Edelstein, and Anthony Stacey. The meeting was going to be secretly taped so that David and Countess Renate could hear how it went. The meeting was held in Luis's boardroom, both as it could easily hold all the participants and as it had all the technological means for such a presentation to include audio-visual material if needed.

Armand started by reminding everyone that there had been not one attack—which everybody knew about—but three attempted attacks using viruses. He said that they believed that the viruses were assumed to have originated in China, though he was careful to add:

"This is the main weakness of our work: we cannot pinpoint the actual source of the viruses. Though experience suggests that they could well come from China, we cannot prove that they did originate there. Any laboratory which is capable of sophisticated viral manipulation could have created them."

Armand then discussed the fact that the first two attacks used the same kind of virus, a cousin of Covid 19, while the third used an enhanced avian flu virus. As Armand was speaking, Mark kept observing all the various participants in the meeting, looking for any reaction which might give him some clue. While Luis appeared totally *au fait* with all that was being said, Mark noted that Angelo seemed quite surprised, though he did not say anything. He thought that there could well be a very simple explanation: Angelo had not been in the loop when it came to the details of the various virus attacks. He only knew that there had been a virus attack, the first. So, Mark gave him the benefit of the doubt, thinking that the severity of the attacks might only then be hitting him.

Before passing the microphone to Oshima-San, Armand suggested that a short pause might be in order given the amount of tea and coffee that had been offered.

■ ■ ■ ■ ■

The private jet had just received permission to land at San Jose Airport on Mindoro Island. Its flight plan indicated that he had taken off from Mischief Reef, in the Spratly Islands, one of the island reefs under the control of China.

The pilot and first officers started the last phase of their approach. They successively extended the aircraft's flaps, the high lift device on the trailing edge of the wing which reduces the stalling speed of the aircraft and thus allows the plane to fly more slowly as it is gliding toward the runway. They did that in three gradual steps so that the lift remained sufficient for the airplane to stay aloft as its speed slowly decreased. The final setting for these flaps was at a thirty-degree angle to the wing, which allowed the airspeed to fall to about 180 knots. When about 1,500 feet above the altitude of the runway, the first officer lowered the landing gears, slowing the plane even more to about 155 knots as the pilot added some engine power to counter the increased drag.

A short while earlier, as the pilots were using a full instrument approach, they intercepted the localizer and checked that the plane remained on the glide slope by looking at the indicator, a needle on the instrument panel which tells the pilot whether the plane is on, above or below the slope. Just before touching down, the pilot who was flying the plane flared the nose of the aircraft up, touched down and engaged his reverse thrusts to transfer the weight of the plane from the wings to the landing gears as soon as the main gears had hit the runway. With the first officer in radio contact with the airport control tower, and once the speed of the jet had come down sufficiently on the main runway, he told the pilot to turn onto a taxi way and bring the plane to a crawl, as it was rolling on the tarmac to the point where the local tower had indicated he should park.

■ ■ ■ ■ ■

With Oshima-San deep into his presentation, Mark noted that the demeanor of Fernando Solano, the secretary of Defense, suddenly appeared to change. He seemed to have been surprised, though Mark could not believe that his surprise was in any way related to Oshima-San's words. Mark walked calmly toward him and asked if everything was all right. Fernando simply replied that his cell phone had just buzzed. With Mark still right behind him, Fernando took his phone out of his right pants pocket and looked at it. He told Mark that this was very important and immediately got up, apologizing that this was a call he had to take.

A few short minutes later, Fernando came back into the room as discreetly as he could and walked to the seat occupied by his colleague Bambi Ruizon the Secretary of Health. They exchanged a few words, after which Bambi rose from his chair and followed Fernando into the hallway just outside of the boardroom. Mark was observing the ballet and was even more surprised when Bambi, who had just come back into the room, motioned to Aaron Meyer and Ehud Shamir that they needed them as well. Mark immediately guessed that the matter was very serious, though, sitting in the room as Mile Loeb he had no standing to ask whether he could join his Israeli colleagues. The interlude lasted no more than five minutes after which Fernando, Bambi, Aaron and Ehud came back into the room and took their seats. Mark was surprised that nothing was immediately said, though that silence lasted but a couple of seconds. Then Fernando Solano stood up, apologized to Armand and Oshima-San that he needed to interrupt their presentation, explaining that he had important news. He declared:

"Friends, we have just had one hell of a lucky break."

■ ■ ■ ■ ■

Back at San Jose airport, a few seconds after the plane had come to a complete stop and been connected to an auxiliary power unit, just as the door to the cabin was being opened, three border police cars converged onto the aircraft. The flight attendant, who was wearing a military uniform, which no one could immediately identify, walked down the stairs ready to help his two passengers disembark. That is when he noticed that the three police cars had parked quite close to the aircraft, making it impossible for it to move. Two police officers stepped out of their respective vehicles, while the flight attendant could see out of the corner of his eye, that at least two other officers in the third car seemed to have weapons at the ready. His surprise was complete when the most senior of the two officers told him that the aircraft had to be inspected before anybody disembarked.

One of the two gentlemen in civilian clothing who had been passengers came to the door of the plane and seemed somewhat agitated. He asked in strongly accented English what the problem was. He was told firmly but politely that all airplanes landing in San Jose that day had to be inspected by custom and border police officers. The gentleman initially claimed Hong Kong diplomatic status and said that no one would be allowed to enter the aircraft before he had had a chance to talk to his ambassador. The policemen did not appear terribly surprised by his request. They immediately offered him the use of their police radio to contact his ambassador. The gentleman looked increasingly uncomfortable, as truth be known, the Chinese Ambassador in Manila would have had no knowledge of the mission or even of the individual who was asking to talk to him. His initial outburst seemed to be a bluff which fell totally flat. He could not have known that the officers had received their orders directly from the Secretary of Defense. They had been instructed to remain courteous, but to remain inflexible.

■ ■ ■ ■ ■

With everyone back in the boardroom, Luis stood up:

"Gentlemen, as you have known for a while, all three wells of the Wilson deposit have been connected. Again, as you also know, we are still maintaining lower than possible production levels because the onshore infrastructure is not yet ready. However, I am happy to report, as Anthony had previewed, that now that Coast Guard protection is visible in the vicinity, we just made a crucial decision."

He paused and looked quite excited to see everyone hanging onto his words. He added with a big smile:

"This morning, we reached an important milestone. We started producing at a rate of 50,000 barrels a day."

He paused again and then added with great emphasis:

"This is more out of our field than the country has ever produced from all its wells combined."

A hearty round of applause followed, after which Luis called his assistant. She walked into the board room with a colleague carrying both glasses and a couple of chilled bottles. They then offered a cup of champagne for everyone.

■ ■ ■ ■ ■

Meanwhile, back at the airport, with his bluff having failed lamentably, the gentleman in the suit was still trying to stop the effort of the border police, Yet, as the conversation was going back and forth, an airport employee, escorted by another border police officer approached the plane's hold and opened its door. He had started removing its contents. This triggered all sorts of menaces from the irate civilian occupant of the plane. Border policemen remained impassible although the senior police officer on the scene placed a call to Fernando Solano. After having asked the officer to describe the package he had found in the hold, Fernando Solano asked

Bambi to join him in the hallway of Luis's boardroom. With Bambi's acquiescence, Fernando decided to impound the plane and asked the policeman to have everyone on the aircraft taken to the terminal.

The capture of the plane which had landed at San Jose in Mindoro unfortunately did not provide sufficient proof to implicate the Chinese directly in the biological attacks. The two passengers on the plane were civilians and they refused to speak when questioned. Their passports were issued by Hong Kong, but they were fake. The gentlemen seemed to be of North Korean descent, but this conclusion was only based on facial features, which cannot really be relied upon.

The contents of the hold of the plane were however given to Armand and Oshima-San who were thus invited to extend their stay in Manila. Mark was not surprised when he learned that the contents were limited to three small glass test tubes containing a gel-like substance. The test tubes were carefully sealed with wax. There were also three hermetically preserved Petrie dishes. The tubes were packaged in a small wooden box, so that they could not touch each other. The box contained enough shock-proofing material to ensure that, even if it was dropped, it would not break nor would its contents. Similarly, the Petrie dishes were sufficiently isolated from one another that they could not break because of some random shock. Eventually, Armand explained that the Petrie dishes contained the nourishment needed for the viruses to remain alive:

"My guess is that the Petrie dishes are emptied into whatever containers are used to place the viruses on location. Once the growth medium has been set, the jellified liquid in a test tube is transferred into the container."

He paused and quickly added:

"By the way, the package confiscated at the airport also contained a few sheets of water-soluble paper. This gives us the answer to an earlier question: the terrorists manufactured the container bowls, and everything else which could be argued to involve some 'technology' is provided by the Chinese. In short, the terrorists were planning to plant another three containers. Obviously, the key question is where. But that we'll never know."

It did not take long for Armand and Oshima-San to report that the solutions contained viruses of the same type as the last attack, a variant on the avian flu. With the agreement of Mike and Ehud, they adopted a different approach to their "discovery" than earlier. Rather than keeping everything secret, they chose to make their findings public. Though neither Armand nor Oshima-San could directly implicate anyone directly, they still held a press conference during which they were able to show the plane which had been impounded, the individuals who were in the planes, civilians as well as military, and to share the results of their analyses, with the direct implication, with appropriate graphs, that the containers held viral agents.

The two civilians professed total ignorance of what the packages that were on the plane contained and who put them there. They argued that someone must have placed the merchandise there without telling them. Nobody believed them. But the police officers had to admit that they could not prove anything in a conclusive manner. When asked why they had chartered another, smaller plane, the civilians simply replied that they wanted to spend some quiet time at the beach. They were able to point to the contents of their luggage which ostensibly did contain the expected bathing suits and assorted beach paraphernalia. They also produced pilot licenses to explain why they did not need to book a pilot for the smaller plane, pointing out to the fact that their licenses did not allow them to operate any aircraft with more than one engine.

The crew was comprised of airmen officially based on Woody Island, but they could only point to their local commander as the person who gave the orders. The individual, located on Woody Island, was prohibited from answering any questions on the grounds that he had not done anything wrong and had a duty to China. He only said that the airmen were North Korean air force officers detached to Woody Island for training purposes. Even when they finally agreed to say a few words, the crew and their commanding officer proclaimed total lack of knowledge as to the contents of the packages as well. Mark noted how smart the planners had been as it would appear that they had never used the same jet to fly into the Philippines.

Fernando and the Filipino Government elected not to detain the civilians or military personnel. That this was in keeping with diplomatic norms was only a part of the rationale. The other justification was quite simply that there was no hard evidence that linked the individuals and the viral solutions, other than they had travelled on the same private plane. The four individuals were, as is typical, expelled from the Philippines, though they had to pay landing fees for their jet as well as the fuel needed for the return trip.

■ ■ ■ ■ ■

Mark had just finished his second cup of coffee, the first since he had arrived at the Israeli Embassy where he had set up office, when Ehud barged into his humble office:

"We're in luck. The enemy has made a mistake. The mole is Angelo . . ."

Calmly, Mark smiled at Ehud and said:

"You're gonna to explain right?"

"Absolutely. Should Nate be here too?"

Seconds later, when all three of them were installed in Ehud's office, which was more comfortable and provided a seating area, Ehud explained:

"Angelo received a message on his phone. Quote: 'what's happened to your other phone? It does not work. So, I must use this one. Why did we not hear from you what the response to our last notices was? You must continue to provide us with the information you need, if you want your mother to stay alive.'"

EPILOGUE

TEL AVIV, ISRAEL

Telling this story has been made much easier by the fact that throughout its development I maintained a healthy distance from it. Most of the hard work was carried out by my Lieutenant, Mark Levi, and our local *Mossad* head in Manila, Ehud Shamir. I should of course start with profuse thanks to all those who were kind enough to share with me details or developments that I did not witness firsthand. I am sure they know how much I appreciated the help they provided.

The call which Angelo received on his work cell phone effectively sealed his fate, unfortunately in more ways than one. It first taught Mark and the team that Angelo had two rather than a single phone, explaining why we never found out about his calls to update his masters. He made them using a phone we did not know existed and thus did not monitor. It was almost child's play for Wong Hai Chock, the cyber security expert of Countess Renate in Singapore, to find out and trace the call Angelo had received on his business phone.

Once told that we knew, Angelo melted down and confessed. His story turned out to be quite sad, right from the start. He had been told he was orphaned and adopted by a Luzon couple of Indian ethnic origin when just a baby and had no reason to doubt the story.

A few years ago, as is often the case with adopted children, he tried to trace down his natural family. He had become wealthier than he would have ever hoped to be thanks to Luis and decided to use some of that money to find out more about his roots. It was relatively easy to find the village where he was born, as the data was on his adoption papers. Digging further, he travelled to the village. That's where he was in for a real surprise.

He learned that neither of his parents were deceased. His father was a member of the Moro Nationalist Front and had over time climbed to be near the top. His mother, to whom his father was not married when she became pregnant, had been forced to give the baby up for adoption, as she did not have the means to support him. Though her relationship with Angelo's father initially was one of youthful passion if not true love, it changed over time. Not because of her, but because of Angelo's father. He started dating other women and Maria Angel, Angelo's mother, was humiliated in front of the villagers, while Arturo, his father, let it be known that she was off limits to all people who valued their lives. She was effectively captive and had no means to escape.

Eventually, when Angelo discovered the truth, he was furious and wanted to help his mother leave the village, being sure that he would find a way, with Luis's assistance, to relocate her to Manila. His mistake was to go to his father and tell him that he wanted to take her along. That's when Angelo started being the victim of Moro blackmail. He was escorted out of the village, told never to come back and instructed to inform his father of any development on the oil exploration front if he wanted his mother to stay alive and well.

He thus started to betray Luis despite all the respect and affection he had for him. After he was found out and had told his story to Luis and through him to Ehud and Mike Loeb, he was allowed to stay out of prison, though he would have eventually stand trial as indirectly responsible for the death of the victims of the first viral attack. Without telling Luis anything, he contacted a local mercenary group to organize a mission to try and free his mother in a semi-military expedition. The operation failed miserably and both he and his mother died in the crossfire.

■ ■ ■ ■ ■

With no trace of either the submarine or its drone, there was no way to point the finger directly at any official Chinese involvement. Careful inspection of the bottom of the sea near where the submarine had been hit by the torpedo fired by Mark allowed a couple of twisted metallic pieces to be retrieved. They could not be traced to any submarine directly, though they were suspected to be part of the rudder mechanism. The only relevant insight was that they seemed to belong to an older vessel. This was the only semi-hard fact that suggested that the submarine might well have been of North Korean origin, validating the broader thesis that China was likely acting through North Korean surrogates.

Suffice it to say that many of us are convinced that even if the operation was somewhat rogue it looked way too well-organized and to call on way too sophisticated methods and equipment to have been hatched by some junior officer. Thus, whether official or not, someone high enough in the hierarchy had had his or her hand in this. We hope that the fact that they failed so lamentably will teach the perpetrators a lesson. We ensured that a few discreetly placed leaks were made available so that the operation did not remain a total secret.

Luis and his company prospered, with the production from the Wilson field eventually allowing the Philippines to become an energy exporter. He was awarded the Philippine Legion of Honor. The award is conferred upon a Filipino or foreign citizen in recognition of valuable and meritorious services. It is awarded by the Secretary of National Defense in the name and by authority of the President of the

Republic. Fernando Solano made an exception to the general rule that it should be the primary order of military merit when he conferred it on Luis and on Eli Abelman, for their roles and dedication in making the country energy independent and actually turning it into an energy exporter.

Signed: D.H.